What the critics are saying…

ಜಾ

Persephone's Wings

"…one of the most amusing stories I've read in ages…just the right blend of make-believe, romance, humor and sex to please just about any reader…" ~ *Romance Reviews Today*

"I was expecting a light-hearted sexfest but there's a true romance story in here as well. Thorne and Persephone are perfectly matched for each other. Fairyland will never be the same after this passionate couple get together…" ~ *Sensual Romance*

"…The snappy dialogue had me laughing while the love scenes left me very hot and bothered…It's different, it's funny, it's hot, the romance is wonderful and the characters are all lovable." ~ *In the Library Reviews*

"…This is one of those books you cannot put down until the last page, and then only to take a cold shower. There was not one forgettable character in the entire book." ~ *Fallen Angel Reviews*

Wingin' It

Gold Star Award "…Funny, uplifting and erotic are definitely words that come to mind as you read this story. Wingin' It is certainly a must read and goes to my "keeper" shelf. Once more Sahara Kelly delivers … and how!" ~ *Just Erotic Romance Reviews*

Recommended Read "…an absolutely delicious read! Ripple's sarcastic sense of humor, and biting wit had me laughing out loud more than once…With motherly bumblebees, spider tailors, butterflies with great abs for transportation in a pinch, and short tempered wasps; Wingin' It is the Alice in Wonderland for adults" ~ *Fallen Angel Reviews*

"The characters are fantastic, the dialog is hilarious, and the scenes are so creative…There's also lots of super hot erotic stuff going on as well so make sure you've got some ice water handy." ~ *ECata Romance*

"Ms Kelly pokes fun at so many aspects and absurdities of modern life that I couldn't keep track, I just kept laughing! …a totally different, sexy, entertaining fairy tale. And like most enduring fairy tales the moral of this story shows us that true love is a treasure that often comes when least expected." ~ *The Romance Studio*

For Rachelle

Wicked Wings

What tells one heck
of a story!!

Sahara Kelly

Hugs Sahara Kelly.

ELLORA'S CAVE
ROMANTICA PUBLISHING

An Ellora's Cave Romantica Publication

www.ellorascave.com

Wicked Wings

ISBN 1419955144
ALL RIGHTS RESERVED.
Persephone's Wings Copyright © 2003 Sahara Kelly
Wingin' It Copyright © 2004 Sahara Kelly
Edited by Jennifer Martin
Cover art by Syneca.

Trade paperback Publication August 2006

Warning:

The following material contains graphic sexual content meant for mature readers. This story has been rated E–rotic by a minimum of three independent reviewers.

Ellora's Cave Publishing offers three levels of Romantica™ reading entertainment: S (S-ensuous), E (E-rotic), and X (X-treme).

S-*ensuous* love scenes are explicit and leave nothing to the imagination.

E-*rotic* love scenes are explicit, leave nothing to the imagination, and are high in volume per the overall word count. In addition, some E-rated titles might contain fantasy material that some readers find objectionable, such as bondage, submission, same sex encounters, forced seductions, and so forth. E-rated titles are the most graphic titles we carry; it is common, for instance, for an author to use words such as "fucking", "cock", "pussy", and such within their work of literature.

X-*treme* titles differ from E-rated titles only in plot premise and storyline execution. Unlike E-rated titles, stories designated with the letter X tend to contain controversial subject matter not for the faint of heart.

Contents

Also by Sahara Kelly

ဆ

Tales of the Beau Monde 1: Inside Lady Miranda
Tales of the Beau Monde 2: Miss Beatrice's Bottom
Tales of the Beau Monde 3: Lying With Louisa
Tales of the Beau Monde 4: Pleasuring Miss Poppy
The Glass Stripper
The Gypsy Lovers
The Knights Elemental
The Sun God's Woman

About the Author

୨୦

Born and raised in England not far from Jane Austen's home, reading historical romances came naturally to Ms. Kelly, followed by writing them under the name of Sarah Fairchilde. Previously published by Zebra/Kensington, Ms. Kelly found a new love - romanticas! Happily married for almost twenty years, Sahara is thrilled to be part of the Ellora's Cave family of talented writers. She notes that her husband and teenage son are a bit stunned at her latest endeavor, but are learning to co-exist with the rather unusual assortment of reference books and sites!

Sahara welcomes comments from readers. You can find her website and email address on her author bio page at www.ellorascave.com.

PERSEPHONE'S WINGS

જી

Dedication

෪

This book is dedicated to those who believe in laughter,
fairies and fantasies - and that dreams can come true. And
to my writing Partner, whose steadfast support and
confidence helps me believe in them too.

Chapter One

Persephone Jones tugged uncomfortably on the lapels of her ill-fitting brown jacket and pushed her glasses further up on her nose.

"I'm sorry, Mr. Marshall, I don't quite understand."

"You've been most satisfactory, Persephone. In fact, your organizational skills are quite extraordinary. The office has never run so smoothly. But now we no longer have any need for your services. I'm sad to say that as of today, we are terminating your contract. We shall, of course, be sending a glowing reference to the temporary agency."

"Of course."

A hollow feeling settled in the pit of Persephone's stomach. Once again, she'd worked herself out of a permanent job. She sighed.

"Thank you, Mr. Marshall." Rising, she held out her hand and got it firmly shaken by the older man.

"I know you'll do well, Persephone. Your talents are really quite amazing when it comes to getting a management system up and running efficiently."

She smiled weakly as she left his office. Yeah, right. She was so good that within a month no one needed her anymore.

Her desk seemed unfamiliar to her as she returned to her cubicle and found some thoughtful soul had put a box next to it. Soon she was packed and gone, few people even stopping to say goodbye. Such was the lot of a temporary employee.

Here yesterday, forgotten today.

And once again, no one needed her.

Perhaps it was that fact that hurt the most. Temp work was fine when you couldn't decide what to do permanently, but it never really allowed friendships to build, especially when one was cautious by nature and not the sexiest woman on the block.

Persephone closed the door of her apartment behind her, dropped the box on the floor and stood silent for a moment. It was ten-thirty on a Tuesday morning, and she was home. It was all wrong.

She shook out her raincoat and hung it up, realizing that once again the heating system was on the fritz. It had to be close to eighty degrees and she was breaking out in a sweat.

Tossing her suit jacket over a chair she went into her bedroom, stripping off her blouse and skirt and pulling awkwardly at her pantyhose. One day, she promised herself for the fourteen millionth time, one day she'd try thigh highs, but until then, it was pinch and roll, tug and wriggle.

Finally free of her nylon torture, she stretched her arms, breathing comfortably.

The mirror over her dresser reflected her image back at her. Average height, average brunette coloring, average weight.

Huge breasts. The curse of the Jones women had struck Persephone with a vengeance, and she winced as she noted the sharp cleavage and firm swell of her breasts above their lacy underwired support.

Someone else was watching, too. Someone with a dark and slender tail, eyes of gold, and a set of long whiskers of which he seemed extraordinarily proud.

"What do you say, Pat, old fellow?" asked Persephone, slanting a quick glance at her very best feline friend.

Pat, whose name was actually short for Patent Leather because that's what he resembled in Persephone's opinion, wrapped his tail elegantly around his feet and looked at his mistress.

"They're big, yeah, but they could be considered sexy by some, I suppose." She turned sideways and studied her profile.

Pat's ears flicked back and forth and his golden eyes followed her movements.

He licked his lips.

"Well, I'll take that as a compliment." She grinned at the cat.

Pat had come into her life about a year ago, entering unannounced through her window and onto her kitchen counter where he obviously liked what he found. He suffered through a trip to the vet, bit the man when he suggested neutering, and had remained staunchly at Persephone's side ever since.

His wants were few: a clean box, the occasional catnip treat, and lots of loving. He also had a lace fetish.

Persephone had been puzzled when she began finding her lingerie in a damp heap when she got home from work, until a little bit of undercover spy surveillance resulted in the sight of Pat nestling into her underwear and blissfully licking the lace until he reached some sort of advanced state of euphoria.

She wanted to feel outraged, but the warmth of his body nestled against hers in bed at night more than made up for his eccentricities. It helped ease the loneliness she sometimes felt at not having a human body to cuddle up to.

So they co-existed in a state of friendly affection. Persephone told Pat all her problems and shared her thoughts with him, while Pat returned the favor by eating the food she put out for him, cherishing her undies and snuggling up at night. If he felt like it, of course. He was, after all, a cat.

"You know it's my birthday today, don't you, Pat?" She posed this rhetorical question as she went into the kitchen with Pat padding behind her. She didn't bother with clothes. The underwear was more comfortable, and until the heat decided to turn off or explode she was better off wearing next to nothing.

"I'll forgive you for not getting me a present." She gazed forlornly at the birthday card from her parents. *Happy Birthday, Dear. Enjoy the day. Mom and Dad*. Ten dollars had been enclosed.

She sighed. She loved them, but would have been very happy if they ever decided to emerge from their sheltered TV-sitcom existence and acknowledge that she was now twenty-seven years old. Perhaps they might even realize that ten dollars didn't get much more than a newspaper and coffee anymore.

She hadn't seen them in almost five years, and even the weekly calls had dwindled to monthly, and then semi-occasionally. She sent them a card now and again, and shrugged it off. Closeness had never been part of their family motto.

She went to the fridge and opened it, vaguely hoping that a "Miracle of Saint Whirlpool" had occurred and magically produced an assortment of delectable goodies since the last time she'd checked it.

Nope, no miracle today.

Only a cup with one egg white in it—going hard, some leftover mashed potatoes from her Sunday dinner—going soft, a piece of cheese—variety dubious, a container half full of milk and the cupcake she'd swiped from the employee lunch room. There was also something that looked like it might have been lettuce in a previous incarnation.

She pulled out the cupcake, looked at Pat and shrugged. "Hey, it's my birthday. The frosting may be a bit hard, but hell, it's a cake. Now if I can just find…" She rummaged in her drawer and pulled out a used birthday candle.

Sticking it in the top of the cupcake, she gazed at it.

"Okay, Pat, this is it." The cat crossed the kitchen and jumped silently onto the table. "Hey. You know that's against the rules." He purred and looked at her through slitted eyes.

"Yeah, I love you too."

He rubbed his head against her breast and purred again.

"Watch it, there, fella. I might get to like that too much. It's been almost a year since I let a guy get that fresh." Like she'd had a choice. Men were as scarce as hen's teeth in Persephone's life, and her words simply brought that fact back to her.

Sighing, she pulled Pat closer to her body and placed a smacking kiss right between his ears. "Thanks for the birthday nuzzle, sweetie." She reached for the matches that lay next to the candle in the center of her small table and lit her little birthday treat.

"Happy birthday to me." Persephone sang the words softly to herself as her eyes filled with tears. This was one sucky birthday.

"Okay, Pat. I'm going to make a wish now." She smothered her pain, and stared at the candle. "What shall I wish for?"

A harsh tongue swept over the lace on her bra, sending a little shiver down her spine.

"Oooh. Bad cat. Reminding me of what I haven't got, haven't had, and god, do I want. Well, perhaps that should be my birthday wish. Fabulous, fantastic sex with fabulous, fantastic, magnificent lovers. Lots of them. Oh, and a good-paying permanent job, too."

Drawing in her breath, she blew out the candle and closed her eyes, wishing with all her might as the smoke swirled upward around her face.

It seemed very pungent smoke for a small cake candle. Her nose tickled and her eyes felt funny.

All of a sudden she felt very drowsy, and wanted nothing more than to lay her head down on the table.

She felt Pat's body rumble with another loud purr and sensed his face as he brushed his whiskers over her breasts. Another long slow lick to the lace of her bra brought a sleepy smile to her face.

"Awww, Pat. Pat the cat. What a guy."

Persephone's eyes closed, and she sprawled over the stained white Formica.

Pat watched interestedly as his mistress disappeared.

* * * * *

The first time Persephone awoke, she was aware of nothing but an extraordinary amount of pain radiating out from her spine to every single nerve ending on her body.

She moaned, and something cool and soft stroked her face.

"Easy now, sweetie. Just breathe slowly." The voice was gentle and comforting, and a very delicate fragrance permeated the air around Persephone's face. It just begged to be sucked down into her waiting lungs.

She lapsed back into unconsciousness.

The second time she awoke, she blearily opened her eyes to see two creatures hovering over her.

She closed her eyes and swallowed past what felt like the Sonora desert in her throat.

"Here, sweetie. Drink." A hand raised her head slightly and something smooth and cool nudged her lips apart.

She sipped the liquid that brushed her mouth, and then sipped some more. It was refreshing, sweet with just a slight tang, and the taste reminded her of the scent of flowers.

"Mmm," she sighed, finally opening her eyes again. The creatures were still hovering. She squeezed her eyelids shut.

"Okay." She cleared her throat. "When I open my eyes I see two creatures fluttering over me. I am in a coma or dead. It was my birthday, if I remember correctly. Therefore, some enormous cosmic joke has been played on me, since nothing could have put me in a coma. I must be dead."

A merry laugh greeted this statement.

"On the other hand, I suppose the heating system might have blown up, thus causing my apartment to collapse and putting me in a coma."

"Very logical, sweetie."

Persephone opened her eyes again. The figures had stopped hovering and were now standing on either side of her bed.

Tentatively she reached out a hand and poked the blue one.

"Ow. Mind the shirt. It's new."

"Oh shit." Persephone sucked in a sharp breath. "You're solid."

"Well, thank you. I think. I have actually dropped a couple of pounds."

"Who…what…where…"

"You're stuttering, dear. Take a deep breath." A hand gently stroked the hair away from Persephone's face. The hand then unobtrusively wiped itself on a towel.

"You need a bath, too. My goodness, you humans get dirty in a flash, don't you? A quick trip between dimensions and you pick up all kinds of grime."

"We humans?" Could that pathetic squeak have actually come from Persephone's throat? She gazed at the man, if that's what he was.

Tall, with long golden hair, he was clad entirely in blue. His tight fitting shirt was a marvel of tailoring, and his tighter-than-tight pants left nothing about his strong and muscled figure to the imagination. He wore a deep blue braided belt that looked like it was the finest leather, and it matched the deep sparkling blue of his eyes.

His shirt was several shades darker than the soft blue of his skin, however.

"I'm Salvias."

"I thought salvias came in red." Persephone struggled with a number of issues, prime amongst which was that she was talking about horticulture to a blue man. Being. Creature. Whatever.

"Oh, sweetheart. I can come in whatever color you'd like." He grinned. "But call me Sal, why don't you? Salvias is such a mouthful, isn't it? Or…" he coyly nudged Persephone in the ribs, "…so Clover likes to say." He giggled. Really giggled. A blue man was giggling next to her.

Unable to process this information successfully, Persephone gave up and turned to her other side.

The lovely being standing there smiling at her was definitely feminine. Sort of.

"Hello, I'm Clover. And you're quite lovely, you know…" She allowed her hands to trail delicately up Persephone's naked thighs while her green eyes feasted on the sight of her rather prominent breasts.

"You do realize that there are those of us who'd pretty much kill to have those, don't you?" The woman nodded with awe at the nipples pointing at her.

That she was stark naked began to register with Persephone, but in light of the fact that she'd just had a conversation with a blue man, it seemed rather unimportant.

"Thank you, Clover." She gulped, eyeing the beautiful green woman.

"Now, now, Clover, time enough for that later. We've got to get Miss Persephone up and about." Sal bustled around the room and gathered wispy draped things in his arms. His wings brushed the low ceiling.

His wings.

Aha. He had wings.

Big ones.

Persephone swallowed. "Um, excuse me." Sal turned with a smile. "Did you know, er—how do I put this, do you know you have wings growing out of your back?"

Sal giggled again. "Why you silly thing. Of *course* I have wings. All fairies do."

"Well, that explains the blue," muttered Persephone, glancing over at Clover. *Her* wings were neatly folded behind her.

"Don't mind Sal. He is a bit on the flamboyant side. There are fixed-wing fairies and swing-wing fairies, and Sal, well let's just say his wings swing more than anyone's."

"And I didn't hear you complaining, Miss Nice-in-her-Notions. Certainly not last night when I made those wings of *yours* shake like aspen leaves." Sal pouted teasingly.

Clover laughed, tossing her long green hair over her pale green shoulder. "That's absolutely right, my love. That tongue of yours is a killer." She grinned down at Persephone. "Just you wait 'til you feel it tickling its way up into your sweet pussy."

Persephone blinked.

"Not until she's bathed, Clover. I'm looking forward to some fun as much as you are, but we've got to get that awful *earthy* taste off her skin. And her hair, well…" Sal clicked his tongue and sighed. "We'll work on it. But first, something to wear."

He held out what looked like an armful of fluff held together by a bit of pink mist. "Here you are, lovey. I think this pink is just right for you. It'll bring out the *leeedle* touch of color in those lovely cheeks of yours." Seeing as he was gazing at her buttocks as she eased herself off the bed, Persephone was left in no doubt as to which cheeks he was referring to. Her other cheeks blushed.

"What's this?" She stared at the thing he was offering.

"*This*, as you so bluntly put it, is your robe. Here…"

He slid her arms into a soft mass of pinkness and Persephone gasped as it tumbled down to her thighs. It hid nothing.

"I…do you see…this is completely…I can see *right through* this."

"Mmm…so can I." Clover licked her lips on the other side of the bed. The sheer want in her green eyes stirred Persephone's hormones in a new and unusual way. She'd never been stared at with such lust before.

She should have been shocked. She wasn't. She was tickled — er — pink.

Chapter Two

"Where on earth am I? And what am I doing here?"

Persephone emerged from her small room with Clover on one side and Sal on the other. A long corridor stretched out before her.

"You're in Fairyland, dear," answered Sal. "Didn't you know?"

"Fairyland. Right." She looked around her as they moved along the corridor to see something that resembled a cross between a sophisticated office building and a rabbit warren.

Open doors revealed computer workstations, busily humming or displaying screen savers. Soft buzzing tones indicated some kind of telephone system, but it was more of a chime than a ring.

"What am I doing here? How did I get here?" Persephone asked the questions again, vainly trying to accept the notion that she was, in fact, in Fairyland, not in the psycho ward of some well guarded mental institution.

Her eyes darted around, noticing that the walls were cleverly crafted to look like dirt encrusted roots, slithering this way and that between the doorways. She glanced down at the floor. Soft green moss, or carpet which looked amazingly *like* soft green moss, cushioned her footsteps.

Not Clover or Sal's footsteps, of course, because they weren't making any. They were flittering gently just above the floor and holding onto Persephone's hands. She got the feeling that she was anchoring them as much as they were leading her.

The draft made by their wings stirred the soft silky robe and she felt a whoosh of cool air swirl up around her buttocks.

"Mmm…who do we have here?"

A deep voice sounded behind Persephone, and a pair of warm hands slid up beneath her robe and around her stomach to cradle her breasts.

She gasped and tried to turn, but found herself held tight against a very hard and warm body.

"Good morning, your Majesty," dimpled Clover.

"Your…your…*Majesty*?" Persephone struggled to free herself, but the arms binding her to his body were strong and his hands were now rolling her nipples between his fingers in the most enticing way.

"Persephone, this is King Oberon." Sal waved his hand behind her, and she once again tried to turn and see who was there.

"Sssh, little one. Don't move for a moment. Let me enjoy you."

The deep voice rumbled against her back and made a spot between her shoulder blades itch frantically. She wriggled.

A laugh met her struggles. "Oh yes, Sal. This one will be a definite asset," and on the word "asset," Persephone felt a pressure between her buttocks.

Something warm and damp tickled between her shoulder blades as his tongue hit the exact spot that was irritating her. She jumped as a thrill of pure sexual electricity shot from her back to her breasts to her clit.

The pressure between her cheeks increased, and she found herself going up on her toes as a very firm cock slid into the space between the top of her thighs. She breathed a little easier as scary visions of anal sex diminished and the cock contented itself with a slow sensual glide along her pussy lips.

Sahara Kelly

The hands continued their assault on her now-harder-than-rock nipples, and she felt herself getting quite warm and wet in places that probably shouldn't be warm and wet in public.

"Uh, your Majesty? Um, Sal, Clover?" Persephone felt the color flooding her skin as she got more and more turned on.

Clover was watching Persephone's body with intense concentration, and Sal was grinning at whoever stood behind her.

"Wings, Sal, I think. This is one hot little recruit…"

At the rough command, Sal moved in front of Persephone and spread his wings wide, screening her from the casual passer-by. Or flitterer-by. Or whatever fairies called their pedestrians.

Knowing her mind was rambling, Persephone tried to tug her hands free.

"Hey guys, we shouldn't be doing…Sal, what…?" Her head tipped back and met a wall of flesh and her eyes caught a glimpse of a dark, finely trimmed beard and a pair of gleaming black eyes.

Brilliant wings were hovering over her, which, combined with Sal's, pretty much guaranteed their privacy. Without her realizing it, the fairies had drifted her over to a wall where a convenient corner hid them from most of the corridor.

The hands separated, one staying firmly on her breast and the other slipping down to the moistness between her legs.

"Go ahead you two," said the voice of Oberon, King of the Fairies.

As if released from some kind of paralysis, Clover and Sal jumped into the game. Sal tipped his head and flicked out his tongue.

It had to be at least six inches long and Persephone felt her eyes widen as she watched it circle her free nipple. Dear heavens, no wonder he'd shaken Clover's wings last night.

Rough and raspy, it teased and tantalized her flesh in concert with the King's hand. She choked in a breath.

Which she promptly lost as Clover placed her hand over Persephone's mound and coaxed her clit out of hiding.

Oberon's cock was sliding freely now, rubbing itself between her thighs high up against her cunt, and getting well bathed in Persephone's juices. His tongue was working that itchy spot on her spine and reducing her to blithering idiocy and the hand that wasn't teasing her nipple was guiding her hips into a rhythm that she found echoed her heartbeat.

Combined with Sal's tongue and Clover's oh-so-talented fingers, Persephone was hopelessly swept up into a whirlpool of sexual sensations. Her body turned into one shivering sexual organ and within seconds she was trembling incoherently.

"Go ahead, darling. Let it out for us," the deep voice urged.

"I can't…oh god…please…" Stuttering and incoherent, Persephone gave up the battle and "let it out."

She came with a sharp cry and for a second or two blacked out as waves of orgasmic sensations crashed over her from her toes to her eyebrows.

"Good girl," said Oberon, jamming his cock up hard along her pulsating pussy to catch every last twitch.

"Oh my, Persephone. Very nice indeed," agreed Sal, with a final loving swirl to her just-about-dead nipple. "In spite of the taste."

"Mmm, you're going to do just fine, lovey," echoed Clover, smiling from ear to ear and sucking her fingers clean of Persephone's juices.

Gently, Oberon eased himself from between her legs, away from her trembling body and moved around her, letting her have her first good look at him.

She couldn't help it. She gasped.

He towered over her, dark, shining, smiling and sexy as all hell. He was unselfconsciously tucking his massive and still-hard cock back into his pants as she stared at him, and grinning at her with such great good humor that she couldn't help but smile back.

His huge wings were almost blinding, covered with myriads of twinkling colors that sparkled and flashed as he moved. A tiny coronet banded his forehead with a glowing stone centered on it, but not glowing anywhere near as brightly as his eyes. His long hair tumbled onto his wide shoulders and his goatee was closely trimmed and tidy. He made her tingle just by looking at her. Must have been some kind of magical fairy aftershave, decided Persephone. And boy, did it work.

"Welcome, Persephone. On behalf of all of us here in Fairyland, we're glad you're with us."

She was seized with an absurd desire to curtsey. She restrained herself.

"Thank you, er—your Majesty. I don't suppose you'd care to tell me what the heck I'm doing here?"

He shook his head. "You'll get all that stuff from Sugar at Orientation. Don't worry your pretty head over it. Just relax, I know you'll fit in just fine." His attention was wandering. "Sal, you seen Tits anywhere?"

"No, your Majesty. Not since last night's party. "

Oberon sighed. "Damn the woman. I'll have to go hunt her down. Right this minute." He turned back to Persephone with another killer grin. "Thanks to you, honey."

He stroked her face and then turned with a swoosh, launching himself into the corridor and streaking off in a blur of sparkling wings.

She turned to Sal. "*Tits*?"

"Yeah. Titania, the Queen."

"He calls the Queen, *Tits*?"

"Well sure," answered Clover, grabbing Persephone's hand and encouraging her along the corridor again. "He may be restricted to coming in the back end of the mushroom with the others, so to speak, but he loves his queen's frontal assets as much as any husband."

Persephone's head spun. "Mushroom? Back end? I don't get it."

"You will, babe."

* * * * *

Two floors down and several corridors over, the suite that held the offices of the Fairyland website and weekly Internet newsletter echoed with the sound of crying. The large front room held two occupants, and on the rear wall was a closed door bearing a neatly carved sign saying *Thorne Leatherfly, Editor*. It could just as easily have read *Thorne Leatherfly, Miserable Bastard* as far as Cobweb Glitterworm was concerned.

She sobbed delicately into her handkerchief, tears rolling from her eyes like tiny shining jewels. Cobweb took her Victorian fairy image very seriously and lost no opportunity to let her fragile pearlescent tears cascade down her porcelain complexion. In fact, there were times when she actively sought out the opportunity. Those times usually resulted when no one was paying her much in the way of serious attention.

Norman Elderbranch wanted to take Cobweb very seriously. He wanted to take her in an assorted variety of serious positions, in a variety of serious places, and bring her to an untold number of serious climaxes.

He wanted to see those delicate and fragile fairy wings of hers tense into rigid spikes and then shudder violently as she came in mighty waves right down to her little caterpillar-skin booties. Which he would, of course, have taken off her sometime earlier. Or maybe not. Especially if they were the lavender ones with the spiked heels.

He wanted to watch her as he brushed his beard across her teeny fairy tits, and maybe rubbed her dainty fairy clit with it. He certainly wanted to observe her reactions as he put his pointy hat to good use. Perhaps he'd even try those new chains the gnomes from the forge had made a couple of weeks ago. Cobweb would look lovely in silver chain restraints, moonlight and his cum.

He sighed. There were no rules against fairy-gnome sex, but sometimes it was bloody hard convincing the fairies of that fact.

Not to mention that there were no gnome women around at the moment who would give him the time of day. The birth rate was soaring in favor of males, which made for a pretty testosterone-laden bar scene. And everyone knew you didn't fuck around with another gnome's woman. There were a few males singing soprano in the gnome chapel who'd tried it.

And so he sat patiently, passing delicate handkerchiefs to the object of his current lust, and trying his best to hide a major hard-on beneath his tunic and away from her dewy blue eyes.

Cobweb sniffed.

"And then he yelled at me *again*, Norman. That's the third time this week and all because I'd forgotten to get the graphics ready for the current issue. I didn't *know* I had to do all that stuff, I thought someone else would. And I only took this job as a favor to the King. *No one* else wants it. And why should *I* get yelled at when it's not my fault, I'd like to know."

Norman ventured a delicate caress of her shaking wings. Of course, if she'd done her rather simple job in the first place, she wouldn't have brought Leatherfly's temper down on her head, but then again, this was Cobweb, mistress of the hurt feelings and emotional scenes. Her breasts trembled as she sobbed in a breath. Norman's cock twitched and he cursed under his breath.

"Poor dear. Leatherfly is a jerk. He shouldn't have come down so hard on you. Don't cry, sweetie." He continued his caressing strokes.

Cobweb hiccupped and blew her nose loudly.

Norman, spellbound by the feel of her wings, ignored it.

"Um, Norman?"

"Yeah, darling?"

"You're drooling on my skirt."

Norman jumped back. "Ooops. Sorry. It's just that you're so — I mean your wings are just — and when I touch them, I — "

Cobweb gave a watery giggle. "Why Norman, I think you like me."

Norman, whose cock was about to explode inside his little red trousers, smiled tightly at her. He wondered if his beard was on fire yet.

"You're sweet," said Cobweb, reaching out and unerringly finding one of his seventy-nine erogenous zones. The one right behind his left earlobe.

He groaned.

"You know, I've heard it said that gnomes are very — er — impressively built." She glanced at his tunic that fell to his thighs and hid whatever secrets lurked within his pants. "Is it true, Norman?"

Norman bit down on the inside of his mouth hard enough to draw blood. "Wanna find out, sweetheart?" He couldn't help asking, he was fighting his gnome instincts here. Instincts that screamed at him to throw a chain on this tootsie, lash her to the nearest tree root, and fuck her every way to Tuesday until she fainted from coming so often and so hard.

"Well…I was thinking of going to Neville's 'Gnome Away From Gnome' for a few drinks tonight…"

Norman's heart leapt. Neville's had a well deserved reputation for hot and sexy entertainment, hot and sexy patrons, and dark, convenient alcoves where the patrons could indulge their need for hot sex. He cleared his throat.

"What a coincidence. I was thinking of going there, too. Perhaps we could meet there." His fingers kept up their stroking on her wings and he noticed her pupils getting larger as he moved toward her back.

Her tongue flicked out and licked her lips as he brushed against her skin and back up along her wing rib.

"Norman," she whispered. "I like what you're doing."

"I'm glad." His voice was rough.

"Oh, my," she gasped, as his beard parted and coiled itself around her small breasts. "I didn't know gnomes could do…" She gasped again.

"There's lots we do that you might find pleasant," grunted Norman, very close to losing control.

"Like what?" she breathed, eyes drifting shut as he continued touching her with his hands and his beard.

He eased himself between her thighs, allowing his hips to spread her legs wide. Sitting on her office chair, she was at just the right height for a little gnome gnookie.

His fingers crept up her leg and under the soft billowing silk of her fairy skirt. Her fairy flesh was warm and fragrant and he shuddered as he found her fairy clit.

"Cut it out, you two. If you're gonna fuck, do it somewhere else, not in my office on my time."

The Editor's voice shattered the mood and sent Cobweb into another flood of tears.

If fairycide had been legal, Norman Elderbranch would have cheerfully murdered Thorne Leatherfly. He could have used his cock to do it too, seeing as it was now harder than marble and would make an excellent blunt instrument.

But gnomes are nothing if not patient, and Norman yanked his hormones back from the brink. He looked over at his boss.

"You're a jerk, Leatherfly. Go harass some other sprite, will you?"

Thorne's mouth curled in spite of himself. "A jerk, huh?"

"Yeah. Just because you haven't gotten laid recently, don't be such a pissass to the rest of us, okay?"

Cobweb gasped at Norman's daringly blunt language, but Leatherfly merely laughed.

"Norman, you're a brass-balled terror. God knows why I keep you around. Now put that little flippety-gibbet down.

You're getting her all stoked up and I can smell her from here. I need you to get me a list of new recruits for the newsletter, and please, try not to fuck this up, will you? If we're late again with this damn thing, my ass is grass."

Chapter Three

The bathing chamber Persephone found herself in looked like some kind of insane vision of a kitchen store. Enormously oversized cereal bowls were plumbed in as baths, and fragrant steam rose from the upended butter dish that doubled as a shower.

"Whoa. Freaky." The words slipped out as Persephone gazed, wide-eyed, around the strange room.

"What's freaky, darling?" asked Clover, busying herself with towels and bottles.

"Well, all this kitchen china. And it's huge, too. Your designer must have been smoking something really strange that day." She waved her hand at the screened off sections where four eggcups were neatly lidded in front of small white tanks. "I mean, eggcup *toilets*?"

Sal and Clover glanced at each other.

"Into the tub with you, Persephone. We'll explain as we wash you." Sal dumped a container full of what looked like little flower bells into one of the cereal bowls and urged Persephone forward, pulling her pink cloud off her as she passed.

At this point, she was getting quite used to wandering around with nothing on but her skin. Her back itched and she wriggled to hit the spot.

"How's that?" asked Sal, rubbing the exact place where she had an irritated patch of skin.

"Aaaaah." Persephone sighed and closed her eyes in bliss, surprised to find her nipples instantly hardening. Must be something in the air.

"Come on, a good scrub will make you feel much better. In you go." Clover turned off the faucets and Persephone lowered herself into the water, sniffing at the delicate lily of the valley fragrance and dodging the flower petals still on the surface.

"So, what am I doing here?"

Clover fussed around with soaps and washcloths. "Well, you must have a skill we need, I guess. What do you do, Persephone?"

"I'm an office management consultant. I can make your office efficient, and save you money at the same time."

Sal shook his head. "My goodness. Such talent. And she fucks well too."

"Yeah, about this fucking thing...does everyone here live around the concept that a fuck a day keeps the fly swatter away?"

Clover snorted. "Persephone. This is Fairyland. We like sex. We're good at it. Adjust, okay?"

"Well, I'm trying to. But I don't understand why I'm here, how I got here, and whether I can go home again or not."

Sal dunked her head and she came up sputtering. "Hey." She spat a petal across the tub and wiped her mouth.

"Sorry, dear. Got to get those tangles taken care of." He filled his hands with shampoo and began to work it into her hair.

"You will get all that information and more from Sugar at Orientation, sweetie. Right now, the most important thing is for you to relax and let your body adjust to the new sensations that being in Fairyland are going to cause."

Persephone looked a bit nervous but Sal's fingers continued their soothing massage and soon she felt some of her tension ease. "This is deluxe, guys." She smiled, leaning back and slipping up to her chin in warmth. "So, tell me about Oberon, mushrooms and back doors."

Persephone closed her eyes as Sal continued shampooing her hair and Clover began soaping her body.

"Well, you know Oberon and Titania are our King and Queen?" Clover paused at her toes.

"Well, of course. Everyone who's read any Shakespeare will tell you that."

"Pah," snorted Sal. "That man didn't do us any favors, thank you very much. You should see what Peaseblossom and Moth get up to. They think just because they're among the older fairies they've got license to…well, never mind."

Clover glowered at Sal and ignored his interruption. "King Oberon kind of got a reputation for his wandering ways, even though it's part of fairy nature to have lots of sex. And Queen Titania got really pissed at the thought he might carry on doing it with someone else even after they were married. So she put a spell on his cock. He's only allowed to do the ass mambo with other fairies. Anything else, and he can't get it up for a month. And we fairies have *very* long months."

Clover grinned appreciatively while Sal winced.

"Smart lady. I mean fairy. Or fairy Queen. Oh sheesh…" Persephone dipped her head at Sal's urging, rinsing the shampoo from her hair.

"Don't worry about it. You'll get used to it after a while."

"Which brings me to another question. How long will I be here? Assuming of course that I am here and not having one hellaciously fine fantasy in my mind while my body is seriously sedated and drooling in some padded cell someplace." She noted Clover's detailed attention to her thighs and tingled a little as the soapy hands worked their way upward. She wriggled in the water.

"Well, you've been recruited, of course. And I must say that you took the metamorphosis very well too. You must have had quite a bit of sugar this morning. We find that humans who have plenty of sugar in their system do better at handling the change than those who don't."

Persephone's brows shot up, and not just because Clover had reached her pussy with her soapy fingers. "Change? What change?"

"Why the size differentiation, dear."

"What size differentiation?"

"Your size differentiation."

"My size differentiation?"

Sal sighed. "Why do I feel this conversation is going nowhere? Yes, Persephone. Your size differentiation. You are now in Fairyland. What was a foot in your world is an inch in ours. You are now approximately five and a half inches tall."

Persephone's jaw dropped. She looked blankly around the room. "These are real bowls," she breathed.

"Of course. We use whatever we can from your world. Cuts down on our factory production costs, and the unions appreciate the chance to stagger their work shifts rather than go flat out all the time."

"Holy shit."

Clover giggled as she swiped between Persephone's legs and up over her belly. "You'll get used to it, honey. At least the change left you with these lovelies." She passed her hand reverently over Persephone's gleaming breasts.

"Hoookay. I think we're done, and Orientation is coming up. Do you feel clean?" Sal gave a last squeeze to Persephone's hair.

"I don't know what I feel. I'm in shock."

"Oh come on, sweetie. You'll do just fine. Come on now, out you come…" Sal held out a huge towel and enveloped Persephone in it as she stepped out of her bowl.

Comments about snap, crackle and pop seemed inappropriate, but Persephone couldn't help a few random thoughts about breakfast cereals. She shook the images away as Clover began running some kind of heated comb through her hair.

Sal smoothed a lotion all over her body, taking extra care around her breasts and her back.

She couldn't help it, she sighed as his hands massaged her glowing skin.

"Oh my, Sal, that feels soooo nice." She smiled happily.

"Well, dear, usually we'd go a couple of steps further at this point, seeing as both Clover and I enjoy a good fuck in the bathing chamber with our clean recruits. But because you've already come once this morning, and with a little bit of a rub from the King's cock, too, we'll pass for right now."

Persephone smiled lazily, part of her wondering why she wasn't running screaming from the room and the other part slightly disappointed. "Can I take a rain check?"

Clover laughed. "If you want one, lovey, it's all yours. Those," she nodded at Persephone's chest, "are going to haunt my dreams. I'll be ready to play any time. Just say the word."

"Now, Persephone, your clothes. I picked pink and white for you, and with your mahogany hair I think it was the right choice," said Sal, bustling to and from a closet with the intense concentration of a fashion designer backstage at a fall showing.

"Brown, Sal. Brown hair. Nothing mahogany about it. But, wow…these are cool…" She held out the softest pink leather pants that Sal had placed on a chair.

"They go with this." Clover passed her a white and pink leather halter, which barely covered her breasts and left her back naked.

She slid into the garments, amazed at how well they fit. "No underwear, I suppose…"

Two horrified expressions greeted that statement.

"Never mind. Forget I asked."

Sal led her to a tall mirror on one wall and, with a theatrical gesture, presented her to herself.

Persephone was rendered speechless once again.

The image that met her eyes wasn't the Persephone Jones she remembered. This woman glowed, with breasts that thrust proudly from a soft white leather bra and a body that seemed made for the low-slung pink leather pants. Her hair tumbled around her shoulders in a deep, rich fall of tangle-free curls. Sal stood next to her, holding a pair of dark pink boots.

"Oh. My. God."

Sal grinned. "Amazing, isn't it? Actually, it's the dash of nettle in with the sunflower oil in the shampoo that does it. Yes, very nice, Persephone. Very nice indeed."

Sal's gaze was resting on her breasts, and Persephone noticed a bulge growing beneath his tight blue pants.

For some reason, the sight turned her on. Seriously turned her on. She had no idea why. "Sal? Are you *quite* sure we're pressed for time?" She turned to him and reached out for the front of his trousers, running her hand up his fly. Clover was standing behind her. Close behind her. So close that Persephone could feel her warmth.

"I, well I don't…" Sal's response to Persephone's touch was gratifying. His bulge assumed mammoth proportions.

"I mean, it's a shame to waste all this clean recruit, and no underwear, isn't it?" Persephone couldn't believe what was coming out of her mouth, but she was driven by some uncontrollable urge. An urge to get some relief with these two darling fairies who'd bathed her and dressed her like she was a doll. She wanted to thank them. And she realized suddenly that she was horny as hell.

Wild sex seemed like a good way to kill two birds with one stone.

She felt, rather than saw, Sal glance at Clover.

"Well, I suppose if we don't spend *too* long…" Clover grabbed Persephone's hand and pulled her from the bathroom to an adjoining room where couches and mirrors were set up around small tables. It looked rather like the elegant foyer of an exclusive ladies room, which was probably just what it was.

Within seconds, Sal and Clover shed their clothes and undressed Persephone. She felt hands all over her and her pulse quickened at the brush of their wings and the touch of their hands on her clean flesh.

They lifted her off her feet and lowered her gently to an open backed couch, where Clover hovered near enough to reach Persephone's breasts.

"Oh god, you can't know how much I've wanted to do this," she sighed, lowering her mouth and suckling.

Persephone's hips jerked as Clover's mouth made contact. Sal settled himself between Persephone's thighs and under Clover.

Persephone realized what an amazing difference wings could make. They added a whole new dimension to sex, for a start. Clover hovered at exactly the right position to enjoy Persephone's breasts, while Sal could reach Clover's clit with his amazing tongue.

Meanwhile, Persephone was finding out that fairy cock was as impressive as fairy tongue, regardless of its color.

A wonderful blue cock had just knocked at the door of her cunt, and she rushed to let it in.

She widened her legs and Sal slid his cock deep into her warmth, surprising a groan of pleasure from her. She was already aroused, hot, waiting for him. This was not the way it usually was.

"Oh, Persephone," muttered Sal, using his wings to help his rhythm as he thrust himself deep into her channel.

"Oh, Sal," breathed Clover, around one of Persephone's nipples.

"Oh shit," gasped Persephone as for one brief second she wondered what in the hell she was doing, getting fucked by two fairies.

Then she felt her orgasm creeping up on her and she gave up wondering anything at all.

* * * * *

Elsewhere in the Fairyland complex, Norman Elderbranch hurried back to his office with a piece of paper in his hand.

When he'd read the list of new recruits, he'd noticed one line in particular and an idea was forming in his devious little mind.

He'd sent Cobweb out for nectar, although why she couldn't drink coffee like everyone else he had no idea. But one lightning memory of the feel of her silky thighs under his hands, and he'd have gone and milked the flowers himself if she'd wanted him to. Gnomes forgave a lot when sex was involved.

"Yo, boss," he said by way of greeting.

Thorne Leatherfly raised his unusual gold eyes and stared at his assistant. "What?"

Undaunted by this chilly welcome, Norman crossed the room and put the paper on Leatherfly's desk.

"Lookee here…" His stubby finger tapped one name on the list. "I notice that in our new recruits for this month we've got a…what was the phrase…office—"

"—management specialist. Yeah. I see. What about it?"

"We need one."

"Huh?"

"We need an office management specialist. Cobweb is fine, but she's not going to run the office the way it should be run."

Leatherfly narrowed his eyes. "If this is some devious plan of yours to get under her wings—"

Norman blushed. "Hey. I don't need devious plans for that. It's already underway. What I'm saying is that this office needs to be run right. I don't have the time to handle your stuff as well as the rest of the site, and even though I'm supposed to be your assistant, you and I both know I do the coding better than anyone."

Leatherfly adjusted his wings and put his fingertips together, watching Norman. "So my thought is, let's grab this office management body, let Cobweb come work for me in coding, and we'll smooth out the running of the site in next to no time."

"Right. So you end up with Cobweb right where you want her, *chained* to your desk, and I get some raw newbie who can't tell her wings from her ass, and is probably going to collapse into tears every time I walk past her."

Norman blushed again at the vision Leatherfly's sarcastic words had aroused. He sighed. "Yeah. That's about it."

"Okay. Good idea. Do it."

Norman glanced up at his boss in surprise.

Leatherfly grinned. "What's the problem? You're right. We need more help. And qualified help at that. You know I spent some time checking out potential recruits and making recommendations. That was one of the areas I paid special attention to. If this recruit is listed as an office management specialist, then that's what we'll get. We'll deal with the tears thing as it happens." He sighed, and shuffled some papers. "We sure need another pair of hands."

Norman swallowed his joy. Cobweb's cunt seemed about twenty steps nearer all of a sudden. He allowed himself a microsecond to enjoy a little fantasy of her hovering upside down between his legs.

"Hey, Norman. Get your mind out of your crotch, damn you. When's the new recruit coming in?"

Norman jerked himself back to reality and adjusted his pants. "Er—I think they're in Orientation now. She should be here within the hour."

"Cool. What's her name, by the way? Why don't they ever put names on this list; bloody inefficient if you ask me." Leatherfly rustled more papers in frustration.

Norman pulled a second sheet from his pocket. "Wait, I've got it here…um…let's see…" He ran his fingers down the paper. "Yep, here we are. It's Persephone. Persephone Jones."

Thorne Leatherfly astounded his assistant. He leapt from his chair with an oath, bashed his wings on the doorjamb and was gone before Norman could catch his breath.

Well, well. Wasn't that interesting? With typical gnome curiosity, Norman returned to his desk and checked the recruiting recommendations list that had been posted after the last batch of scouts had returned. He knew the magic of Fairyland couldn't be correlated with the passage of mortal time, but he figured he should be able to get a pretty good idea of when Leatherfly had been "outside."

Yes—there it was. Two fairy years ago. And what do you know? Mr. Thorne Leatherfly had wholeheartedly recommended the acquisition of one Ms. Persephone Jones for her office management skills.

A wry grin curled Norman's lips. He'd bet his last beard hair that Leatherfly was interested in a heck of a lot more than her typing skills.

It was mildly surprising that no one had thought to let Thorne know his personally selected recruit was now on her way. But then again, given the fact that the sun had been particularly bright for the last few days, the nectar had been running hot and sweet and the fairies imbibing freely, he supposed it shouldn't come as much of a shock.

He raised his nose and sniffed. Cobweb was returning, her scent preceding her by a few moments. His cock stirred hungrily at the thought of her fragrance all over his hands and the rest of him as well.

He wiped the grin off his face as she delicately fluttered back into the office.

"What was that all about? Mr. Leatherfly almost knocked me over," she whined, as she gracefully folded her wings and crossed her legs at the ankles.

"Oh, just the boss being the boss," answered Norman, drinking in the sight of her once again. "Tell me, Cobweb." He eased himself up to sit casually on her desk. "Do you like to wear bracelets?"

Chapter Four

"Well, that about wraps up the important issues of insurance and benefits, and so on."

The words percolated through Persephone's muddled brain as she fidgeted on the extremely uncomfortable chair in what looked like a conference room furnished in early Victorian torture devices.

Of course, this strange assortment of furniture was probably accounted for by the fact that an assortment of different beings were attending this Orientation session.

Persephone was one of five humans, and she could only guess at what they had been recruited for. The other two women could have been teachers, librarians or high-priced hookers. Well, probably not the latter, seeing as they both took copious notes and ignored the rest of the room.

The two guys were pretty nondescript. One had a prominent ink stain on his shirt and a pocket protector, which pretty much announced his technological tendencies to the world. The other—well, if the Bluebell Bar and Grill needed a country and western singer, this dude would fit the bill. From his trail-worn boots to his sweat-stained hat on the floor beside him, he trumpeted his western origins loud and clear. Maybe it was round-up time down on the Bumble Bee ranch and they needed help with the branding.

Persephone stifled an almost hysterical giggle and brought her attention back to the lecture. The squirrel next to her frowned as she fidgeted once more. Now there was a novel experience. She'd never had a squirrel frown at her before. Arrogant little rodent.

The Orientation was being conducted by Sugar. Sugar, it turned out was short for Sugar Plum Fairy. Although Sal had whispered that she actually had some kind of a Russian multi-syllabic name, she was known to one and all as Sugar, and she took her role very seriously. The pink tutu and the little white-feathered earmuffs left her identity in no doubt whatsoever.

Unfortunately, Sugar had the name but not much else, being built along lines that more appropriately described the Marine Corps than the Corps de Ballet. She might have been what Tchaikovsky had in mind for his creation, but she wasn't anything like her namesake who flitted across the stage during the Bolshoi's last production.

Sugar Plum was light years away from fairylike. And she probably should be re-thinking the whole tutu thing as well, seeing it was giving her a wedgie the size of the Grand Canyon.

Her constant wriggles and leg stretching did little to alleviate her discomfort, and Persephone felt for her as she watched her surreptitiously yank the offending fabric out of her butt for the fifteenth time. But her next words blew all thoughts of wedgies and tutus clean out of Persephone's mind.

"Now, to close this Orientation, we must discuss the issue of wings. Unfortunately, only recruited humans are eligible, so we shall say goodbye at this point to our other new friends."

The squirrel got up from its seat next to Persephone and glowered at her. She frowned back, restraining the temptation to tell it to go bury its nuts. It fluffed its tail in her direction.

She flipped it a mental finger.

"That's right, please close the door." Sugar twitched her butt as she looked at the five remaining humans.

"This is my chance to explain a few salient points to you folks that don't really apply to the other recruits." Sugar smiled happily around the room at the rather confused faces looking back at her.

"Firstly, I expect you all wondered how you got here? Yes? Yes? I can see I'm right."

Persephone realized Sugar would have made an excellent lounge entertainer. Any minute now she was going to ask where they were from and how long they'd been married.

"Well, you have all been chosen for your skills, of course, let me see…" Sugar referred to her notes. "We have a librarian and a junior high school teacher." She nodded to the two rigidly composed women who managed to look proud and embarrassed at the same time. "We have a computer hardware technician who specializes in storage devices." Mr. Inkstain blushed. "Um, then there's a livestock consultant."

"Yup, that'd be me, Ma'am." Mr. Branding Iron tapped his forehead in a polite salute. Sugar tittered.

"And our office management consultant." Persephone managed a social smile.

"Now, Fairyland needed folks with your particular skills, so our scouts checked around and selected you lucky recruits."

"Why?" Ms. Librarian snapped out the question. "Why me?"

"And me?" barked Ms. Teacher, not to be outdone by a mere librarian.

"Our research is most thorough. We try to select recruits from those who have little to leave behind. We clearly wouldn't take anyone who had a responsibility to their family, or who might be a valuable member of their community or their workplace."

Persephone digested this. "So, we're selected because we're useless to just about everyone?"

Sugar laughed heartily at this, her cleavage shaking with her mirth.

Persephone waited, not smiling at all.

"No, no, no, my dear. You couldn't be more wrong. You are *very* valuable. You have been selected as the very best at what you do, and also with the added advantage of no permanent ties to the mortal world. We're fairies, not savages, you know."

Sugar shot a reprimanding look at Persephone. "We need your skills. We don't take mothers from their families."

"Okay. I get that. But how long do we stay? Are we here forever? Do we get to go back? I still have parents, you know…"

Sugar nodded. "We know. There are…criteria…Persephone. Things that must occur in order for you to fully accept your status as a resident of Fairyland. If, as sometimes happens, things don't work out, you are returned to your previous mortal existence with no recollection of this place at all. If all goes as planned, and you become a full member of our happy family, then arrangements are made for you to contact your remaining family members, either by mail or by phone. We actually have a new satellite cellular system going online shortly…" Sugar looked breathlessly excited.

"Fine, fine." Persephone had no patience for cellular wonders. She'd been bugged by too many salesmen in the past. "What criteria?"

Sugar looked blank.

"You said there are criteria. Things that must happen before we can stay. What are they? If they happen do we get a choice?"

"Do you want one?"

Sugar's words slipped into the room like a cool breeze, bringing a shiver to Persephone's flesh. It was a loaded question, all right. In a moment of brutal honesty, she admitted she had nothing to go back to. But was this a better alternative?

She didn't know.

"The criteria, Sugar?" Ms. Teacher voiced the question that still hung over Persephone's consciousness.

"Well, that's easy. Wings, of course."

"Wings." Persephone echoed Sugar's statement with a wry twist to her lips.

"Yeppers. Wings." Sugar fluttered hers with delight. "Pretty, aren't they?"

"Yes. Wings." Persephone repeated herself, just to emphasize to Sugar that they'd all got that point, and that Sugar's wings were lovely, thank you.

"Well, to be a successful resident of Fairyland, you have to grow wings. Now, all humanoids who are recruited have the wing DNA implanted. Not all humanoids are able to activate it."

Sugar laughed, a tinkling sound with hints of the 1812 Overture. "That takes a special kind of person. Of course, we hope you'll all be that kind of person…"

"So, how can we tell?" Mr. Inkstain asked the obvious question.

"Just wait and see if the growth responds to the activation stimulus."

"And the activation stimulus would be…" prompted Persephone.

"Well, it's quite easy really. You just have to have—er—relations."

"Relations?" Mr. Branding Iron boomed. "Ain't got no relations, honey. Family's all dead and gone, like old tumbleweed."

"Quite." Sugar looked perplexed. "And the name is Sugar, not Honey. But that's not exactly what I meant by 'relations.'"

Ms. Teacher looked horrified. "You don't mean what I think you mean, do you?"

Sugar blushed, her abundant expanse of creamy skin coloring softly. "Probably. Yes."

"So what does she mean that you don't think she means, but she does?" asked Mr. Branding Iron, obviously stretching his intellect as taut as his jeans.

"Oh for god's sake," muttered Persephone. "She means you've gotta fuck, cowboy."

"But I don't wanna fuck cowboys," he whined.

Persephone's eyes met Sugar's in a moment of female bonding that transcended species.

Sugar smiled. "Good. I'm glad you all understand. The more you—um—indulge, the bigger your wings will become and the faster they will grow. There is a limit, of course, otherwise, my goodness, there wouldn't be room in Fairyland for all our wings."

Sugar looked around with a little giggle and fluttered her quite sizeable wingspread gently. She must be one hot little bedbug without that wedgie, thought Persephone.

"Oh, and I should add that doing it by yourself doesn't count. You must, you simply *must,* have a partner. Any partner is fine, of course. Gnomes, yes, quite acceptable. Elves, most satisfactory. Goblins, well, I have to admit their breath can be, shall we say, less than fresh at times, but they have other charms. We are basically quite diverse in our activities. Of course, you'll want to experiment and find out who and what suits you best."

Sugar looked around the room. "If they don't grow, then, well…I'm afraid you'll be returned to the mortal world. There is one other circumstance too, that will send you back to the mortal world."

"Oh yeah?" Mr. Branding Iron was fidgeting on his chair, and Persephone couldn't decide if he was embarrassed by this conversation or wanted to get on with the fucking and grow himself the dangdest pair of wings.

"Yeah. I mean yes." Sugar bit her lip nervously. "In the event that any of you find your wingmate…" she held up her hand to forestall any questions, "you'll be required to make a Nuptial Flight to cement your bond. Should you fail the Nuptial Flight, you will immediately be returned to the mortal world and all memories of not only Fairyland, but your love for your mate, will be erased."

The room had turned silent as Sugar spoke. "Your wingmate is someone special for whom your heart beats faster. The one person who can awaken something deep inside you that has never been touched before. The one person who can mate with you and create life. It's a very special thing, and doesn't happen too often. That's why the requirements are very precise and must be completed perfectly. If you fail…the alternative is bleak indeed."

Persephone shivered, as if someone had walked over her grave. A wingmate.

Was there one for her here? Someone to fill her loneliness? If there was, then she owed it to herself to stay and explore the possibilities. After all, if the choice were between an empty apartment and an equally empty life or the chance to find her "other half," then she'd be a fool to turn it down.

"So, we fuck around, we get these here wings?"

Mr. Branding Iron boomed out his question, obviously immune to the thought of a wingmate.

Sugar nodded.

Persephone felt a little twinge between her shoulder blades as she thought of her experiences with Sal and Clover earlier. Surely she should have some kind of a wing by now if fucking was all it took. She'd had two fabulous orgasms with three fairies so far. And, dammit, one of them had been the King. That was a case of starting at the top. Shouldn't that have gotten her to the single-engine Cessna stage of development? At least?

She raised her hand. "Excuse me, Sugar?" she asked.

"Yes, dear?"

"Where do they grow and how can we tell they're growing?"

"Good questions. Firstly, they grow from your spine right between your shoulder blades."

Persephone's hand automatically slid behind her to that single itchy spot.

"And you'll be able to tell when they start growing because they'll itch like crazy." Sugar laughed. "Oh, and although that spot will itch, it will also become quite special to you. But," she dropped her lashes and peeked coyly at the group, "I'm not going to give away any more secrets. Some things are better left for you to find out on your own. Now, if there are no more questions?"

No more questions?

Persephone didn't know where to start. She was in Fairyland, having sex with strange creatures, probably growing wings, although she couldn't tell yet because she was still itching and had no mirror handy, and had engaged in a visual confrontation with a squirrel.

Oh yes, she had more questions. She wanted to know more about wingmates, about Nuptial Flights and the love of her life. If he was out there.

But Sugar wasn't, apparently, going to be the one to answer them. Gathering her little goodies together and giving her butt one last tweak, Sugar was already walking from the room in that curiously flat-footed style affected by ballerinas since the first one thought that deforming her foot so she could be an inch taller would be a good idea.

Persephone sighed and headed for the door. She hoped someone, maybe Sal or Clover, would be outside to help her find her way around. Did she have her own room? Was she rooming with someone else? Or worse, some*thing* else?

She was the last to leave, and as she did, her back began to itch again. *Really* itch, this time. She saw no alternative, but gently leaned against the doorjamb, rubbing the offended spot against the wall.

She sighed with relief.

"Why don't I help you with that?" A deep voice intruded on her moment of bliss and she turned.

Her jaw dropped.

She found herself looking at a vision of sexual magnetism. If Harley Davidson designed fairies instead of choppers, this guy would be their poster boy.

Long, muscled legs were encased in black leather pants, not too tight, but snug enough to hug his thighs and other interesting parts *really* nicely. A white T-shirt with no sleeves topped the pants, and matched the untamed look about his unusual gold eyes and jet-black hair. Straight and shiny, it fell past his shoulders to lie softly against his chest. Just like she'd do if she got half the chance. A tribal tattoo circled one solidly cut bicep.

His thick chain belt clanked as he neared her, and she glanced upward at the wings that were folded firmly above his head.

They looked just like shiny black leather with the occasional silver stud down the ribs.

She shivered.

His hand slid behind her back and went directly to the source of her itch.

He rubbed.

She shivered again, this time unable to contain the moan that his touch brought to her throat. He stroked her skin as his golden eyes held her gaze, and watched as she bit down on her lip while trying not to squirm.

His fingers were sending waves of semi-orgasmic pleasure through her body. Her breasts were throbbing and she wanted to leap on him and wrap her legs around his hips. Tight. So she could get that bulge in his leather pants right up against her needy pussy.

She gasped as he slipped the ties on her halter-top and freed her breasts.

His head dropped and he fastened his mouth around her hard nipple, tugging and pulling with his tongue.

She moaned, closing her eyes and letting her fingers drift up to the black silk of his hair.

"I'm Thorne Leatherfly." He moved away a little, breathing hard. "So for god's sake don't call me Pat anymore."

* * * * *

Thorne was practically beside himself with lust. He'd finally managed to get those beautiful tits into his mouth, and he resented the fact that conversation, not to mention efficient breathing, required that he remove them.

But he slowly became aware that the woman in his arms was staring at him with an expression resembling a cross between outright horror and what she'd probably looked like the first time she'd tasted snails.

"You? You're my…my…*cat*?"

He pressed her even closer, letting her breasts rub against his T-shirt, and growling deep in his throat at the sensation. "I'm not your damn cat. Do I look like a cat? Do I *feel* like a cat?"

He thrust his hips into her body and drew a groan from deep down in her gut as his hardness slammed against her heat. Even the leather pants they wore couldn't stop her cunt from burning him.

"So why did you say anything about Pat?" She gasped again as he dipped his head for a brief suckle. "You certainly seem to have some of his tendencies. Although he preferred my bra."

"No, I didn't," he muttered, flicking her nipple to a state of impossible hardness with his eager tongue.

"That does it."

She wrenched herself away from his hold and jerked her halter back into place. "You can just put that talented tongue away, mister. I don't know who or what you are. You may be a Hell's Angel Fairy or something. Or maybe you're wanted by the FBI. How the hell should I know?"

"FBI?" Thorne's eyebrows rose.

"Yeah. Fairy Bureau of Investigation." Persephone snickered.

Thorne closed his eyes and sighed. "Persephone, I'm not a Hell's Fairy, wanted by any law enforcement agency, nor, at this moment, am I your cat. Can we go someplace and discuss this please?"

"Will you keep your mouth away from my boobs?"

"Do I have to?"

"Yep."

"You're cruel."

"Oh, give me a break…" Persephone flung up her hands in a gesture of frustration.

Thorne laughed. "Come on, honey. Let's find ourselves a cup of coffee. Looks like you're gonna need it, seeing as you'll be working for me from now on."

"Excuse me? Working for you? Hey, says who? Last time I looked, Oberon was King. So who died and made you Top of the Toadstool?"

Thorne froze and pulled her back into his body. "You met Oberon?"

Persephone leaned back and smirked at Thorne. "Oh yeah. Did I ever."

Thorne's golden eyes narrowed into fierce slits and he crushed her so tight he knew she'd have trouble catching her breath. "No one, and I repeat, no one, puts a hand or a wing on you from now on. You got that?"

His heart pounded with a combination of lust and anger, seasoned with a dash of fear. He was awfully afraid he held his fate in his arms, and that Oberon, damn his wings, had gotten to her first. He also had a scary feeling that his days as an unencumbered source of virile fairy pleasure to the female residents of Fairyland were just about done.

Persephone Jones could well be his mate. His wingwoman.

A small part of him shouted out against the twists and turns of fate and that he wasn't ready to settle down with just one woman for the rest of his life. The rest of him just wanted to shout out while inside Persephone.

Chapter Five

Persephone found herself being ruthlessly dragged along darkened corridors and away from the bustling and active business end of Fairyland. Now the halls were quieter, the doors closed and numbered, and she realized this was the living quarters for some of the creatures she'd met.

Stopping in front of a large door, Thorne maneuvered the handle and pushed her inside as soon as it opened. It slammed behind her with a solid thunk, and it dawned on Persephone that she was now alone with some kind of buffed-up fairy-cum-stud who considered her his exclusive property.

Oh dear. She probably should scream or something. Well, perhaps she would. In maybe a month or two.

However, there was no time like the present to get one thing straight between them before they went any further.

"I don't belong to anyone, Mr. Macho-Fetish-Gear. So cut out the domination crap right now, okay?"

She was ignored.

Right. So much for asserting her individuality.

Thorne busied himself in what appeared to be his kitchen, and Persephone couldn't resist the urge to peek around his apartment.

The ceilings were very tall, helpful when one had wings, she supposed. The decor was pretty much what she'd expect from a bachelor. Some leather chairs, a lot of chrome and glass, a batch of magazines featuring semi-naked fairies, an old pizza box and a large pot of something called "Wonder Wing Wax."

And then there were the windows.

Persephone gasped as she stood in front of the floor-to-ceiling sliding windows and looked outside for the first time in what seemed like a lifetime.

She felt, rather than heard, Thorne cross the room and stand behind her, his body radiating heat against her bare back.

"It's beautiful, Thorne," she breathed.

"I know," he answered softly.

She was grateful that he gave her the time to appreciate the scene before her. Greens in every shade imaginable painted the landscape outside Thorne's windows. They seemed to be high up in a tree, because branches and leaves shaded the small deck that jutted away from the windows, and the ground looked to be far below.

It was a far cry from the brick wall and the occasional glimpse of sunshine that her apartment windows had offered.

The bright sunny sky was dotted with small flying things, and every now and again a blinding flash could be seen as the sun glanced off a delicate wing.

"The kids are playing right now, learning how to fly."

"Kids?"

"Yeah, you know, little sprites, small wings? Clumsy fliers, too." He laughed as one swooped upside down beneath a branch with a shout.

"I didn't know. There's so much I don't know," said Persephone, more to herself than to Thorne.

"There's time, Persephone. Don't rush it," he answered, coming even closer. "I've put some coffee on."

A thrill of desire made her shudder as she realized that Thorne had also taken his clothes *off*. The feel of his nakedness behind her turned her on with a vengeance, and she made no demur when his hands unfastened her halter and tossed it away.

He moaned with delight as her breasts filled his hands to overflowing.

"I knew I'd love these babies. I knew it. They used to drive me mad, especially when you'd ask me if they were too big." He rolled them lovingly around, taking Persephone's breath away.

"So, are you going to tell me how you come to be here when you should be curled up on my quilt enjoying a nap? *Pat*?"

He tweaked her nipples energetically, making her squeak.

"I did warn you not to call me that," he breathed against her neck. He licked her shoulder and with one hand quickly unsnapped her pants and let them fall to her ankles.

She moaned as she felt him hard and thrusting against her buttocks. The heat of his touch was incredible.

"So, you don't deny you are my cat?"

"*Were* your cat. No, I *was* your cat. Oh hell, you know what I mean."

"No, I don't," she answered, shaking her head. Carefully, because she was quite concerned that the least movement on her part might send her into some kind of orgasmic frenzy.

"You want to hear about relativistic theory and the space-time continuum?"

"Noooo…" she moaned.

"How about the recruitment service that transforms fairies on a regular basis and sends various divisions out to locate the right people for Fairyland?"

"Noooo…" she repeated herself.

"Good. Just accept that it's magic. I was there scouting you out, now you're here. That's all that matters." His tongue moved down to her spine.

With the first slide of his wet warmth across her wing buds, Persephone was a goner. Her pussy was soaking to the point where her juices were tracing cool tracks down her thighs. Her nipples were harder than agate and Thorne seemed to be obsessed with tugging and pulling and rolling and squeezing them and driving her slowly into insanity.

Her hips began to move, rubbing and pushing against him, and he worked his tongue a little more firmly against her wing buds.

"What's happening to me?" she whispered, as she pushed his hand harder against her aching breast.

"Touch yourself. I don't have a free hand at the moment," he urged, between licks and flicks to her back.

Ignoring the fact that she stood naked in front of twelve foot—excuse me—twelve *inch* glass doors, and halfway up a tree to boot, Persephone obeyed Thorne's command and slid her hand down to her pussy.

"I can smell your body," moaned Thorne. "God, you taste so good…"

"What are you doing to me? Why is this so…sooo…" Persephone's breath caught as her fingers found her clit, and the merest touch sent shudders through her.

"It's your wing buds, darlin'. They're a sexual organ…"

"Oh god, are they ever…" Persephone thrust herself against Thorne, pulling his body closer, forcing his hands to rub her breasts harder, and teasing her clit with rapid movements of her own fingers.

His cock slid between her buttocks as he nibbled around her wing buds and forced his tongue into unknown places.

Her legs trembled.

This was something completely out of her realm of experiences. Her lungs felt as if they could scarcely draw enough oxygen to keep her conscious, yet her body was alive to every breath Thorne made. His tongue burrowed into a place in her spine that acted like an "on" switch for the rest of her body. She sobbed as she rubbed her clit and writhed against him.

Suddenly, she felt him inside her and gasped with the joy of it. She heard his intake of breath.

"Don't move for a second, doll. Just hold it. I need to feel you for a minute or two." His tongue slid gently over her flesh, his hands caressed her breasts and he moved deeper into her ass with a little thrust.

Into her *ass*.

"*Thorne*!" The screech could have shattered crystal.

"Easy, babe. Easy."

"Thorne, I've never…" Visions of lubricants and condoms and safe sex lectures flashed before Persephone's eyes.

"Relax, honey. This is Fairyland. Am I hurting you?"

She paused for a moment. "Come to think of it, no, you're not." She tried tightening her inner muscles, only to hear a grunt from Thorne behind her.

"And does it feel good, babe?"

He slid back and forth a little, very gently, while administering fluttering little licks to her wing buds.

She melted. "Oh yeah…" This was magic the way it was *supposed* to be.

Her arousal revived itself within seconds, and she moved from a plateau of pre-orgasmic heat to an approaching explosion within moments.

"Please, babe, please…" begged Thorne.

"What? Anything, oh god, Thorne…"

"Just keep doing that," he groaned, as he thrust deeply into her with his tongue and his cock.

Her fingers found her clit, now oh-so-ready to be tugged and encouraged into doing its job and sending her off into bliss.

Persephone's buttocks tightened, making Thorne sob with pleasure.

His tongue found the perfect spot on her wing buds as her own fingers found the perfect spot on her clit.

She shattered into a million cosmic pieces, taking Thorne with her.

His cry deafened her, and his shivering body filled her. His wings rustled and shuddered around the two of them, adding another dimension to her orgasm. She'd never experienced anything like it in her entire life.

She closed her eyes and moved her hand away from her now-extra sensitive clit.

With a little gasp she realized something else.

Her feet weren't touching the floor.

Slowly, gently, Thorne lowered them both back down to ground level, then simply held her against him. She could feel his cock as it relaxed inside her, and that was also something uniquely special.

"Thorne," she said.

"I'm here, honey. I'm here."

"Oh, Thorne." Disgusted at her complete inability to come up with anything more than his name, Persephone just closed her eyes and allowed her body to come back to whatever passed for normal in this strange place.

"Oh, Persephone." Clearly Thorne was having the same problem.

Not so the goblin who watched them. "Well, *shit*, dudes. Now *that* was a good one."

"Oh—fuck," said Thorne.

* * * * *

"Hi, Thorne," said the goblin. He wrinkled his already-wrinkled face into what passed for a grin. "That was one helluva bang, boy. Up the ass, too. Whew. Damn near got my nubs into a twist and shot my load right along with ya."

Short and hairy, the creature leaned nonchalantly against Thorne's couch, stumpy legs crossed and belly fat flopping over his rather grubby white silk trousers. His wings were on the stubby side and looked like someone had spilled ketchup on them some time ago.

"Who the hell are you?" Persephone found her voice and it reflected her outrage. Well, she was as outraged as she could be given that she was standing stark naked in a post-orgasmic fog and talking to a goblin.

Thorne was clearly having trouble holding back his grin. "Persephone, allow me to introduce Phuque."

"Thorne, please. Get your mind out of the gutter. Who is this?"

"This is Phuque." He paused, as Persephone frowned at him. "P-H-U-Q-U-E."

"Hiya Toots." The little man waved a rather grimy finger at Persephone. "Real nice set of honkers you got there, lady. Can I have a lick?"

He zoomed up to Persephone's breasts with his tongue hanging out.

Before she had time to flinch, a leather-clad wing rib slapped Phuque back down onto the floor.

"Damn, Thorne. That hurt."

"It was meant to. Touch her and die."

"Really?" Phuque stroked the stubbly hairs that passed for a beard. "Well, well. Whaddya know. You never told me that before about any of them. In fact, I remember when you an' me an' those two from France, you remember? The highfalutin' one who screamed when you pulled her skirt down and stuck your tongue up her…"

Another lash with the wing rib shut Phuque up.

Persephone had struggled back into her clothes and was regarding Phuque with a good deal of distaste.

"So, let me get this straight. Your name is Fuck? Like…like…well, like in *fuck*?" Her hips moved forward slightly, the gesture conveying her meaning.

"Well, yeah. Of course, some people pronounce it 'Fook,' but you probably know me better as Robin Goodfellow. You know…" His eyebrows waggled at her. Not a pretty sight. "Ahem." He cleared his throat. *"I'll put a girdle round about the earth in forty minutes."*

Persephone frowned.

"*If we the shadows have offended, think but this and all is mended*?" Phuque tried again hopefully.

Persephone's expression changed. "Ooooh. Now I know. You're *Puck*."

He sighed. "Well, I suppose it's better than that sissy-boy Robin shit. But that's the thanks I get for helping create one of the greatest plays ever. Do you know…" He led Persephone to the couch and sat down beside her, legs dangling.

Thorne shrugged and slipped back into his pants.

"…I was the one who gave Bill that damned idea for that fucking play. I even allowed him to use my name. Did I get a word of thanks? Nope. Any credit? Nope. Did I see a fucking ducat out of those productions? A percentage of the gate from the Globe? Not a pisspoor penny."

He shook his head in mournful sorrow. "All I get is grief. I didn't tell Bill to make the Queen a pain in the ass, did I? He did that all himself." Phuque absently scratched his crotch.

"So, what does Queen Bitch do? Well, every stinking night she creeps up there and changes Bill's script. Of course his spelling sucked, and he was writing my name like he heard it. So she goes and quote *corrects* it unquote. No F's like he was writing it, but a "P" instead. I mean, I ask you. Would it have been so bad to have had a fairy named Fuck helping out Bottom?"

Persephone bit back a giggle.

"It's okay, honey, you can laugh." Thorne slid in next to her and cuddled her protectively next to him. "That's one of his jobs, to—what's the phrase—"*jest to Oberon and make him smile*"? He does it quite well. Most of the time."

"Yeah, right." Phuque farted loudly. "That's for you, piss boy. Anyone who dresses like the inside of a Chevy shouldn't get bitchy with me."

"Was there something you wanted, or did you come by just to be your usual pain in the ass?" Thorne looked at Phuque with distaste.

"Hah. Don't you two talk about pains in the ass. I mean, sheesh. Oberon could have gotten a few tips from you two. Fogged up my glasses, you did."

Persephone lowered her eyes, while Thorne just snorted. "You don't wear glasses, you've seen it all before, and you're not about to tell Oberon anything because he's still mad at you for trying to goose the Queen at the last party."

Amazingly, the grumpy little goblin colored up. "She's a stuck up bitch, that's what she is."

Thorne turned to Persephone. "As a little back history here, you might be interested to know that our friend Phuque has had a severe case for the Queen for, what is it, two, three hundred years now?"

Another fart greeted this statement, and Phuque turned his face away from the pair on the couch with a pout.

"Unfortunately, Phuque made the mistake of trying to get it on with Peaseblossom..." continued Thorne.

"...Mustardseed."

"Beg your pardon, Mustardseed, when she was bending over some flower or other, harvesting nectar. Well, as you can imagine, most fairies, and other creatures too, come to think of it, don't take too well to having their butt cheeks spread and their asses reamed when they're not expecting it."

Persephone blushed. Obviously she wasn't "other creatures" because she'd enjoyed it immensely.

"*You*, my love, were expecting it. Or at least ready for it." Thorne's low whisper made her shiver.

"Anyway, Mustardseed took her complaint to Queen Titania, who decreed that history would remember this lad as mischievous Puck, not lusty Phuque, seeing as he'd tried to live up to his name once too often. Since then, he's lost no opportunity to piss her off, in the vain hope that she'll change her spell and put his real name back into Bill's scripts. And possibly screw him senseless as well."

Persephone gazed at Phuque. "Don't get your hopes up, little fella."

"Little fella? *Little* fella?"

Thorne sighed. "You've done it now."

"Let me tell *you*, hooters, better women than you have trembled and begged for this…" His hands fumbled through his pants and whipped out a quite impressive cock.

Persephone, who had just taken care of some very impressive cock attached to a much more impressive Thorne Leatherfly, merely smiled. "Quite nice, Phuque. Now put it away. There's a good boy."

Thorne stood up while Phuque was still sputtering. "Come on, rat." He grabbed Phuque by the scruff of his rather ugly neck and dragged him to the door. Phuque's wings fluttered madly but he was helpless against the muscled strength of the arms that held him securely.

"Now. Did you have a message for me from Oberon or did you come here just to get your ass kicked out again?"

"Oh yeah. Jeez, Leatherboy, go easy on the back will ya? Keep that up and I'll be humping *your* ass in a minute."

Thorne dropped him quicker than a hot potato.

"His Royal Pain-in-the-Ass-ness wants you to bring Miss Big Bazooms here to Neville's tonight. Party time. See ya, Stud-dud."

With a snicker and another loud fart, Phuque was gone, leaving a quiet room and the definite scent of marsh gas behind him.

Thorne leaned against the closed door and sighed.

Chapter Six

Persephone gazed out of Thorne Leatherfly's tall windows, not really seeing what was before her, but pondering what was within her.

Thorne had fussed and fidgeted around after Phuque had left, finally pressing a hard kiss on her lips and telling her to rest.

"Make yourself at home, Persephone. It's your turn to curl up for a nap on *my* bed." His sensual lips twisted in a wry smile.

In answer to the question in her eyes, Thorne gazed at her, his unusual golden irises flickering with his changing moods. "You are staying here with me. That's all there is to it. No questions, no arguments. You're mine." He'd turned to the door. "I have to go back to the office for a while, so settle in and try to rest up a bit. It's likely to get wild tonight at Neville's."

With a wink and a flick of his wings he'd left, leaving Persephone with the taste of his mouth on her lips and a million or two questions in her mind.

Settle in, he'd said. Yeah, right. She'd begin by unpacking her suitcases. No, wait, she didn't *have* any suitcases. Obviously, *Leatherhead* had overlooked the fact that she hadn't so much as a change of underwear, not that she *needed* them because no one here wore any, but it was the principle of the thing.

She'd wandered around the empty apartment and found the bathroom. Suppressing a giggle, she'd used the eggcup and then showered. Thorne's towels—black of course—were softer than kitten fur, and she'd swiped a robe that looked like midnight velvet and was long enough to polish the floor behind her as she walked.

So she was clean, warm, dry, and wondering if she could raid his fridge, if he *had* a fridge, and if he did, would it be full of nectar and moonbeams?

Nothing ventured, nothing gained, decided the intrepid Persephone. She left the windows and moved to what seemed to be Thorne's kitchen.

Oh happy day. She found the coffee. And it was the good stuff, too. It was in a French-press style coffee pot, but she could manage. There was some milk in the small fridge, hopefully not from aphids or anything, and even a couple of frozen waffles. Now *this* was more like it.

Wiping the remains of her late breakfast from her plate, Persephone jumped as a melodious chime filled the room. She couldn't smell smoke, which eliminated some kind of Fairyland fire alarm. She'd turned off the toaster, so that wasn't doing it. She couldn't see any kind of telephone. Then the sound came again accompanied by a tap on the door.

Aha. The doorbell.

Pleased with her deduction, Persephone opened the door.

"Hi there. I'm Cobweb." A tinkling voice emanated from a glistening white ball of fluff.

"Really. I'd have said dust bunny, but what do I know." Persephone leaned against the doorjamb.

"Mr. Leatherfly said I should drop this off with you." The delicate little creature hovered over the doorstep with a large box in tow, supported by five fluttering moths, one at each corner and one, presumed Persephone, as a back up in case one of the others got a flat wing?

She moved back, waving Cobweb and her entourage into the apartment.

"Oh, thanks. This has been a bit awkward. Where shall I have them put it?"

"How about right here," said Persephone, pointing to the coffee table.

"Super. Okay boys, down here, please—gently, that's it. Thanks so much." Cobweb fluttered her wings and blew little fairy kisses at the departing moths who fanned their wings as they assumed a precise formation and zoomed off.

"Now," said Cobweb, closing the door behind them. "Let's get to know each other, shall we?"

Persephone gulped.

"You must know that *everyone* is all agog because you're here with…*him*."

Cobweb's perfect golden ringlets shuddered on the last word, and she looked around fearfully.

"You mean Thorne?"

"Sssh. Yes. *Him*."

"Er—something wrong with *him*?"

Cobweb's huge blue eyes got impossibly huger. Persephone suddenly remembered the racks of Victorian-themed cards in her local store. Cobweb would have been a perfect model for each and every one of them. Her heart-shaped face shone with innocence and delight, and her whole body glowed with warmth. She was a natural for the ones about the perfection of giving and sharing, endless love and stuff like that.

"Wrong with Mr. Leatherfly?" Cobweb's little giggle sparkled across the room. "Oh no. Of *course* not. Not if you don't mind the fact that he's the biggest motherfucker to hit Fairyland in a hundred years, he's got a temper that could slice the dick off a goat, and most days I'd like to tell him to take his head and shove it so far up his ass he can see daylight."

Persephone's jaw dropped and she lost her breath for long seconds.

"Oh, sorry. I forget to watch the language sometimes." Cobweb colored prettily.

"Um." Persephone was at a complete loss for words.

"Are you going to open the box?" The delicate little beauty skipped to the large package and let the sunlight dance off her wings as her tiny fingers twitched the ribbons apart.

"Sure." Persephone followed her, feeling fat, lumpy, and un-fairylike.

"Oooooh…" Cobweb's exclamation filled the room. "Persephone. Look at this…"

This was a leather dress of sorts. Vivid pink at the hem, it faded through all the shades of pink until the top where it was almost white. The front was cut low and the back non-existent. It was softer than the finest chamois and Persephone wanted to roll herself up in it and wriggle for about a week. She noticed a nice pair of matching boots.

"Oh my. This is really cool." She stroked her hand along the fabric like she would pet a dog. "What on earth is it made of?"

"Hmm. It's imported. Probably locust leather."

Persephone drew her hand away quite sharply. "Oh. Really?"

Cobweb giggled. "It's a very fine piece of fabric. Don't be worried about it. It's treated very carefully and run through a special process before it's even touched by fairy hands. That's what makes it so soft. And expensive, too. Well, you must have Mr. Leatherfly in the palm of your—" Cobweb glanced at Persephone's cleavage, "um—hand."

Persephone blushed.

"So tell me…" Cobweb scootched her bottom along the coffee table a little nearer Persephone. "What's he *like*?"

"What's he like? Don't you know what he's like? You've already described how you feel about him."

"Well, I haven't worked for him for very long, and he's a bit of an asshole really, in the office, that is. At least *I* think he is. Norman says he's really quite nice, but he never seems to pay much attention to *me*." She pouted prettily. "What I meant was…" She scootched even closer. "What's he like to…well…*you know*…"

The fairy that had no problems with a multitude of foul curses apparently was unable to use the word "fuck" as a verb. Persephone shook her head. "Sorry. I don't believe in flit-and-tell."

Cobweb pouted. "Oh come on, share a tidbit. All that lovely leather? Those studs, those wings?"

"Nope."

The doorbell chimed on Cobweb's pleas, and with some relief Persephone opened it to find Sal hovering over the doormat.

"Sal, bless you. Come on in. Just the man I need."

"Oh darling. They all say that. Go ahead, use me, abuse me. I *love* it. Hi, Cobweb darling. *Love* those booties…"

They exchanged air kisses, two dazzling beings hovering off the floor. Persephone yearned for a camera. It was a photographic moment that would have assured her fame and fortune for the rest of her life with Paranormal Weekly.

"Well, I'm going to toddle along, Persephone. I heard you're coming to Neville's tonight, so I'll probably see you there." Cobweb gave an entrancing little chuckle. "I've managed to get a date with Norman Elderbranch. He's the most gnarliest thing, you know." She sighed theatrically. "Have you tried a gnome yet?"

Persephone shook her head, eyes wide.

"Oh, my dear, you don't know what you're missing. They can do the most amazing things with their beards. I can't wait to see the ones in the floor show. With that kind of inspiration I'm definitely going to get Norman out of his hat tonight if it kills me." She giggled and fluttered off, leaving a tiny trail of glitter behind her.

Sal sighed and closed the door behind her. "She's been at the nectar again, I guarantee it. Sugar imbalance does that to some fairies. Turns them into raving nymphos."

He grinned.

Persephone grinned back. "You got stock in the nectar company?"

"Yup. Went up two points this morning, too." Sal laughed merrily. "So. We're going to Neville's tonight, are we?"

"I guess *we* are. At least that's what Cobweb told me."

"So how is Mr. Leatherbulge? Built for speed or distance?"

"Sal. I didn't tell Cobweb anything, what makes you think I'm sharing stuff like that with you?"

Sal pouted. "But darling. I've sucked those gorgeous tits, too, you know. Even now the taste is still rattling around in the back of my throat." He tipped his head back and made gargling noises. "Mmm. Vintage human with just a dash—the merest soupçon—of vanilla."

Persephone burst out laughing. "Oh, cut it out. Come see what I'm supposed to wear tonight and tell me about these damn wings. You can scratch my back too, if you wouldn't mind. It's itching like the devil…"

"Um, Persephone." Sal looked surprisingly embarrassed. "I don't think I can do that anymore."

"Do what? Scratch my back?"

"Uh, yeah."

"Whyever not?" Persephone frowned at him.

"Well, see, it's your wing buds that are itching."

"Yeah, I know. Believe me I know." She rolled her shoulders against the fabric of her robe.

"Well, you see…oh dear, how to explain this. My mother did it so much better. Here, come sit down by me and hold my hand. Don't be scared now…"

Sal fussed her into the couch next to him and far from soothing her, he twisted up Persephone's nerves into a taut knot.

"So, what is it? Am I dying or something?"

"Oh, dear heavens, no." Sal looked aghast. "Nothing like that."

"Then *what?*

Sal winced as Persephone's screech rattled the lampshade. He took her hand in his and stroked it soothingly. "You're becoming a woman fairy, darling."

Persephone burst out laughing. "God. If this is about my period, don't bother. I already know."

Sal blushed. "Silly thing. No. Now listen to me, this is important."

Persephone stifled her giggles, trying to look appropriately impressed.

"When you were brought here, you had fairy DNA implanted, which enables you to grow wings, right?"

"Right. We covered that at orientation."

"Good. Now what you may not realize is that your wing buds emerge from a brand new orifice in your spinal area. An opening that is full of the most exquisitely sensitive nerve endings…"

"Sensitive nerve endings. Yeah—I kind of figured that bit for myself." *With a little help from Thorne's clever tongue.*

Sal took a deep breath and continued. "Well, you are developing what we call a thrusterbud."

"A what?"

"A thrusterbud."

"A thrusterbud." Persephone frowned. "What the hell's a thrusterbud?"

Sal seemed to be searching for words. "Let's see, I can probably best describe it as a new seat of sexual pleasure, a new gathering of nerve endings designed to bring you to the most amazing climaxes of your life."

Persephone tried to absorb exactly what Sal was saying. Her eyes widened and her hand involuntarily slipped behind to her back. "You mean—dear god. This is…Spinal Clit?"

Sal's mouth dropped, his eyes widened and for two seconds he was struck dumb. Then he began to giggle, and it grew into a bout of hysterical laughter that brought the tears to his eyes.

He coughed and sputtered and started over again, clutching his stomach as he roared.

Persephone would have slapped him on the back, but at this point wasn't quite sure about touching anything on anyone anywhere.

She settled for fetching a glass of water, putting it down on the table and waiting for Sal to stop his guffaws.

"Oh heavens, my darling. I'm so sorry you're Leatherfly's. You could have brought so much sunshine into my life." Sal took a deep breath, glanced at Persephone and started laughing all over again.

She sighed. He looked like he was in for another extended session with his giggles, so she grabbed her dress and went into the bedroom to slip it on.

Thorne's bedroom was a surprise. Huge, of course, and dominated by a giant bed which looked like it had been wrought out of a fight with some mammoth branches. Twisted and gnarled, they fingered their way across the headboard and poked up at either side, in a weird kind of natural oak paralysis. The bedding was lush, featured several shades of black—no surprise there, but was accented by a rather ragged pink bunny.

Persephone bit her lip as she picked up the little fellow and cuddled him. He bore the signs of having been much loved over many years, and she felt her heart stir at the thought of the massively male Thorne sleeping with his bunny. It was rather disarming, and she smiled as she stroked the soft bunny fur.

She tucked him back onto his pillow and turned to the dress.

It slid over her body like warm air, hugging her hips, and caressing her breasts into an impressive cleavage. She grimaced, but then remembered the feel of Thorne's mouth and fingers on her body.

Maybe these were not such a bad thing after all.

She fastened the catch behind her neck, and then couldn't resist turning and peering over her shoulder at her bared skin.

Sure enough, there were tiny wings peeking out from between her shoulder blades.

She gasped at the sight. Wings. *Wings!*

Her very own wings.

They caught the light with a little glitter, and she noticed the light pinkish reflections. So she was going to be a pink fairy. She could live with that. She reached back and carefully touched the only one she could comfortably reach.

It was an odd sensation. Almost a tickle, but not quite. Almost like a kiss, but again—not quite.

She gently brushed the skin around her wings.

Aha. There it was. A sexual zing shivering through her body that bettered any she'd felt with her vibrator. Even when it had new batteries in it.

She whipped her hand away, feeling almost naughty at touching that part of herself. Her thrusterbud.

She chuckled.

"Cute, aren't they?"

Sal was leaning in the doorway, watching as Persephone turned this way and that, admiring her new assets in the mirror.

She blushed. "I, um—they're growing, aren't they?"

"Yep. And pink, too. I'm glad to see I was right about that."

"Any significance to the color?"

"No. Just means you won't be wearing much orange this season." Sal raised his eyebrow at her.

"I don't do orange anyway," she muttered, flexing her shoulder blades. "So how do these things work, Sal? Like am I going to be able to actually fly, or are they just a real handy hair dryer?" The whole business of flying still seemed rather surreal to Persephone.

Sal grinned. "Of course you're going to be able to fly. Not *yet*, they need to grow some before you can actually achieve lift off, but you'll do the flight prep course, get into training, you'll be all set."

"God. Flight school? Is that physics and velocities and stuff?"

"Nah. Just how not to hit anyone and how to land without ramming a goblin up your ass by mistake."

"No flap twice when making a left-hand turn or something?"

Sal snickered. "Nope. Nor shout or make beeping noises when backing up."

Persephone started to giggle. "Not even little flashing turn signal lights or white lights on my butt for reversing?"

Sal held up his hands. "For god's sake don't get me started again, will you? You're too funny for words." He crossed the room and grabbed Persephone in a huge hug, planting a wet kiss on her cheek.

"You're going to have soooo much fun here in Fairyland, Persephone. Of course, whether Fairyland is going to be able to stand the shock, I don't know."

"And whether you can stand the shock of having your wings ripped off and shoved up your ass is another matter. *Get your hands off her.*"

Sal rolled his eyes. "Ah. His Master's Growl." He turned to face a lividly angry Thorne Leatherfly who was staring at the two of them with ferocious intensity. "Hi, honey. How was your day?" Sal batted his eyelashes at Thorne.

Thorne growled again.

"Oh, cut it out, Thorne," sighed Persephone. "Stop acting like a spoilt twelve-year-old. Sal was keeping me company and making me laugh. He's a friend, for god's sake. He helped me when I got here, found me clothes, got me clean, and…" Her voice trailed off as she briefly remembered what else he'd done.

"Yeah. Sure." Thorne folded his arms across his chest and gazed at her.

"Oh, darling. You know me. Love 'em all, and they all love me right back." Sal fearlessly tapped Thorne on his solidly muscled chest. "I think she probably is your wingmate, you know."

Thorne's head tipped sideways and he narrowed his eyes. "Oh, yeah?"

"As you so succinctly put it, yeah. The signs are right and you're both responding properly. You'd better fill her in on the details of the Nuptial Flight thing, by the way. The wings are starting."

Thorne's eyes whipped over to where Persephone was standing, a frown beginning to wrinkle her brow.

"Hey. You two. I'm here, you know. It's considered rude to talk about someone like she's not even there." She tapped her toe and placed her hands squarely on her hips. "So, if there's something I should be told, I'd appreciate *someone* doing it right away."

"She's all yours," grinned Sal, blowing a kiss to Persephone. "And of course if she doesn't work out for you, Thorne sweetie, I'm still here. You know what leather does to me." He sighed and fluttered his wings.

"Flit off, Salvias," said Thorne rudely, but without any real heat.

"I'm gone. Just a trail of fairy dust in the wind."

He was, too. That fairy was damn good at making a dramatic exit.

Chapter Seven

Thorne stared at Persephone as silence filled the room. Without Sal's distracting presence, he became more vividly aware of her. She just looked so *right* standing at the foot of his bed. Like she belonged there. He felt himself walking toward her, his feet carrying him toward his goal without his conscious volition.

"So, honey," she said nervously. "How *was* your…umph."

He plastered his mouth to hers.

Hungry for the taste of her, his lips couldn't wait. Her breath was sweet, her body smelled of flowers and woman, and he wanted her more at that moment than he could ever remember wanting anything for the past three hundred years or so.

He kept his hands glued to his sides and just let his mouth feed on her.

Turning his head to align their lips more perfectly, he breathed in her sigh as she opened for him and welcomed him inside.

This was different. This was special. Something about the way their lips met in perfect alignment sent chills down Thorne's wingribs.

He fought the urge to grab her in his arms, preferring the delicious torment of permitting only the touch of their mouths.

Persephone let him know in no uncertain terms that she had other ideas.

She moved closer to him, mewling in the back of her throat as his tongue stroked her softness.

He could feel the heat of her body as she stopped a mere wings' width away from his chest. One hand rested gently on his forearm as the other slid up to his shoulder and around the back of his neck.

She was holding him to her, letting him play with her tongue.

Her hands sifted through his hair and touched his neck lightly. He shuddered.

She closed the gap between them, pressing the softness of her breasts against his body.

He could feel her nipples hardening against him as his tongue plunged deeper and more aggressively into her mouth.

She sucked it, played with it, coiled her own tongue around it, and met him, move for move.

His leather pants groaned as his cock swelled rapidly.

"Damn, Persephone," he breathed, pulling back and resting his forehead against her. "You're so beautiful."

Persephone froze at his words.

He raised his head in query. "What? You don't think you are?"

She stared at him and shook her head slightly. "Thorne, no one has ever said that to me before."

"No one?"

"No one."

"The world is full of fools, Persephone. Complete and utter fools." He raised his hand and gently ran his fingertips down over her shoulder to her elbow and her wrist. He raised her hand to his mouth.

"You're incredibly lovely." He slid her pinky finger into his mouth and sucked it, watching her eyes widen.

"And you taste better than the finest honey." He coiled his tongue around her finger and caressed it as he pulled it out of his mouth. Her ring finger was next. "You kiss like no one I've ever kissed before." The ring finger was followed by the middle finger.

Persephone's nipples were pushing against the soft leather and making enticing little nubbins appear on her halter dress.

"You smell like fresh flowers, twilight and snow," he whispered, as her forefinger disappeared between his lips to be worshipped by his tongue. He could scent her arousal now, adding fuel to his smoldering fire.

"And you touch me in places I've never known. You make me think of things I've never thought of, and when I'm away from you I want to be with you." He released her finger with a little pop.

His hands opened hers and squeezed the fullness at the base of her thumb. She moaned. He brought it to his mouth and bit gently, making her squirm.

"Thorne," she whispered.

"You loved me unconditionally as a stray cat, and let me share your warmth, your home and your bed. Will you do that with me now, Persephone?"

His mouth enveloped her thumb and suckled it, sliding it out again with a brush of his lips.

"Will you share my warmth, my home and my bed? Will you love me unconditionally?"

* * * * *

Persephone looked deep into Thorne's glowing golden eyes, trying to see the man behind the wings. She'd known he would be something special as soon as he'd first touched her, and places deep inside her had responded to him as never before. But was it too soon? She'd been in Fairyland for less than a day. Sure it seemed like a lifetime ago she was in her kitchen with her cat and her cupcake, but it was still only hours.

Then she set those thoughts aside and looked within herself. The answer was clear. Seize this chance or spend a lifetime regretting it.

"Yes."

The dam broke and Thorne seized her in a grip of iron. A wicked grin curved his handsome mouth and his eyes gleamed brilliant gold.

Persephone felt her heart melt just from the glory of looking at him. And he was all *hers*.

Daringly, she tipped her hips and rubbed against him.

He moaned and she smirked. This could be more fun than she'd ever imagined. A handsome, horny fairy, fairly tripping over his tongue to get to *her*, Persephone Jones. My, my. What a birthday.

"Shit, honey. There's nothing I'd like better than to tumble you onto our bed right here, right now, and…" His hips thrust back, sending chills through her as his incredibly hard cock rubbed her in *just* the right place.

"Oh yeah, Leatherfly. Oh yeah," endorsed Persephone, eyes closing with pleasure.

"But…" He eased himself away from her with a wince.

"But what?"

"We have to go out."

"*What*?"

"Look, if it wasn't Oberon himself, I'd be the first one to say fuck them all and you'd be stark naked underneath me right this second. But he is the King, and it's damn near a royal command. We *have* to go."

Persephone sighed. "I suppose. It was too good to be true, wasn't it?" She shrugged herself back into a more normal frame of mind. The one that said how unlikely it was that Mr. Perfectly-Slick Studded Wings would actually be falling head over landing gear for someone like her.

Hands slid up her sides and around her back.

"Oh, no, baby, it wasn't too good to be true. Not yet." His fingers darted around her tiny budding wings and she gasped as they stroked her sensitive flesh.

"God, Thorne," she breathed.

"Yeah, honey. Just imagine…" His touches flickered and fluttered on the twelve million nerve endings that were all hard-wired to her cunt. She could feel her juices leaking from her and her breasts ached for his mouth, his hands, his wingtips, any part of him to ease their need.

"Dear heavens," she sobbed, all but coming apart under his touch. She grabbed the first thing that came to hand, which turned out to be his cock. His indrawn breath matched hers as his fingers moved faster.

She ripped the zipper down and shoved her hands into Thorne's pants, cradling the erection that fell readily into her hands.

"Oh my, you're…you're incredible," she said, entranced by the thick and hot length of him. She ran her hand up and down, and circled the base, squeezing firmly.

His gasp pleased her, although she almost lost her concentration as his fingers found a new and entirely incredible place to massage around her thrusterbud.

"Thorne, I'm going to—" she choked, flinging her head back and hanging onto his cock for dear life.

"I know babe, I know…" His voice was as tight as his balls, and she felt the veins in his cock twitch as he groaned loudly.

She couldn't believe what was happening to her. Thorne was coming into her hand, hot and alive and pulsing in her grasp. His fingers were driving her to insanity, and he hadn't even touched her clit or her breasts. Her entire body shook and trembled from his touch on her back and when he savagely pulled the front of her dress away from her and fastened his mouth to her nipple it was almost a relief.

His tongue pulled and suckled and his teeth bit down as his finger penetrated into the mystery of her thrusterbud.

She screamed. And came. And came. For what felt like hours.

Spasms shook her from head to toe, deliciously painful cramps rocketed through her spinal column to echo the clenching of her womb, and her cunt wept tears of delight.

She collapsed into Thorne's waiting arms, exhausted, sated, and happier than she'd ever been in her entire life.

"Holy fucking-A."

Thorne's words dropped into the now-quiet room like machine gun fire, jerking Persephone out of her stupor.

"You brought me off with a hand job. I can't believe it."

Persephone blushed. "Well. So much for romance." She straightened herself and moved out of Thorne's embrace.

He seemed quite stunned, just looking down at himself and the wet stain he'd left on his clothes.

"You weren't exactly idle, either, you know." She pulled her halter top back into place and refastened the tie. Her back ached a little and she winced.

"You okay?" His concern warmed her heart.

"I think so. That was something else, though. What, I'm not sure, but definitely in the category of *something else*."

Thorne looked at her uncertainly. "Does—er—does that mean it was…good?"

Persephone hid a grin. "Yeah, Thorne. That means it was…fabulously spectacular. Bells, fireworks, earth moving, that sort of thing."

Thorne regained his customary expression. "Well, of course it was. Nothing but the best for you, babe." He moved toward the bathroom then turned back. A wide grin spread across his face.

"Well, okay. I guess it *was* good for you."

She glanced over at him with a puzzled frown.

"Look at those beauties."

She swiveled and checked the mirror. Where there had been a pair of small baby wings, there was now a matched set of quite respectably sized wings, glittering softly in the growing darkness of their room.

"Wow…" she breathed. "Wow. Sugar was right. Sex works."

Thorne chuckled from the bathroom. "You said that right, honey." He emerged a few moments later, clean, changed and smiling. "Let's go party, Persephone. I want to dance with you, hold you against me, make a public display of ourselves and let Fairyland know you're mine. And most of all, I want to come home with you. Sleep with you after making love to you. Hold you all night and wake up with my arms warming you and my wings around you."

Persephone's eyes filled with tears. If this was a dream, please don't ever let her wake up. If it was the answer to her birthday wish, then thank you to the gods of birthday wishes. She'd never make another one.

"You're on, Leatherfly. Let's go rock Fairyland, and then come home and rock the Universe."

* * * * *

Persephone wasn't quite sure what to expect when she entered the dark and dusky interior of Neville's "Gnome Away From Gnome" that evening, and it showed in the hesitant expression on her face.

Thorne had no such problems. All his attention was focused on his beautiful wingwoman.

"Hey Thorne."

"Hi, Leatherlover…"

"Thorne baby. How've you been?"

The chorus of female greetings that flowed over him as he walked Persephone past the tables toward the back of the club bounced off his wings like raindrops.

He could feel a slight tension in Persephone's spine, however, as he rested his hand just above the swell of her buttocks.

"Come here, often, Leatherfly?" she asked, with a dry tone to her voice and a raised eyebrow.

"Not anymore," he answered, slipping his hand even lower and squeezing her buttocks.

He was satisfied with the slightly cross-eyed glance she gave him and the falter in her stride.

He led her to a larger booth where a couple was already seated.

"Hey, boss." Norman Elderbranch stood and shook hands with Thorne, staring all the while at Persephone. Next to him, Cobweb dimpled at the two of them.

"Persephone, this is Norman Elderbranch, my right hand gnome, and I think you've met Cobweb Glitterworm?"

Persephone smiled and shook hands with Norman, trying hard not to bend down to his level too obviously. Thorne was touched that she'd even consider it.

"Hello, Norman. It's a pleasure to meet you. And Cobweb, lovely to see you again."

Thorne hid a grin. The professional Persephone had just peeped through, regardless of the fact she was dressed like a horny fairy's wet dream and had wings that sparkled like pink diamonds. He couldn't wait to get her in his office. Actually he was having a hard time waiting to get her anywhere. He considered the possibility of dragging her off to the bathroom for a quickie.

"Don't you think so, Mr. Leatherfly?" Cobweb's delicate voice grated on his aroused body and wrenched him back out of his fantasy.

"Um, yeah. Whatever."

Persephone glared at him and Norman grinned.

"What? What'd I say? It's loud in here, I didn't catch everything."

"Oh, sit down," said Persephone, tugging him onto the banquette next to her. The waitress hovered next to their table with a pad in one feeler, a tray balanced between two others, a cell phone and pager in yet others, and a pencil poised to take their order.

"Hi Mayfly. Looking good. How're the kids?"

"Great, Thorne. Thanks for the toys, by the way. My son loved that truck."

Thorne blushed and looked away.

"So, what'll it be, Persephone?" Norman asked.

"I have no idea, Norman. What does one order in Fairyland? Usually I have a light beer…" Persephone tilted her head and looked at the little fellow.

"Oh, Persephone," tinkled Cobweb. "Beer's way too heavy for us fairies. Why don't you try something light and sweet?"

"Like nectar, I suppose?"

"Oh yes, absolutely. All the in-crowd just loves it. Especially the honeysuckle one."

"There goes Sal's stock, up another couple of points," she whispered to Thorne as the Mayfly took their orders.

Thorne grinned, needing no further explanation. "I've got some, too."

She punched him gently, then turned the hit into a caress and took his breath away. "D'you think the King and Queen will be here soon?"

"I wouldn't doubt it," answered Thorne. "They hate to miss a good time."

"Real party royals, Persephone," added Norman. "Of course, they've had a couple thousand years to practice, and if you could hear them tell their tales about the old times and the parties they had back then, whew. It'd melt your wing wax."

A blast of sound interrupted their conversation, and Persephone leaned back into Thorne's arm with her glass of nectar in her hand.

"Dancing?" She looked up at him with a smile that made his heart ache.

"Not yet, sweetheart. We get a floorshow first."

"Oh cool." She turned a little and brushed his side with her breast. He felt his pulse rate leap and fought a battle with himself to keep his hands out of her tempting cleavage. For the moment, anyway. "I love live entertainment. Is it a band, a singer? What is it? A rock group?"

Thorne swallowed. "Er—not exactly."

"Faireeeeeesssss and Beeeeeeings…" a loud voice blasted through the speakers that were placed around the room. "Neville is proud to present for your entertainment this evening…direct from the Fairyland Palace in Las Vegas…the *Canterbury Belles.* Accompanied by their Gnimble Gnomes."

A roar of applause filled the room at this announcement.

"As a special treat, the Gnomes have invited a Guest Gnome to perform with them this evening…put your hands together for *Gnaughty Gnicholas.*"

Thorne swallowed and prayed that his wingwoman was broad minded.

Chapter Eight

The lights dimmed over the raised stage, and Persephone slid her hand into Thorne's as she waited for the show to begin. She was having a wonderful time. The nectar was delicious—Cobweb had been right—and she was considering a second glass. She had a hunky fairy all her own who couldn't seem to get close enough to her or stop touching her. And she was about to watch what was probably some kind of risqué floorshow.

And it was still her birthday. Life didn't get much better. Or odder, but then again, who said normal was fun?

A drumbeat began and two cloaked figures slid into the spotlight. Delicate veils swathed their wings and blended with the softness of their cloaks, hiding most of their bodies and sparkling under the lights.

The bodies swayed in time with the drumbeat, and behind them Persephone could see a line of smaller figures, silhouetted against the curtains at the back of the stage. Their pointy hats gave them away. They had to be the Gnimble Gnomes.

The drums picked up and a mournful guitar began twanging out a sad refrain.

In perfect timing, the two cloaks fell to the floor, revealing two female fairies.

Persephone gasped. They were wearing stardust and not much else. And boy, were they stacked.

"They're not real, Persephone, don't worry. Implants, you know." Cobweb leaned over the table and patted Persephone's hand reassuringly. "They wouldn't be able to fly if they were real. But since Tinkerbell went Hollywood and got herself a pair, every would-be fairy 'star' figures she's got to have big—um—

well, you get the idea." Cobweb stuttered to a halt, obviously realizing she was talking to a woman who possessed star qualities of her own that were quite real, and owed nothing to the surgeon's skill. She blushed a little and sat back next to Norman, whose beard twitched slightly.

Persephone shot a glance over at Thorne, only to see him frowning at Cobweb. A drum roll brought her attention back to the stage.

The Canterbury Belles slipped the rest of their veils off and were revealed as glorious red-winged creatures with softly silvered bodies and tiny red thongs that sparkled and glittered brightly. Their breasts were bare and pointing at the audience as they began to sway to the music.

Their movements became slightly more provocative.

Their hips began thrusting in a gently rhythmic fashion, bringing a few calls of approval from the crowd. As they continued their dance, the gnomes behind them filed out into the spotlight, marching slowly to the drumbeat and swaying in time with the girls' hips.

These, realized Persephone, were not your everyday, sit-next-to-the-tub-of- roses-on-the-front-lawn, gnomes.

Their tunics looked like shiny blue satin, cut long in front, their hats stiff, pointy-sharp and decorated with sequins, and their red trousers were transparent. When they turned, Persephone was treated to the sight of five little gnome bums, just barely covered by their tunics.

She stirred. Thorne's hand gripped hers tighter and he settled her practically on his lap, folding his wings around her protectively.

She snuggled in with a smile and a sigh of contentment and returned her attention to the cute little gnome bottoms that were bouncing around on stage.

"Oooh, Norman," cooed Cobweb from the other side of the table. "You'd look good in that."

Persephone stifled a chuckle as Norman slid as close to Cobweb as he could, tucked his hand behind her back and whispered something in her ear, making her giggle and shiver.

Persephone could just imagine where his hand was and what it was doing. She glanced up at Thorne to catch sight of his eyes burning down at her. He folded his other wing across their bodies and slid his hand into the pocket of her dress.

Well, that was fine, until Persephone realized she didn't have a pocket in her dress.

"I had this made especially for tonight," whispered Thorne, licking up the outside of her ear as he spoke.

His hand had passed right through the hidden slit in the leather and was even now resting above her pussy, stroking, caressing, moving softly over her skin.

Her back itched like hell.

"I won't touch your thrusterbud here, babe. Some things are best kept for more private surroundings."

She sighed as his fingers speared through her pubic hair.

"But we have other options. Just keep watching the show."

Persephone did as she was told.

The gnomes had cleared away the veils and removed their hats, placing them in two pointy piles at either side of the stage. The Canterbury Belles, pleased to be free of their draperies, were now running their hands lightly up and down each other's bodies, turning, twisting, moaning, and generally making sure that everyone got to see their nipples as they were pulled and tweaked, and their breasts as they were lifted and offered.

The audience was getting increasingly restless, with several moans indicating patrons who were doing a lot more than lip-synching with this particular act.

The music sped up a little, heightening the sexual tension, and with a little drum roll a new gnome leapt onto the stage.

This, deduced Persephone, must be Gnaughty Gnicholas.

It wasn't a difficult deduction.

Gnicholas was practically gnaked.

His costume was completely transparent, and although Persephone had no idea what the general cock size was for an average gnome, Gnicholas had to be outstanding when measured by any standard.

He was hung like a—well, whatever began with G and was really huge. She couldn't think of anything because she was stunned at what she was seeing.

"Never realized gnomes hid such secrets, did you?" said Thorne quietly.

"Dear heavens," she answered, stomach fluttering as his hand moved against her skin.

Thorne grinned. "Look at Cobweb," he whispered.

Persephone risked a glance across the table. Cobweb's eyes were the size of saucers and her mouth hung open in a rather unflattering manner. Norman, on the other hand, grinned like an idiot, clearly waiting for Cobweb to make the connection.

Cobweb turned to Norman. He turned the grin down a couple of notches, and smiled at her affectionately.

She licked her lips and swallowed.

Norman pulled her onto his lap and fluffed her wings out to either side.

At that point, Persephone ducked down behind the protection of Thorne's wings. There were some things that she probably shouldn't be watching.

From her shielded cocoon she returned her attention to the show. And was completely distracted by Thorne, whose fingers were teasingly playing with her hair, her flesh, and now, her clit.

Sheesh. This was something else.

Gnicholas had assumed a position on his knees and was beckoning the Belles with his hands raised.

They fluttered over to him, and hovered, one on either side, hands above their heads in wanton pleasure.

Fascinated, Persephone stared as Gnicholas' beard began to twitch and divide itself into two streams of hair. It parted cleanly and each side seemed to develop a life of its own. Beads of sweat began to glisten on Gnicholas' brow.

The beard halves began swaying, almost like puppets on a string. They crept up the thighs of the Belles on either side of him, and Gnicholas closed his eyes in concentration.

With a grunt, he tipped his head slightly, and each beard half slipped under the thong of a Belle. His erection grew.

The girls moaned.

The beard trembled and with a mighty roar, Gnicholas commanded his beard to pull.

It yanked the thong off each fairy, leaving them gnude. Persephone shook her head in disbelief. She was thinking in gnome.

The crowd applauded, whistled, honked, screamed, and generally signaled its appreciation.

But Gnicholas hadn't finished.

The Gnimble Gnomes rushed around the stage, and within seconds had assembled something that looked like a velvet-upholstered mushroom. Gnicholas reclined on it, and allowed them to wipe his brow, and feed him sips of restoratives. The fairies had hovered off to either side of the stage, where they were flitting over the pointy hats, spreading their legs and teasingly flying down to brush their pussies against them with little giggles.

The music was raucous, pounding, and Persephone could feel it through her seat and through Thorne's fingers.

Not content with touching, Thorne was now softly rubbing her swollen tissues, teasing her clit with his nearness, yet not bringing her to full arousal. She fidgeted slightly, wanting more of his warmth.

"Easy, love. We have time."

Persephone gritted her teeth, then remembered that two could play almost any game. She slid her hand across his lap and found something that felt just right in her hand.

Thorne sucked in a breath.

She grinned. "You're right, Thorne. Plenty of time." *Gotcha.*

The music changed, and the lights on the stage dimmed, throwing the Gnimble Gnomes into shadow.

Gnicholas was alone in the spotlight, and as he lay back onto his mushroom, his transparent pants tented against his huge erection.

The fairies, summoned by a clap of his hands, fluttered to him and eased his pants away, leaving him free and upstanding in the center of the stage.

An awed silence fell as the audience considered the magnificence of a fully engorged virile male gnome.

His cock was standing straight and proud, as Gnicholas clasped his hands behind his head in a pose of casual magnificence. The head was broadly flanged and deep red, and the veins running down its length were hard and prominent. He could have modeled for Michelangelo, mused Persephone, wondering what Thorne would look like on a mushroom like that. She'd love to find out.

Gnicholas spread his legs, displaying an equally impressive set of balls, and with a click of his fingers the portion of the stage he occupied began to rotate. No one was going to miss the spectacle of this gnome's equipment.

A spattering of applause broke out and within moments, Gnicholas's genitals got a standing ovation.

He reached down and proudly waved his cock in thanks, sending a couple of fairies into a swoon.

The Belles, meanwhile, had flown high above Gnicholas while he rotated in splendid display. Now, as the movement slowed, they fluttered down, hanging in the air next to his body.

Persephone watched, fascinated, as they flew. The mere thought of being able to do that sent a shiver of pleasure through her. No, wait, that was Thorne's fingers.

He was about to sink one deep into her cunt. Oh god. She closed her eyes, not caring if she missed the show.

"Put your leg over mine," hissed Thorne, tensing under her fingers. She'd almost forgotten that she had a very nice fairy cock in her own hand. She had to gather her thoughts for a moment before she realized what he wanted her to do. Quietly, she raised one thigh and draped it over Thorne's. She was now open to his searching hand.

And he searched. And thereafter found.

She gulped, fighting back the urge to moan.

On the stage, the fairies seemed to be in much the same state. Gnicholas had divided that magic beard of his again, only this time his progress was unhampered by anything as mundane as a thong. This time, his beard clearly played with two fairy clits that now glistened with fairy juices.

It was quite clear what was happening to them, because they were now hovering upside down, giving the audience a perfect view of their pussies, and enabling them to begin working on Gnicholas.

The gnome was about to receive the blowjob to end all blowjobs from two fairies whose heads were bobbing around his cock and his balls.

Persephone's attention was torn. She'd never imagined anything like what she was seeing, and she'd never imagined anything like what she was feeling.

Oh shit. Decisions, decisions.

Thorne's fingers made it easier, and without realizing it, she closed her eyes on Gnicholas and concentrated on Thorne.

He must have sensed her attention, and his fingers plunged deep into her cunt. He moved them slightly, bending them, twirling them, pulling them back out to toy with her clit, then plunging them back in.

Her breasts ached to the point of pain and she wanted to squirm down onto his hand and drive it deep inside her.

She clenched her fist around his cock, only to have him gasp and push her hand aside with a wing rib.

"I can't take it, honey. Once in my pants today is enough. I can wait. This is for you. Open your eyes and watch the show, while I watch you. Think what it might be like with you hovering over me, sucking me into your mouth like that…think about all the different ways I'm gonna fuck you when we get home…"

Persephone broke out into a sweat. Her back itched fiercely, and her clit screamed for release.

On stage, the fairies were getting pretty stoked up themselves, almost fighting over whose tongue was going to lick Gnicholas' balls and whose mouth could take him the deepest. Gnicholas, for his part, let his beard do all the work, only occasionally reaching out and tweaking an available fairy nipple. The music was reaching a crescendo, as was the act.

With a scream, one of the fairies collapsed, shuddering, into a twitching orgasmic heap of red and silver glitter. Seconds later the other one fell, only she toppled into rigidity, thighs clasped, body taut and breasts shaking.

Gnicholas sighed, and reached down to his still rock-hard cock. He grinned at the audience, as if inviting them to share in his amazing abilities. With a couple of strokes he enlarged his awesome cock even more, then lay back and thrust his hips upward in time with the pounding drums.

Suddenly he raised his hand, the drums ceased and there was a moment of complete silence.

Then he roared, and released a mammoth cloud of sparkling fairy dust in a gushing geyser from his cock. It was followed by five simultaneous smaller explosions of fairy dust from the five Gnimble Gnomes who'd been busily stroking themselves in time to the beat of the music. Five little sets of buttocks tensed, five little beards shuddered and twitched, and five little gnomes toppled exhaustedly to the floor.

The audience went wild.

Persephone saw none of it. Thorne had just made her come.

* * * * *

"So how *did* they do the sparkly thing?" Persephone's head rested on Thorne's chest and his chin gently grazed her hair as they danced together on the still-glittering stage. "Please don't tell me I'm stepping in gnome-cum."

He chuckled, tightening his hold and adjusting his hands to grip her buttocks even closer.

"It's theater, honey. All theater."

"Well that must have been one hell of a special effect. I guess."

"Sorry you missed it?"

She snorted, burrowing deeper into his shirt. "You've *got* to be kidding. Hey, I could probably see gnomes jerk off any time I wanted to. But having you touch me like that, well. *Well.*"

Thorne's heart bounced. He distinctly felt it. "You know, Persephone, we're going to have to talk soon."

She stilled. "Oh, god. You want to *talk*?" She pulled away from his heat and blinked up at him. "Is this where you tell me that it's been fun, but it's time to move on? Or you need more space? Or now that you've had my wings, you don't need to buy the flight deck? Or something?"

Thorne was startled into wrenching her back against his body with a smack. "Hell no, Persephone. What's your problem?"

"Bethides a broken nothe?" she snuffled.

"You really think *that's* what I want to talk about? When I know damn well you can feel *this*…" His hips thrust his cock against her softness and he knew she couldn't miss the point.

"Look, this's and that's aside, I *don't know* what you want to talk about. I don't know how to do things like this guy-girl stuff. I'm real bad at it in my world, as if you hadn't noticed, *Pat*. And now it's turned into fairyguy-fairygirl stuff. I'm completely lost."

The tremor in her voice touched Thorne someplace he'd thought hadn't existed. He wanted to take Persephone to some remote island and convince her that she was a priceless jewel. That she was worthy of the best any relationship had to offer. And his was the best. And he'd like to fuck her lots, while they were there, too.

He sighed. "Honey, what I need to say to you is important. To you *and* to me, and it has nothing to do with moving out, needing space, or sex. Well, maybe sex. Yes, actually mostly sex."

Persephone shook her head. "This is one damn confusing world, Thorne. Can we just dance right now?"

Thorne grinned and pulled her into the rhythm, loving the feel of her breasts as they rubbed against him and the way their bodies fit together. Her hands were around his waist, and every now and again his neatly folded wings felt a little flick as she brushed her fingertips against them.

It was amazingly erotic, arousing, and affectionate, which was not a word he usually used. "Persephone—let's go home."

The words were scarcely out of his mouth when a noisy commotion at the door heralded the arrival of Oberon and Titania.

The party was now officially underway.

Chapter Nine

Persephone wondered about fairyland protocol. Did it include sneaking away from a crowded nightclub before the King and Queen noticed you were there?

She glanced around, then up at Thorne. Apparently not.

His expression was a mixture of frustration and distaste, which was quite flattering, but not very encouraging. It looked like they were going to have to stay.

In fact, it was mere seconds before Oberon waved to Thorne and gestured him over to their table, hurriedly prepared by Neville himself. The fact that he'd had to evict two drunken fairies, a gnome who was trying to get it on with one of them, and a squirrel stealing the peanuts from their snack bowl, made no difference to Royalty.

They were here, and their table was in the center of the club. The rest of the world should be ready to pay homage.

"Hey, Leatherfly. Get your ass over here and bring your wonder boobs girl with you."

Oberon's voice rang over the crowd, making heads turn and Persephone wish for a minimizer bra.

"Thorne, darling…" a voice purred. "How *lovely*. Still living up to your name, I see?"

Queen Titania had appeared at Thorne's side and linked her arm through his, guiding him back to the table. She amiably ran her hand over Thorne's pants.

Persephone wondered if there was an appropriate way to tell a reigning monarch to keep her fucking hands to herself. She wasn't *quite* sure, so she contented herself with tightening her grip on Thorne's other hand.

His fingers flexed as he responded to her twitch. Apparently, he was no happier than she was.

Titania was a surprise. Not the eye-popping cross between Michelle Pfeiffer and Tinkerbell that Persephone had been expecting, the Queen was actually quite short. She also possessed a very healthy set of hips.

Long, reddish-blonde tendrils escaped from a rather untidy knot of hair on the top of her head, which she'd secured with what looked like blades of grass. Her dress was haphazard at best, and one side kept slithering away from a shoulder, only to be yanked up absently by Her Majesty as she chatted with Thorne. Her skin was amazing, the color of rich cream with a subtle blush, and she had lips that probably should have been declared illegal.

Her waist was small, her breasts adequate, and her blue eyes held a blend of curiosity and good humor, with a liberal helping of sensuality on the side. She was an intriguing mixture of earth mother, fairy, Queen and sex goddess. Someone who made you wonder if she was going to cook an exquisite apple pie, grant a Royal pardon, or simply fuck someone's brains out.

Persephone sighed with envy and realized why Oberon was so smitten.

Speaking of the King, Persephone wondered where he was. The pair of hands that slid around her body and cupped her breasts gave her a clue.

"Gad, Thorne. This one's a real handful, isn't she?" Oberon's deep voice chuckled behind her. The King certainly liked to plaster himself up against women's backsides.

He was about to tweak her nipples when a whirr of black swept past her eyes. With a movement almost too quick for her to see, Oberon darted out a hand and stopped the leather-clad wingrib that had nearly lashed his hands away from Persephone.

Silence fell on those around the table and Titania's left eyebrow rose in interest.

"Well, well, Thorne." The Queen's lips twisted wryly. "Not many would dare to warn the King away."

"I…" Thorne had turned pale, as if the enormity of what he'd done was just sinking in. He met Oberon's narrowed gaze with worried eyes. "Your Majesty, I…"

Titania didn't give him chance to finish his sentence. "Oh, shut up, Thorne, you're forgiven. I can't stand pissing contests. Oberon, get that mulish look off your face and your hands off Persephone's tits. Where, I might add, they shouldn't have been in the first place. Especially with your *wife* in the room. "

A smothered laugh greeted those words as Titania took her seat and beckoned Persephone over. "Come here, child, next to me. We'd better make friends with each other pretty quickly, or these two brainless hulks will be squaring off at each other like rams butting heads in the spring."

"Your Majesty, Ma'am, I…" stuttered Persephone. Of all the things she'd expected from Royalty, this *wasn't* it.

"Relax, Persephone. Oberon's an ass. Always has been. It's probably why I love him. Of course, Shakespeare got the whole damn thing wrong. Should've turned Oberon into the ass, not Bottom. But what can you expect from a horny Elizabethan with a fetish for chatty love scenes? Tell me about Thorne instead. When did you fall in love with him?"

Persephone's jaw dropped. "I—uh…well…"

"You ever going to get a full sentence out, do you think?" Titania grinned at her.

"Probably not. The way things are going, I doubt if I'll ever be coherent again," Persephone replied with a laugh. "But as for loving Thorne? I couldn't say. It seems like forever."

Titania smiled. "Just the right answer, dear. Just the right answer."

Her smile grew as the men returned to the table and slid in next to their women.

"So, did you two finish your pissing contest?" asked Titania acidly, as her husband dropped a kiss behind her ear.

"Yeah." Oberon smirked. "I won."

"Only because I let you. Your *Majesty*," retorted Thorne.

"Oh, for Chrissakes," groaned Titania. "Keep this up and you are soooo out of the big bed tonight, buddy…" She smacked Oberon soundly on his chest, which had absolutely no effect whatsoever.

"Thorne, please," whispered Persephone, still not quite sure how far friendship with Fairy Royalty was supposed to go. He simply responded with a look that was for her alone. She blushed.

"So. About your Nuptial Flight plans?"

Titania's words stopped Persephone's train of thought dead in its tracks. "Pardon me?"

"The Nuptial Flight. Yours and Thorne's."

"Er, we haven't actually discussed that yet," answered Thorne.

"Well, no time like the present. Are you familiar with the Nuptial Flight, Persephone?"

The Queen's question was phrased in a very businesslike way, much as she would have asked for Persephone's cell phone number or mortgage rate.

Unfortunately, the answer to the question was similar as well. Persephone didn't have a cell phone, or a mortgage, and hadn't much of a clue what a Nuptial Flight was.

She simply shook her head. "Only what I got at Orientation."

"Well, let me explain." The Queen settled her hips more comfortably. "Fairies enjoy sex, and lots of it. You've probably guessed that by now." She grinned in a most un-royal manner. "But there are some fairies who are lucky enough to find their true mates. Their wingmates, if you will. For those couples, a

Nuptial Flight is permitted, and, if they're very fortunate, children follow."

Persephone remembered the little sprites flitting around the tree outside Thorne's window and smiled.

"Not every fairy couple is blessed, but we don't have any birthrate problems currently, so something must be working right. But it *has* to take place between a perfectly matched pair of mates. A certain kind of behavior has to be exhibited by both parties, like extraordinary possessiveness, passion and extreme desire along with lustful urges. We've gotta know that little ones will be raised in the right kind of home."

Persephone knew her cheeks were boiling and didn't dare glance at Thorne.

"But above all, there has to be a deep affection present, a real respect for, and a major devotion to, one's mate. There has to be love. *That's* what makes the Nuptial Flight something incredible."

Titania closed her eyes and shivered, and for a moment Persephone could have sworn that everyone within a ten-yard radius got a sizzle of sheer sexuality right through their bodies.

She slipped her cold hand across the banquette and found Thorne's. He grasped it and held on like it was a lifeline.

"So, what do you think?" asked Titania looking pointedly at the pair of them. "Do you think the Nuptial Flight is for you?"

Persephone bit her lip. "Can you tell me a bit more about it?"

Titania grinned. "Nope. I think you two should go home now, and then Thorne should tell you. In detail. And then, I think you should both stop by my office tomorrow morning sometime, and we'll talk about schedules. In fact," Titania ran her tongue over her full lips and glanced at Oberon, who couldn't take his eyes off her glistening mouth. "I think I might take my man home, too. His memory seems to require refreshing."

Oberon fidgeted, and looked surprisingly self-conscious. For a moment he was simply a man who wanted his woman with an embarrassing level of need.

"Make that late in the morning, will you guys?" continued Titania, leaning provocatively toward her husband. "Oh and Oberon, do me a favor, darling?" She purred at him.

"Anything, babe, you know that…"

"Get Phuque out from under the table. He's slobbering over my thighs."

* * * * *

Thorne had gotten them away from Neville's in record time, reflected Persephone as the door to their apartment closed behind them.

Once Royal permission to leave had been granted, they'd been out of there so fast they'd probably left skid marks. If wings left skid marks, that is.

Persephone winced as one wing bumped into the doorjamb.

"Easy, sweetheart. They take a little getting used to," said Thorne, as he moved around the room lighting candles.

"Candles?" she asked, a little shiver of excitement brushing her skin.

"I thought perhaps I should try and do this right." Thorne looked surprisingly unsure of himself. "After all, I intend to seduce you tonight, so I probably ought to set the stage, at least." He grinned.

"Oh. You're going to seduce me, are you?"

"Yep." He lit a couple more candles, then stepped to the window and pulled the drapes back.

Persephone gasped. The night sky shone with the brilliance of more stars than she could ever remember seeing at one time, and a sliver of crescent moon peeked over the shadowy treetops.

Every now and then lights flickered in the darkness, making the scene appear unreal and magical.

"Fireflies?"

"Yep. Fucking."

Persephone couldn't help the choke of laughter. "God, everything's about fucking with you fairies, isn't it?" she wheezed. "It's so unexpected. When you've spent your whole life thinking fairies live at the bottom of the garden and put dewdrops on roses, it's a bit disconcerting to find that most of the time they're thinking about having sex, doing sex, showing off how to do sex, and watching sex." She shook her head in amusement.

"Any complaints so far?"

Thorne was behind her. What was is with these fairies and their get-her-from-behind fetish? She decided to ask.

"No complaints, but one question. Why is it you all seem to like holding your women in front of you?"

Thorne's hands slid around and cupped her breasts, and his cock swelled into the crack of her buttocks. "You have to ask?" He rubbed himself against her. "It's probably the wings thing. The bigger they get, the harder they are to manage, so fucking like this gets a bit more challenging. There are other ways to explore once the wings are fully developed. Of course, there are those of us who just like a real nice ass, too. Do you mind?" He pressed her hard against him.

"Well, no. I suppose not…it's just that…just that…" Thorne's tongue traced a path from her shoulder toward her wings and she began to shiver. "Has the seduction begun?"

"Oh, yeah," he whispered, blowing on her damp skin.

"Okay."

"You were in any doubt?" His fingers rolled her nipples through the leather.

"Thorne?"

"Yeah?"

"Stop talking and fuck me."

Thorne obeyed.

He turned her away from the window, gathered her in his arms and flew her to his bedroom, taking her breath away. But before she could exclaim, he had her stripped and naked in front of him.

His clothes seemed to melt away, and then, finally, he pressed her warmth against him, skin to skin, breast to chest, cock to pussy.

She moaned at the pleasure, and grabbed his head, bringing his mouth to hers in a demanding kiss that she knew promised everything and offered more.

His arms slid around her, one hand cupping her bottom, the other fondling her thrusterbud.

She moaned again as tremors shuddered through her, and she felt her legs turn to jelly.

"Let's get comfortable," said Thorne in a hoarse whisper.

He urged her down onto his bed, tossed the hapless pink bunny onto the floor and tugged an oddly shaped pillow beneath her spine.

"It cushions your wings. They're new and tender right now. This gives them room to move and yet you can still relax."

Thorne was right. She lay back, feeling the pillow support her lower back and her upper spine and neck. Her wings lay open on the bed, but not compressed. And her thrusterbud was still available to Thorne's busy fingers.

She sighed as she settled herself.

Thorne pulled back, resting on his knees between her outspread legs, and watched as she found the best way to arrange her wings.

"God, watching you do that, I can't remember ever being so turned on…ever wanting to be so deep inside someone that I lose myself. I want to lose myself in you, Persephone."

He slid his hands up her thighs and leaned forward, brushing a kiss and some hair over her belly and breasts.

She ached, and spread her legs wider in invitation.

"Thorne, I need you. Right now. No messing, no soft nibbles or kisses, just your cock in my cunt. Now. This minute. Oh god, I'll die if you don't…"

Persephone's words were dredged from her soul. Her body needed Thorne's to survive. If he didn't fuck her now she'd die, without question. He was hard, handsome, he smelled right, and he was hers. She knew it with every single fiber of her awareness.

Burning gold eyes stared deep into dark pools of dusky chocolate. Their gaze held as Thorne moved forward and brushed his cock over Persephone's pussy, spreading her juices around and soaking both of them.

"Oh, so good, soooo good," he whispered, still staring into her eyes.

"Yes," breathed Persephone, trying not to writhe. "Please, Thorne, more."

"Always, love, always." He pushed forward, grasped his cock and guided himself slowly into her fiery heat.

She sighed, feeling as if years passed while he slid himself into her body. Without breaking their gaze, she raised her thighs and clamped them around his, encouraging him to go that extra little bit deeper.

Their bodies met, curly hair tangling, Thorne's balls touching Persephone's cunt.

They froze.

"I'm there."

"I know. I can feel you, Thorne." Persephone's eyes were wide with amazement.

"You feel—I don't know—you feel like boiling silk around me. It's incredible." Thorne's voice reflected his awe. "It's like nothing I've ever felt before."

"You can say that again." Persephone was afraid to breathe, afraid to move, afraid to lose this exquisitely magnificent sensation caused by a perfectly proportioned cock touching her womb.

Then Thorne moved.

The world, as Persephone knew it, ended.

Her cunt lit up with currents of sensation as Thorne pulled back and then thrust home once again.

He tenderly slid his hand behind her to touch her thrusterbud and she felt her cunt contract violently around him.

He grunted, but continued to move, using his other hand to gently tease her clit. A slight draft and hint of a rustle told Persephone that his wings were supporting him.

She latched her ankles around his back to hold him to her.

"I'm not going anywhere, sweetheart," he said roughly. "Hang on to me if you want, but I'm not going anywhere."

Beyond speech, Persephone just hung on.

Thorne's cock touched all the right places as his hips drove it home again and again. She wanted to come right away, and yet she wanted to wait, to let the sensations build naturally.

His touches on her thrusterbud were driving her insane, magnifying everything his cock was doing, everything his fingers were doing, and everything her body was feeling. It was like having twelve people making love to her body while one perfect cock fucked her into a blissful state of idiocy.

She knew she was closing in on the orgasm-to-end-all-orgasms and she reached up to Thorne to hold him near.

He lowered himself so that his chest just brushed her breasts, and she slid her hands around him, reaching for his wings. Heedless of what she was doing, she just let her hands caress him wherever they fell as her body rose higher and higher toward the peak.

She felt his wings stiffen under her hands as his cock throbbed within her cunt.

"Persephone…" His rough shout was preceded by an incredibly forceful slamming thrust that nearly bounced her into the headboard, made her wings rattle, and slapped so hard against her clit that it toppled her over into her own orgasm.

She couldn't even scream his name. She just screamed.

Waves of sensation rolled over her again and again, and she locked her legs around Thorne to stop herself from being buffeted off the bed. Her muscles clenched, her womb contracted almost painfully, and she felt her cunt lock onto Thorne's cock with a vise-like grip. Even her eyelids were pulsing in time with her climax. This was truly a life-altering fuck.

It seemed to take years for the aftereffects to ease.

Eventually, she realized that her difficulty breathing had nothing to do with the fact that she was about to die from unbelievable orgasm-itis, and everything to do with the fact that Thorne had collapsed in a heap on top of her and was now crushing her into the bed with his weight.

She poked at him, gently.

His response was not entirely unexpected. "I'm dead."

Chapter Ten

In point of fact, Thorne realized he'd never felt quite as alive as he did at that moment, in direct contradiction to what he'd just said.

Persephone's muted giggle told him she wasn't taking him too seriously, but her movements did encourage him to fold his wings together and roll languorously off her damp body.

He couldn't repress a moan as his cock slid from her warmth and he felt her answering shudder. He knew without words that she'd been pretty much blown away by the whole thing too.

He dropped a kiss on her shoulder and cuddled her to him, putting one hand possessively on her breast.

"Is it always like this?"

Her question drifted to his ears, and he wondered if she knew she'd asked it aloud.

"No, sweetheart. It's never like this. This is…well, this is something outside my experience."

Persephone struggled to arrange her wings behind her so that she could rest her head on his chest.

"Damn, these things take some getting used to." She fidgeted into a comfortable place. "Do you really mean that, Thorne? That this…what we have between us…it's out of the ordinary?"

Thorne chuckled, letting his amusement rumble through him and into Persephone. "Honey, if it were any more out of the ordinary, we'd be on a National Geographic special. 'Unusual Physical Responses to Sexual Stimuli as noted by the Fairy

Participants.' In other words, babe," he pulled her even closer and dropped a kiss on her nose, "you blew my wings off. It's never, ever, been like that before."

Persephone sighed gustily, feathering the hairs that whorled across his firm flesh.

"I didn't know. Sex for me has been nice, sort of. I mean it was something that happened when I got into a close relationship with someone, but to be very honest, I could take it or leave it. This—" she waved a hand over Thorne's body, "—this, I don't ever want to leave. If I wasn't so dead myself, I'd take more, right now." She sighed again.

"We've plenty of time, sweetheart." Thorne closed his eyes and felt the warmth and pleasure of holding his wingmate in his arms.

"Tell me about this Nuptial Flight."

Thorne grunted. "Now?"

"Yes, now. Please. I'd rather hear it from you than someone else. Especially if it's going to be bad news. Everyone seems to think it's a big deal, so it probably hurts, right?"

Thorne hugged her. Somewhere along the line his Persephone had acquired a major case of negativity toward life. He was going to make it his mission to completely eliminate it.

"It doesn't hurt, honey. In fact, I'm told it is the most breathtaking, life-changing experience two people can ever have."

"Okay, so it's sex, then, right?"

Thorne chuckled. "Of course. Nuptial? As in marriage?"

Persephone stilled. "This is marriage we're talking about?"

"Yep."

"Well, isn't there something you've forgotten?" Persephone idly tugged at his chest hairs.

"Ouch. No. I don't think so. Find Persephone, fuck Persephone, fuck her some more, take a Nuptial Flight together and live Happily Ever After with plenty of great fucking. That's how it goes. And I'll get to the 'fuck her some more' part shortly…"

Another tug brought tears to his eyes. "Ow. Cut that out, will you?"

"Listen, you arrogant leather bug. Don't you think you ought to find out how *I* feel?"

Thorne couldn't help but rise to the bait offered by that statement. His hand slid to her nipple and caressed it, bringing a hitch to her breathing.

"Oh, babe, I *know* how you feel. And it's amazing."

"I didn't mean *that*…"

He laughed. "I know. And I also know how you *feel*, Persephone. You couldn't have taken my cock so deep inside you and then sucked me dry with your wonderfully hot cunt if you hadn't been crazy about me."

Persephone opened her mouth to respond, but Thorne stopped it with a quick kiss.

"You'd never have opened your ass for me this morning, if you hadn't been crazy for my touch. You'd never have snuggled next to me at Neville's and let me make you come if you hadn't wanted my fingers in your pussy. Your nipples wouldn't be peaking right now if they didn't want my lips to do this—" He leaned over and gently licked and blew kisses on one breast.

"And most of all, Persephone, you wouldn't be here right now if you hadn't already given me the most important part of you. Your heart."

He rested his head on her chest, listening to that organ as it pounded beneath his ear.

"Hear that? Can you hear your heart beating? It's in sync with mine." He took her hand and placed it over his heart. "This doesn't happen too often, honey. When it does, every fairy knows it. It's like there's a big drum somewhere deep inside us, and if we're really lucky, we find someone who makes that drum sound, and shakes our whole body. It's a sign that we're meant for each other. That we can mate and have children. If you want. *That* is something we should talk about."

Thorne pulled back from her chest and pressed his lips to her shoulder. He didn't seem to be able to get enough of the taste of her. He nibbled his way down her arm, keeping one hand firmly on her breast.

"The Nuptial Flight simply takes all these things and makes them into a special moment. One that can only be shared by two compatible fairies. We all have sex, but few of us mate. And once we do," he raised his head and stared at Persephone with every bit of intensity he could muster, "we mate for life."

He resumed his oral adventures over her body, running his tongue around and into her navel. He smiled as he heard her suck in her breath.

"But Thorne?"

"Mmmm?" He found a sensitive spot just inside her hipbone and flicked at it with his tongue, and enjoyed watching the goose bumps that he produced.

"Do I get a choice?"

"A choice?"

"Yes, a choice. A chance to say 'yes,' or 'no,' or 'I don't know, can I have some time to think about it?'"

"No." Thorne's tongue moved further down to her pussy. He sighed in contentment.

"No? Ohmigod."

Correctly deducing that it was his tongue that had produced that last exclamation, not the conversation, Thorne merely grinned and continued what he was doing.

A few moments later, he raised his head. "Do you want to take the Nuptial Flight with me?"

There was silence for a moment or two, during which time Thorne felt his world come to a screeching halt.

"Of course I do."

The world started up again. Thorne sighed and buried his head in his lover's pussy, finding her swollen flesh with his lips and her secret folds and caves with his tongue.

Persephone moaned. "I just accepted an offer of marriage from a fairy whose face is between my legs. I don't believe this."

"Happy birthday, my love," answered Thorne between sucklings.

"Thank you," she sighed, opening her legs even more.

Thorne was in seventh heaven. His wingwoman had pledged herself to their Nuptial Flight, they'd had fabulous sex, and now he was doing one of the things he really adored—bringing her to an orgasm with his tongue.

She began to moan beneath his lips and her juices ran freely, sweet as lilac dew with the tang of lemon blossoms. He couldn't get enough of her.

His tongue found her clit and she gasped as it curled around it and tugged. He knew he'd been perfecting his oral talents for something special—this looked like it was "it."

He slid two fingers inside her as he continued to abrade, tease, love and encourage her clit. Her moans provided a backdrop to his actions, and her legs began to thrash next to him.

He covered one thigh with his heavy arm and slid a knee over the other shin to keep her still and open for his pleasure.

Her hands slipped into his hair and she tugged.

"Thorne. I can't stand it—"

"Yes, you can…" His voice trailed off as he buried his face in her pussy, moving his fingers inside her. He searched for that special spot, curving his hand and flexing his fingers until a shout told him he was there.

"Relax, babe. Let it happen."

"Dear god, Thorne…" Her voice faltered as he moved his fingers over that little puffy nubbin inside her.

His tongue kept up its frantic attack on her clit and found a rhythm that echoed the movement of his fingers.

She sobbed and struggled, muscles twitching and cunt weeping.

Thorne could feel the tensions begin to shiver through her. As her thighs hardened, her skin became tight to his touch and her breathing quickened.

Thorne was merciless, driving her as far and farther than he thought possible. He became seized with the need to take her somewhere she'd never been, and following his instincts he gave an extra hard flick to her clit and started her orgasm.

With the first spasms he stopped everything, just froze in position, fingers still, tongue a breath away from her clit.

"*Thorne.*" The strangled cry surprised him.

He smiled and counted to ten.

Then he started all over again.

After doing that twice, he had a feeling that neither of them would survive this night. She'd die from the orgasm she was heading for, and he would probably die when she killed him out of frustration.

It was time.

His fingers resumed their teasing friction within her liquid cunt, but this time his tongue found a place just beneath her swollen clit.

"Now, Persephone. Hang on, love," he muttered.

Beyond speech, the woman beneath him grunted.

He thrust his tongue up against her clit from beneath and flickered his fingers inside her. After a moment or two, her entire body stiffened.

"Here we go, babe," he breathed, stabbing her with his tongue.

Persephone couldn't even scream, apparently.

Gasping, she let her body go, succumbing to waves of orgasmic pleasure that rolled through her and onto Thorne's fingers and tongue.

He buried his face in her cunt, and pushed into her, hard. If he could have climbed inside her while she was coming, he would have done so. Instead, he just held her tight to him and let her ride it out, sharing whatever he could.

She trembled and shook from the force of her climax for what seemed like hours. The walls of her cunt grabbed Thorne's fingers, and when he pulled them out and thrust his tongue inside her they grabbed that as well.

Her body pulled at him, her clit throbbed before his eyes, her juices soaked him, and he felt on top of the world.

As she slowly receded from the ecstatic peak she'd been trembling on, her body relaxed in Thorne's arms.

"You okay?" He had to ask, even though he held the answer tight against his heart.

"No. This time *I'm* dead."

* * * * *

Persephone awoke to the soft sound of birds singing outside her window, and the sweetest smell this side of paradise—fresh coffee.

She sighed in contentment. She was achy, sticky, and sore, and her wings were a bit cramped, but she had been well loved and couldn't have felt any better.

Well, okay, that was an incorrect assumption. Because at that moment, a blatantly naked Thorne walked in with two mugs of coffee, and she reached paradise. Completely ran over it, actually, and passed on into someplace even better.

Her throat choked on the words that were welling up inside her and she just smiled.

"I love you, too." His low murmur caught her by surprise.

"How did you know?"

"That you were going to say that? I saw it in your eyes. They told me that you feel wonderful, that you're happy, and that you love me. And that your left lower wing is cramping a bit."

Persephone gazed at him, startled. "You can tell all that from my eyes?"

"Well, most of it. Not all of it. The wing cramp is pretty evident, because this little bit here has a dent in it…" He reached over and smoothed her wings.

It felt like a warm kiss and gave her a major glow in her heart and other places.

"My god, Thorne, when you touch my wings—" She looked at him, shyly.

"That's it, honey. That's one of the things that tells us we're good for each other. Wings are a very sexual part of a fairy's body, but with a wingmate, well—off the scale."

"Yeah. I know." She grinned. "Is one of those for me?" Persephone nodded at the mugs of coffee he'd set down on the bedside table.

"Well, actually, Phuque is coming over for breakfast."

"*What*?"

"Kidding." Thorne snickered. "God, you're easy."

"Huh. I haven't had my coffee. No fair teasing before coffee." She buried her face in the mug and inhaled the fragrance. Yes, she was definitely a not-before-my-coffee person.

Although, as her eyes swept down the wonderful length of Thorne Leatherfly, who reclined on the bed next to her sipping his coffee, she decided there might be something to be said for ditching the coffee routine and going straight to the sex.

Thorne's cock was obviously ultra-sensitive to thought vibrations. It swelled before her eyes.

"God, even your cock's psychic."

Thorne's bellow of laughter rattled the rafters. "Honey, that's not psychic. That's horny. That's a guy in bed with his woman. That's said woman looking at said cock with lust in her eyes."

"Did not."

"Did too."

"I—well, perhaps just a little."

Thorne grinned. "How about a lot?"

Persephone grinned back. "Can't help it. You're yummy."

"Yummy?"

"Yeah, Mr. Black Leather and Studs. Yummy."

Thorne leaned near her, bringing the fragrance of coffee and man with him. "And is 'yummy' a good thing?"

She closed her eyes and sniffed deeply. "Oh yeah…"

Thorne sighed contentedly. "Cool."

Persephone opened one eye. Wasn't this where he was supposed to jump her bones and remind her that caffeine wasn't the only thing that could curl her hair in the morning?

"Okay. I think you're ready to hear about the Nuptial Flight, aren't you?"

Ah, the intrusion of practicality. She sat up and pulled the covers around her chest. Now he was finally going to fill in some of the blanks.

"Yes. Please, Thorne. Tell me all. Spare me none of the lurid details." Her mouth quirked. "Kidding."

Thorne rolled his eyes. "Well, basically, it's a flight that we take together, much like a ceremony in the human world. It's a declaration of our intent to live together and raise children together as mates."

"Well, that's cool. Sort of a fairy wedding?"

"Sort of."

"There's more, isn't there?"

"Well, yeah."

Persephone sighed. "Go ahead. Tell me the rest."

Thorne shifted a little. "Um, we have to have sex during the flight."

"Hmm. The mile-high club for fairies?"

"Not exactly." Thorne looked down into his coffee mug. "Sex during this flight is by thrusterbud alone. Something physical happens when a fairy orgasms during the Nuptial Flight. For males, it's an extra added jolt to the sperm or something —"

Persephone couldn't believe that Thorne was actually blushing. She spared his embarrassment and kept a straight face.

" — While for the female fairy, her ovaries get a push and she becomes fertile."

"Ah. So the Nuptial Flight is necessary for conception? It activates the breeding mechanism, so to speak?"

"Exactly." Thorne looked relieved. "So as long as you can fly real fast, we'll have no problem.

"Um — Thorne?"

He glanced over at her.

"How do I fly?"

Chapter Eleven

Persephone fidgeted at the edge of the group standing in the sunshine. This was her second day of accelerated flight training, and she was nervous.

The first day, Thorne had rushed her into the classroom, demanded and insisted that she be part of the class, and threatened the teacher with all manner of bodily disasters if he didn't get her into the air.

Queen Titania had been pleased to grant approval for their Nuptial Flight, and seeing as Midsummer was three days away, that was decided on as the best possible time. Assuming Persephone could learn to fly before then.

Thorne assured her she could.

Persephone was terrified she couldn't.

The first day had been filled with a variety of classroom topics from the basic rules of the air — leave plenty of room around little ones and be polite to other flyers — to wing care. So *THAT* was what one did with wing wax.

There'd been little hops with the instructor and his aides, and she'd panicked the first time her feet had left the ground. But it gradually became more natural, and with her rapidly expanding wingspan she forgot about her nerves and began to enjoy the feeling.

She'd arrived home, exhausted, aching, weak and bleary-eyed, and Thorne had taken one look at her and shoved her into the tub. Followed by a thorough washing, a none-too-gentle toweling-off, and a rather depressing tucking-in to bed. It seemed that everyone knew just how physically demanding flying lessons were.

Now she was going to take her first solo flight.

"Go ahead, Persephone. You're next. Just like we practiced, remember?"

She remembered. A twitch, a thought and an indrawn breath and she was aloft.

She, Persephone Jones, was flying. It was astounding.

"Turn to your left, Persephone." The loud voice of the instructor boomed over the megaphone.

She'd been inordinately surprised to find that her instructor was actually a hummingbird, but when she thought about it she couldn't think of anyone better qualified to teach flight dynamics to fairies. The aviator sunglasses perched on his beak threw her a little though.

She made the prescribed left turn, and resisted the urge to yell "Wheeeeee" at the top of her voice.

"Very good. Now ascend please. Try for five wingspans."

She complied with his instructions, remembering his description of the distance over the horizon being measured roughly in the width of one's lower wing taken relative to the observer. Or something.

She simply pointed her nose up and fluttered.

Unfortunately, not much happened.

She went up some, fluttered, and went up a bit more. But there seemed to be a barrier she couldn't break.

Sweating, she dropped back to the ground and executed a neat two-point landing on both feet, immediately tucking her wings safely behind her as she'd been taught.

"Very nice indeed, Persephone." The hummingbird nodded at her.

"Yeah, but I didn't get too high."

"Well, dear, that's to be expected. It's those." He angled his beak in the direction of her breasts. "Not as aerodynamically impossible as the bumble bee, I'll admit. But they'll keep your altitude and velocity down, that's for sure. No reason why you can't fly though. Shouldn't be a problem."

"But…but I have a Nuptial Flight day after tomorrow."

The bird was silent. "Oh dear. Oh my. That could be a problem. My goodness."

"What can I do?"

"Well, I don't exactly know, Persephone. This isn't a common problem here in Fairyland. Look, maybe the Queen will have an idea, or your mate—" The hummingbird paled as he realized who he was speaking about.

One part of Persephone's mind was fascinated with the fact that a hummingbird *could* pale. The other was shivering at the thought of not being able to mate with Thorne.

"Oh lord." She bit her lip. " I'll deal with it. But you say I am quite capable of flying normally, right?"

"Certainly. You have a nice smooth style, your wings are balanced and adjusted, and you handle them well. I'll get you a diploma, because all you need now is practice. Just make sure you fly during the day, and have a buddy nearby until you get some mileage on those wings."

Persephone nodded her thanks and waved to the rest of the class who muttered to each other and cast sympathetic glances her way.

She wanted to scream at them all that she'd find a way to mate with Thorne somehow, but right now, all she wanted was to be held. Close. Preferably to a really nice chest that smelled of Thorne Leatherfly.

And the best way to do that was to find the chest that was attached to Thorne Leatherfly.

She knew he'd be at the office, so she headed that way. They'd managed to spend some time there the day before, with Thorne filling her in on the website they maintained, the mailings they took care of, the ads and contests they ran and the newsletter they published before rushing her off to flight school.

She was astounded to realize that **www.fairyland.web** was actually a major enterprise. She also looked forward to managing the office into far better and more efficient shape than it was in at the moment.

There was also the matter of the rather nice couch in Thorne's office that they'd used after Thorne had told Norman to hold his calls for half an hour. He'd also locked the door.

None of these things were in her mind at the moment, however, when she let herself in.

"Hey, Persephone, how's the flying coming?" Norman Elderbranch grinned at her through his beard.

"Not too good, Norman. Is Thorne in?"

"Yep. What's up, sweetheart? Anything I can do?"

"I don't know…" Her voice caught on a sob, and before she could say any more Thorne Leatherfly hurtled through his office door and pulled her into his arms.

"Wassamatta? Are you hurt? Did someone hurt you? Are you okay? Do you need a doctor?"

Norman leaned against his desk and folded his arms, watching as his boss made a blithering idiot of himself.

"Uh, boss?"

"Shut up, Norman. Can't you see there's something wrong with her?"

"Yeah, she can't breathe. Give her some room, why don't you?"

Blushing, Thorne backed off. A little.

Persephone sniffed. "Sorry, Thorne. I didn't mean to scare you, but we have a problem, and I don't know how to solve it."

"Tell me, babe. We can solve anything together."

"Oh god." More tears fell and she sobbed on his chest.

Norman sighed and reached for one of Cobweb's little handkerchiefs. He passed it over to Thorne, who nodded his thanks.

Thorne wiped Persephone's eyes. She took the handkerchief and blew her nose loudly. Norman winced.

"Okay. I'm all right now." She took a deep breath and looked at Thorne. "It's my boobs."

Silence fell in the room while the fairy and the gnome considered her words.

The gnome recovered first. "And very nice they are too, Persephone. Is there something wrong with them?"

Norman's calm question restored some balance to her world and Persephone looked gratefully at him. "No, not really. It's just that they're too big. I'm not aerodynamic, you see. I can fly, but not very high and not very fast. I don't know if I'm going to be able to make the Nuptial Flight with you, Thorne…"

Thorne held her close.

"I see the problem." Norman stroked his beard and ignored a glare from Thorne that should have shriveled his cap to ashes. "Lemme think."

"Honey, we'll do something. We'll go to the Queen; we'll talk to Oberon. There must be people around who know about this sort of stuff. I'm sure we can find a way around it. Nothing is impossible."

Persephone sighed and hugged him. "God, I love you, Thorne Leatherfly. And it'll kill me if I can't make the flight with you. But you know I'll always love you regardless, don't you?"

There was absolute silence in the room for a heartbeat.

"Persephone…" Thorne buried his face in her hair.

"Oh no. What?" she breathed.

"Persephone," said Norman quietly. "If you can't consummate the Nuptial Flight, you must return to your own world, and Thorne's DNA will be altered to become compatible with someone else. Neither of you would be able to stand the pain of knowing you're wingmates yet cannot mate."

Persephone's flesh turned to ice as she recalled Sugar saying much the same thing at Orientation. "I'm doomed."

* * * * *

"Well, screw that." The words were out of Thorne's mouth before he realized it. Then he knew it was the truth. "She's mine. She's destined for me and I won't leave her or forget her." He glared at Norman. "And we'll find a way to beat this."

"Got any good plastic surgeons in Fairyland that give drive-thru breast reductions?" Persephone tried to lighten the moment.

"Don't even consider the possibility," growled Thorne. His fingers twitched and he knew if they'd been alone, he'd have his hands full of those wonderful breasts of hers right this minute. They were *his*, dammit.

"There may be a way."

Norman's quiet murmur wrenched Thorne's attention away from Persephone's assets.

"Norman, if you think, even for a second, that you know a way to handle this—" Thorne's heart was in his throat as he stared at the little gnome.

Persephone gripped his hand hard.

"Gnomes are pretty amazing beings, Persephone." Thorne leaned toward her reassuringly. "Much of the lore of Fairyland has been saved by gnomes. They're a vital part of this society, because I honestly don't think fairies would have survived without the practical down-to-earth abilities and knowledge of the gnomes. If Norman says there might be a way, then you can bet your boots there might be a way." He glanced over at the gnome. "Right, Norman?"

Norman stared blankly at the pair of them, stroking his beard. His eyes were unfocused, and Thorne could almost see the circuits accessing databanks within that extraordinary mind that lurked beneath his red pointy hat.

Suddenly he snapped his fingers. "Got it."

"Got what?" Thorne and Persephone echoed each other with the question.

"Calamus."

Thorne looked at Norman and then at Persephone who raised her shoulders in query. "Okay. I'll bite. What's calamus?"

Norman drew in a deep breath. "If I remember correctly, calamus is a stimulant. We haven't used it for years, but a couple of generations ago it was real popular, especially with some of the woodland witches who swore it made them fly faster and further."

"Is this some kind of drug?" Persephone sounded a bit doubtful.

"Not at all." Norman frowned at her. "Nobody does drugs here in Fairyland. Why bother? There are spells for most everything one could want. But *not*—" he added quickly "—for something as important as mating. That's got to be a natural, magic-free rite. However, there's nothing in the rules about an herb or two."

Thorne and Persephone looked at each other.

"What do you think, honey?" he asked, watching as she chewed on her lower lip.

"I don't know. I've never had any kind of a stimulant, unless you count coffee. What does it do, Norman? Do you know?"

"Not until I've got some research out of the way, no. Let me go hunt up some old records and download some of the information for you. Give me an hour or two, Thorne. How's that?"

"That will earn you the biggest and best raise I can manage, Norman."

"And we'll name the first one after you," added Persephone with a little grin.

She couldn't see Thorne's frown, but Norman could. He chuckled. "Let's not go that far, Persephone. We'll discuss names for your kids after you have 'em. First things first." Rubbing his beard for luck, Norman toddled off to do research, and Persephone snuggled into Thorne's arms again.

"I don't want to be here right now. Let's go home." Thorne tugged Persephone to the door.

"Fine by me. I can't think of anywhere else I'd rather be."

Thorne caught his breath as he realized that home meant Persephone. Not his apartment where his stuff was, but anyplace he could be with Persephone would be home to him. He held her even tighter as they walked back through the corridors.

He was not, he promised himself, going to lose her. Whatever it took, whatever he had to do, he was staying by her side. Forever. Until there were no more fairies at the bottom of anyone's garden.

* * * * *

The door slammed behind Persephone with a comforting thud, and she sighed as she crossed the room to the windows. Thorne came up behind her and snuggled her into his favorite spot, tight up against his chest with his arms around her, cradling her breasts. His cock moved slightly as she tucked her bottom back against him.

They both enjoyed the feeling, as they watched the last of the sunlight fade.

"Persephone," said Thorne quietly. "There is something else that might help us with the Flight business."

She tipped her head and looked over her shoulder at him. "Really? Tell me."

He gazed out of the window. "I don't want to."

She frowned. "I don't understand, Thorne. I want to make this Flight with you, more than anything in the world. Tell me what I can do and I'll do it. I have to walk through fire? I'll do it."

"Would you have sex with someone else?"

She froze. "What are you saying?" The words fell in whispers from her suddenly cold lips.

"Honey, you need to increase the size of your wingspan, right?"

Persephone nodded, getting an inkling of where this conversation was going.

"And sex helps, right?"

"Yes."

"So how would you feel about having sex with maybe more than one person?"

She swallowed. This was not something she'd considered. "I don't quite get it, Thorne. I know what you're saying, but I don't want anyone else but you. How could it possibly work with someone else?"

"Well…" Thorne held her tight against him, like he was telling her without words that she was part of him. "Suppose, for example, I was to ask someone else to join us, and we could kind of share an experience."

His voice was rough, and Persephone didn't dare meet his eyes. She was afraid of what she might see. The way he held her told her this was painful enough for him, and whatever decision she made would only add to the burden.

"I guess—I guess a lot would depend on who, and exactly what kind of rules we'd have…"

"How about Sal?"

She blinked. If it had to happen and it had to be someone else, she couldn't imagine anyone better. A shiver crossed her body as she considered the impossible combination of herself with her own wingmate and the incredibly sensual Sal.

"You really think it might work?" She turned to face him, knowing what she had to do.

His eyes told her of his conflict, and she reached out to cup her palms against his cheeks.

"Thorne, I will do anything in this world, in *whatever* world, to take the Nuptial Flight with you. If I don't, my life will be nothing."

His eyes glistened as he watched her.

"If you think that adding Sal to our bed for one night will help my wings grow, then I'll do it. "

Thorne sagged in relief.

"With one condition…" She raised a forefinger and tapped him on the nose. "If we need rules, you get to set them."

"Me?" Thorne nearly squeaked in surprise.

"Yes, you."

"Why me?"

"Because I love you, and I believe you love me. You know what it will take to get my wings growing some more, and only you can set the boundaries and guidelines for us. Whatever you say we can and cannot do, goes. You tell us who gets to put what where, and we'd better be clear about it up front. Okay?"

Thorne swallowed, and gently bent his head to kiss her. His lips touched hers softly and reverently, and he smiled as he pulled back.

"I don't think I could love you more than I do right at this minute. You are a constant surprise to me, Persephone Jones. I took the liberty of contacting Sal before we left the office. He'll be here shortly."

Persephone quirked an eyebrow. "How did you know I'd say yes?"

"Because, if I may quote, I love you and I believe you love me."

Damn the man, thought Persephone. When he was right, he was right.

Chapter Twelve

"You *what*?" Thorne Leatherfly's roar must have rocked the entire world of Fairyland, thought Persephone as she stood behind him in astonishment.

"I brought Clover along for the fun." Sal stood in all his sparkling blueness, with an ecstatic smile on his face. "It was pretty obvious what you needed. Everyone's talking about my darling girl over there and her wonder boobs. It was only a matter of time before you realized that there's nothing like a good orgy to put the inches on your wings."

Thorne shut his mouth with a snap. "This is not going to be an *orgy*." Sputtering through clenched teeth, Thorne slammed the door and turned as Sal and Clover fluttered over to Persephone.

"Sweetie, this is going to be such fun. God, Clover and I couldn't wait. Actually, we didn't wait." He giggled as he whipped out two bottles of something from under one wing. "Happy Nuptial Flight, my love." He kissed her on both cheeks and would have gone for the mouth but Thorne was too fast for him.

"Enough, Sal."

Sal pouted, but moved over as Clover gave Persephone a big hug. "I'm just so excited, Persephone," she said. "I'm dying to see Thorne without his clothes on and you know I *love* these." She glanced down at Persephone's breasts and rubbed her own against them.

Persephone was shocked to feel a thrill run through her. She'd never felt any interest in exploring her sexuality with other women, but this was something different and her curiosity was aroused along with her hormones.

She glanced at the men and surprised them staring at her and Clover. If they'd been cartoon figures, their tongues would be hanging out.

At that moment, Persephone made a decision. She had to do this for her future, for her happiness, and for Thorne. So, dammit, she was going to enjoy it. Privately, of course, but this would be just for herself. A little memory to tuck away for some far distant evening when she was alone.

She grinned at Clover. "It should be fun, shouldn't it? Wanna get started?"

"Wine first, I think," said Thorne, grabbing the bottles and all but running into the kitchen for glasses and an opener.

"I think Mr. Big-Bad-Fairy is nervous," stage-whispered Sal to Persephone. "Don't worry, love, we'll take care of both of you. When it comes to orgies, you've come to the right place."

Persephone giggled as she looked at the magnificent figure of Sal, glittering blue, and Clover, bubbling over with green and laughter. She guessed she had come to the right place.

An hour or so later, when she sprawled mostly naked on the couch with Clover, she was *convinced* this was the right place.

The elderberry wine was perfect, and having met up with an empty stomach had rendered Persephone completely relaxed and happy. Clover had suggested strip Trivial Pursuit, and in spite of cleaning up in the Movie category, Persephone had lost the bulk of her clothes when it came to Sports.

The guys had fared slightly better, both still had their pants on, but Clover, who despaired of ever remembering anything useful, was stark naked. Persephone found herself fascinated by Clover's neatly trimmed and shaped green pubic hair. Almost like one of those carefully groomed putting greens, she thought, as she stared at it.

"Go ahead—touch," offered Clover, sensuously spreading her legs.

The room had darkened, and there were only a few candles lit high up on the walls. The atmosphere was close and warm, and for a moment Persephone forgot where she was and simply let her inquisitive instincts take over. She forgot she'd suggested rules, to be set down by Thorne. She forgot there were two guys watching. She forgot everything but the need to touch.

Reaching out, she tentatively brushed her fingertips over the green softness. To her amazement, Clover sighed and slid further into the couch. Getting bolder, Persephone slid her fingers across Clover's mound and dipped down a little, just flicking against her pussy lips.

There was a moan, but from whom, Persephone couldn't guess. She was vaguely aware of some fidgeting in the chairs across from her, but she was so interested in what she was doing that she paid no attention.

She slipped off the couch and onto her knees, moving between Clover's thighs. Clover reached out and cupped Persephone's breasts with her hands.

"God, honey, these are magnificent."

Persephone looked up and smiled, and Clover moved toward her and dropped a kiss on her lips.

Startled, Persephone jumped and touched a hand to her mouth. It had been soft, sweet, and different to kissing a guy. Not unpleasant, but different.

Clover smiled at her, watching her every move and gently rolling her nipples around as they hardened beneath her skilled fingers. "Touch me some more, Persephone, touch me like you like to be touched," encouraged Clover, opening her thighs even wider.

As Persephone slid her fingers to Clover's pussy, warmth surrounded her and she felt a very naked and aroused Thorne Leatherfly behind her. She was vaguely aware of Sal as he moved behind the couch and slid his hands down Clover's body to grasp her breasts. Thorne pressed himself against her, plastering his hard body to her softness.

Somebody moaned, and Persephone realized it was her. She found Clover's clit with her fingers, just as Thorne found hers.

"Sit forward a bit, Clover, there's a good girl," said Sal roughly. He stepped over the back of the couch and slipped down to rest right behind Clover, his thighs outside of hers and her back pressed against his chest. He dipped his head and sent his tongue someplace behind Clover.

Probably, thought Persephone, the same place that Thorne was playing with on her own spine...her thrusterbud.

A particularly teasing push of Thorne's tongue coupled with a flick of his fingers, and Persephone was no longer in doubt who was moaning. It was definitely her. Of course, the echo might have been Clover, who was now starting to get seriously wet around Persephone's fingers as Sal's tongue worked its magic.

"You taste so good," breathed Thorne almost silently in Persephone's ear. "Your thrusterbud is warm and silky and feels like heaven against my tongue. When we fly high together, I'm going to fuck you here..." He slid his tongue back into the groove and reduced her to slavish idiocy and a puddle of liquid sex.

His cock was growing harder and firmer against her buttocks and she wanted to spread her cheeks and welcome him inside. Absently, she teased Clover's clit, most of her mind focused on Thorne and what other arousing things he found to do with her body.

Thorne's hands gripped her hips, pushing and moving her to where he wanted her. He slid his cock up her cleft and sought her tight ring of muscles. She groaned with the sensation of his hardness pushing against her and briefly took her hands away from Clover to pull at her cheeks in wanton invitation. Thorne was no slouch. He pressed firmly and she opened to let him inside. It was as if she'd been doing that all her life, and with Thorne, too. She was once again astounded at the way their bodies melded into one. She smiled.

* * * * *

His cock slid in like he'd been made for her. Once again, Thorne was amazed at their perfect fit. Whether he was buried to the hilt in her sweet cunt or pressing himself deep into her ass, it didn't matter. This woman was his, now and forever.

He slid back gently and pressed forward again, listening to her responses, learning what she liked, finding new places to explore with his fingers while his cock massaged her darkest and most secret places.

She was melting in his hands, and he was harder than he could ever remember being. If he'd been human this would have been hurting her, he knew, but Fairyland was full of sexual magic. The magic that let fairies fuck their chosen partner any way they wanted, without difficulties. Consensual sex was the recreation of choice in Fairyland for just this reason, thought Thorne.

Never one to indulge in group sex, however, this was a new experience for him, although he'd be damned if he'd let anyone know that little fact.

And it was turning out to be more fun than he'd expected. Mostly because Sal was keeping his distance from Persephone and staying behind Clover.

At that moment, Sal obviously decided that distance wasn't quite what he wanted, and with a mighty groan he lifted Clover off the couch and brought her back onto his lap and his cock.

The huge shudder from Clover told Thorne that Sal had accomplished his goal.

Both men were now buried balls-deep inside their women.

Both their women were still touching each other.

It was a major turn on, and Thorne was majorly turned on. Keeping his tongue busy around Persephone's thrusterbud, and his hands on her clit, he managed a quick glance over her shoulder to watch as she played with Clover's pussy.

He mimicked her hand movements, pressing and rubbing as she did, and was thrilled to sense her response.

He could see Clover's eyes fastened on Persephone's breasts, and her hands moving over and around them, playing with them, pushing them together and tugging on the hard nipples.

Clover's own breasts were hidden in Sal's hands, and she was beginning to bounce a little as Sal's hips thrust his cock into her cunt.

Thorne had to admit that the sight of Persephone and Clover touching each other was incredibly arousing. Smart enough to know that neither Sal nor Clover were any kind of a threat, he let go of his tensions, and allowed himself the freedom to enjoy this rather unique situation.

He opened his mind and his senses to the sounds of their lovemaking. The rustle of their wings as they moved and shook, and the hiss of skin on skin as hands touched, caressed and urged to excitement.

He could smell Persephone's arousal as her juices flowed over his hands, and a faintly different fragrance told him that Clover was doing the same thing to Sal's cock.

His breathing was rapid and his ears caught the choked breath of Persephone as she tensed beneath him.

He knew she was near her peak, and he hoped Clover was too. His knees locked, and as this wasn't the best position to enjoy his own climax, he fluttered his wings a little, to take the pressure off.

It looked as if Sal had been waiting for some move just like that. He fluttered his wings, and in response Thorne slowly rose from the floor, keeping himself firmly buried in Persephone.

Sal rose simultaneously, keeping Clover tight against his crotch.

Within seconds, all four were hovering over the couch, Persephone and Clover pressed face to face by the movements of their partners.

Thorne knew he was pressing Persephone's breasts against Clover's and it made him even harder. His hands, working their magic on Persephone, brushed against Clover's clit and made her gasp.

Persephone's arms opened and she hugged Clover, reaching around to touch Sal's wings.

Muscles tensed, breaths came in choppy little pants, and as two sets of tight male buttocks thrust, the two soft female bodies between them embraced.

Clover exploded first.

Tearing her mouth from Persephone's, she screamed shrilly, shuddering violently as Sal's strong hips pounded her cunt from beneath. Within seconds Sal too was shaking and crying out in hoarse gasps.

Persephone's buttocks tightened against Thorne and he slid his tongue as deep as it would go into her thrusterbud opening.

Combined as it was with his fingers thrusting deep into her cunt, it was more than enough to finish Persephone.

She shouted out his name and tossed her head back onto his shoulder, going rigid beneath his touch. Her legs swung wildly back and she locked her ankles around his, pulling him further into her.

The strong spasms within her ass began to have their own effect, and Thorne felt himself slipping over the edge.

He squeezed Persephone tight, dropped his head to her neck and gently held onto her with his teeth. He came in a massive eruption that sent his brain cells into overload and detonated a million tiny white explosions in front of his eyes.

His savage shout echoed round the room into the silence and he sank slowly to the floor, still buried in Persephone.

That, he thought cloudily as his mind began to fall asleep, was really fantastic. Really, really fantastic. Really, really, really…

* * * * *

Persephone gradually awoke to the knowledge that she was in bed. She couldn't remember how she got there, but she was snugly comfortable and she could smell the wonderful aroma of Thorne's coffee perking.

Something wet and warm was playing with her toes.

She smiled as a tongue slid over her big toe, tickling between it and the next one, and flicking underneath. A hot mouth engulfed it, sucking and pulling back and making her grin.

She stretched, eyes closed, and hummed her pleasure.

She'd never had her toes sucked before, and it was surprisingly pleasant. Especially coming as it did on top of a night of blazingly hot group sex.

Her clit throbbed, reminding her of how much fun she'd had last night. It had been late when Sal and Clover had finally staggered from Thorne's apartment. Tired, but satisfied.

She turned in response to the hand on her foot, rolling onto her side and folding her wings behind her. She opened her eyes and looked into the sleeping face of Thorne Leatherfly.

Shit. If he was sleeping, then who…

"Oh fuck."

"Okay, honey, gimme a minute," said Thorne sleepily, reaching for his cock.

"No, not that." Exasperated, Persephone dug Thorne in the ribs.

"Ow."

"I meant—Phuque." She nodded to the foot of the bed, where the little goblin was enjoying the hell out of her toes. He had a hard on the size of a Louisville slugger that was poking through his fly, and Persephone's foot was covered with drool and half in his mouth.

"Eeeuwww." She wrenched it away with a massive tug. God, she'd never be clean again.

"Phuque, you bastard. What the *hell* do you think you're doing?" Naked and angry, Thorne Leatherfly was quite intimidating, mused Persephone, watching her wingmate towering over the little fellow, who was unrepentantly licking his lips.

"Hey, bro. Don't get your dick in a twist. All I did was taste her. And only her toes." He sighed dramatically. "I really wanted to suck her off, but I figured you'd do something stupidly emotional like kill me, so you should thank me for just waking her up from the feet, so to speak."

He gazed at Thorne with innocent eyes, totally unimpressed by the massive towering anger poised above him.

"And I put the coffee on, too."

Thorne relaxed slightly, and allowed Persephone to tug him back down onto the bed. "*That* may have just saved your sorry ass, you little…" Thorne shook his head. "Words fail me."

Phuque raised his nose and sniffed. "Smells like your cock didn't. So the orgy went well, did it? I do note, by the way, that I *wasn't* asked. Now, me and Mr. Hardstaff here," he stroked himself lovingly to indicate of whom he spoke, "We coulda made a huge contribution to the festivities, and I do mean *huge*." He winked at Persephone. "Know what I mean?"

Persephone sighed.

"I'm not gonna be angry that I wasn't asked, or at least try not to be, and I'm not gonna let it hurt my feelings. I'm just gonna figure that you all didn't know any better. And that if you did you'd have been afraid that the girls would've left you guys in a flash after having me." He grinned wickedly. "After all, you know what they say…"Once you've had Phuque, all other guys suck."

Persephone snorted. "You made that up."

Phuque scrambled off the bed and tucked "Mr. Hardstaff" back inside his pants. "Whatever. But I didn't make up the fact that the Queen wants to see you right away."

"Well, thanks for telling us *right away*, asshole." Thorne was still slightly angry, and his frown made it no secret. "After all, you could have come in here, uninvited, and done something totally off the wall like suck my woman's toes. But no, good little Phuque came right in and politely delivered his message."

"Sarcasm, Leatherchump? You don't know the meaning of the word 'sarcasm.' Let me tell you…"

"How about you don't, Phuque. Just toddle off, there's a good goblin, and we'll go see the Queen." Persephone leaned toward Phuque. "You'll only make him worse. He hasn't had his coffee yet."

Phuque's eyes wrinkled out of sight as he smiled at Persephone. "You got it, babe. Smart one you've got here, Leatherzip. Hope you two get to make that Flight okay."

"Thanks, Phuque. We'll be seeing you soon, I'm sure," said Persephone, encouraging him out of the room and trying to hold up the blanket she'd grabbed to cover herself at the same time.

A growl from Thorne sent him scurrying off and the door slammed shut behind him.

"I swear to god I thought it was you," said Persephone as she dropped the blanket back onto the bed and stretched.

Thorne's eyes roved her body and she felt the urge to purr.

Then his expression changed. "Holy shit…Persephone, come look." He almost dragged her over to the wall mirror and turned her around, forcing her to look over her shoulder.

She gasped at what she saw.

The most enormous pair of pink wings stared back at her.

"Thorne, oh my god, Thorne…" Her eyes filled with tears of joy as she looked at the growth spurt their activities had stimulated.

"Hell, woman. Those are fantastic." Thorne couldn't take his eyes off them as she spread them gently, watching the light sparkle from the delicate membranes.

"D'you think they'll be enough?" She turned a worried look on him.

"I'm no flight engineer, but those babies look like 747 jumbo jet quality to me. We'll make it, sweetheart. Don't sweat it."

She went into his arms without a moment's hesitation and sighed at the contentment she found there. It was unquestionably the one place in the world she belonged.

Chapter Thirteen

"Go away, Thorne."

The Queen's firm command rang in Persephone's ears like the sound of doom approaching.

"But, your Majesty—" she muttered, painfully aware of the warmth of Thorne's hand slipping from hers.

"Persephone." The Queen needed to say no more. Today she was every inch the monarch, sitting elegantly on a raised throne, wearing a very smart pale gray pinstripe suit and dark pumps. The ensemble contrasted beautifully with her magnificent gossamer wings.

Thorne leaned over and gave her a hard kiss goodbye. "I love you." He whispered the words to her as he pulled away.

Titania, however, was the Queen. She missed nothing. "That's why she's here, Thorne. Don't worry. All will be well if I have anything to say about it. Go away and come back at midnight, ready for your Flight."

Thorne's eyebrows rose, but he obviously knew better than to argue. An instant later he was gone, leaving a little whorl of dust in the air and an emptiness in Persephone's hand.

"Come, child. Let's walk." The Queen stepped down from her dais and kicked off her shoes. "God, I hate those things. Some days one has to play the role, though, you know?"

She pulled her jacket off, carefully sliding it past her wings. "Aaah. That's much better." She grinned, and in a flash the royal ruler was gone and a laughing woman had taken her place.

"Now, let's go see what we can do about this situation. I see your wings have grown some since yesterday. I guess Sal and Clover helped, huh?"

Persephone blushed. "Does *everyone* know?"

"Well, there may be a couple of June bugs who missed the announcement," chuckled Titania. "Don't sweat it, girl. We love to have something spicy to talk about and you catching Thorne is the spiciest thing to happen this month. Everyone's rooting for the two of you. Thorne's a good lad in spite of the leather thing. He ought to cut back on a few of those studs, mind you. Perhaps when you're mated you could do something about that."

Persephone stared at Titania, fascinated. "You think so?"

"Well of course. You should have seen Oberon before we were married. Phew. That was one plug-ugly bug of a guy. He was trying to go for the extra-macho muscle boy look. It was all the rage with the knights back then. He had a haircut that looked like some kind of pudding got dumped on his head. He was covered in pimples from the junk he ate, and the chain mail he'd had spun from spider's webbing chafed him raw. God, what a mess." Titania snickered.

"I straightened him right out." Her face took on a distinctly provocative expression.

"I'll just bet you did," agreed Persephone.

"But enough about him, this is what I want to show you…" She led Persephone through a large door and out onto a beach.

Persephone gasped, choked, and coughed until her eyes watered. "What the heck…?"

"It's my private beach. I'm really a fan of the ocean, you know. Can't get there too often, so my sweetie conjured this up. Don't swim out too far or you'll hit the wall on the other side, but it's pretty close to the real thing, wouldn't you say?"

Persephone said nothing. She was completely overwhelmed by the sand beneath her feet, the cries of the seagulls wheeling overhead, and the soft shush of the waves as they lapped at the shore. From what she could see the beach went for miles, and a light mist obscured the horizon. A large sun had risen over the ocean and sparkled like any postcard from the tropics. It was incredible.

Persephone had to laugh. "Absolutely fantastic, your Majesty."

"Hey, call me Titania here, okay? I'm off duty for a while, so it would be nice to just be friends."

Persephone grinned. "I'd like that a lot, Titania."

"Good. Now strip."

Persephone's mouth hung open as she watched Titania shuck off her clothes and stretch, stark naked, under the warm sun.

"Come on. Time's wasting."

Blinking, Persephone began to take off her dress. Titania walked over the sand to a small beach hut and pulled out two inflatable rafts.

"We're gonna catch a few rays, maybe ride a few waves later, and have ourselves some fun, sweetie," she called, tossing one raft to Persephone.

"Okay." Persephone wondered about sunblock, lifeguards, sharks, and other beach related dangers. Then she remembered that she was in Fairyland. If Oberon could make an ocean, then he damn well ought to be able to keep the sharks out. Not to mention the icky seaweed that wrapped around one's ankles like dead fingers. Ugh.

"Now here's what you do…" Titania splashed around in the shallows and Persephone followed her in, unsurprised to find the water pleasantly warm.

"See these two straps? Those are for your feet. And this hole lets your wings get a good dunking. Salt water is really good for strengthening them, so just let the water swish around them. Don't try to move them underwater, you'll tire yourself out, and we want you in tip top shape for tonight's Flight."

Persephone followed Titania's instructions and found herself floating on her back in the sun, wings swirling in the water beneath her and her legs awkwardly spread with her feet tucked into little notches at either side of the raft. It was sort of like an inflatable examining table with rubber stirrups.

The warmth of the sun quickly penetrated her pussy, however, and she found it very relaxing. Especially as it didn't seem to bother the Queen of Fairyland who floated happily next to her with her fire-red mound displayed for the world to admire.

"This is nice, Titania," she sighed. "And private too. I've never been skinny dipping before."

"You've missed a wonderful thing, honey," said Titania lazily. "Now, all we need are the…oh good. Here they come."

Persephone raised her head to see several rather large fish swimming their way. "Umm, Titania?"

"No prob, sweetie. I asked these guys to come in today especially for you. Well," she coughed politely. "Actually for me, too."

The fish were close to them now, smooth and pale pink, and water droplets shone brightly off their fins as they broke the surface.

"These are sucking gouramis."

"Oh. How nice."

Titania giggled. "You've probably heard of kissing gouramis. Well, these guys do the same sort of thing, only they suck. And they love it. There's not too many of them around these days—they were real popular a while back and didn't get a chance to breed as much as they should have. So they're almost an endangered species now. We protect these guys, and they'll drop by as a favor now and again. Just watch."

Titania brushed her hand through the water as one of the fish circled her raft. It raised its head and allowed her to stroke it softly, then bobbed back down under the water and swam beneath her.

Seconds later it emerged between her legs, and placed its mouth directly over her pussy. She moaned.

Persephone felt her eyes bugging out of her head. And they probably got even bigger when she felt a pair of cool lips attach to her mound too. She went rigid and looked down over her stomach at the friendly face of her own personal sucking gourami.

Huge lips that would make Mick Jagger faint with envy were wrapped around her pussy. Some kind of harsh tongue wriggled around her clit and its eyes grinned at her.

Within seconds she couldn't swear to anything at all, as this amazing denizen of the deep caressed her clit, and sucked her cunt until she was a trembling mess of writhing need.

A scream from Titania didn't even distract her.

The current seemed to be slamming the creature into a wonderfully arousing rhythm against her body, and Persephone slid helplessly into an orgasm with a cry of pleasure.

A few minutes later, she raised her head to see Titania grinning at her. "Not bad, huh?"

Persephone grinned back. "I'll never mock Charlie the Tuna again."

"I can stay for another hour or so then I've got to go. But you get to enjoy the day here, Persephone. You see, this actually counts as sex, and your wings should be well on their way to full extension after undergoing what I like to call gourami therapy."

"All *day*?" She squeaked out the question as another gourami came up between her legs and swirled the waters around her sensitive clit.

"Oh yeah, all day. It's quite an experience. You'll find a hammock over there for when you're done." Titania waved a hand up the beach. "You'll probably need it. We'll wake you in plenty of time for the ceremony, don't worry."

Persephone could say nothing at all.

Another sucking gourami was about to live up to its full potential.

* * * * *

Thorne Leatherfly was in an unusual state. At least it was unusual for him. He was nervous. The Queen had all but kidnapped Persephone, he had taken a couple of days off from his job, and he was about to get married. He sighed.

Time to go harass someone. Perhaps Norman was finished with his research and had some news. It had been a lot longer than the two hours he'd originally promised.

Thorne ran the gnome to earth in his office.

"Yeah, I found a couple things." Norman sipped his coffee as he watched his boss with narrowed eyes. "I don't know if you're gonna like them, though."

Thorne ran his hands through his hair in frustration. "Let me have it."

Norman picked up some papers and clicked open a website on his laptop. "Okay. Here's the scoop on calamus. It's certainly one of the stimulant herbs, but fell out of favor because it was rather risky in its usage. It's now no longer recommended."

"Sheeeeit." Thorne hissed out the expletive as his world crumbled around him.

"Look, boss, just because it's not recommended, doesn't mean we can't use it and doesn't mean I don't have any." He leaned over and pulled a small vial from his desk drawer.

"I got this from my grandmother—don't ask—and she said to put five drops in tea."

He placed the small deep blue bottle in front of Thorne, who stared at it as if his whole world was inside. Which, he mused, it might well be.

"It's a gamble, boss. It might well work and guarantee you guys a fabulous Nuptial Flight. But it might also have some kind of a negative effect on Persephone. There were rumors of seizures and some kind of heart problems. I wasn't able to find out much about things like reactions or long-term damage estimates or anything like that. Those files are long gone."

Thorne took a deep breath and stared at the bottle. He lost himself in thoughts, dreams and visions of Persephone. His heart ached for her, his body yearned for her, and his soul felt incomplete without her.

He knew, in that instant, what he had to do.

"Thanks, Norman. Remind me to give you a raise," he said as he leaned over, grabbed the bottle and turned for the door.

"I always do. I never get it," said Norman to his boss's retreating butt.

"You will this time," yelled Thorne over his shoulder. "I just hope I'm around to give it to you."

* * * * *

Persephone struggled to consciousness from a dream that had her tangled up in chains of silk and Thorne's arms. She found herself caught in the webbing of the hammock, and with a sigh she eased herself free.

Amazingly enough her legs supported her, and she slowly crossed the sand to the water, letting her muscles ease and her body stretch. The sun had set a little while before and its glow still turned the sky to a variety of wonderfully unimaginable colors.

The stars were coming out. It was her wedding day. Well, wedding night.

Whatever it was, it was special.

She fluttered her wings tentatively. They seemed to be bigger, fuller and they snagged what ambient light there was and turned it into pink crystalline glimmers. Yes, uncounted numbers of orgasms courtesy of the sucking gouramis had certainly helped.

Now, however, the time for wing growth had passed. It was the Nuptial Flight that lay ahead of her. She took a short flight across the beach, trying her wings out, drying off the salt and shaking them free of any sand particles.

There—she felt a definite increase in her climbing power. With a little ping of pleasure coursing through her, she bit her lip in excitement. She could do this. She really could do this. All it would take would be a prayer, a breath, a lot of love, and Thorne.

Always Thorne. For him, all this had been worth it. The playtime with Sal and Clover, the aqua-orgasms with the gouramis, every bit of it.

She stroked her hand over her naked belly and imagined it filled with Thorne's child. In that moment she saw her. A little dark-haired imp demanding black leather boots from her doting father.

Tears clogged her vision as she wished for that to happen more than anything else in the whole world.

A sound behind her drew her back from her private meditations and she turned to see Clover quietly watching her.

"Persephone? The Queen sent me. It's time."

Chapter Fourteen

A huge moon hung low in the night sky as Persephone and Clover made their way across a smooth lawn to the terrace where a crowd had gathered. Persephone tried to stand tall and proud in the gorgeous pink silk gown that Clover had brought with her.

She was showered, buffed, powdered and even had a fresh application of wing wax. Her bare feet felt the soft grass and her body seemed extra sensitized to the swish of the silk around her ankles. The gentle night air brushed over her bare back—no surprise to find yet another halter gown. The fastenings at the waist were all that kept her decent, but she felt special all the same.

A cloud of tiny fireflies approached her and circled around her head. She laughed as they spun and danced in a crazy pattern, and cast little shadows across her arms.

She knew Thorne would be waiting with the crowd.

As she neared, she could see him. His robes were black silk. Well, hell, if he'd been wearing crimson she'd have fainted from surprise. As it was, he looked magnificent. She knew that Titania and Oberon were there, smiling from their dais, but she couldn't keep her eyes off Thorne.

His wings gleamed in the moonlight, his studs were spotless, and his body beneath his robes called to her. As she neared the flagstone, he moved toward her, holding a sprig of apple blossom in his hand.

Holding it out, he beckoned her to him.

She smiled shyly and accepted the blossom, transferring it to her other hand and placing her fingers into his warm grip.

His eyes told her a thousand things, but most of all that he was hers.

Persephone knew that this was her destiny. Being with this man, this fairy, this spirit, at this time and in this place, was where she was meant to be. There could be no question about it.

Thorne led her to a small carpet before the King and Queen.

Persephone glimpsed Clover moving over to stand at Sal's side, and realized that Norman and Cobweb were there too. In fact, there was quite a large crowd.

Her hand trembled for a second, but the reassuring squeeze she immediately felt from Thorne helped her regain her confidence. A little.

The King rose and held out his hands to the couple.

"Friends, fairies, enchanted beings. It is our joy to bless the Nuptial Flight of our devoted subject Thorne Leatherfly and his destined wingmate, Persephone Jones. Their love will be sealed by this mating Flight and their lives will be intertwined forever. As will their spirits when their wings fail and they move to their next great adventure."

Persephone felt the sting of tears in her eyes. It was sooooo beautiful, and she'd always been a sucker for weddings.

The King turned to Thorne. "Thorne Leatherfly, will you pledge your magic to this woman for eternity? Will you salute her with your wings, worship her with your body and cherish her with your heart?"

Thorne turned to Persephone and gently tapped his wingtips together. "In front of our monarchs I do so pledge."

Then it was Persephone's turn. Titania rose and faced her. "Persephone Jones, will you pledge your magic to this man for eternity? Will you worship him with your body, cherish him with your heart and bear his children in your womb?"

Persephone turned to Thorne and met a gaze that turned her insides to mush. Swallowing, she answered. "In front of our monarchs I do so pledge." She felt her wings give a little involuntary flutter.

Oberon and Titania joined hands. Oberon spoke reverently. "You have pledged yourselves to one another. We recognize and honor this pledge on behalf of Fairyland. May your union bring joy and fulfillment. May your mating be fruitful, and may your line continue unbroken for generations to come. In honor of this occasion, Her Majesty and I grant you, Persephone, the right to a new fairy name. From this moment on you shall be known as Persephone Blossom, mate of Thorne Leatherfly."

The King grinned wickedly, lightening the somber moment. "You may have one minute to kiss. Any more and I'll kick your asses."

"Well, Persephone Blossom?"

Thorne held his arms open and grinned. Persephone shook the tears from her eyes and took full advantage of the minute offered by Oberon.

"Keeerist. The minute's long over, you horny overstuffed sofa. Get to the good stuff, will ya?" The groaning tones of Phuque broke the emotional silence and sent a laugh rippling through the crowd.

Oberon held up his hand again, after giving Phuque a healthy smack upside the head. "It is time to fly, children."

Thorne held on to one of Persephone's hands, and turned to the dais. "If I may be permitted, Your Majesties, I have something I need to say." He pulled a small blue vial from under one wing and held it up to the moonlight.

"You all know of our concerns about this Flight. Well, it turns out that this little bottle of calamus might be the answer."

The crowd muttered and fidgeted and looked interested. Oberon and Titania waited, as did Persephone, for Thorne to continue.

"However…" He unstoppered the bottle and held it upside down. "I'm not going to use it."

The contents trickled out into a blue sparkling puddle on the ground. Persephone choked back a gasp, wondering if her future had just been poured out of a bottle and into nothingness.

"You're not?"

Thorne heard the agony in the question as Persephone whispered it into the silence.

"No, I'm not." He squeezed her hand. "I have a good reason. Bear with me, sweetheart."

Turning back to the dais, Thorne took a deep breath and proceeded to rattle a pair of metaphorical dice in his brain. This was going to be the biggest crapshoot of his entire life.

"Your Majesties. Fellow fairies. Friends. Even you, Phuque." A slight murmur of amusement sounded from the crowd.

"I discovered that this herbal preparation might have helped Persephone with her flight problems. But I also found that I could not guarantee its success and that it could have serious or possibly even lethal side effects on her. I could not take that risk."

Persephone tensed next to him.

"I have pledged myself to Persephone, my wingmate. But in the event that our Nuptial Flight fails, I request a boon. I cannot conceive of losing this woman. My life and my soul are hers in so many more ways than I ever imagined possible."

Persephone sniffed next to him.

"If we fail to achieve our Flight together, I ask to be returned with Persephone to her world."

Silence fell as the true meaning of Thorne's words sank in.

"You realize you cannot return as yourself. It would have to be in your cat manifestation," warned Oberon with a frown.

"I understand that, your Majesty. "

"No Thorne, you can't," choked Persephone. "You cannot do that. Give up your life here and become a cat permanently? No. I won't allow it."

Thorne turned to her and pulled her close, feeling the tears on her cheeks through his thin silk robe. "Yes I can. I will not live without you. To be at your side in whatever shape or form destiny decrees is my goal. I cannot do anything else."

Titania cleared her throat loudly. "God, Thorne, you're really something." She turned to the King. "Why didn't *you* ever do something like that, you jerk?" She sniffed again and wiped tears from her eyes as she elbowed Oberon.

Oberon winced. "Nice going, Leatherfly. Now look what you've done."

Thorne shrugged. "She's my woman. That's all there is."

And he meant it with all his heart. Standing there with Persephone tight against him made him whole.

"Very well." The King and Queen turned to the couple, after a few moments consultation. "We shall agree to grant your boon. Should your Flight not achieve mating, then you and Persephone will awaken in her world. Her memories of this place will be as a dream, and you will be her cat permanently."

Thorne bowed his head in agreement. "I understand."

Persephone's hand grabbed his like a vise, but he knew she'd no longer argue now that permission had been granted.

"If I may, your Majesties." Her clear voice rang out. What was she going to do now?

"I'd like to go on record as saying I don't like this deal particularly, and would have taken that herb if it would have helped, regardless of the risks. Anything for the man I love." She turned and her heart shone in her eyes as she gazed at Thorne.

"Oh barf. Get to the fucking before I vomit." Phuque farted loudly and ruined what was turning into a three-hankie soap opera. Thorne was profoundly grateful. He'd had his little moment, bared his soul, and now he wanted nothing more than to fly away from their Majesties and the assembled crowd. He wanted his wife to himself.

The King sighed. "Very well. Our flatulent friend has reminded us that midnight approaches. Persephone, come here please—Thorne, to the Queen."

Thorne took a deep breath and tried to quell the shaking in his gut.

This, as they say, was it.

* * * * *

Persephone neared the King's outstretched hands with a puzzled frown on her brow. She had thought they'd simply take off after the ceremony, but apparently there were some final pre-Flight instructions.

The King reached for her gown and unfastened it, allowing it to slide to the floor and leaving her naked before them. She noticed the Queen doing the same to Thorne.

"Our blessings on you, Persephone," boomed the King's voice. He leaned closer and whispered, "Give him a good fuck, babe. You can do it, I know."

Oberon then winked at her. "I give you the royal kiss of favor to send you aloft with our token of joy." The ritual words fell from the lips that neared hers. A certain glint in his eye told her that this wasn't going to be a polite air kiss to each cheek.

She was right.

Oberon grabbed her in a lip lock to end all lip locks, sliding his tongue past her barriers and encouraging her to open her mouth to him. She felt something pass onto her tongue and her eyes opened wide with shock.

Oberon pulled back with a grin, and placed his fingers on her lips, shutting her mouth firmly. "A little something from us, sweetheart. You don't think we're gonna let these lovelies go back to your world, do you?" He casually flicked her nipple, and probably would have gone further, if his attention had not been recalled by a very strong clearing of his wife's throat.

Thorne glowered at him, but Titania looked at Persephone. Blushing, Persephone returned her gaze.

The Queen winked.

Thorne took her hand and turned her away from them all. "Let's get the hell out of here, babe."

Only too ready to agree she followed him, slowly at first, then faster until they were running, then touching the ground in spots, then, without her realizing it, they were aloft.

Cheers followed behind them, but in seconds they were too far away to hear them.

The night claimed them and hid them from view as Persephone swallowed the refreshing peppermint-tasting whatever-it-was that Oberon had slid into her mouth.

She felt a wonderful tingle. The air whooshed past her naked body, stimulating every single cell. Thorne's hand held hers in a firm grip and they seemed to be getting really high, as the trees below dwindled to dark amorphous patches.

"Thorne…" she cried, loving the feeling of flying free next to him. Her breasts tingled.

With a neat bit of fancy flying, he swooped around and under her, flying faster than ever but with his body plastered to hers.

She felt his warmth and the breeze from his wings as his lips touched hers.

She exploded. Stars sparkled in her vision and her whole being seemed to come alive.

"Oh god," she sighed, as his head dropped down to her breasts and his rapidly expanding cock brushed her thighs. The total lack of any kind of fear led her to experiment with her own flying maneuvers and she allowed her speed to fall off slightly. This put her on a level with his cock.

She grinned and reached out, pulling herself to within centimeters of the rich ruby head. Her tongue flicked out and licked a path around it, then paused, waiting for the rush of air to chill the moisture.

She heard Thorne groan and smiled to herself, repeating her actions and adding a little swipe of her tongue to his balls, too.

No slouch, Thorne spread his legs and slipped his feet around her. This put his toes next to her wings and as they moved they brushed Thorne's feet. The feeling was sensuous and arousing, and she responded by taking him deeper into her mouth.

His response was gratifying. She felt the pulses in his cock as it hardened even more, and his hands ran through her hair. His moan told her that she had probably got this part of the Nuptial Flight right. She licked and sucked and cradled his sac in the softness of her palm as they flew through the night sky.

Finally, Thorne gasped. "No more, wait. Give me a minute…" He slowly allowed his body to slither beneath hers, suckling her breasts and tracing a line down her stomach with his tongue as he went.

Reaching her pussy he paused, loving the moist folds with a hungry touch and teasing her clit out into the cool air.

He swiveled and rose behind her, dropping a light love bite on her buttock as he arranged himself over her.

This was where her wing strength was crucial, she realized. With Thorne in that position, she would not have full throttle, as it were. She would have to hold steady on minimum power.

She gritted her teeth. She could do this. Oberon's magical candy was still sending shivers through her gut, and her wings felt invincible. The juices from her cunt felt cool against her flesh as the wind blew them to dryness.

It was the most sensual experience she could ever have imagined.

She could not have imagined, however, what would happen when Thorne slid up her back and touched his cock to her thrusterbud.

Sensitized by her Flight and aroused by Thorne, her thrusterbud was ready for action.

At the touch of his hot hardness, it went into overdrive. Sizzling tingles scurried through her muscles to her clit and her cunt. Her ass clenched. Her nipples jumped and marbled in seconds.

Again Thorne brushed her with his cock and she felt a drop of moisture on its tip. Again, her body responded wildly.

She sobbed out a gasp of pleasure. "Thorne—" she shouted, "my god, Thorne."

She couldn't have heard if he'd answered, because at that moment, Thorne pressed his cock deep into her wing opening and rubbed it against her thrusterbud.

If she'd had brakes, they would have locked and left a trail of rubber a mile long.

As it was, she screamed. Her body arched into an impossible bow, thrusting her breasts into Thorne's hands. Her wings were locked, her body shuddering, and she could feel her wings clamping around Thorne's cock.

His guttural cry echoed across the star filled sky.

His hips pounded against her as her body spasmed. Her cunt contracted violently, sending her into another series of orgasms.

"Persephoneeeeee…" Thorne's wild shout topped off her ecstasy. She knew she was coming with a ferocity and depth she couldn't begin to imagine.

She closed her eyes and rode it out.

She couldn't breathe, couldn't think, could only feel. Feel her own body as it responded to this new stimulus, and feel Thorne's body as he emptied his body and his soul into her keeping.

Finally, he withdrew, and a totally new kind of feeling filled Persephone.

She turned, flapped her wings and stared at Thorne.

He was grinning from ear to ear. "I love you, wingwoman."

"We did it, didn't we?"

"Yep. We didn't need any herbs, thank god. Just ourselves."

"And maybe a little magic from your fairy friends," laughed Persephone. "I think we owe the King and Queen a private thank you for some very special candy."

Thorne grinned. "Titania told me that Oberon was going to slip you a little something extra. I guess they use it now and again to crank up the volume. Did it work?"

Persephone just smiled. "What do you think?"

Thorne slowed their descent by taking her in his arms. "I think I'm nuts about you. I know I'm glad we succeeded, and I can now honestly tell you that I'm really happy I don't have to go back to eating cat food and licking your bra. I'm even gladder knowing you'll be here with me for the next five hundred years or so."

"Only five hundred? Well, I guess we'll just have to make every minute count." Persephone kissed him back and sighed as they resumed their flight.

"One last thing, sort of a verification. Just hold my hand and you'll see…"

Thorne pulled her alongside him and together they flew as high as they could, shivering slightly as the air chilled around them.

Then Thorne stopped her with a tug. He leaned over and kissed her. "Hello, Mrs. Persephone Blossom Leatherfly."

Persephone felt herself returning his grin. Thank god she didn't have to embroider towels with her married name. "Hello, Mr. Leatherfly."

"We're going to descend now, and as we do, your wings will settle into place and your thrusterbud will close up considerably. As it closes it leaves a trail…well, you'll see."

Persephone was puzzled, but figured Thorne probably knew what he was talking about. She simply placed her hand in his, content that it would be there for the rest of her life.

They turned, and began a gentle downward glide.

Sure enough, Persephone felt a new sensation in her wings. More assured and stronger, they carried her smoothly and a couple of twinges in her back told her that Thorne had been right.

"Look, honey," urged Thorne, pointing behind them.

A trail of sparkling dust stretched out behind them, like the tail of a comet.

"What is it?"

"It's us. Our essence. My cum and your juices have blended. The magic we've made is trailing from us across the sky to show everyone below that we're mated. Forever."

"Does that mean no more thrusterbud fucking?"

Thorne laughed aloud. "We'll figure it out, babe. Never fear. Where you and I are concerned, everything's magic and nothing's impossible."

Persephone, reflecting on the truth of his words, smiled and put her arms around her husband's neck as they flew home.

Together.

Epilogue

Phuque, entering from stage left, stares out across the audience.

"Okay, listen up, you sex-starved readers! If you were expecting some of that classical 'you-have-but-slumbered-here' crap, you're shit out of luck. Fairyland—yeah right. I know what you're sayin'. You're sayin' that's a load of frog manure. That no one can fly, grow wings or have sex up the ass without a lot of lubes."

Phuque glances around angrily, and farts.

"Well, that pretty much sums up my feelings about you all. You gotta believe something special happened out there with those two. You wanna call it 'luuuve' and get all mushy, well that's fine by me. Just don't sob all over my chest, it makes my nipples itch. All I'm sayin' is that you gotta believe in something. Those two did, and look where it got them? Mated, disgustingly happy, and fucking like minks. According to the noises, anyway. And I still find it damn hard to figure that Thorne Leatherdick. Go back to being a cat? Huh. I sooo don't think so."

Phuque leans against column, folds arms and thinks for a moment.

"Mind you, for a set of bazooms like Persephone's? Well, yeah, maybe there's a few things I'd do too. But you know what?"

Phuque leans forward intently.

"It's really all about believing, ain't it? Believing that if you love someone you can accomplish the impossible. Believing that love is out there somewhere for all of us. Believing in a happy ending. Believing that Fairyland exists someplace, maybe in your heart or your mind. Or maybe even in this story you just finished. And speaking of finished…"

Phuque turns and levitates off the stage by about three feet.

"Now that you have, it's time for me to get the Phuque outta here."

WINGIN' IT

જી

Dedication

ॐ

This book is dedicated to friendship.

Neither time nor space can loosen these bonds, once formed. Friends know that love and laughter are gifts best shared, since once given they are returned tenfold. A dear friend of mine reminds me of this every day…thanks, Partner.

And it's also dedicated to a very special group of people now living in assorted countries, who proved — despite commonly held theories — that one can go home again. And have a helluva lot of fun while doing it.

To my personal vineyard fairies — thank you. You'll always be at the bottom of the garden in my heart, and I'll always be there with you.

Chapter One

"Aaaargh."

The scream erupted from Ripple's throat as she opened her eyes to see the ground hurtling towards her at a frightening rate of speed. The wind whipped her wings straight back behind her and she was helpless to stop her fall.

This was the worst hangover *ever*.

Curling into a ball, she covered her head with her arms as best she could and waited for death. Nasty, messy, splattered-on-some-sidewalk death.

Why had she had those two extra shots of tequila? She should've known they were a mistake when the first one had gone to her wings, making them all but useless, and the second had made that fairy from Hackensack look like a hero from a romance novel. He'd flown her to the top of the Empire State Building, and fucked her up the ass beneath a starlit sky.

She thought it had probably been fun, but couldn't, right at this moment, remember.

Which was probably a good thing, since she didn't want her last thoughts in this life to be of a vague sexual encounter with some faceless dork.

It was bad enough that she was going to end her days with a mouth that tasted like the inside of a dead caterpillar and a headache that would surely kill her if the fall didn't.

Her short hair lashed around her ears, making her eyes water, and her rate of descent blew a screaming wind through her belly-button ring. It whistled like some weird musical instrument, orchestrating her departure from this world.

Fuck, fuck, *fuck*.

She pried one eye open and looked down. *Oh yuck…bad idea*. Swallowing down a mouthful of vomit, she blinked and closed the eye again. It was frickin' *dark*.

Where the hell was she? Central Park? Over the East River? Oh God forbid—please—not Long Island. She *hated* Long Island.

She struggled to remember the night before, but it was a blur. She knew she'd probably fell asleep up on that damned skyscraper. She vaguely recalled thunder. Oh shit. Perhaps she was over the water?

Urgh. Like most fairies, Ripple wasn't thrilled with the idea of getting her wings wet. Hers had a distressing tendency to frizz in humid weather, and getting them soaked just made her flat-out miserable. Not to mention that she didn't have a wing dryer tucked into her low-riding jeans, and she'd have to go borrow one, which always pissed off the person she "borrowed" it from, since she had a bad habit of not returning stuff she borrowed.

She meant to. She just forgot most of the time. Hey, shit happens. Live with it. That was her motto.

A couple of wet clouds whisked by and chilled her, and she ventured one more look at her life before it ended. Light filtered in past her fingers, and she opened both eyes this time, wide.

The world beneath her was quite extraordinarily green. And getting greener by the minute.

Where was the concrete? That heady scent of pollution and exhaust fumes? The early morning glitter of sunlight on the piss puddles left by last night's human drunkards?

Huh. This was, in a word, *odd*.

She wrinkled her nose and tried to flap her wings a bit against the onrush of air that smelled remarkably…clean.

But it was to no avail. Even fairies couldn't avoid the inevitability of the laws of physics. In this case, gravity. It was waaaay too late for her to request a repeal of *this* particular law.

The greenness got…greener, and Ripple closed her eyes tight as the sun peeked over the horizon and pierced her skull with what felt like sharp knitting needles.

This was *it*.

Goodbye cruel world, I hope New York will miss me.

Maybe a miracle will happen and I'll miss New York and hit the Hudson River instead.

God, don't let me shit in my jeans. They're new, and I finally got a pair that fit right…

She clenched her teeth, pulled her legs and arms tight into her body and prepared to die.

* * * * *

"Aaaaaaiiiiiyyyyeeeeeeee…"

"Aaaaaargggghhh…"

"*Fuuuuuuck…*"

"Oui…oui…*ouuuuuiiiiieeeeee…*"

Ripple's eyeballs rattled in her head as she crashed into a pile of something soft and warm and writhing, the impact of her collision lessened by…what?

She rolled over onto what felt like a cool damp bed and risked lifting an eyelid. Holy shit. It was moss. She'd heard about it, but never actually seen any. Carefully she extended one finger and stroked it. *Nice.*

"*Merde…*"

The voice was breathless, and Ripple opened the other eye, fighting to focus both pupils on *one* thing, not the twenty-seven that shimmered in front of her. Her head was pounding, her wings felt like they'd been run over by a stag beetle, and she had a nasty feeling she'd pissed in her pants.

Her vision settled down at last, and the blur resolved itself into two fairies. Two naked fairies. Two naked female fairies, one of whom was frowning at her and the other lying sprawled on the moss with a blissful expression on her face.

Sahara Kelly

"Ah, *bon Dieu*, *cherie*. That was…that was *extraordinary*." The fairy on the ground sighed and stretched.

The other fairy fiddled with her strap-on dildo. "Perhaps, *cherie*, but I had little to do with it, I think."

"That last thrust…mmmm."

Ripple cleared her throat. "Ahem."

They glanced at her. "*Bonjour.*"

Oh swell. French fairies. This must be Soho or Greenwich Village, maybe. Now she was gonna have to deal with that snooty European thing. She struggled to her feet and sighed.

Yep. Pissed my pants.

"Hey guys. Um. Sorry about the crashing stuff…"

Strap-on shrugged. "'Tis no matter. You gave me that extra little push that sent *ma cherie* into ecstasy, I think."

Ma cherie grinned. "*Merci. Merci beaucoup.* I truly saw heaven today."

"Riiiight." Ripple flexed her shoulders and gently tried her wings. "Ouch."

"Oh, *cherie*, you are hurt…" *Ma cherie* got slowly up from the ground, steadied herself, fluttered her wings and walked over to Ripple.

"Huh? I thought you were *Cherie*…" Ripple froze as soft hands stroked her wings.

Both fairies laughed. "*Non.* And *oui.* We are both *Cheries.*"

Uh-huh. With a bad case of identity crises.

Strap-on finally unlatched her strap-on, and dropped it to the ground. She smiled. "I am *Cherie-huit* Chardonnay. This is *Cherie-douze* Chardonnay."

"Oh my God. You're sisters?" Ripple was broad-minded to a fault, but this?

"No, no…you misunderstand. We are both Chardonnays, yes, but of different vintages."

164

Two pairs of hands stroked her now, caressing her wings, tousling her already-seriously messed hair, and…and…

She gasped as they brushed the curve of her breast that dipped from beneath her torn crop top. "Uh, girls?"

"So pretty, isn't she, Huit?"

"Mmm," said Huit.

Not "strap-on", must remember that.

Douze's head lowered and a long tongue flickered out, tasting Ripple's belly ring.

Hoookay. This was pretty weird, even for The Village.

"Chardonnays, huh? Any relation to the wine?" Ripple tossed out the quip before their hands ventured any further. She had a slight feeling she might get aroused if they kept this up, and that would pretty much kill her reputation as a hot tamale back in good old Manhattan.

Ripple gets off with two lezzy fairies in the Village. She could damn near see the headlines and hear the whispers in the clubs.

It worked. They both withdrew and stared at her curiously. "But of course," said Huit. "We *are* the wine."

"Didn't you know?" said Douze. "You're in the Chardonnay vineyard."

"I am?" Ripple smacked her ear with her hand, just in case she'd gotten something stuck in it, like an elephant. "I could've sworn you said I was in a vineyard."

"You are." They spoke together.

Great. French stereo. Just what her headache needed.

She tried again. "And this vineyard would be…where?"

"Why, in the valley, of course." Now it was fucking *surround* sound.

"Which valley?" Ripple would have ground her teeth, but was afraid if she did the top of her head would blow off.

"The Loire Valley. You're in France, *cherie*."

"Holy *shit*." Ripple blinked at them while her mind tried to absorb the information, gave up, and took a nap.

Suddenly a *whop-whop* sort of sound broke the quiet around them and Ripple gasped as it got very loud very fast.

Incoming. Instinctively, she ducked, grimacing against the blur her movement caused behind her eyeballs. *Remind self never to watch* Apocalypse Redux *again.*

A crashing sound and a rustle of wings alerted her to the fact that the "incoming" whatever it was had landed.

"Girls…girls…he's coming. He'll be here soon. Better get a move on."

Ripple turned slowly as the Chardonnays gasped in horror.

"Oh *merde*. He's coming *here*?"

"He wasn't due back 'til next *week*."

Hoookay. This was all getting a bit much for a simple girl fairy from the Big Apple. Ripple stared at the newcomer.

And there was a *lot* to stare at. And all of it stared right back at her.

"Who the hell's this?" The bumblebee placed two of its arms—legs—whatever firmly on its hips, or whatever passed for hips in the bumblebee world.

"Our friend." Huit slid a hand familiarly down past Ripple's wings to land on her backside, and squeezed.

"Not *that* much of a friend, honey." Ripple moved out of reach.

"What are you doing here?" The bee sounded cross, and a frown wrinkled its eyebrows. Bumblebees had eyebrows. *Who knew*?

"Aww, c'mon, *cherie*. She's our friend. She fell on us, pushed Huit just at the right moment, and I?" Douze's eyes glazed. "I orgasmed like *never* before."

TMI, Cherie. Damn Chardonnays. Always knew there was a reason I didn't go for white wine.

"How nice." The bee tapped one of its other…appendages. "Be that as it may, *he's* coming. Soon. And there's bound to be trouble."

Huit and Douze glanced nervously at each other. "Oh *merde.*"

Merde. Ripple knew that word very well. And it summed up how she felt, right about now.

"Well?" The bee stared at her, the Chardonnays held hands, and Ripple…

She did the only thing she could think of.

She threw up.

Chapter Two

"Ohhh—you pooooor dear…" The bumblebee's expression changed into one of deep concern. "Just look at you. Are you hurt? Come on…let's get you cleaned up. What your mother would think, I can't imagine…"

Helpless, Ripple allowed herself to be picked up and snuggled into the bumblebee's ample breasts. This was one helluva big critter. And a female one, too, which explained the sudden nurturing thing.

She was knee-deep in a small pool before she realized it, being efficiently stripped by Nurse Bee and her two helpers. Who were a little too enthusiastic for Ripple's liking. She didn't need her pussy scrubbed for God's sake.

Shit. Nor *that* spot either.

She backed away, stumbled and fell, going under and coming up coughing and spewing water. *Fuck.* It was the final straw.

"Now cut that *out*."

Ripple rose wrathfully from the stream, wings hanging sodden down her spine and chilling her butt. She spat a piece of weed from her mouth. "I don't know where I am or why I'm here. But I do know *one* thing."

She glared at Huit and Douze. "I'm a straight wing fairy, okay? No hard feelings, but keep your hands to yourself."

Two identical pouts crossed two pairs of rosebud lips.

"My name is Ripple, I'm from East Elmhurst, New York, good old U. S. of A., and where I live we don't grope pussy unless specifically asked, you got that?" She shook her body free of water droplets and dragged a hand defiantly through her short hair.

"*Okay*?"

The girls nodded, and Ms. Bumble tsked.

"Ripple. Pretty name. I'm Bee17." She closed the gap between them and proceeded to rub Ripple down with various portions of her thorax. Since she was covered by a thick soft coat of fuzz, the sensation was rather like drying off in an expensive hotel towel.

"Bee17. Hoookay. No surprise there." Ripple noted the enormous wingspan and wondered if the Pentagon knew about her.

"New York? Really?" Huit's eyes were wide. "How exciting. I've never met anyone from New York."

Douze giggled. "You've never met anyone who wasn't a Chardonnay, darling."

Huit's expression changed. "Except…*him*."

Ripple frowned as she stepped out of the water into the sunshine and spread her wings to dry. *Fuck*. She could've used some of that new Sassoon wing-smoother. They were gonna frizz something fierce. "Who's this '*him*' everybody's talking about?"

Douze and Huit exchanged glances as Bee17 rinsed Ripple's clothing efficiently in the pool and tsked again.

The girls settled themselves delicately around Ripple's damp wings. "Well…" began Huit. "He's—he's…"

"Oh for heaven's sake." Douze rolled her eyes. "He's a pain in the arse, is what he is."

Ripple raised an eyebrow. "He's a guy, I take it. Most of 'em *are* pains in the ass, one way or another. What's your point?"

Douze folded her hands. "He's the leader of the vineyard fairy kingdom. Do you know about the vineyard fairies?"

"Only the ones I've seen after a night of too much wine," snorted Ripple. "I think I threw up on a couple of 'em."

"Do that a lot, do you dear?" Bee17 looked over maternally. "Perhaps I should make you a nice cup of chamomile tea. Settle your stomach."

Ripple ignored her. "Go on. Tell me about this leader jerk. The pain in the…'arse'."

"Well." Douze tucked her legs beneath her and absently fondled Huit's breast. "We vineyard fairies are responsible for the vines. The grapes. The whole harvest, actually."

Ripple's eyes widened. "Wow. Heavy job, girlfriend."

Douze laughed. "Oh we don't do very much, really. We just make sure that the right flowers get pollinated, that the crops mature on schedule, that the humans know when it's time to harvest the grapes, that sort of thing."

"Ah." Ripple fought a yawn. The sunshine was warming her nicely now, and although Douze's recitation was interesting, that life didn't sound like one she'd enjoy. Where were the clubs? The parties? The midnight trips down the ventilation shafts into Saks to whip through the reduced-for-clearance section?

"And we fuck," Huit added.

Ripple sat up. "You what?"

"We fuck. A lot." Douze grinned. "You see, we Chardonnays…well, we're rainbow fairies."

Ripple blinked. "Huh?"

"We prefer same-sex fucking, Ripple," said Huit gently.

"Ah. Okay. Uh…" The next question seemed logical. "So where do all the little Chardonnays come from?"

Douze sighed. "Volunteers."

Damn. This was getting more bizarre by the minute. "Volunteers?"

"Oui. Volunteers. Every season a few Chardonnays volunteer to cross-pollinate with the opposite sex." Huit wrinkled her nose. "Rather distasteful, and messy, but necessary."

Ripple shook her head. What these girls are missing.

"And that brings us to *'him'*." Douze continued her story. "*Monseigneur Pinot Noir*." She spoke the name with scared reverence.

"Give it up, babe. I'm not gonna quit asking." Ripple's interest was well and truly caught.

"This year, he's Philippe Gustave Emile Pinot Noir. The Monseigneur of the Pinot Noir family."

"Like a Godfather or something?" Ripple tilted her head.

"Sort of. *They're* more common in the Sicilian vineyards, though, I hear." Douze went on. "The Monseigneur has a very special job, and that only in champagne years."

"Is that like dog years?"

Huit frowned at her. "*Pardonnez-moi*?"

"Never mind. What's a champagne year?"

Bee17 entered the conversation. "A champagne year is when conditions are right for the very best grape harvest. When there are enough Pinot Noirs to…to…blend with Chardonnays and produce a magnificent crop of champagne grapes."

"Ahhh." Light was beginning to dawn in Ripple's fuddled mind. Her headache was clearing up too. "And lemme guess. Sex is involved, yes?"

"Yes." Huit sighed. "He picks a Chardonnay, and they make the 'Noble Mold' flight together."

"Whoa." Ripple held up her hands. "Time out. Back up the truck here, babe. A 'Noble Mold' flight?"

"You really don't know much about wines, do you?" Bee17 sighed.

"Only how to uncork 'em with my teeth. Go on…"

Douze went on. "Yes, a Noble Mold flight. The leader of the vineyards must…er…spurt his seed over the vineyards."

"Eeeeuwww." Ripple wrinkled her nose.

"His...semen...dapples the grapes and makes the Noble Mold grow. And of course, he has to do it with a Chardonnay, since the blend of their juices strengthens the effect of his...semen." Douze blushed.

"So." Ripple digested the information. "This Pinot Noir guy gets jerked off by one of you Chardonnays while making a low altitude pass over the vineyards?"

"Essentially, yes."

"Sounds like loads of fun." Ripple curled her lip. "For him."

"Oh, well, he is returning the favor, of course. The Chardonnay chosen for the flight is...er..."

"Getting her flight clearance, too?"

Douze nodded at Ripple's attempt at humor. "Yes indeed." She sighed. "It's quite lovely, actually. An amazing sight."

"Wait a goddamn second here..." Ripple interrupted. "You mean people get to frickin' *watch* all this jerking off?"

"But of course." Two pairs of eyes stared at her in surprise. "It's a very important moment to all the vineyard fairies."

"Lord, you people are fucked."

"Well, yes. That too." Huit giggled as Douze's hand fell to her pussy.

Ripple sighed. "I didn't mean that, and *cut it out*. I ain't a vineyard fairy and it makes me..." She squirmed. "...itchy."

"Sorry." Douze gave Huit's pussy a final stroke and pulled her hand away. She lifted her fingers to her lips and licked away Huit's juices.

"Okay. That does it. I'm gonna barf again." Ripple's stomach churned.

"Oh no you're not, Mademoiselle Upchuck." Bee17 slapped her sharply around the ear with one wing.

"Ouch. What the hell was that for?" Ripple winced.

"I've just washed your clothes, you grub, and I'm damned if I'll do it again. And you two…" Her multifaceted eyes glared at Huit and Douze. "Keep your hands off each other for five minutes. You can see Ripple isn't used to our ways."

"Yes, Ma'am." The stereo was back on.

Ripple stood carefully, unfurling her wings and fluttering them in the sunshine. It dawned on her that she was buck naked, but for her belly button ring, and not bothered in the least.

The last time that had happened she'd been in Times Square on New Year's Eve riding the ball down at midnight. This time she wasn't even drunk.

Weird.

A sudden stillness fell over their little patch of vineyard paradise, and a tall shadow blocked the sunlight from Ripple's drying wings.

She shivered and turned around.

Hooookay.

It had to be *him*.

* * * * *

The first thing she noticed was his height. He was a good deal taller than your average fairy, and it was no wonder he was blocking out the sunlight.

The second thing she noticed was his hair. A deep red with glints of purple where the sun caught it; Ripple knew there were people at Clairol who'd probably kill to get just exactly that color. It was long, too, flowing well past his shoulders in silken glory.

The third thing she noticed was a distinct warmth flowering between her legs. *Fuck.* He was downright *gorgeous*. Silk pants in a blood red-purple shade flapped gently in the breeze, and his pristine white shirt was unbuttoned just enough to show off a very nicely muscled chest.

His wings were folded neatly behind him, reflecting odd shades of blue and purple and red like an oil slick on a rain puddle. And his eyes?

Well, if he'd stop staring at her crotch, maybe she could get a look at them, too.

"Yo. Buddy." She snapped her fingers at him. "My pussy ain't gonna say hello."

A gasp rang around the glade, and she realized their little group wasn't alone. Mr. High-and-Mighty Purple Hair had brought his retinue along with him.

Half a dozen matching wasps were standing at attention behind him, and she wished she had a can of Raid stashed around someplace. Wasps made Ripple—uncomfortable. They were short-tempered, argued a lot, and thought themselves God's gift to fairies in the fucking department.

They weren't. They were wiener-dicks.

"I *beg* your pardon?" A rich voice boomed into the silence.

Oh *that* got his attention. Eyes of the deepest purple were now fixed on hers. And they didn't exactly send off come-jump-me messages, either. "Were you addressing *me*?"

Ripple's eyes narrowed. Arrogant piss-ass. "Yeah. Since *you* were the only one gluing your eyeballs to my crotch, I sure *was* addressing you." She stepped forward and stuck out one finger. New Yorkers trembled when Ripple stuck out that particular finger.

She jabbed it firmly into his chest. "Let me tell you something, my friend. Where I come from it is *not* polite to stare at a woman's snatch, okay? Especially when you haven't been introduced." She glared at him.

He glared back. "Do you know who I am?"

"Yep. You're the asshole who seems to think he can take inventory of my pussy without a hello. Ain't gonna happen, dude. Don't care if you're the King of the World and this is the Titanic. It *so* ain't gonna happen."

Ripple turned around and stalked away.

Only to find herself surrounded by wasps, weapons drawn. She stopped short.

Of course, to draw their weapons, wasps had to turn around and bend over. It was kind of like being mooned by a bunch of furry-assed teenagers with first strike capabilities. Or something she'd seen at the last Yankees game.

She sighed and shook her head. "Call off your hounds, your Godship. I am not about to kill anyone. I'm just pissed off, hungover and frickin' confused."

"And bald."

"What?"

"Your…what did you call it…*snatch*?" He nodded his head towards the junction of her thighs. "It's bald."

She was *soooo* not having this conversation.

Grabbing her jeans from the nerveless hands—or whatever—of Bee17, Ripple tugged them up and zipped them with a sharp jerk. Never mind that they were still damp and stuck to her butt cheeks like wet toilet paper. She'd be damned if she'd let her beautifully depilated pussy provide entertainment for some over-opinionated French lecher.

She struggled into her cropped top, fluttering her wings a little as one tip caught on the shoulder.

With an oath, he strode over and freed it, tugging it down and brushing her breast while he was at it.

"Hey…" she snarled at him.

"Oh, *mon Dieu*. Do you *never* shut up? How about you lose the attitude and tell me who the hell you are and what you're doing in my vineyards."

"Attitude? *Me*?" Ripple was irate. "I end up here after a night's fun, and I don't know how. Last thing I remember was falling asleep on top of the Empire State Building." She glared at him. "That's in New York City, buster, in case your geography's as weak as your eye control."

He glared back. "So, Miss *New York City*. What the devil are you doing *here*?"

"*I don't fucking know, all right?*"

They were nose to nose now, and all but screaming at each other.

"*Well what the fuck do you know?*" His face was turning red as he hollered the words up her left nostril.

"That you're a *loudmouthed pain in the arse*, Mister Pee-nose Noir." Ripple yelled back, feeling the bile rise in her throat. "And I'm gonna yark on you if you don't quit deafening me."

"Now that's quite enough, both of you." Bee17 marched forward, pushing them apart like a referee at a boxing match. "Behave yourselves." She wiggled her thorax threateningly.

"You, Philippe, should know better than to shout at a guest that way. I'm appalled. What would your vintage say if they could hear you now?"

"They probably can," muttered Huit.

A glare from Bee17 shut her up.

"And you, Ripple, for heaven's sake stop throwing up on everybody and everything. I don't know what you do in this New York City place, but if it involves so much…what did you call it…*yarking*? Well, all I can say is I don't want to visit it, thank you."

The wasps tittered.

Ripple drew back and sucked in air through her nose. "Yeah." She swallowed and nodded at Bee17. "What she said."

Philippe straightened, glancing around at the mostly silent throng. A blush spread over his cheeks and he frowned. "My apologies."

He spun on his heel and stalked off, followed by his guards, who sniggered. One even spread his fur and flashed Ripple with his cock.

Yep. It was a wiener. Even France couldn't produce a wasp with a dick worth shit. She curled her lip at him.

"Bring her." The command was barked over his shoulder as Mr. High-and-Mighty strode back down the path, wings glistening in the morning sun.

The wasps closed ranks and one came a tad too close to her ass for Ripple's liking.

"Buzz off, buddy. Another inch and that wiener of yours will be gracing a bun at the next cookout."

Philippe glanced back. "W2. Rear guard means standing at the rear. Not fucking it."

W2, huh? No wonder I hate the IRS.

Surrounded by her "guard" and accompanied by Bee17 and the Chardonnays, Ripple left the clearing and the stream behind, passing along a quiet lane. The air hummed with sun and leaves, and bunches of grapes hung heavy from the vines on either side of them.

It was idyllic, gorgeous, and Ripple would have sold her left tit to be sucking up exhaust fumes from a NYC transit bus.

She was out of her element, surrounded by a bunch of weird, snot-nosed foreigners half of whom were deviants, had wasps…wasps!…marching in formation beside her, and her wings were frizzing.

This was so not a good day.

Dear Diary. Today I took a trip. To Crazyville. And met one helluva good-looking guy. Did not — repeat not — throw up on him.

"Uh…hey." She cleared her throat and caught Huit's eye. "Where we going?"

Huit smiled nervously and glanced at Douze.

"The Choosing."

Ripple sighed. Once again Le Stereo French made absolutely no sense whatsoever. Pretty much like the rest of this nightmarish experience.

Another of the wasp guard snickered and winked at her. His hair was heavily slicked back with a sheen of gel. Enough to lube a '57 Chevy and have plenty left over for a couple of lawnmowers and a chain saw.

Ripple curled her lip. "Lemme guess. WD-40, right?"

Surprisingly, a quick bark of laughter sounded from His Godship. It was immediately stifled.

Hmm.

Chapter Three

Ripple tentatively fluttered her wings.

Thank God they were drying out and not too badly frizzed. She sure could have used them, since these heathens had made her walk — *walk* — for what seemed like endless miles. Like they'd never heard of taxis? Or public transportation? A handy butterfly with a good set of abs?

Sheesh.

With all the disdain of a native New Yorker, Ripple perched on the end of the small bed and examined her feet. They'd never be the same.

She'd been force-marched through that damn greenery to a Chateau that could have skipped off the promo posters for a Gothic romance movie, separated from her new friends, the lezzies and the bumblebee, and pushed into this — cell-like room. Which was locked.

And then deserted.

Fuck wine. Gimme a Margarita any day.

She squelched down the memory of that real fine male ass that had occupied much of her time during that trek through the vineyards.

She'd always been a sucker for a nice pair of buttocks, and Mr. High-and-Mighty sure had a set of the best.

She licked her lips, then told herself off. *Cut it out. You shouldn't be thinking hot sex right now. You should be thinking of getting the fuck out of this madhouse. Mad Chateau. Whatever.*

Besides, he clearly wasn't for her. He was gonna jerk off some Chardonnay dolly over a bunch of grapes.

Lucky her.

Now cut that out!

Ripple's internal dialogue was interrupted by the entrance of another large bumblebee. "Strip."

Huh. Obviously this one had had her nurturing gene removed at an early age.

"I will not." Ripple stood up and put her hands on her hips.

"Yes you will." The bee advanced on her threateningly and bared her teeth in a snarl. *Jesus.* Bumblebees had teeth too.

"Why?" Ripple stalled.

"Because I told you to."

"Oh yeah? Gonna make me?" No chick from Manhattan was about to be intimidated by a furry-assed bully.

"Yesss…" The bee produced the biggest pair of scissors Ripple had ever seen. "And I won't be too careful about where I cut either."

Hookay. Chicks from Manhattan were also smart and knew when they were outgunned.

Carefully, Ripple stepped out of her clothes. "You'd better take damn good care of these." She passed her jeans to the bee. "I had to promise a blowjob to my tailor to get them to fit right."

The bee snorted. "It figures." Her look spoke volumes. *Foreign trash.*

"Well, you know how spiders are. They're so frickin' glad to get a little without having their heads bitten off afterwards…"

Ripple was blabbering. She knew it, and the bee knew it. Being stuck in a dungeon-place while wearing designer jeans was one thing. Being naked in it was another.

Fucking Bee-stapo! "You sure this isn't a German vineyard?"

The bee clacked her scissors loudly.

"Okay, okay. Don't get your pollen sacs in a twist." Ripple struggled free of her crop top, sighing as she handed that over as well. "Now what?"

The bee pulled a piece of fabric from one of her leg pockets. "Here."

Ripple looked at it. "Toilet paper? How kind."

"It's your garment."

"*Riiiight.*" The thing was about a foot or so square. And just about transparent. Ripple's window sheers had more heft to them.

"Put it on or stay naked. It's all the same to me." The bee gathered Ripple's clothing, stuffed it into another pocket and rumbled off, letting the door clang shut behind her.

Shit. Now what?

She twisted the small piece of fabric into an assortment of shapes. It was like trying to do origami with wet noodles. Apparently she had a choice of which of her private parts she could cover, since the frickin' thing refused to stay put in one particular place. The holes in it seemed designed to let her nipples stick out, or her ass, depending on where she tied it.

Hell. I paid attention during Fashion Week. I watched those designers turn less than this into a seven-hundred dollar ensemble. C'mon girl. Get it into gear.

An hour or so later, she was…for lack of a better word…dressed. Sort of. Providing she didn't move, sneeze or fart, she should be okay. Most of the important bits were now *draped* at least, and although a good puff of wind would evaporate the damn thing, Ripple felt a little more confident.

And hungry. What she wouldn't give for a Reuben sandwich on rye. Her mouth watered. Perhaps they were gonna starve her to death?

Well fuck it. She'd been promising herself a decent diet plan for a while. Now was as good a time as any to start.

The sound of footsteps and the rattling of the door interrupted her thoughts once again. *Now what?*

"Hello."

Oh fuck. It was *him*.

Her tongue stuck to the roof of her mouth as she stared at him. He'd removed his shirt, brushed his hair, probably shaved and showered, and he looked a damn sight more tasty than a Reuben sandwich.

This must be the *intimidate-the-prisoner-with-a-fabulous-chest* interrogation technique. Hell. She'd talk. Whatever secrets he wanted, she'd spill 'em.

"Uh...hi."

Ripple licked her lips.

* * * * *

Philippe entered the room with a certain degree of trepidation, which was unusual for him. This odd little creature with her bald pussy had captured his attention to a highly abnormal degree, and he wasn't sure whether he liked it or not.

"I realize we have not been formally introduced." He tried not to stare through her transparent clothing.

"You've met my crotch, however."

Her tone was challenging, and he grinned. "A very nice one it is, too. I'm Philippe Gustave Emile Pinot Noir." He bowed.

"I'm Ripple Amanda Jennifer Elizabeth Corianthus Smith."

"Really?"

She grinned back. "No, but I figured I'd take how ever many names you have and raise you one."

He laughed. "You are very strange, Ripple Smith. And probably hungry." He took a tray from someone outside the door and closed it firmly. Then he opened it again with a muttered apology as a portion of wing was whisked out of the jamb with a whimper. "Sorry."

Ripple, damn her stupid name, giggled at him. He ignored it and uncovered some wine and a couple of fresh croissants.

"Oooh. You must have read my mind." She reached hungrily for the food.

I hope you didn't read mine. "I realize our hospitality has been a little lacking, and for that I apologize. But there are circumstances…" He paused.

"Oh yeah?"

Yech. She even spoke with her mouth full. Why he couldn't get this brash creature out of his mind he had no idea. Right now she was looking at the wine like it was poison.

"Uh…this is wine, right?"

Brilliant. "Yes. One of our better years, too."

"Can't drink red wine. Gives me a migraine. You got any soda? Diet something? Root beer?"

Philippe blinked. "*Merde.* You are a Philistine, aren't you?"

"Certainly not. I'm Protestant." Ripple devoured the last of the bread and licked her fingers. With a very nice tongue. Philippe's cock appreciated the sight.

"So what's these circumstances?" Ripple belched slightly and waved her hand. "'Scuse me."

He sighed. "You really are from New York City."

She tapped her fingertips on the tray. "Jeez, buster. What the hell have I been saying all along? You people got grapes in your ears or something?" She shook her head. "I was in the Big Apple for a party last night. Or whenever last night was. Had a couple of drinks, you know? A good time?"

She looked apologetically at him. "And with all due respect, there was no wine involved. Just tequila."

It was Philippe's turn to wince. *Tequila*? Eeeeeuuuuwww.

"Anyhooo…" She continued her tale enthusiastically. "Things were really cooking at my favorite club, and there was this guy…" she broke off and blushed. "Aw…what the hell. You're unshockable, right?"

God only knows when it comes to you, cherie. Philippe nodded.

"So anyhooo…we took a quick flight up the Empire State building, did it under the stars and I fell asleep." She looked pained. "Okay. So it was more like passed out. But he was damn good. Knew his way around an ass, lemme tell ya."

Philippe bit down on a sharp pang of lust. She liked ass? Hell, he'd show her ass like she'd *never* had before. But she was still talking.

"Next thing I know, I'm flying high and falling fast. I land on a couple of your Chardonnay gals doing the strap-on thing, and here I am. End of story."

Philippe pondered her tale. "There were storms over the last couple of days. Big ones. My best guess would be that you got scooped up in one of them. The prevailing winds run west to east—"

"Look, Mr. Big Chest Philippe Andrew George whatever. Prevailing-schmailing. I don't really give a rat's fart about that stuff. I want to know how to get home, and out of these…these *green* places. I think I'm allergic. I might get a rash."

He let his eyes roam over her creamy skin, most of which was exposed. "Don't see any signs of a rash yet…"

She hunched a shoulder and turned her back on him. "Yeah, well. You never know."

There was just the slightest tremor in her voice that told him she wasn't quite as brash as she would like him to believe.

And her ass? Ooooh, *yessss*. It was a *very* nice ass. All tight and rounded and curvy and—he was drooling.

He closed the distance between them. "Don't worry, *petite* Ripple. We'll figure out a way to get you home."

He stroked her wings and she shivered. "Uh, don't do that."

He kept up his delicate touches, just brushing the ribs and lightly caressing that special spot where they grew from her spine.

She gulped. "You really shouldn't do that."

"Why not?" He dipped his mouth and licked her wing bud, that exquisite place on all fairies that was pretty much hardwired into their sex organs.

"Because…" She trembled. "Because I don't like it."

He peeked over her shoulder and noticed her nipples, hard as stones and poking through the sheer netting. "Your body tells me otherwise."

She folded her arms across her chest. "It's cold in here."

Philippe smiled "Then perchance as a good host, I should warm you."

He tugged the drawstring on his pants and stepped out of them with ease. "Is this better?" He plastered his body to her back, gasping as her wings brushed his own nipples. Oh yes. That was *much* better.

"Uhh…" She swallowed, hard.

He pressed himself against her, letting his cock rub her body. His wings took over, lifting him into the air and positioning the now-swollen head right above her wing bud.

He pushed himself forward.

She squawked as her own wings fluttered, she lifted off the ground and her legs spread wide. "Jesus fucking Christ—what the…"

His hands crept around her, dipping beneath the fragile hem of the pretend dress and finding the smooth folds of her alluring pussy. Images of that shining flesh had been driving him mad for hours.

His cock had dragged itself down her spine as she'd risen, and they were now hovering, effortlessly, clasped together.

With Philippe exactly where he wanted to be—tucked into her warm cleft.

* * * * *

Oh, fuck those fickle fingers of fate. The ones that were teasing her pussy and making her shiver against this super hunk of heat fluttering behind her.

Ripple bravely fought for composure. At least she wanted to imagine that's what she should be doing.

Okay, so she wasn't. *Sue me. I've got him exactly where he wants me. And it's…super-cali-whatever.* She doubted any flying nanny had ever thought of doing it in quite this way.

His cock was nudging her, finding its way between her butt cheeks with unerring accuracy. For a minute she wondered if someone had tattooed a target on her ass without her knowing about it. Fuck *here*, please.

His fingers played over her bald pussy. They spread the lips apart, searching out all those very nice places that were guaranteed to unlock the dam of juices that flooded her thighs when somebody touched them.

Like he was doing. Right this minute.

And fuck him, he knew it, too. Philippe smeared those hot liquids around, swirling intricate—and probably Impressionist, knowing the French—designs on her skin. She was turning into a work of oversexed art beneath his hands.

She ripped off her stupid bit of netting. *Better. New York Fairy as Lustful Slut. A nude in wet pastels.*

Let's see 'em hang this one at the Metropolitan.

Within moments, he'd found her ass. Not a real challenge, of course, since the damn thing had a mind of its own and was sort of presenting itself in the right place to the right thing.

Ripple leaned forward a little, shamelessly encouraging him. She was surprised at the level of need she felt, to have that fine piece of male flesh introduce itself to her more-than-ready female flesh.

C'mon, French dude. Let's do the dark dance here.

Philippe was certainly up to the challenge. With surprising ease he slid that lovely cock of his into her tight passage, combining his entrance with delicate little flicks against her clit.

She moaned. Honest-to-God, romance-novel-heroine moan.

It was *that* good.

"Ahhh, *Ripple*…" The low growl surprised her for a second or two, so lost was she in the feelings of him filling her ass and bringing her whole body to an amazingly high level of arousal.

"Yeah," she groaned. "Oh yeah. Do it, French-boy."

He thrust harder. "I am not a *boy*, Ripple…"

Damn straight. His cock stretched her, expanded within her, sent shivers of pleasure up her spine to her wing bud and generally turned her inside out. And *then*—just when she thought for sure she was gonna come—hard—he started to move.

Hands and cock in concert, he fucked her, bringing her higher than ever with strokes of his fingers, followed by strokes of the rest of him. Breathless, she gripped the windowsill, legs spread wide now, needy and hungry for whatever he could give her.

His body smashed against hers, his balls slapped her thighs, and when he finally plunged two fingers deep into her cunt, she lost it.

Completely and abso-fucking-lutely *lost* it.

"Aaaargh!" For the first time in her life, Ripple screamed out an orgasm, shocking the shit out of herself. Philippe's fingers were merciless, coaxing her from one peak to the next, plunging in as his cock withdrew and then pulling back as his cock buried itself up her ass once more.

She rocked violently against him, wings taut and rigid as plate glass. There was no air…she couldn't breathe for long seconds, and then she felt him. Hot jets of come exploded into her body and Philippe cried out as well.

"*Merde*…"

Their wings were a tangled mess, Ripple's thighs were soaked, her wing bud was humming a symphony, and she was shaken to her core. Holy fucking *Frenchman*. Maybe there was something to be said for wine, after all.

The strength of his wings alone held them aloft for a few moments as the last of the shudders died away.

Then even Philippe surrendered and they tumbled to the floor.

As they did, the door opened.

"Bon Dieu—*Philippe*. I might have known it. What the *fuck* do you think you're doing?"

Philippe yanked a wing out from under Ripple, cursing luridly and with great emotion.

She blinked, wondering if he'd teach her a few of those words. They had to be pretty foul, but they rolled off his tongue like music.

"I'd have thought that was obvious." His tone was terse, and earned him a slap upside the ear from the stern fairy who had entered Ripple's cell.

Ripple straightened her own wings, tried to close her legs which had gotten locked around Philippe's wrist somewhere along the line, and pulled her Manhattan training to the fore. *Never look embarrassed. If at all possible.*

"Ripple, *cherie*, may I introduce my mother?"

Okay. Not looking embarrassed soooo wasn't going to work.

Chapter Four

"*Philippe!*"

The woman was clearly irate. Ripple didn't need to see a sign around her neck saying "pissed-off fairy" to catch her drift. Her gown was elegant, hugging some quite nice curves, and her wings glittered silver in the sunlight.

"What *is* the *matter* with you? Wasting your precious essence on this…this…" She waved her hand at Ripple.

Who narrowed her eyes as her temper rose. "Hey. *Lady*. You may have birthed a red-hot poker, here, but that's no damn reason to look at me like I'm something your caterpillar dragged in." She struggled into what was left of the pink piece of tissue paper she'd been given to wear. "I'll have you know I'm kinda out of my depth here with you crazy people. I'm from New York. We don't treat people with disrespect there, okay?"

She put her hands on her hips and stared angrily at the older woman. Who, it was to be hoped, had never been to New York, and wouldn't know a boldfaced lie when she heard one.

"Mother, I…" Philippe staggered a little as he stood.

"You. Shut up." A pointed finger reduced him to silence.

Shit. She's better with the finger-thing than I am.

"You." The finger aimed right between Ripple's eyes, making them cross. "Who are you?"

"I'm Ripple. From New York. Vintage East Elmhurst. And I gotta tell you something. Great sex from your kid here notwithstanding, I'm getting pretty fed up with this whole damn place."

The silver wings trembled a little, and Ripple watched, fascinated, as a smile began to curve a full pair of lips. "*Great sex?*"

And that was definitely a twinkle in those grey eyes if Ripple had ever seen one.

"Shit, yeah. The best. Your boy did you proud, Ma'am." *Oh sure. Be polite to a woman while complimenting her son's sexual prowess. Jeez, Ripple, you sure know how to fuck up a conversation.*

"My name is Shiraz. It would appear you have met my son. Intimately." She turned to the door. "Philippe, go away and clean yourself up. You are a wart on the ass of this vineyard, sometimes."

Philippe choked.

"Ripple—come with me. We must get you something decent to wear and find out what the fuck is going on. Why you're here, and how to get you back where you belong."

"Hey...don't blame me for this bit of nothing. One of your bees threw it at me under threat of death-by-scissors." Ripple felt honor bound to defend her fashion statement.

Shiraz paused. "That would be Gerda. She's been hanging around the Alsace bees again. I'll speak to her."

"Well...good." Lost for a response, Ripple glanced at Philippe. He shrugged, spread his arms wide helplessly and left.

Shiraz beckoned Ripple. "Come on, New York. Let's see what can be done to straighten out this clusterfuck."

Hmmm. For a European fairy, Shiraz had a damn good grasp of basic English.

Ripple had no choice but to follow her.

* * * * *

Philippe watched from an alcove as his mother led Ripple away down the stone corridor. He tried to keep his gaze above her butt, but failed dismally. Those nicely rounded cheeks still glowed from where he'd crushed his body into them, and his cock stirred at the memory.

Merde. Why now? Why had fate and some kind of freak storm dumped a woman into his arms that he could really get a heavy dose of lust for?

He wiped his hands over his face and smelled the scent of her pussy, which lingered on his fingertips. Tart and tangy, she was so different from the ones he took with regularity. Sex with her had been—uplifting. To say the least.

No duty was involved. No "excuse me, I'm the current Lord of the vineyard and I'm going to fuck you now"…none of that.

Just sheer unadulterated lust…need…desire…all the good things he'd sort of lost touch with since becoming Monseigneur.

He cursed again as he took himself off to his suite. Only to curse even more when he found a guest awaiting him.

"*Daaaahling*…what do you think?" The figure pirouetted. "Isn't it just *divine*?"

Just what he needed. A pink Chardonnay. He closed his eyes and pinched the bridge of his nose. "*Bonjour*, Soix."

Soixante-Neuf Chardonnay turned once more, proudly showing off his new ensemble. "Isn't this just the bee's knees?" He pouted. "No. Wrong analogy. Those bees have the worst knees I've ever seen in my life. Isn't it just…too much?"

"Probably." Philippe sighed and blinked at the pink confection that graced his friend. Glittery little dangly things cascaded from a high collar, and matched the same glittery things that were embroidered on his belt. The pants must have been spray-painted on, since every damn fold of skin was clearly delineated. Along with what looked suspiciously like some kind of pouch holding his genitals snug against his body.

"What's that?" He gestured at Soix's crotch.

Soix giggled. "That, dear boy, is a *codpiece*."

"I thought they went out several hundred years ago."

"They did." Soix smirked. "I intend to bring them back in again." He glanced down. "Only underneath the clothes this time. So much more fun to discover a package within a package, don't you think?"

Philippe shook his head. "What do you want, Soix? The sun hasn't set yet. You didn't haul your ass out of bed and dress up like pink frosting just to show me your codpiece."

"I wish you'd let me show you what's in it." Soix looked longingly at Philippe's crotch.

"Stop it. You're a Chardonnay, I'm a Pinot Noir. We both know where our interests lie, okay?"

Soix tsked. "Such a shame. Such a *waste*." He paused and sniffed. "Although…my extra sharp fairy senses tell me that perhaps you *haven't* been wasting your talents recently…"

Philippe, to his surprise, blushed.

"Aha."

Philippe disappeared into the shower and yelled back over the sound of the water. "You don't have extra sharp fairy senses."

"Do too."

"Do not."

"Do too, you bastard. Wasn't it me who figured out which little tootsie was trying that pheromone spell on you?"

Philippe spat shampoo out of his mouth. "Wouldn't have worked anyway."

"She didn't know that."

The mist from the wing-shower heads caressed Philippe as he fluttered beneath them. It was relaxing, and he grinned as his friend brought back a few good memories. It distracted him, at least, from his more immediate problems.

Finally he emerged, naked, and strolled to his closet, dragging out a pair of dark silk pants and slipping them on.

"Tease." Soix sighed.

Philippe grinned. "Enough already. We are not fucking, sucking or doing any kind of Chardonnay weirdness. *Comprends*?"

"You don't know what you're missing, *mon cher*." Soix shrugged, then settled himself on Philippe's bed, tucking his wings behind him and his knees up under him. "So. If you won't let me have any fun, at least you can tell me the latest. Who is she?"

"Who?" Philippe shook his wings dry and toweled his hair.

"You know who I mean, you *beast*." Soix shook his finger at Philippe. "This new one. The one they slapped in the dungeon. The one you went to visit. The one who, shortly thereafter, screamed loud enough to rattle the grapes in Hungary. If there are any left."

"*Dieu*. Gossip really does get around these old walls very quickly, doesn't it?"

"Well, darling, of course it does. Especially when it's the Monseigneur who's making some little stranger scream out in ecstasy." Soix paused. "It was ecstasy, wasn't it? You weren't…um…getting all Gewürztraminer on her ass, were you?"

"*Soix*." Philippe looked outraged. "I'm not into that stuff. You know that."

"Okay. So it was ecstasy. Good. Tell me *all* about it. And her." He leaned forward eagerly.

Philippe sank down in a chair and stared at his friend. Where to start? At the beginning would probably be best. "She's an American. From New York. Don't know how she ended up in my vineyard…and her name's Ripple."

"Ripple, huh?" Soix frowned. "What the hell kind of vintage is that?"

"I don't know. Never heard of it. But then again, who knows what these Americans are up to these days? There are all kinds of rumors about some Nappy Valley trying to do wines too."

"No. *Really*?"

Philippe shrugged. "Doubt they'll have much luck. After all, the best wines are *French*. Everybody knows that…"

Soix snickered. "Everybody except the Italians, Hungarians, Germans, a couple of Swiss and maybe a Croatian or two…"

"You know what I mean."

Soix creased his smooth brow in thought. "American, huh? Seems I did hear of some very strong upper level winds recently. The jet stream's been really active. The bats put out a high-wind alert not too long ago…" He snapped his fingers. "I'll just bet she got caught up in it somehow."

"That's pretty much what I said, too." Philippe paused. "I think. She agreed. I think. Sometimes what she says is hard to follow."

"But the rest of her isn't, I take it?"

There was silence for a moment or two as Philippe considered his answer. "No. The rest of her is…unique." He jumped up from his chair and strode to the window. "She's not like any fairy I've ever seen. No long flowing locks, just a tumbled mess of brownish spikes. No sense of style whatsoever, a sort of ring-thing in her navel, and she shaves her pussy hair."

"*No!*" Soix gasped.

"Yes." Philippe's cock stirred once more. Damnation, Ripple had really gotten under his skin. "She's abrasive, confrontational, spits out what she thinks without a moment's notice, hasn't a delicate bone in her body, swears like a drunken wasp…"

"And fucks like a dream?" Soix finished the sentence as Philippe's words trailed off.

"Yes. Yes indeed."

"And you're smitten." Soix nodded sagely.

Philippe whirled on his friend. "I can't afford to be *smitten*, Soix. Not now. Not with the Choosing so close. If I'm smitten, as you so politely put it, I'm seriously fucked." He frowned. "And not in a good way."

"Hmm."

Philippe ignored the interruption and started to pace. "If I let myself get any more…*smitten*…with Ripple, I won't be able to pick a Chardonnay for the Noble Mold flight. You know that. And you also know damn well what'll happen next."

Soix pursed his mouth. "Urgh. I see your point."

"I thought you would. If I can't get it up for the Chardonnay who is chosen for me, there'll be no flight.. No flight means no champagne this year and profits will drop like a rock for everyone, not to mention the reputation of our vineyards. We'll lose face, the Gewürztraminers will lord it over us like the gods they think they are, boasting that their champagne grapes will outshine ours this year, the Cabernets will start pushing for one of their own Sauvignons to replace me as Monseigneur, and there'll be more in-fighting than either of us wants to even imagine."

"Fucking politics." Soix stood and stretched. "Where is this little troublemaker right now?"

"With my mother." Philippe's voice was gloomy.

"Oh *merde*."

"You can say that again."

* * * * *

"So that, in essence, is *that*." Ripple licked honey from her fingers as she sat across a small table from Shiraz. "Now you know it all. Or as much as I do, anyway. I got fucked in New York, fucked by the weather, and now fucked by your son." She glanced over at the older woman. "Um…sorry. That was a bit blunt."

Shiraz waved the objection away. "No problem. Better to be honest, here, I think, given the current situation."

195

Ripple glanced around the suite of elegant rooms. Real swanky—sort of like the Ritz meets Hollywood and gives birth to luxury. She wasn't complaining, however, especially since Shiraz had ushered her into a really nice state-of-the-art bathroom, let her clean up and even loaned her a wing dryer.

A decent set of clothes had been forthcoming, and although it was more in the style of the traditional fairy than Ripple was used to, she decided that swanning around in floaty things wasn't all that bad. For right now anyway. She still wanted those jeans back, though. She hadn't sucked off Sid the spider for nothing.

"That was good. Thanks." The remains of a small meal lay between them, accompanied by the usual wine, which Ripple regarded with a wary eye. "You folks sure like your wine, don't you?"

Shiraz sighed. "Ripple, here our life *is* the wine. It's our reason for existence."

"Um, yeah. I sorta picked that up. The Chardonnay gals…odd names…even odder sex life…" She grinned and tried a small sip of the golden liquid. "Hey…this isn't bad, ya know?"

"Don't overwhelm me with your praise," smiled Shiraz.

"So…if you don't mind my asking…what the fuck is going on here?"

"Going on?"

"Yeah, honey, *going on*. Like why does a stranger get slapped into a dungeon before she can say 'Hi, how's it hanging?' and what's this 'Choosing' thing that's got everybody's wings in a cramp?"

Shiraz drank her own wine and sighed. "It's both simple and complex, Ripple. And to answer part of your question, all strangers are sequestered and interrogated upon arrival here in the vineyard these days."

"Ah. Well if they all get Philippe's preferential treatment, I'm guessing there's probably a line a mile long outside…" Ripple giggled.

Shiraz smiled back. "No, they don't. You got a special dispensation."

"Ah. That's French for a good ass-fucking, is it?"

Shiraz laughed. "I like you. It's clear you're not a saboteur or spy. You're refreshingly honest, see things differently, and make me laugh." She stood, flexing her wings. "I don't mind telling you, Ripple, it would be nice to talk about some stuff with you…get your perspective. For some reason, I think you can be trusted."

Ripple straightened her shoulders. "I like you too. Thanks. And yeah. My word as a New Yorker. I can be trusted." She held out her hand.

Shiraz blinked and took it. "Thank you."

The two women shook hands and then looked a bit self-conscious.

"Why do I feel like we oughta head out for a beer and the nearest ball game on TV?" Ripple covered her emotions with an attempt at humor. "Of course, you guys don't have *real* football, only that pretend soccer stuff, and with my luck I'd end up watching some three-hundred mile bicycle race. I'm guessing NASCAR hasn't made it big over here yet."

"Mass car?"

Ripple shook her head and said a mental farewell to some of her more erotic Jeff Gordon fantasies, sparing a second to mourn the one that always took place on the hood of his Chevy. "Never mind. Tell me stuff."

"You have heard about the Noble Flight, yes?" Shiraz glanced at Ripple, who nodded. "Well, for some time, there have been…factions…who question the right of the Pinot Noirs to make this flight. They insist that other vintages should be allowed to participate." Shiraz snorted.

"Uh…sounds democratic to me. What's the problem?"

"The problem, dear Ripple, is that on the rare occasion when another vintage has made the flight, the Noble Mold sucked."

"Oh."

"Yes. Oh." Shiraz shrugged. "There're no two ways about it. The best Noble Mold, and thus the best champagne grapes, comes from…er…the come of a Pinot Noir and a Chardonnay. That's just the way it is."

"And the Monseigneur? How's he chosen?"

Shiraz smiled. "Believe it or not, the grapes choose him."

"Uh, Shiraz? You sure you ain't been tippling your own vintages there, babe?" Ripple stared at her.

"Sounds crazy doesn't it?"

Crazy? Lady, you have no idea. "Kinda, yeah. So what happens? The grapes all stand up—although they're round so how can you tell?—and yell 'we want *him* to come all over us', or something?"

"Not quite." Shiraz chuckled. "Although I sort of like that visual." She shook her head. "No…what happens is that at the right time of year, all the eligible males walk the pathways in the vineyards at midnight. One male will make the flowers open when he passes."

"Oooh. Sounds…*lyrical*." Ripple dragged the word out of some rusty schoolbook buried in her memory, behind the limericks, the words to a Nine Inch Nails song and the choicest graffiti she'd read recently.

"It is."

"Okay." Ripple ticked the points off on her fingers. "We've got ourselves a male sperm donor, he's gonna choose a Chardonnay, they're gonna jerk off in front of an enthusiastic audience, and the world's supply of champagne is undiminished. New Year's Eve can go on as planned. What's the problem?"

"The problem is that this year, the political situation is…is extremely fragile. We have reason to believe that some Merlots are egging on the Cabernets, stirring up trouble, which they love to do. Whispering into certain ears that the Pinot Noirs are not up to the job anymore." Shiraz looked worried. "It's no secret that the Pinot Noirs are a small vintage. We don't breed well."

Ripple considered this. "That explains the spy thing, I suppose."

"Absolutely. Any little thing the Merlots could use against us, they would. The Cabernets have a new leader who is a helluva lot more likely to fuck us over than blend vintages. And if he starts a power struggle, the Gewürztraminers would march in and overrun the lot of us."

"And bye-bye champagne." Ripple frowned.

"Exactly." Shiraz tossed her long hair back over her shoulder. "It's happened before. The humans put it down to weather conditions, but *we* know those years when there were no usable champagne grapes were basically those years when politics won out over the Noble Mold flight." She shuddered. "It was awful."

"So this Choosing thing is real important?"

"Yes. It begins today. The Chardonnay women who volunteer to take this flight will be presented to the Pinot Noir vintage in a Vault ceremony. Each will be accepted. Then within a few days, when the moon is high, the Choosing will happen."

Ripple bit her lip. "And that's when Philippe gets to do his thing?"

"Sort of. He has to get a hard-on from one of the Chardonnays. That's how the Choosing occurs."

"Jesus. Good thing this doesn't happen in Manhattan. A girl could get chosen a dozen times a night." Ripple chuckled. "If she's lucky."

Shiraz smiled weakly back. "Well, I suppose. But this choosing isn't about the body. It's based solely on the wing buds. That's all the Monseigneur will see."

"Whoa." Ripple blinked. "You mean the poor guy's gotta get himself a boner from some girl's *back*?"

Shiraz raised an eyebrow. "Ripple, did Philippe touch your back when you two were…um…fucking the daylights out of each other?"

Ripple froze. Then shivered as she remembered that instant when her world had shifted three parsecs to the right.

"I see he did." Shiraz snickered in her turn. "The wing buds are the key, Ripple. Something about them—and we don't know what—produces the male response necessary to create the Noble Mold semen."

"Ah."

"The candidates are screened by a special arrangement of shrubbery. No clue as to their identity is permitted. The Monseigneur will examine each wing bud, and when he comes to the right one…"

"He will come."

"Well, hopefully not at that moment, but yes. Essentially, his cock will recognize the right wing bud, signal its approval, and the whole process begins."

"He pops his cork here and corks pop in Times Square at midnight."

"What?"

"Never mind. It's all very…*magical*, Shiraz. Like real fairies."

"*Chère*, we *are* real fairies."

Ripple snorted. "Live in New York for a bit. The only magic there is in the miracle of markdowns at Saks Fifth Avenue. Although there's a baker on Seventh who has a way with bagels…"

She stopped herself. "Well, honey, it seems like you guys have the same old political shit driving you nuts that the rest of the world does. I'm sorry to hear it. Wish I could help."

Ripple stood and stretched. "Thanks for the food, babe. It was great, and your son's a pip. But with all due respect, it's time I was thinking about getting the fuck out of here and heading back to the good old U. S. of A."

"Uh, Ripple?"

"Mmm?"

"You can't leave."

Chapter Five

Philippe stood silently on the dais as the throng before him muttered, fidgeted, coughed and then finally settled down.

A blast on a very loud set of trumpets heralded the beginning of the Vault Ceremony, and he sat down on his special chair, trying not to let his wings droop with boredom.

His mother was off to one side, and he'd looked in vain for a glimpse of Ripple. He knew he shouldn't, but damn it, his head kept harking back to the memory of his body buried in hers. He was thinking with the wrong head again.

A procession of green aphids wandered slowly onto the slab flooring, preparing to offer their recital to the guests. It was traditional, although why the ladybugs hadn't eaten the lot of 'em, Philippe never could figure out.

A flash of white caught his eye. It was Ripple. She was standing in back of the Chardonnay vintage, next to…oh *bon Dieu*—next to Soix. Philippe couldn't begin to guess what he'd be telling her.

Things were going from bad to *merde*.

Their gazes clashed for brief seconds, and Philippe *knew*. His mother had told her that she was now stuck here. The recipient of his seed, an honored "guest", she was stuck here. No one who'd been fucked by the Monseigneur could leave. Not until after the Noble Mold flight, anyway.

Her eyes were a blend of anger, confusion, fear and…something else. Something he sincerely hoped was at least half the lust he was fighting right at this moment. He sighed and turned his unseeing gaze back to the green mass struggling to stay in formation.

He really would have to see her after the ceremony. Talk to her. Try to apologize, perhaps, if he could. *Oh sure, you hypocrite. Apologize for the best sex you've ever had, and then do it again. If she's willing.*

A round of applause jerked him from his thoughts, and he watched the blushing little aphids scurry away. Wings rustled, throats were cleared, and another trumpet blast announced the procession of Chardonnay candidates.

Here we go.

* * * * *

"You do have a delightful ass, you know."

Ripple rolled her eyes. The pinkly frou-frou Chardonnay standing next to her was running appreciative eyes over her backside. He'd introduced himself as soon as she'd peeked into the Vault chamber, and taken her under his wing, metaphorically speaking. It was a sure bet he wasn't gonna be taking her in the literal sense of the word.

Soixante-Neuf Chardonnay. Figures a Chardonnay would be named after a sexual position. And this one was about as swing-wing a fairy as she'd ever met. He was also charming, funny, and Ripple liked him from the get-go. *So I'm a fag hag fairy now, too.*

"I know, Soix. And it ain't gonna do you any good, is it?" She hissed back her response as about a gazillion aphids attempted to do some kind of formation routine. This was not a good idea when more than two feet were involved, and aphids had God knew how many.

Soix sighed gustily. "Just wondering what Philippe saw. Why he's all ass over wingtips about you. And if you want to share any juicy details, you can trust me not to blab." He looked hopeful.

Ripple couldn't stop her grin. Damn, this dude was cuter'n a button. "Got the hots there yourself, Soix?"

Another sigh stirred Soix's shining mass of silky hair. "Always, *cherie*. From the moment Philippe and I met, I pined." He clasped one hand dramatically to his breast. "I yearned. I dreamed of the moment when he'd surrender to the inevitable."

Ripple snorted. "Yeah right."

Soix looked injured. "I did my best. My passion was boundless, but alas—unreciprocated."

"No kidding."

"Hey. I'm a pretty good lay, you know." Soix wrinkled his nose.

"Don't get huffy. I'm sure you are. But Philippe's gotta be about the straightest wing guy I've ever met. Testosterone oozes out of him like juice from a peach. He sooo ain't gonna ride down your road, babe."

"Tell me about it." Soix shrugged. "We've managed to stay friends, though, over the last couple hundred years or so." He looked at Ripple's ass again. "So naturally I'm curious about you. Why he was in such a hurry to visit you in your cell and…and do whatever he did to make you scream." He fanned himself. "Oh my God. I'm having a hot flash just thinking about it."

"So don't think about it. Have fantasies later, okay? I need the four-one-one here."

"*Pardon*?"

"Information, dude. Tell me what the fuck's going on with this 'Miss Make-a-Boner Chardonnay' contest." Her gaze roamed the dais. "And tell me who's who, too."

"You do bird impressions?" Soix raised a perfectly plucked eyebrow.

Ripple frowned at him.

"Sorry. Thought you were doing the mating call of the spotted owl."

She frowned at him some more. "Don't make me use the finger on you."

Soix shuddered theatrically, holding up his hands. "No, no…not…the *finger*."

His performance got him some angry looks and a few "ssshhs". He sighed. "I'm so underappreciated." He rolled his eyes. "What do you want to know?"

Ripple nodded at the dais. "Who're the dudes up there with Philippe?"

Soix squinted at the crowd. "Well, let me see. The ones in the nicely tailored dark green, no decoration, maybe leather or perhaps velvet—so hard to tell from this distance—"

"*Soix*… I swear to God…"

He chuckled. "They're the Cabernet Sauvignon representatives. Humorless lot. Good fashion sense, but not much else." He pursed his lips. "The fellow in unrelieved black leather, and trust me that's a very cheap leather too, is a Gewürztraminer. Nasty bunch if half of what I hear is to be believed. Arrogant and a bit heavy on the fetish side of things."

Ripple stared at the group. Political undercurrents must be wafting around that crowd like a fart at a Mexican restaurant, and stinking just as bad.

"I don't see any Merlots, but you can bet that delectable ass of yours they're here somewhere. Stirring up trouble, starting rumors, doing whatever they can to fuck things up." Soix's lips curled.

"Why?"

"Because they fucking *can*, that's why." He caught himself up. "Sorry. It just pisses me off that some people have nothing better to do than screw up the world we're trying to peacefully fuck around in, you know?"

"I hear you." Ripple nodded. "It's the same all over, honey."

"It sucks."

"Yep."

"Speaking of sucking…" Soix raised an eyebrow.

"No." A blast of sound made Ripple jump. "Oh goody. Here come the brides."

Soix giggled next to her. "At least the aphids are done. I'd hate to think of them getting squished by the parade. So messy, all those green guts everywhere…"

"Shh."

This time it was Ripple who shushed him. She wanted to watch the Chardonnay fairies as they made their slow progress into the room.

Holy fucking vitamin-enriched conditioner, Batman!

Ripple blinked as a dozen or so Chardonnay women fluttered gently above the stone floor and into a line before the dais. She hadn't seen this much silky blonde hair since the Gwyneth Paltrow look-alike contest over on Lexington Avenue.

Then, the prize had been *all-you-can-drink-'til-you-pass-out*. This time the prize was much greater.

Philippe.

"What happens now?" She dug Soix in the ribs with her elbow making him squawk.

"Ouch. Watch the body, *cherie*. Bruise this and you'll make a lot of guys unhappy."

Ripple ignored him, eyes glued to the blonde blur hovering in front of Philippe. "What's next?"

"Nothing, really. They'll just do a little dip thing—see?" He nodded at the lineup. "She just did it. It signifies that she has freely volunteered for this, and is willing to make the Noble Flight with Philippe if she's picked."

Ripple ground her teeth.

She didn't need the visual image of Philippe getting off with any of these…these…*blondes*. They were fragile, delicate, would have given a greeting card company an orgasm on the spot, and made her feel like a hippo stuck in a butterfly enclosure.

"Ah." It was all she could do to force the word between her clenched jaws.

It went on, each of the Chardonnays making her bow…curtsey…whatever…in front of Philippe and the other dignitaries.

And not a one of 'em looked worth more than a dime.

Not to Ripple, anyway. A day at her spa, a few hours with her hairdresser, and she could look like that too.

Sort of.

She let a healthy dose of anger fill her and squash the nasty little pang of jealousy that threatened to squeeze her heart clean out of her chest.

"I've seen enough," she grunted out the words.

"Me too. All this blonde is giving me a headache." Soix grinned. "And there's a different kind of blond waiting for me elsewhere."

Since the line had pretty much finished flashing its tresses at Philippe, others were starting to take their leave, and Soix maneuvered them both into the crowd. "I'm going to take you to that nice suite Shiraz gave you, and leave you there, *cherie*, is that okay with you?"

"Sure, honey. Whatever." Ripple's spirits dragged along behind her, so deep in the mud they probably left ruts.

"Chin up, Ripple. They may be blonde, but you're…"

"What?" She looked at him. "Brunette? Sort of brown with touches of frosting? Overly endowed with hips and wearing a belly button ring?" She turned her eyes away. "Don't sweat it, Soix. I know what I am, who I am, and the only thing I don't know is how to get the hell out of here."

Soix paused at an impressive set of doors. "And you're really nuts about the big guy too, aren't you?"

"Me?" Ripple snorted. "Nah. Fuck 'em and leave 'em, I say. This girl belongs in New York, not in some green vineyard."

Soix dropped a light kiss on her hair. "Nice try."

His whisper echoed after him as he half-danced, half-fluttered off, leaving a delightful floral fragrance behind him.

And one rather confused New York fairy.

* * * * *

"*Yooooou make me feel…*"

Philippe paused outside the doors to Ripple's suite and tilted his head, listening.

"*Yooooooou make me feeeeel…*"

Merde. What the hell was she doing? Casting some strange American spell? Chanting an ancient ritualistic rite of sunset?

"*Like a something-or-other…*"

Slowly, without knocking, Philippe eased open the door and peeked inside.

"*dum-dum-dee-doo…*"

Ripple was…hell, he didn't know what she was doing, but it sure was fun to watch. Standing on a low table, she was turned away from him, eyes closed, wings thrown back behind her, and a hairbrush clasped firmly in her hand.

"*I used to feeeeel…whatever…dum de dum dum…*"

Her hips were swaying, feet wide apart, and she was apparently singing, although not anything Philippe could remember hearing.

"*Oh shit—*"

She'd opened her eyes and seen him watching. Pity. He'd like to have watched the rest of the performance.

"Don't you people believe in knocking?" Ripple's eyebrows snapped together. "I could've been naked in here, ya know."

"Yes. I know."

She blushed bright pink, strangely at odds with her aggressive stance. "Well, whatever." She glanced at the hairbrush, as if surprised to find it in her hand. Then swallowed and stared at Philippe. "I was singing, okay? I get nervous, I sing. You don't like it, tough shit."

She clambered down off the table and tossed the hairbrush back onto the bureau.

"I didn't say I didn't like it." *Nor did I say that all the bats within three kilometers are probably shuddering in pain right now. I'm not that stupid.*

She fluttered her wings behind her, and turned to face Philippe, hands on hips. "So whaddya want, Boss-boy? Haven't you done enough to this chick already? I'm stuck here now because I got an ass full from you. I have no idea how to get home. I can't find my jeans, have to wear this...tent thing..." She fluffed her skirts with a sneer. "And I'm pretty much screwed."

"Really?"

"Well, what the fuck would you call it?" She stuck out her chin.

Philippe repressed the urge to nibble on it. "Perhaps you could look at it as being our guest for a little while?"

"Guest?" She snorted. "Oh sure. Here for the wedding, right? The entertainment to be provided by aphids and blondes who probably share a brain cell. The grand finale will be watching a super display of fireworks against the night sky, only this time it won't be *Stars and Stripes Forever* in the background, but some kind of porn show."

Ripple turned away from Philippe, annoying him. He wanted to see her face, read her expressions. There was something under this anger of hers. Something he wanted to explore.

He gripped her shoulders and spun her around. "You know what has to be done. You're a bright woman. Why are you so pissed off?"

She refused to meet his eyes. "Fuck if I know."

"Ripple?" He slid a hand to that stubborn chin and raised it. "Could it have anything to do with the fact that I'm the one who has to make that flight?"

Sahara Kelly

She shut her eyes. "Nope. And it's pretty fucking arrogant of you to make that assumption."

"Ripple?" He stroked her cheek. "I'm an arrogant asshole. Arrogant enough to believe that you're lying to me." He closed the distance between them, bringing his chest up against her breasts. Her nipples hardened immediately.

She opened her eyes and stared at him, heat flickering behind her gaze. "Go away."

He pulled her closer. "As in *go and never darken my door again* sort of go away?"

Her gaze dropped to his lips. "Yes."

Philippe slid an arm around her, letting his hand rest low on her spine just above the swell of her buttocks. "You never want to see me again."

"That's right." Her wings shivered delightfully, their delicate fronds just brushing his arm.

"And you'd never even *think* about fucking me again."

"Absolutely not." The voice was low and husky.

"Not even when you know how hot it can be between us?" Philippe nudged his hard cock into the space between her thighs. She immediately spread her legs, welcoming him.

"*Nooo…*" It was a groan of pleasure.

"Not even when you're wondering how it would feel to have me buried deep in your sweet cunt, Ripple? After I've loved every little bit of you…" Philippe rubbed his chest against the silk over her nipples, smiling slightly at her gasp. "Every *inch* of you with my tongue." His hand dropped lower behind her, cupping her ass and squeezing gently. "And I would lick every single inch, Ripple. I'm very thorough in my attention to detail."

"Absolutely not. No way in hell." Ripple's arms slid around his neck. "It so ain't gonna happen, Philippe."

"Too late. It already has."

And he kissed her.

210

Chapter Six

For a first kiss, it wasn't bad at all, thought Ripple as her wings melted. His lips were firm and sweet and his tongue forced his way into her mouth with demanding ease.

So what if she'd welcomed it? *So sue me.*

He was right about the tongue thing, though. Like a creature with a mind of its own, it flickered around the cavern of her mouth, learning it, memorizing it, and returning again and again to duel with her own tongue.

He pressed their bodies even closer as Ripple tried to peel her face away from his, and breathe.

Philippe did things with his fingers behind her and her fairy gown floated to the floor. "So you don't want me to touch you?" It was a growl that made her shiver.

"Absolutely not." She struggled to keep her New York state of mind.

Philippe dropped his own pants—God, those drawstrings were handy little buggers—and his cock thumped into her belly. "And I shouldn't do *this*, for example?"

He dragged himself down her body, letting his hands wander where they would, tweaking her nipples, kneading her flesh and finally settling between her legs which obligingly parted for him.

"No, you certainly shouldn't do that." *Go New York. Hoo-rah. That's telling him.*

"Or this? Right here?"

Ripple gasped as his mouth fastened on her pussy and began its magic all over again. She reached out blindly and found a convenient pair of shoulders to hang on to. "No, definitely not. Uh-uh. Especially not *there*!" She shifted to the left ever so slightly.

He tongued her, grasping her buttocks hard. Oh *fuck*. The man's mouth was driving her completely nuts. He seemed to have an instinctual feel for exactly the right spots to suck, the ones to nibble on and the ones to lick.

"So you're never going to let me do this?"

Ripple's wings tensed and fluttered as his tongue thrust into her cunt and his nose buried itself in her clit. She lifted off the floor as he sought out her juices hungrily, feeding on her with all the enthusiasm of a starving hummingbird in a bush full of hibiscus.

Her bush was full of Philippe. Or would be if she hadn't waxed it off. Her thigh crept involuntarily up his body to rest comfortably on his shoulder, and his hair grazed her inner skin. She moaned a little. "Oh no. I'd never let you do that. Ever."

Her scruples were staring at her from beneath lowered brows. *Take a hike, guys. I'm involved in an intense battle of wills here.*

"Mmm." Philippe hummed.

And Ripple decided that some battles were worth losing. She hung out the mental white flag, surrendered, and prepared to be invaded, occupied, overrun and fucked out of her skull.

Both her thighs were now resting on Philippe's shoulders as her wings flitted madly and lifted her to the right position for his mouth. Her hands twined in his hair and then dropped it, as she sighed and writhed in his grasp.

She ached. She was on fire. This was something new to Ripple, this furious burn that swept over her. Her breasts heated and she slid her palms up her torso to grasp them, finding too little relief in the touch of her own hands.

Philippe groaned into her cunt and she risked a glance down between her legs.

He was *watching* her. Dark eyes hot and alive with desire, he was watching her. It was such a frickin' turn-on. Here she was, fluttering her twat into the mouth of a hotshot French honcho, letting him give her the best oral she'd ever had in her life, and he was watching her with a hunger of his own.

Well, whaddya know?

She rolled her nipples between her fingers, choking on her own cry of pleasure as her touch shot down to her clit and mingled with the sparks from Philippe's tongue. And teeth. He ground his face into her like he could devour her whole.

Fuck it, dude — go ahead. Eat me.

But apparently her cunt was only an hors d'oeuvre. Philippe dragged his face away from her and eased her thighs down. *Shit. You need chips or something? You sure as hell got Ripple-dip all over your face.*

Panting, Ripple stared as he stood up. Panting even more, she felt his hands squeeze her butt hard and lift her. As their eyes locked in a gaze that was almost astonished, Ripple's breath left her altogether.

Philippe slid his cock between her parted thighs and lowered her down…down, impaling her, filling her, and finally holding her tight against his crotch.

Holy fucking…*fuck*.

She blinked. "*Jesus. Philippe.*"

He smiled, albeit rather tightly. "Yes. Jesus. *Ripple.*"

She figured he was saying her name, not giving her a command, but what the fuck. Experimentally, Ripple tightened her inner muscles around his cock. He filled her perfectly, touching all the right places, rubbing her where she needed to be rubbed and holding her where she needed to feel the heat of his hands.

It was — well, it was Fourth of July, New Year's Eve and Christmas, all rolled into one fabulous package. That was now well and truly buried in her cunt.

And then he moved.

Ripple forgot about New York, her jeans, tequila and anything and everything that usually occupied her mind.

She couldn't remember her own name. She didn't even care to try. The only thing that mattered now was moving with him, sliding up and down his cock, wrapping her legs around him to get him closer, nearer, *deeper* inside her.

They had to be a mile off the ground, because her wings were fluttering madly, helped along by one strong hand that had crept up from her buttocks to her wing bud.

Oh holy Tinkerbell! This was a whole new magic kingdom, one Ripple hadn't ever imagined visiting.

Their thrusts increased in intensity, Philippe's lips curling back from his teeth in a beautiful snarl of passion. Ripple shocked herself with that thought. *Where the hell did that come from?*

Then she realized her own teeth were bared as she damn near fought him for her orgasm. It would be a battle to see who came first.

It was a matter for some debate whether it actually mattered.

Debates could wait. Ripple hung on for dear life and let go.

* * * * *

Philippe was lost.

Lost in the scent of her, the feel of her, the slight sound of her wings as they fluttered wildly about behind her. Even the delicate shiver of her wing bud was an arousal all by itself.

Fucking this woman—this New York fairy— was, in a word, extraordinary.

Deep in her cunt he felt the ripples inside her squeezing his cock as she lived up to her name. *Mon Dieu*. He wanted to scream, cry out, fill her, leave her and fill her all over again.

His buttocks were cramping with the force of his thrusts, his wings ached as they achieved an amazing rigidity, and he knew he couldn't hold back. Couldn't, this time, play the emotionally detached lover, intent only on distributing pleasure.

Been there, done that, come on schedule, and left flowers.

Not this time. Not with Ripple. She was sucking his soul dry with her cunt, her enthusiasm matching his and driving him onwards to some mystical place he'd never been before. She was making him wild, pushing him over the edge into someplace new.

He was sweating, for God's sake. Fairies seldom sweat. But he was, droplets trickling down his face and spine. The vineyard had disappeared; the political situation was less than nothing in his mind. All he had was Ripple.

And she was more than enough.

Reaching the limits of his endurance, Philippe threw his head back on a shout. "Now, Ripple…*mon Dieu*…come *now*!"

For a moment, Philippe could've sworn he blacked out. Then light exploded behind his eyeballs as he orgasmed, deeper inside a woman than he'd have believed possible. Her scream echoed around his brain as his fingers dug into her, holding her closer than a second skin.

Their bodies meshed, writhed, shuddered in a mutual climax of earth-shattering proportions. Philippe's balls blew up like hand grenades, emptying their cargo in a massive spurt from his heaving cock directly into the shuddering cunt of the woman falling apart against him.

Her thighs were locked around him in a rib-cracking embrace, her nipples hard enough to carve scars into his chest, and her head was thrown back, neck cords taut, as she reached for the stars alongside him.

Somehow, Philippe kept his eyes open as his orgasm eased, and he watched Ripple fly away into the cosmos on a rocket fueled by her own climax.

God, she was beautiful. Unique. Unafraid to let the feelings out, go where her body took her, relish this wondrous moment they shared. She lost herself in the spasms they had created together, and he held her tight as she shivered herself back down to earth again.

They were drenched in sweat, juices and his come. Sticky, sated, and aching now, not from desire, but from the release that had come with it.

Philippe dragged the two of them over to Ripple's bed, and heedless of wings, wetness or the antique quilt they were about to ruin, tumbled them both on top of it.

They lay, panting. Philippe gulped down air and pulled a bit of hair from his mouth. Ripple's breasts were heaving as she struggled for breath, nipples softened now, rosy peaks on creamy mountains.

Her hair stuck out in damp tendrils, her wings still shivered with aftershocks as she settled them more comfortably around her, and a wave of tenderness washed over Philippe, leaving him as shaken as his orgasm had done, only moments ago.

She blearily opened one eye and found him staring at her. She cleared her throat. "Okay. We definitely shouldn't do that. I *certainly* don't want you to do that." The other eye opened. "Not for another ten minutes, at *least.*"

Philippe gave up the struggle against his emotions. It was the wrong time, the wrong place, the wrong woman...the vineyards would be plunged into chaos if not all-out war, and his name would be mud.

He didn't give a flying shit. Ripple was *his.*

He grinned.

Chapter Seven

Ripple finally drifted towards sleep with the memory of Philippe's smile branded into her brain cells.

They'd showered together, loved some more, and when she'd mentioned to him that she'd dated a sword-swallower and proceeded to demonstrate some of the finer techniques she'd learned by deep-throating his cock, Philippe had damn near passed out beneath her.

It was good to reduce a guy to a quivering lump of jelly. Leave it to New York sophistication to teach these stuffy Europeans a thing or two.

A twinge in her thighs reminded her that she might not have been the only one doing the teaching. She sighed and cuddled into Philippe's embrace. *Hoookay.* So there was something to be said for all this wine stuff, and a *lot* to be said for the fairies who made it happen.

Especially when they made it happen to her. She'd discovered she did, in fact, have a g-spot, and probably an h- and i-spot as well. He'd hit all of 'em and made her bells ring louder than St. Patrick's on Easter Sunday. If she'd known sex could be like *this*...

Her song rumbled around her brain. *Oh yeah, Aretha baby...you got it right. He sure does make me feel like a natural woman...* Her wings twitched. *And a well-fucked one, too.*

Sighing, she snuggled into the pillow. All things considered, this was a helluva nice vacation.

It got less nice when the covers were disturbed some time later. Darkness permeated the room and Ripple sensed Philippe peeling his body away from hers. "I must go, *chère*." Light kisses brushed her cheek. "Sleep now. I'll be back later."

"Mnrunmpf." Ripple wasn't at her best when awoken from a post-multiple-orgasmic sex coma. She grabbed the bedclothes and tugged them up, sinking back into blissfully exhausted oblivion.

Only to be interrupted as the covers were dragged off her once more.

"Quit it, Philippe…" She grumbled and tried to reach for the sheet, only to encounter something extraordinarily furry. *What the fuck…?*

Somebody muttered a phrase that sounded remarkably like "foreign trash", and then darkness descended. Well, even more darkness, since it was dark to begin with. Whatever *this* darkness was, it wasn't normal. It was smothering, smelled shitty, and as Ripple struggled, panic set in.

She was being suffocated. There was a weight over her mouth and nose, and whatever or whoever it was apparently had no intention of removing it.

She dragged in a breath. Big mistake. Her head swam, her thoughts faded…*oh fuck*…

* * * * *

"*Aaargh.*"

Ripple screamed her way back to consciousness as what felt like a bucket of cold water was thrown in her face. She opened her eyes and blinked, shaking her head dry. Standing next to her was a bee, holding an empty bucket.

Okay. So her senses still worked. She *had* been doused with a bucket of cold water. She glared at the bee. "Hey, asshole. Ever hear of 'wake up'? Works just as well and doesn't mess the hair."

The bee curled its lip at her and stalked off.

Ripple tried to move and follow it, but found herself immobile. *Hmmm.* This was so not right.

Refusing to panic, she raised her head slightly. *Holy fucking Dom whatever.* She'd died and gone to fetish heaven.

Ripple blinked as she stared around the large cavern she found herself in. Dim lights flickered on stained walls, bare flagstones floored the place, and along the ancient brickwork, chains had been nailed into spots high above the ground.

Ripple swallowed as she realized there were still a couple of fairies…um…hanging around. Faces to the stone, they were spread-eagled, manacled by wrist and ankle, bare assed, and…and…

Oooh, shit. That was *soooo* gonna leave a mark.

A large, leather-clad fairy with tattoos all over one shoulder was brandishing a whip, raising red lines on the buttocks of one of the prisoners. Or whatever. The fairy turned, and Ripple's jaw dropped as she realized this was a woman. Solid breasts were bare, nipples large and pointed, swinging free in time with her lashings.

And the chained fairy was moaning, groaning and yelling, "More…more."

More? What the fuck was with these freaks?

She struggled to stand, then remembered she couldn't. Nervously she glanced down at herself. Naked as a jaybird, she was tethered to some sort of wooden device. A fetish party she'd gone to in the Bronx flashed through her mind. *Holy fucking St. Andrew's cross.*

She was tied to an X-shaped contraption that some idiot had named after a Saint. And she was secured damn tightly too.

"Don't bother to struggle. You won't escape, and damaged skin will piss him off."

Ripple turned her head to see the bucket-brigade bee smirking next to her. They stared at each other. Pieces clicked into place. "Gerda, right? The one with the thing for the Alsace bees?"

Ripple knew she'd got it in one when the bee drew herself up proudly. "I serve my Master with pride and humility."

Ripple noticed the leather collar that now adorned the place where a bee's neck usually was. On anyone else it would've been a helluva belt. There were studs on it and carefully crafted letters. "Do Bee a Slut". *Cute.*

More noises drifted through the room, and Ripple tried to focus on the bizarre scene unfolding around her.

On the side of the chamber across from the hanging ass-whippees, there were a number of other fairies in assorted positions in assorted contraptions. They all looked uncomfortable, but all resulted in the same thing — the presentation of buttocks to whoever cared to walk past.

And plenty of fairies were walking past. Tools and implements were neatly arranged by each bottom, apparently for the delectation of the would-be smacker. This was...like *soooo* not Ripple's scene. But for a few minutes she watched, unwillingly fascinated by the enthusiasm everyone seemed to be showing for what amounted to a damn good spanking.

Her thoughts harkened back to a painting she'd seen once during a nighttime excursion into some museum or other. Sure, she'd been a bit buzzed, but she'd never forgotten this dude or the weird things he'd slapped onto his canvas.

Hieronymus Bosch. Cool name. She'd promised herself that if she ever got a pet caterpillar of her own, she'd call it Hieronymus. She would pass on the "Bosch" part.

Looking around her now, Ripple figured old Hieronymus must've hit the wine a bit freely, and seen this stuff in his dreams or something. Nightmares, maybe. Whatever.

A slap and a cry distracted her. Jesus...*holy fucking earwigs*! Some poor fairy dude was straddled over a bench, cock and nuts hanging loose, with a bunch of earwigs clipped to 'em. Shit! *That's soooo gotta hurt..* And another dude was whacking into him with a handful of leather things, thongs...whatever they were, they were making his cheeks blush. And not out of modesty, either.

Ripple shook her head. This did not bode well for an *out-of-her-milieu* New York babe. She'd been places, done stuff, but this? Uh-uh.

"Like what you see?" Gerda sneered at her.

"If you're into assholes. Which I see you are." *Sneer at me, will ya? Freaking bee-sub slut.*

Gerda merely smiled. "You will understand." She raised a set of arms and jangled something in front of Ripple's nose.

"Jeez, back off, bitch. I'm not shortsighted, ya know. Although it sure looks like the rest of you weirdoes are."

Gerda obligingly stepped back and ran a length of chain through her hands. All four of 'em. "This is for you, poor slut."

"Hey, I'm nobody's slut, thank you very much."

"You are now." Gerda revealed excruciatingly poor dental care as she curled her lips in yet another sneer.

"Oh yeah? I sooo don't think so. Better bees than you have tried and failed, asshole."

Gerda seemed immune to insults. *Stupid buzzer probably likes them.*

Ripple gulped down her emotions as Gerda reached into her knee-sac and produced a handful of small things.

They moved on her hand. Oh fuck. *Earwigs.*

Now having been an NYC babe for most of her life, Ripple was accustomed to dealing with assorted bugs. Both the insect kind and the fairy kind. She respected life, sucked off spiders for well-fitting clothes, and pretty much ignored the roaches who were forever boasting that they'd inherit the Earth someday.

Seeing as it was gonna take total nuclear devastation to bring that to pass, they were welcome to whatever was left, in Ripple's opinion.

But…and it was a big *but*…she really wasn't too sure about having those earwigs as close as Gerda was bringing them.

Especially when she noticed that they had little D-rings affixed to their carapaces.

With her nasty yellow sneer firmly in place, Gerda proceeded to latch an earwig onto each of Ripple's wing tips. One up top and one at the bottom. It didn't hurt—much—but was damned uncomfortable, all the same. Fairies didn't think much about their wings until something bothered them. Like having earwigs clamped on 'em.

She bit back a mutter of distaste, but Gerda caught it. "Oh it gets better, slut."

I give up. Can't argue with an idiot. "You ever hear of Hieronymus Bosch?"

"Who?"

"It figures." Ripple tensed as Gerda produced the chain and threaded it carefully through the earwig rings. Two larger earwigs appeared and were attached to the chains in their turn.

When Gerda neared Ripple, standing between her outspread thighs, it was panic time.

This was *soooo fucking not happening*. With a pinch and a pull, Gerda clipped an earwig to each of Ripple's nipples.

"Aaargh." The squawk was pulled from her throat as the earwigs clamped around her tender flesh. Her wings trembled. It quickly became apparent that such a move was a really bad idea.

The chains from the top and bottom of each wing led directly to her nipples. Every little flutter sent exquisitely painful little shocks through her breasts and down her body. It was appalling, arousing, and embarrassing, and made even worse by the fact that Gerda was peering interestedly at her pussy.

"Never seen one like yours before."

Ripple clenched her teeth. "Take a good look, then, fuzzbutt. If I ever get loose you ain't gonna be seeing much of anything for a while."

"Tsk tsk. Temper, temper." Gerda grinned, not dazzling anybody with those god-awful teeth. "The Master will see to your…schooling." She darted a last look at Ripple's pussy and then turned and stalked away.

Bees look fucking stupid in black leather stiletto boots.

* * * * *

Philippe Pinot Noir was furious, frustrated and flying around his Chateau like a moth with an inner ear infection.

His balance was off, he bumped into other fairies, growling at them like it was their fault and generally making a major ass of himself. Which his mother took great pleasure in pointing out to him at length.

"You, my son, are making a major ass of yourself."

He snarled at her. "You said that before. At length."

"And I shall say it again until you get the point. All this fussing and fuming is getting us nowhere." Shiraz sighed. "I'm worried too, but we've done everything we can. Now we must wait."

Philippe stalked the length of his mother's suite and back again. "Wait? *Wait*? Just how do you expect me to wait, Mother? Ripple is abducted from her bed, for God's sake, in *my* house." He paused behind a chair and drummed his fingers on the upholstery. "She disappears into thin air from this very chateau, in spite of the guards, the security systems—in spite of all the precautions we are currently taking against spies and heaven knows what all."

He glanced at Shiraz. "Doesn't say much for my leadership or organizational skills, does it?"

"No. But it says a lot about your feelings for Ripple."

"Don't go there."

Shiraz sighed again. "I'm cursed. There's a big black cloud hanging over my head. Your father, may he rest in peace, was an asshole occasionally and he passed those genes on to his son. It's a miracle champagne ever gets made these days."

She straightened her shoulders. "Look, Philippe. I like Ripple, make no mistake about it. And nothing would make me happier than to see you happy. But if you're so hung up on Miss Statue of Liberty that you can't get it up for a Chardonnay, we're talking political ramifications that could shake the grapes off the vines and render the whole damn question rhetorical."

"I know." Philippe's voice was gloomy. His mother was painfully accurate. Fairies were sexually indiscriminate most of the time, but when the right one came along, things changed. Their bodies changed, their lives shifted, and—if they were very lucky—babies happened.

Young ones were a precious gift, given only to those couples who had mated…for life. And mating for life meant just that. Becoming wingmates. No thundering erections for anyone else. Philippe had a growing feeling gnawing at his brain. Ripple might just prove to the only one for him. *His* wingmate.

He needed time to find out, and time was the one thing he didn't have.

A discreet knock at the door made both Shiraz and Philippe jump a little.

"Enter." Shiraz shifted in her chair.

A wasp entered the room. But not just any wasp. This one was very tall, well muscled, and his fur was trimmed to within millimeters of his body. His uniform was a pristine and creaseless dress white, and he held a small hat correctly in the crook of his arm.

"Lieutenant Etienne 'Le Coq' Lépine, W 101st Airborne, reporting, Sir. Ma'am." He nodded respectfully at Shiraz.

Who gaped, and then turned to Philippe. "You called in the HORNETS?"

"Of course I did."

She looked back at the HORNET. "Le Coq?"

He met her gaze unblinkingly. "It's a nickname, Ma'am. We all have 'em."

"Ah." Shiraz's gaze wandered low over his uniform.

Philippe surveyed the wasp. The HORNETS were renowned for their efficiency, skill and daring. Their elite organization specialized in HerOic Resolutions to Nasty Elements along with lots of Terrific Sex—hence the acronym. They were a stealthy group, preferring to work anonymously if at all possible, doing what needed to be done quietly and effectively.

"You understand our predicament, Lieutenant?"

"Information is coming through as we speak, Sir. Our ComHQ is assembling a team. If you could give me your current report, we'll be formulating a strategy and giving the team a green light to go wings-up ASAP."

"Our guest from New York is gone. The bee named Gerda is also missing. We're assuming the Gewürztraminers are behind this abduction." Philippe kept it short and factual.

The HORNET nodded. "Fits with our intel, Sir. We've had the bee Gerda under surveillance for some time. Her developing tendencies to shop for leather and hang around known Gewürztraminer locations tipped us off." He pulled a small notepad from one pocket, transferred his hat to another arm, and thumbed through the pages.

"On the fourth of this month, an order was placed from the Fetish Wear section of www.fairyland.net for a flogger, two sets of leather cuffs and…ahem…a clit clip." He looked up at Philippe. "As you may know, bees are generally allergic to leather and don't have clits, so this order set off a few red lights in our monitoring system."

He returned to his notes. "On the eighteenth, subject Gerda purchased a substance from *The Wicked Witch of the West Spells and Substances Store*. Substance was known to be something that will induce unconsciousness." He thumbed some more.

"Our Crime Scene Forensics Unit has worked the abduction site. HORNET CSFU reports no signs of blood or bodily fluids." The Lieutenant glanced awkwardly at Philippe and cleared his throat. "Other than those expected in such a location."

Philippe blushed as Shiraz smothered a laugh, turning it into a cough.

"Traces of bee hair were, however, retrieved. We therefore deduce…" continued the Lieutenant, "…that your Miss Ripple Smith was indeed abducted by said Gerda, who rendered her unconscious and then removed her from the room by means as yet to be determined."

"Okay." Philippe ran his hand through his hair. "So you guys know who, and how. What next?"

"Well, sir." The Lieutenant snapped his notebook shut. It disappeared smoothly back into his uniform, impressing Philippe. *Damn, these guys are good.*

"As I said before, we're working on an extraction strategy now. It is most likely that the subject has been taken to Gerhard Gewürztraminer's home." He paused and pulled one antenna closer to his ear, listening to something. "Roger that."

He looked at Philippe. "It's confirmed. Our intelligence sources report that several Gewürztraminers were seen carrying a large bundle into Gerhard's house early this morning."

Philippe whooshed out a breath. "*Fuck* it. They've got her." He grabbed for his shirt. "Let's go."

The Lieutenant stopped him. "Sir. Please. This is a job for a highly trained team of specialists. Let us do what we do best."

Philippe shook off his hand. "Look, Lieutenant, I know where she is. God knows what they're doing to her. I want her back."

"I understand that, sir. Believe me I do. But my team is trained in hostage extraction from hostile territories. We go in, do the job right, and get out. Fast. And without political ramifications if at all possible."

The Lieutenant was standing tall, tall as Philippe himself. It didn't take a wizard to figure out why so many fairies had a serious case of lust for these guys. The rumor about wasp wiener-dicks sure didn't apply to HORNETS. They were about as alpha as a flying insect with a stinger could get.

He sighed. "I shall insist upon regular updates, Lieutenant."

"You'll get 'em, Sir. Team W14 is suiting up as we speak. They'll do a HALO drop into the Gewürztraminer compound."

"HALO?" Shiraz raised her eyebrows.

"High Altitude Low Opening, Ma'am. They jump from bats above the radar level and fly down using minimal wing power under cover of the clouds. You'd never know they were there."

"Let's hope the Gewürztraminers don't." Philippe knew he was being sarcastic, but the worry was driving him…as Ripple would say…*frickin' nuts*.

"They won't. Recon is already reporting in, Cencom is compiling data, and the Special Ops team is preparing." He tapped his antenna. "We're hotwired in to the data banks, and we'll be five-by-five shortly. The SIBS is on alert. It's a routine HEO, Sir. It'll be A-OK."

"SIBS?"

"Sub-Ionosphere Bat Squadron, Sir."

"HEO?"

"Hostage Extraction Operation, Sir."

"You guys ever run out of letters?" Shiraz stared at the Lieutenant.

"No, Ma'am."

Chapter Eight

Unaware that back at the Chateau Pinot Noir, crack military teams of HORNETS were brushing up their alphabet, painting themselves in camouflage and preparing to "extract" her, Ripple remained securely manacled to her St. Andrew's cross.

The earwigs had decided to sing for a bit, which was mildly comforting, since their music was not displeasing to fairy ears. Unfortunately, the two bass members of the chorus were the ones attached to her nipples, and every time they went into four-part harmony, she felt it all the way to her clit.

Getting aroused while stark naked, draped in chains and displayed for the delectation of a bunch of freaky Gewürztraminers was really not her thing. Of course, if Philippe had appeared in front of her right at that moment...well, that would've been something else again.

She bit her lip and tried not to think of him. *Yeah right. Like don't breathe while you're at it.* He was probably wondering where she'd gone, but with those Chardonnay dollies flipping their blonde hair at him, she doubted he'd worry much about a gal from NYC. Too much Clairol would make any sane guy lose his marbles.

Tears stung the back of her eyes and she blinked them away angrily. Ripple Smith had never cried over a guy yet. She wasn't about to start now. Maybe later. But not now.

Especially not since a loud blast of music had made everyone jump. It was a short fanfare that would've sent any movie studio into fits of orgiastic promotional delight.

Gerda returned to Ripple's side. "He's coming...he's coming." She bounced up and down.

"That's nice. *Who?*"

Gerda stared at her. "Who? You don't know who?"

Ripple clenched her teeth. "Here's a clue, dimwit. I ask 'who'—it means I don't know *who*, since if I *knew* who, I wouldn't be asking, would I?"

Gerda blinked.

Frickin' bees. This one had fuzz in her ears too.

Fortunately, Ripple didn't have to wait for Gerda's mental processes to catch up, since the rattle of metal and the stomping of feet heralded the arrival of whoever it was that needed a *Fanfare for the Common Fairy* to enter a room.

"*The Master.*" There was a soft thud as Gerda dropped to her knees and lowered her head, her antenna quivering with excitement.

Ripple rolled her eyes. The only time she'd ever consider getting on her knees for a guy was when they were both naked, and even then she'd better be damn sure he was gonna return the favor. *Like Philippe had done so enthusiastically…*

Bad mind.

The entrance of what looked like a small parade distracted Ripple. Up front were two wasps wearing some kind of leather g-strings. Since wasp asses didn't resemble fairy asses, they seemed rather uncomfortable, and their stately progress was interrupted now and again by a slight wiggle of their abdomens as they tried to pry wedgies out of odd places.

Following them was…*jeez.* Some engineer at Harley Davidson's wet dream.

Four fairies, wings dyed black, fluttered in formation. Their long tresses, also dyed black, lay across white skin and emphasized the nipple chains that joined their breasts in glittering swathes. Tiny black leather thongs covered their crotches and below that, long shiny black boots hugged their legs.

The Rockettes do Goth wear. Wouldn't go over too big at Radio City Music Hall for the Christmas show, that's for damn sure.

They were all wearing collars, some with spikes, others with studs, and Ripple blinked as she realized a leash led from each collar to the man behind them.

This was obviously the Master.

"Lower your eyes before Master Gerhard." The order was hissed from between the lips of the kneeling Gerda.

"Fuck that." Ignoring the command, Ripple took a long look at the head of the Gewürztraminer vintage.

And bit back a giggle.

Gerhard Gewürztraminer might be the big Boss-dude, but when it came to the looks department, he'd obviously been shopping in the reduced-for-clearance section.

He was a head shorter than the fairies he had on leashes, to start with. And the image of height wasn't helped along by the paunch that showed a tendency to protrude between his leather vest and the top of his tight leather pants. His wings were…well, the word "mud" came to mind.

A blend of green and grey dappled with an odd mustard yellow blurred their surface, and even the addition of studs and a chain or two didn't do a damn thing for them.

This was the Master? Physically unimpressive, he had a walk that would have qualified him for instant groping on Forty-Second Street. Ripple wondered if he had a giant earwig clamping his butt cheeks together. It was a combination of mince and strut and she had to bite her lips hard not to laugh out loud.

Memo to self. Never order anything with Gewürztraminer on the label.

All activity in the Cavern had ceased with his entrance, and it was oddly silent as the procession clanked its way through the crowd, chains jangling and leather slapping. Along with the odd wasp-butt twitch and rustle.

Finally, they reached Ripple. The fairies separated into two pairs, one on either side and just behind Master Gerhard.

Boldly, Ripple raised her chin and stared at the fairy in front of her. "Yo, dude. Whazzup?"

* * * * *

In her palatial suite, Shiraz Pinot Noir paced back and forth, brow furrowed and wings tense. There was the tickle of a plan budding in the recesses of her mind and she needed time to think it through.

She'd dismissed Philippe—finally—by telling him to go do something before she ripped his wings off and fed them to him. Piecemeal. She'd never seen her son in such a twitter before, and she was privately thrilled to bits.

Unfortunately, she was also seriously worried.

She'd known the minute she'd seen the two of them together, lying in a sweaty panting heap on the floor of the cell, that they were wingmates. Destined by whatever quirky critter ruled the Fates of Fairies to be together for eternity.

Or until some idiot smashed one of 'em to bits while joyriding a stolen dragonfly. She closed her eyes and fought away the memories of her husband's passing. Too young, too soon, and now only a memory that brought bittersweet pain and pleasure to her lonely nights.

She knew Philippe's state of mind. Knew his state of body, too. She'd been there, experienced it, and fortunately, married because of it. Since then…there'd been lovers, of course, but just as an afterthought. No one had driven her insane with lust.

Like poor Philippe was, right now.

Few in the Chateau remembered Shiraz as anything other than Paul Pinot Noir's wingmate. Probably even fewer remembered the scandal and whisperings as she'd strolled in with the Chardonnays for that particular Choosing. She was different, from another region, another vintage, and her flowing purple hair had not endeared her to the Chardonnays.

There had been much discussion about whether she should be allowed to participate. Back then, politics had been simpler, the rules less rigid. Paul had simply said "Why not?" and she was in.

Paul had looked at her wing buds. And before she knew it, he was in *her*, too. They'd made a Noble Mold flight that had redeemed her in the eyes of the Pinot Noirs, the grapes had been phenomenal that year, and all was held to be as it should be.

Now, she was accepted, honored and treated as a Pinot Noir. She seemed to be the only one these days who recalled she wasn't. She knew what a good idea it was to introduce some new genes into the wine vat.

And, Shiraz admitted, she wanted Ripple as a daughter-in-law. It was time to let a little fresh air into the hallowed halls of the Chateau. To move ahead into a new century, get the lead out of the asses of too many old-time fairies who clung to their notions of tradition with a grip that threatened to strangle the vineyards.

To stop the fucking politics, end the games between vintages, and get going on what they did best. Ensure great grapes.

A commotion outside her window drew Shiraz to the embrasure and she looked out to see Philippe marching around, barking orders right and left to a group of HORNETS. They were studiously ignoring him.

Shiraz watched her son anxiously moving from one group to another until finally one HORNET, probably *Le Coq* —and wouldn't it be interesting to see if he lived up to *his* nickname— drew Philippe aside and engaged him in serious conversation.

She heaved a sigh of relief as Philippe nodded and stepped away from the troops, just in time to watch four bats silently land nearby. The light was fading, and her acute hearing caught soft clicks as communications between bat and HORNET team were established.

With a gentle whoosh, the HORNET team was airborne. A sound echoed around the now-still courtyard.

"Hoo-rah."

Shiraz sighed. If anyone could rescue Ripple, she supposed these were the fellows to do it. She certainly couldn't. She'd have her work cut out for her restraining Philippe from following them and turning the entire Gewürztraminer compound upside down in his search for his woman.

She could, however, put *her* end of the plan into effect.

Straightening her shoulders, she crossed the room and opened the door. It was time to call in a few old favors and use some new technology to do it.

There was a spring in her step and a light in her eyes. For the first time in too long, Shiraz had a mission. A purpose to her life other than masterminding cleaning the Chateau and listening to the incessant whining of other fairies about their love lives or lack thereof.

Time to stand up and be counted. Or as Ripple would probably say…*get with the program, girlfriend.*

Shiraz grinned. This was going to be fun.

* * * * *

Ripple found herself the recipient of a rather unpleasant gaze.

Gerhard Gewürztraminer might have believed his eyes to be deep green pools of magic and mystery, but to Ripple they looked more like mud puddles with a scattering of grass clippings. They sure weren't doing a damn thing for *her.*

"You speak strangely." Shit. He lisped a bit too. Not much, but it was there.

"You look strangely." *Take that, asshole. Your serve.*

"I am going to punish you then fuck you."

Whoa. Get straight to the point, why doncha? "Do I get dinner first? A kiss? Chocolates? At least a frickin' introduction? And here I thought Gewürztraminers were described as a 'politely mannered wine'. Somebody fucked up someplace, I guess."

Her retort sent gasps and shudders around the room. The four Goth fairies cringed, and Gerda damn near licked the floor as she bowed even lower.

Gerhard, however, decided to be amused. He curled his lip in a sarcastic grin.

Yep. Lousy teeth. That explained the lisp thing.

"I shall enjoy the chore ahead of me." His eyes flickered down to her shaven pussy. "Very much." He clicked his fingers. "The red one."

Huh?

With a scurry of activity his Goth minions rushed around and finally produced a small flogger with red tails.

Ripple sighed. She had a pretty high pain threshold—hell, she'd had her belly pierced for chrissake—but this was sooo not a turn-on for her. Anger began to roil in her gut. This was too frickin' stupid for words. She'd done nothing but end up in the wrong place and here she was about to be tortured at the hands of an ugly asshole.

Life surely did shit on one sometimes.

"Ah. So the high and mighty leader of the Gewürztraminers gets off on bondage and domination, huh? Well, they do say it's to cover up...er...other inadequacies. Is that true, your Domship? Gotta *leeedle* problem in the size department there, fella?"

Gerhard's eyes squinted at her and he moved closer, taking the flogger in one hand and running the other down her thigh. "You are very brave. And very stupid."

He flicked his wrist, catching her right between the legs with the flogger.

"Ouch." The tails had quite accurately caught her right on the clit. Her wings trembled, tugging on her nipples. *Oh fuck.* Along with the tingle of pain came a distinctly sexual rush.

"You see?" Gerhard continued his light flicks with the flogger. "Pain is good."

"Pain is pleasure." Like the echoes of a chorus the rest of the room answered his words. *Holy fucking catechism.*

"Pain is what's gonna happen when I rip your balls off and shove them up your nose, jerkface. And it *will* be a pleasure. For me." A red haze of fury mingled with embarrassed arousal seeped into Ripple's brain. She struggled with the ropes that bound her. Oooh…one was loose.

She focused on that one loose knot, and did her best to ignore the sting between her legs. Not the easiest thing in the world, and Ripple had never been real good at mental multitasking.

She kept her eyes fixed on Gerhard, refusing to let him see she was one teeeensy bit scared. From a clit flogger to a whatever-else flogger might be only a step away. She liked her skin the way it was, thank you.

"So…" She gasped as another lash caught her pussy lips. "Why *are* you gonna fuck me, dweeb? Is that why I'm tied up? Can't fuck anybody who might possibly run a mile and a half barefoot through thistles rather than let you touch them?"

Er, Ripple? Her sanity crept out of its hiding place and tapped her brain on the shoulder. *Pissing off a guy with a smartass insult while he's lashing your pussy might not be the best course of action just at this moment.*

Gerhard paused. "Because I can, of course. And because fucking you will ensure that my seed will be the one mixed into the Noble Mold."

Ripple blinked. "Uh, you got your facts seriously screwed up there, dude. It's a Chardonnay who's gonna be taking that particular flight."

Gerhard snorted and handed the flogger over to one of his minions without even looking at her. "Our resources are effective, slut. We know you have the Pinot Noir by the short hairs. That he will choose you for the flight."

"Hey. Watch it with the slut thing. They may like it—" She nodded at the openmouthed crowd surrounding them. "But it pisses *me* off."

Gerhard ignored her and reached for her pussy. The one that was sort of kinda like aroused and wet right now. *Sheeeeiit*.

"She is ready. I will take her."

"Jesus. I'm not a quick burger at a Mickey D's drive-through, ya know."

Gerhard was apparently deaf to everything but his own voice. Typical arrogant male asshole.

He stepped back and held out his arms. Obedient to his silent command, the four Goth wannabes moved quickly to him and began undressing him. When they finally tugged his leather pants off—not without some difficulty—Ripple bit her lip.

The Cavern was sighing with excitement.

Ripple was about to laugh her frickin' head off. "Gerhard? Sure it ain't Ger*soft*?"

He frowned. "It seems I need some extra stimulation."

Oh fuck. What was he gonna do to her now? Ripple heaved in a breath and prepared herself.

"Where's *mein Schatz*?"

Visions of archaic torture devices ran through Ripple's brain, leaving nasty footprints behind. The rack? The wheel thing? Or that spikey cupboard she'd seen in some horror movie someplace?

Memo to self. Stick with musicals in the future.

"Here, Master." A woman stepped forward and Ripple recognized her. It was the tattooed fairy who had been happily whacking ass over on the far wall. She had muscles on muscles, the skull tattoo on her biceps was grinning, and she looked a helluva lot more dangerous than little Master Minidick.

"Schatz, pet. Your assistance please."

"Of course, Master. It shall be as you desire." Schatz's wings were jet black, without a lick of light reflecting from them.

Ripple burned to tell her about the latest sheening product. Would've really done this cookie some good.

But Schatz was busy sorting through the tools on one of the tables, finally finding what she was looking for.

Oh *double* fuck. A whip, longer than God-knew-what, was now held firmly in Schatz's hand. And she was licking her lips. This was sooooo not good.

Ripple wanted to close her eyes, but couldn't. It was all too…too…Edgar Allen Poe for words. Schatz took up her position to one side of the St. Andrew's cross and raised her arm, testing the thong of the whip and flicking it a few times.

Then she lashed out—catching *Gerhard* perfectly across the buttocks.

"Ahhhh…yessss…" His head jerked back and his cock…jerked.

Ripple heaved a sigh of relief. If anyone was gonna get a whuppin', she couldn't think of a better target.

After a few minutes, the rest of the room was panting and moaning, and the heat level had upped itself a few notches on the thermometer. Not that this medieval hellhole had one, but if it had Ripple would be reaching for the AC control right about now.

Others had returned to their play, apparently inspired by the punishment of their Master and his evident enjoyment of it. His cock was indeed growing. However, the expression "leaps and bounds" didn't really apply. Ripple sniggered. It was more a case of shuffles and hops.

"Stop." Gerhard's face was flushed and he was breathing hard. He glanced down in satisfaction. "You have done well, Schatz pet."

Obviously a scant three centimeters was considered well-hung in this part of the world. Ripple braced herself to be raped by something approaching the size of a healthy cocktail wiener. Gerhard leered at her as he closed the distance between them.

"And now, slut…"

"Anybody ever tell you your breath is really bad?" Ripple turned her head.

This was it. Her body was about to be polluted with sperm from a frickin' Gewürztraminer. *Eeeeuuuuuw.*

"Wait."

A voice thundered through the cavern, and Gerhard jerked backwards, thankfully taking his foul breath with him.

Ripple coughed and turned her head to see a newcomer leaning casually against a column.

Murmurs spread through the crowd. And Ripple could see why.

This sure as shit wasn't a Gewürztraminer. Tall and elegant, his wings were ruby red, shining hotly in the reflected flames of the lights. A loose white shirt barely met across a broad chest, and was untucked from tight ruby pants. Black leather boots stopped just below his knees.

Her gaze traveled upwards to his face. *Ooooh Mama. Zorro to the rescue.*

Dark eyes drilled into her, or at least one dark eye did. The other was covered with a romantically dramatic patch. *Maybe it's Johnny Depp.*

Silky black hair just touched with grey tumbled long around his wide shoulders, and a neatly trimmed goatee and moustache added a dash of masculinity in spite of the lace ruffles that fell down the front of the shirt.

Oh, frickin' D'Artagnan. Just what I need. A fairy musketeer.

Chapter Nine

Gerhard Gewürztraminer's eyes were not improved by their current posture—bugging out of his head. "C-C-Count *Goriziano*!"

Ripple sighed. These frickin' Europeans had more titles than the goddamn New York Public library. Wasn't there a plain old *Mister* amongst this lot anyplace? Mind you, this dude probably was a Count. He sure dressed for the role, anyway.

The one visible eyebrow rose as he stared down at the now-shrinking Gewürztraminer assets. "Gerhard. Lovely to see you again." He paused. "In all your glory."

Ripple sniggered, only to be hurriedly whacked by one of Gerda's fluttering wings. "Sssh. That's Count Adriano Collio Goriziano."

"Of course. I was just about to say that." *More multiple names too*. These guys had issues. No two ways about it. The name thing and the title thing—talk about pissing contests.

"He's from Friuli."

"I thought that was a pastry." Ripple watched the musketeer stroll casually over to Schatz and take the whip from her hand.

"No, no…the Italian vineyards…oh…watch. He's going to show us how to do this right."

Count Goriziano glanced around him, the forcefulness of his gaze enough to send the Gewürztraminers scuttling back about ten feet. "If you will permit me, Gerhard?"

"Of course, of course…to be punished by the hand of such a Master as yourself…well…*ausgezeichnet*!"

Ripple assumed this was an approval not a sneeze. Although with these German accents it was sometimes hard to differentiate between the two. She sighed. Sauerkraut was probably off her menu now, too. And she wouldn't be able to look at a cocktail frankfurter again without seeing Gerhard.

Schatz bowed respectfully, trembling as the Count tested the weight of the whip. *Oh my. Schatz is gonna shitz.*

There was a miniscule flicker in the Count's wrist and a loud snap echoed through the room. Three Gewürztraminers jumped, one gasped and another passed out.

Pussies. Not a backbone amongst the lot of 'em.

He glanced around, one eyebrow raised. Eyes were apologetically lowered by all the submissives. Hell, with this dude just about everybody was a submissive.

There was another crack and Ripple jumped this time. He'd neatly sliced through the ropes binding one of her ankles.

She blinked and stared at him.

For a split second, she almost believed his one visible eye winked at her.

Oho. D'Artagnan had an agenda, it seemed. And he didn't need any backup musketeers to do it, either. She stayed put, continuing to fidget a little, masking the fact that one wrist was almost loose enough to pull free.

Meanwhile the Count set about his business—whipping the crap out of Gerhard and making him live *up* to his name. He laid the lash down across the Gewürztraminer's ass.

Ripple wanted to cheer. Give her five minutes with that whip and Herr Needle-Dicktraminer would truly appreciate the healing qualities of aloe gel. Flog *her* clit, would he? *Hah.*

Gerhard wriggled in pleasure, leaning towards the Count's blows, his eyes drifted shut and he reached out to grab onto one of Schatz's muscular shoulders. "Oooh…"

Sick. Ripple shook her head. There sure were a lot of crazy fairies in the world.

But whatever the Count was doing, it seemed to be working. From its tidy nest of curly hair, Gerhard's cock was now emerging enthusiastically. It wouldn't have gotten him raves from the "Dick of the Month" club, by any means, but it was a helluva lot more respectable than his earlier attempts at pretending to have an erection.

Another lash, another gasp of pleasure, and another quick flick severing the other ankle. Ripple's legs were *free*.

She stared at the Count. His head dipped slightly, motioning towards the darkened corridor leading from the Cavern. She nodded back.

Gotcha, buddy. When the time is right, make like a bat and get out of this hell.

Gerhard was panting now, along with most of his court. Several fairies were overcome by the excitement, busily groping and flogging each other. Two couples were fucking. Another couple was playing in some sort of swing contraption. There was even a three-way going on with two females and one male fairy. And a lot of leather.

Ripple's breasts pinched slightly as the earwigs released their hold. She looked down. One looked back at her and gave her a cheery wave.

Uh yeah. Whatever. Thanks for the nipple clamps, dudes.

The chain tinkled to the ground and Ripple sighed as her wings were released. She supposed there were some things even earwigs didn't want to watch.

Gerhard was moaning, his cock distended to a magnificent three-and-three-quarter centimeters or so. It was purpling rapidly, the vein pulsing along its…length, if that word could be used in conjunction with this little prick.

His fingers dug into Schatz's shoulder, but she didn't seem to care. She was too busy with her hands down her own leather pants to worry about what her Master was doing.

Ripple rolled her eyes. Group jerk-offs had never been her scene, no matter how "zen" people had tried to make 'em. If she wanted to get in touch with her inner sexuality, she could do it by herself with her newest dandelion vibrator, thank you very much. No audience required.

"Count… I'm going to…oh *mein Gott*…" Gerhard's throat worked as he squawked out his imminent release.

The Count doubled his efforts, flicking through the final ropes that secured Ripple in between furious lashings against Gerhard's ass.

"Wait… I need to…" Gerhard was clearly attempting to recall that he was supposed to be raping Ripple, not enjoying his punishment. "*Aaaahhh*…"

The Count gave him no choice. Expertly allowing the very tip of the whip to snick Gerhard's balls, he finished it.

"Oooh…ooohh—" Gerhard panted, whimpered, threw his head back and thrust his hips forward.

Since he was standing directly in front of Ripple, she braced herself. This was gonna be *real* icky.

She could clearly see his little balls throbbing as he began to orgasm. But instead of the jets of fairy come she expected to douse her naked body, there was a sort of plopping sound.

With a straining ooze, a blob of come appeared at the tip of Gerhard's cock. It was less of a volcanic eruption and more of the popping mud bubble type thing. *Fucking failure all the way around. Couldn't even get up a good head of steam.*

Cries and screams from the rest of the partygoers surrounded Ripple. Apparently Gerhard wasn't the only one coming. Schatz was on her knees in front of him, hand frantically scrabbling at her clit, and licking him clean.

Eeeeeuuuuwww.

This was the moment the Count had been waiting for. "*Volare, signorina*!" He whisked himself around the writhing mess of Gewürztraminers and freed her from the tangle of ropes that still held one wrist loosely. "It is time we take our leave, no?"

"Yes." Ripple wrenched herself away from the St. Andrew's cross. "I'm with you, buster."

He grabbed her hand and rushed her towards the exit. "Can you fly?"

Ripple tentatively tried her wings and grimaced. "*Shit.* They've cramped. Fucking Gewürztraminers."

"*Non un problema.* I have transportation waiting."

Now that's what I like to hear. A guy with his wings on straight. Gimme an Italian with a whip any day.

"Okay." Ripple ran behind the Count, her feet pattering on the stone floor. They were in the darkness of the corridor before the first cries of orgasm began to subside, and outside the Gewürztraminer Cavern shortly thereafter.

She nearly ran into the back of him when he paused at the top of a long flight of steps. "Now what, your Countship?"

He flashed her a wicked grin, all white teeth and crinkly eye. *Damn, this is a cute dude.* "Now we take my Porsche."

Oooooh. An Italian with a *Porsche*. This day was getting better all the time.

He frowned and whisked his shirt over his head. "Here. You'd better put this on, or you'll be a major distraction."

She accepted it. "Well, thanks. Nice of you to say so." She glanced at him. "Nice chest too."

He chuckled and emitted a piercing whistle.

"Uh, Count? You got one of those remote-activated Porsches or something?" Ripple tugged the shirt down over her head. It came to her knees and smelled very nice. Manly, in an Italian sort of way. With a dash of garlic.

"*Non, signorina.* Watch." He whistled once more and a huge dragonfly stirred up the dust as it landed delicately at the bottom of the steps. "Meet Portia."

Ripple sighed. *It figures.*

* * * * *

Adriano Collio Goriziano snuggled himself up against the back of this charming little fairy and slid an arm around her. "Let your wings down, *cara mio*. It'll lower air resistance. We'll go faster."

"Uh, 'kay dude. Whatever." She obediently drooped her wings low, letting him cuddle her even closer.

He relaxed his own wings, and gripped Portia's body with his knees. "Hang on."

Ripple hung on, her knuckles white against the black leather pommel at the front of the large saddle. Portia lifted off smoothly, unperturbed by the additional weight on her back.

"Whoooeeee. This is cooool, your Countship."

Adriano grinned. "Call me Adriano, *cara*. I take it you are indeed Ripple from America, with that bald pussy?"

"The one and only." She relaxed a little as the ground fell away beneath them, and they soared into the night sky. "How'd you know about me?"

She had to turn her head a little to speak to him, and the twist of her body brought his hand up beneath a very nicely rounded breast. Adriano's cock stirred. She was certainly no French vineyard fairy—there was a lovely helping of meat on these fragile bones. "Word spreads quickly here, Ripple. News that you'd arrived got to me probably before you'd reached the Pinot Noir Chateau."

"Jeez. You guys got cable news or something?"

"No need. We have moths. Biggest gossips around and there's lots of them."

Ripple turned some more. *Merda*. Another fraction of an inch and he'd have her nipple right where he wanted it. In his palm.

"So the moths told you where I was? Or what? How'd you know I'd been…um…bee-napped?"

He shifted a little on the saddle as Portia headed towards the hills and the rising sun. "Didn't take a genius. The

Gewürztraminers are looking for a way to get into the whole Noble Flight process and have been for years. Unfortunately, Gerhard of the *molto piccolo* prick is also *molto piccolo* in the brains department."

"No kidding. *Molto piccolo* is Italian for itsy-bitsy, right?"

"Right." Adriano laughed. "You are from New York, then?"

"Yep. That's me. Vintage East Elmhurst." She sighed and leaned against him. "Dunno if I'll ever see Lady Liberty again, either."

"Why not?"

Ripple blinked at him. "Look, Adriano. Sweetie. I got here in some kind of freak windstorm. Even I know the winds don't blow backwards."

He grinned and nuzzled her hair. "You are charming, *cara*, you know that?"

She squirmed against him. "Yeah, well you ain't so bad yourself, dude."

"*Grazie, cara mio.* But we must talk about this whole situation. The wines, the Choosing, Philippe…"

She straightened in his arms. "You know Philippe?"

He plastered his body up against hers. *Cazzo.* She was a warm armful. He sighed. "Yes, I know Philippe."

"So you know about this Choosing crap and all those blondes."

Adriano had to think for a minute to sort that out. "Uh…*si*. You are speaking of the Chardonnays and the Noble Flight, yes?"

"Dunno what's so fuckin' *noble* about it. Getting your jollies in front of a crowd while airborne. Should be called the jerk-off strafing run, if you ask me." She grumbled low and her delightful lower lip stuck out in what would easily have been called a pout on somebody else. Adriano found he'd rather like to taste it.

He blinked the thought away.

"So what's with the patch? The pirate look big in Rome this year?" Ripple changed the subject adroitly.

"This?" Adriano peeled off the patch and stuck it in his pocket. "Merely for effect, *cara mio*. The Gewürztraminers love theater."

She stared at him, then a grin spread over her face. "You bastard. You are a smart devil, aren't you?"

Merda. Maybe he would fuck her after all. "And you are quite…unique."

"Yeah. So I've been told. It's the bald pussy thing, isn't it?" She grimaced. "Swear to God if I'd known what a fuss folks would make over such a little bit of bare skin I'd have left it alone."

Adriano bit his lip to hold in the laugh. "We're almost here."

Ripple turned. *Aaaaah*. Yes. There it was. A nicely budding nipple nestled into the warmth of his palm. Sadly, she didn't seem to notice and Adriano almost wished his cock hadn't. Landing on Portia's hard saddle was going to be a *bitch*.

"Where are we?"

"Just a place I know. Quiet. Pretty. You'll like it." He steered Portia a little with the strength of his thighs and willed his erection away a little lest he impale himself when they touched down.

Ripple heaved a big sigh in his arms. "Listen, my Italian friend. Right now I don't think quiet and pretty are gonna do much for me. I'm ready for concrete, neon and loud noises. Along with about ten shots of tequila and a decent pair of jeans."

"Which I would only have to remove, Ripple *cara*. I can't wait to see that bald pussy of yours again."

She blinked as they slid from the saddle. "Oh. Uhh…oh."

For once, it appeared that Miss New York City was speechless.

Chapter Ten

Get a grip, Ripple-baby. Get a fucking grip.

Ripple slid from the back of Portia-the-Porsche into Adriano's waiting arms. He was one delectable piece of Italian bread and it felt like he'd got a real nice chunk of salami tucked away in those tight red pants of his.

But for some reason, although her body tried to respond in its usual enthusiastic fashion, her head just wasn't there. "I think I'm dying."

Adriano stumbled as he carried her up a small path to a clearing. "*What?*"

She grabbed his shoulder. "Watch your step, buddy. You drop me and you're toast. Got that?"

He chuckled. "If you're dying, what does it matter?"

"Hmm. Point to the garlic team."

Adriano reached a secluded grassy patch and delicately set Ripple down on her own two feet. She swayed a little, then steadied.

Automatically, Adriano reached for her, and to her amazement, she found herself backing away. "Uh…Adriano…your Countship…"

He huffed an exasperated breath. "Ripple, *Dio Mio*. You'd try the patience of a saint, I swear. Sit *down*." He glared at her.

Ripple sat.

"Wait here. I'll be right back." He vanished back down the path towards Portia.

"*Bossy*. Like I'll let some slicked up dude tell me what to do just 'cause he's a Count and rescued me from a bunch of pervs."

"Yes, you will."

Damn, he was quiet. And fast. He'd slung Portia's saddlebags over his shoulders, and Ripple's wings fluttered a bit from the downdraft as the dragonfly took off once more.

"Here. Food and drink. You need both." He tossed a pouch at her and she unwrapped it, finding a hunk of bread, some cheese and — surprise, surprise — wine.

"You people ever hear of soda?"

Adriano curled his lip. "Chemicals. Disgusting."

Ripple tore off a piece of bread and bit down on it. "Chemicals. Good. Fizz. Good. Wine…too much of it and you turn into a Gewürztraminer."

He sat down next to her and rescued the bread. "You ever hear of sharing in New York?"

"Sorry. But I was hungry. Those idiots never thought to feed me. I gotta keep my sugar levels up, ya know."

Adriano grinned and reached for the wine. "So if it's sugar you want, there's none better than the natural ones in this…" He waved the carafe in front of her.

"You trying to get me drunk?"

"Possibly. If it'll relax you a bit."

Ripple snorted. "Better men than you have tried and failed, dude." Her conscience kicked her. "Okay. So not many of 'em have played the Cavalry and saved my ass in the nick of time."

Her conscience kicked her again, harder. "And not many of 'em looked like Johnny Depp, George Clooney and Viggo Mortensen all rolled into one with a dash of Sean Connery."

"Uh…this is a good thing?"

Ripple sighed. "It should be a real good thing. I should be doing my famous seduction bit right about now. You know…smiling, teasing, touching…trying to find *some* way to thank you for what you've done." She raised an eyebrow. "Like that whole breast-in-the-palm bit. Don't think I didn't notice."

Adriano grinned. "I wouldn't dream of it." He swigged the wine again and passed it over to her.

Tentatively she took a sip. It wasn't vile and washed the bread down nicely at least. "You see…" She paused and looked up at the stars, fading as the dawn approached. "It's this fairy-and-sex thing. It's what we do, isn't it?"

"Pretty much, *si*."

"So why aren't I getting turned on about the thought of us…er…doing it?"

"Well, perhaps because I haven't done *this* yet…" He leaned towards her and lightly brushed her lips with his, coincidentally running his hand up her thigh beneath the shirt.

He tasted nice, and Ripple let him kiss her, even parting her lips to encourage him a bit. His hand continued its voyage of discovery, eventually reaching that notorious bald pussy.

His fingers felt good, warm against her mound, comforting in an odd way. But that was all.

Confused, she did what came naturally, opened herself to his touch and reached for his crotch. Oh yeah, this dude *really* knew his salami.

"Mmm." Adriano murmured softly against her mouth. "I like bald."

His fingers parted her folds and investigated the terrain, teasingly and just the way she usually responded to with enthusiasm.

Holy fucking dead. Nothing. Nada. Zippo. Not even a dewdrop.

"Uh, Adriano?"

"What…" His voice was hoarse.

"Dude? Adriano? Mr. Italian Guy?"

He sighed and pulled away from her. "Nothing, huh?"

"Nope. See? I told you I was dying." She flopped onto her back and closed her eyes. "This is fucking *awful*. Must be what a guy feels like when he can't get it up." She frowned. "And I owe you so much, too."

"Ripple." Adriano's voice was stern. "I don't want a thank-you fuck."

"Well, that's good, because it looks like you ain't gonna get any fuck at all, thank-you or otherwise. Since I'm halfway to dead here, you might as well just leave me. Let some icky forest critter pick the rotting flesh off my bones when I'm gone." Tears stung the back of her eyes.

Suddenly she was enveloped in warmth as Adriano pulled her into his arms and cuddled her. "Do not fret, little one. You are not dying."

"Yes I am." She sniffed and wiped her nose on the sleeve of his shirt. "If you can't turn me on, then sure as shit I'm dying, 'cause you're the most gorgeous thing I've seen since…since…"

"Since *Philippe*?"

And there it was. The name that Ripple had been doing her best to put out of her mind. The image of him, so splendid, rose in her mind to smile at her.

And she burst into tears.

Strong arms wrapped around her as she sobbed, soaking his chest and probably half his pants as well. But she let it out, let it go…cried for what could have been but never would be.

Cried for the loss of her home, all that was familiar to her, and cried for the future with Philippe that she'd never have.

She had no idea how long she cried, but eventually the tears softened into hiccups and her practicality surfaced. She blew her nose in Adriano's shirt. "Sorry about that. I don't usually cry. I hate women who cry."

She shifted a bit in his embrace. "You sure you're not cold? Want your shirt back, or anything?"

"Uh, no." He carefully picked a sopping bit of fabric off his chest. "You keep it. Thanks anyway."

Regardless of his protests, Ripple absently used a bit of it to dry her tears from his body. "So you don't think I'm dying here? I gotta tell you, I'm doing shit I'd *never* do in New York." She rested against his now-dry skin once more. "Like this. Drinking wine. *Wine*, for God's sake. Lying damn near on top of a hunk and *not* getting any. Not *wanting* to get any. What the fuck's the *matter* with me?"

Adriano ran his hands gently over her wings and settled them both comfortably. "Not a damn thing, Ripple. You've found your wingmate, that's all."

"*What*?" She struggled, but he shushed her, holding her tight.

"Hush, *cara mio*. Listen to me. You and Philippe, you…fucked, yes?"

Ripple sighed. "Oh yeah. Twelve ways to Tuesday, too."

Adriano's chest rose and fell on a quick laugh. "So there it is. Once mated with the right one, there can be no other."

"No other? *Ever*?"

"Never. It's how it works with fairies."

"Shit." Ripple considered Adrian's words. "But…" She struggled with the concept. "In New York…well hell, I never *knew* what that really meant."

"I doubt there's time to learn the old ways in New York, Ripple. You have a busy life, yes? Lots of fun and fucking?"

Ripple thought. Remembered the Trump Tower Tootsies. Always screwing something new—and that weird hair thing! Urgh.

Then there were the Madison Square Garden fairies—bunch of hockey pucks that lot was, too. But always moving on…to something—someone new. She couldn't recall anyone ever mentioning this wingmate business, other than a joke or two over martinis in some bar.

"I suppose." She was forced to agree with Adriano. The fast-and-furious lifestyle she'd led hadn't exactly been the stuff of traditional fairy tales.

"Well, here in the vineyards, our life is different. There's a purpose to our existence. The wines. There probably was a purpose to the New York fairies' existence too, but it got lost over time and…"

"And with the advent of microchips and megabuildings."

"*Si*. Something like that."

"So…what you're saying is that now I've fucked Philippe—that's it? I'm a goner? No more nookie for this chick?"

"*Si.*"

"Adriano! That's terrible." Ripple's mind refused to embrace the concept of exclusivity.

He chuckled. "Is it? Really?"

"Uhhh…"

"Look. Here we are, resting alone in the most beautiful spot in the entire world, as far as I'm concerned. You've already told me I'm a…what did you call me…a hunk?"

Ripple nodded.

"So—a week ago—let's say…what would we have been doing?"

She thought for a moment. "Fucking our brains out?"

"Without question. And it would have been magnificent too, Ripple. Never doubt that."

"I don't. Honestly, Adriano, I don't." She nestled her head beneath his chin. "I'm sorry."

"Don't be. I know what has happened to you, and I'm happy for you. Philippe is a good man."

"How do you know Philippe?" Ripple's curiosity got the better of her reluctance to speak his name. That *asshole*. Part of her was angry at him for being her wingmate—whatever the hell that entailed. How *dare* he screw up her sex life for the rest of eternity?

"He spent some time with me when he was younger. Many years ago. I might add that much of his technique in the fucking department, he owes to my tutelage."

Ripple sighed. "Oh sure. Tell me that now when I can't find out for myself."

Adriano chuckled. "Never mind. Rest, *cara mia*. You've had a hell of a long day. We'll work it out."

Ripple closed her eyes and for once surrendered to the urge to be held. Just enfolded in strong arms, no sex involved. It was—very pleasant…

She drifted off to sleep with a comfortingly familiar whiff of garlic teasing her nose. Mmmm…*pizza*…

* * * * *

Adriano's mind drifted like a will-o'-the-wisp as he held a sleeping Ripple against his body.

He would have fucked her—in her words—twelve ways to Tuesday if she'd been willing. She was bright, funny, independent and attractive in a unique way. All qualities he'd always found appealing on a personal and sexual level.

He envied Philippe. Theirs would be a life full of ups and downs, certainly. But it would be a life filled with passion, and possibly even children. He regretted he had none of his own. But apparently, a wingmate for him wasn't in the cards.

In typical Italian fashion, Adriano dismissed concerns about the Choosing and the Chardonnays. Somehow *something* would work out. It had to. Fairy law was fairy law, vineyard politics notwithstanding.

He took a moment to wonder what it would've been like to find a special woman, one who would have made his hair curl, his cock rise harder than a branch from an old oak tree, and who would have sent him flying out of his brains when she touched him.

With a mental shrug, Count Collio Goriziano closed his own eyes, tucked his body protectively around Ripple and dozed as the first rays of the morning sun touched the forest around their glade.

Perhaps it was the fact that these rays were blocked that awoke him sometime later. Whatever it was, he blinked himself into consciousness, only to find eyes staring at him. Many eyes.

"Ssssso, Count Goriziano. I find you at lassssssst."

Oh *merda*.

Ripple stirred in his embrace and yawned, rolling away from him as she finally achieved consciousness. "Holy fucking crap. Who the hell are *you*?"

Chapter Eleven

Ripple scrambled to get her brains together, aware of the tension in Adriano. And unable to believe the figure standing before them.

Very tall, blocking the sunlight, he—she assumed it was a *he*—glowed red. Transparent wings were held erect, filtering the bright sunshine. Then he moved. There was a clank and a clatter, and a large sword appeared.

Holy fucking Transformer. This was either the largest red ant she'd ever seen or some kind of Battlebot.

"Rissse, Count. We have mattersssss to sssssettle between usssss."

"Hey. Don't I get an introduction here?" She snapped her fingers at the critter. "Yo. Red dude. Who the fuck are *you*?"

The ant turned multifaceted eyes on her and stared.

Ripple stared back. She'd been stared at by a lot more frightening things than some bug in red armor. Let's see how *he* liked it.

"You do not matter. Leave."

"You are an asshole. *You* leave."

"Ripple." Adriano's voice was cautious. "This is Signor Formica Rossa."

"Ssssso. You remember." The voice was a sibilant hiss. Funny thing that. Ripple had thought only snakes hissed, since those two front fangs made the letter "f" pretty much of a dental impossibility for 'em. Who knew ants did too?

"I take it you two have met?" She straightened her shirt. "Wanna clue me in here, guys?"

The ant ignored her. *Well fuck you too, buddy. Ever hear of Raid?*

"We have met. Some time ago in Tuscany." Adriano stood quietly between her and the ant.

"You ignored my queen. It wassss an inssssult."

Ripple sighed. More pissing contests. "Look, boys. Maybe we should talk about this…"

"There is nothing to disssscusssss." A flicker of movement and a couple more arms appeared clasping nasty sharp pointy things. Whatever else he might be, this jerk was packing some serious heat.

"*Signor.*" Adriano's tone was courteous. "I deeply appreciated the honor your queen did me by requesting me. But…mating with her means death. I wasn't ready to die."

"Hell no." Ripple's eyes widened. "She must be a killer fuck, huh?"

Adriano rolled his eyes to the heavens. "Ripple, you're not helping things here."

"Look." She put her hands on her hips and glared at the ant. "There's gotta be a better way to solve this issue than carving up the Count here like an Italian sausage."

The ant looked down his nose at her. Or where his nose would have been if he had one. "You are insssssignificant."

Oh *that* did it. Out came the finger. Ripple strode fearlessly up to the massive critter and poked him, hard.

"Ouch." She winced. His carapace was rock solid, a dull gleaming red, and had less give in it than the Empire State Building. She stepped back, rubbing her hand. "Okay, Adriano. Take him."

"What?"

"Go ahead. Do whatever it is you folks do when you gotta deal with this shit. Twelve paces, no hitting below the…" She glanced at the ant, "The wherever-his-belt-would-be-if-he-had-one place."

Adriano swallowed. "I really hate this, you know."

"Yeah, I know. But Mr. Red Ass here seems bent on revenge. Or bent on bending you, anyway. So go for it, babe."

Her tone was casual, but her eyes were roaming the glade as she spoke. "I'll just stay out of the way over here, okay?" She spotted a real nice hefty branch that would've doubled nicely as a baseball bat. "*Okay*, Adriano?"

He followed her gaze for a split second, then smiled. "Okay, Ripple."

The ant flicked his weapons. "*En garde.*"

Adriano reached for his saddlebag and produced his own rapier with a sigh. "As I said, I really would like to go on record as positively despising violence."

"Ssssso noted." The ant swung one sword to his face in the universal gesture of fencers saluting each other. "Honor will be sssssatissssfied."

Sheesh. Like ants had *honor*. Ripple could've shown him honor. The last time she'd hung around ants they'd damn near killed each other to be the first to hit the sugar cube she'd lugged into the park with her.

It was too freaky for words and Ripple backed away from the duelists cautiously. The red ant was very big, very determined, and armed better than a Bradley Assault Vehicle. With a body that was just as hard. Frickin' thing was probably bulletproof, too.

What the fuck Adriano thought he was gonna do with his pigsticker, Ripple had no clue, but she watched, fascinated, as he saluted back and assumed the classic Errol Flynn pose, one arm bent slightly behind him for balance, the other with rapier extended. Of course, Errol Flynn looked a bit different, since he'd never had to duel with a large pair of wings in back of him.

Ripple shrugged. Errol's loss.

The clash of swords broke the stillness in the glade, and in a lightning flurry of moves, the duel began.

Even though the ant had more arms than any single species had a right to, Adriano was holding his own. Obviously he'd studied under some dueling master or something. Ripple would've been sort of disappointed if he hadn't—after all, one did expect these things in fairy tales. And she sure as shit was living in one right now.

The ant, however, drew first blood with a small nick to Adriano's shoulder. Ripple gasped, but he ignored it, lifting off the ground slightly and executing an aerial maneuver that would've sent an Air Force pilot into orgasmic ecstasy. The resultant swoop neatly severed one of the ant's arms.

"Wooohooo! Yay Adriano! *Scooooooore*!" Forgetting for a minute that this was an actual duel, Ripple let herself get caught up in the moment and did her best cheerleading impression. "Go Italy. Go Italy. Rah Rah Rah!"

Locked in combat, both the ant and the Count ignored her.

Well hell. See if she'd get pompoms for Adriano the next time he dueled something.

The ant was getting pissed. His lips parted in a snarl and his remaining arms blurred in a flurry of attacks. Adriano fell back a bit against the onslaught. *Sheeeit.* Time to do something.

Ripple stealthily moved backwards until she reached the hefty branch. Trying not to draw attention to herself she picked it up and weighed it in her hand. *Niiiiice.* She hadn't followed the Yankees for so many seasons for nothing. It was all about the hitting, in her mind.

She moved closer to the fighters. In a strange maneuver, the ant swung his sword arm behind him and flicked the blade across the point of his ass.

"Jesus, dude. You never hear of toilet paper? You're gonna hurt yourself trying to clean up with *that* thing…" Ripple blinked at the odd move.

"*Merda*." The curse was forced out between clenched teeth as Adriano battled each and every thrust, parried the ant's lunges and generally did his best to defend himself. Another ant arm went flying, and Ripple ducked as it whizzed by her ear.

Being dis-armed didn't seem to faze the damned thing, though. It kept coming at Adriano with renewed fervor. Fuck it. *Memo to self. Pack a couple of Bazookas for next trip to Europe.*

The ant's lips peeled back from his gums. No teeth, which explained the hissing thing. But apparently he didn't need 'em. Adriano was tiring, understandably, and on his feet now most of the time. His wings were shaking from the exertion and probably aching like fire.

It was time for Ripple to add some New York street tactics to the fight.

She moved quietly to one side, gripped the branch in both hands and assumed the stance of a designated hitter at the bottom of the ninth with the bases loaded and one run needed to win the game.

Adriano had seen her, and turned so that the ant's back would be towards her. She was ready. All she needed was the right moment…and…

This was it! *Batter up*!

With every ounce of force she possessed, Ripple swung her makeshift bat and connected with the ant's head. The clanging concussion from the blow rattled her eyeballs.

It did worse to the ant. He staggered and crumpled, hissing out an odd sound that reminded Ripple of a leaky pressure valve in a radiator. With a desperate last thrust he lunged at Adriano, catching him in the thigh with his sword.

Then he fell, a clanking jumble of red armor and a few remaining limbs. He twitched, then lay still.

"Well, fuck it. About time too." Ripple tossed down her branch and brushed her hands together. "That'll leave a mark." She stalked over and prodded the ant with her foot. "I'd kick you, asshole, but I ain't got shoes on and I don't wanna break a toe on crap like you."

The ant was out of it. Good riddance.

"Nice job, Adriano." She turned to the victor, expecting to see him leaning on his sword and grinning at her.

But he wasn't. He was lying awkwardly on the turf, and gasping.

"*Adriano…*" Ripple ran to him. "What the fuck? He get you someplace?"

Adriano winced. "That last thrust…his sword…fucking *venom*…"

"Oh shit. *Shit, shit, shit*…" Ripple saw the blood oozing from high up on Adriano's thigh and ripped his pants away without a second thought. Jesus fucking Christ. A hairsbreadth to the right and that damned ant would've turned Adriano into a *castrati*.

It was a small gash, but it was turning an angry red. "What can I do, honey?" Ripple frantically tried to wipe the blood away. "Tell me."

"Nothing, *cara*. It's venom. He got me… I'm done for." Adriano's voice was weak and his skin was turning pale as she worked over him.

"*Bullshit*." Ripple's brain worked at faster-than-light speeds. "Venom, huh? That's why he wiped his ass with his sword. Fucking dirty fighter." Okay. She could deal with this. She hadn't hung around an EMT station in the Bronx one summer for nothing.

She had no epinephrine, no defibrillator, and not a clue about proper medical procedures. God knew she wasn't sterile. But she had to do *something*. This dude had saved her life, or at least what was left of her virtue. He'd cuddled her, protected her and generally been all-around Mr. Nice Guy. He'd even let her ride his Portia.

No Big Apple gal would let a buddy like that down.

She had to get the venom out. *Hookay*. There was only one way and it was going to seriously suck. In the truest sense of the word.

"Adriano, I'm going to suck out the venom. Hang on, Italy, okay?"

"Ripple…" His voice was a whisper.

Shit. This was real bad stuff. It simply had to go. Ripple gulped and pushed his flaccid cock out of the way. It was gonna be pretty disgusting, but fuck it. Friends were worth it.

She bent to his flesh, put her lips to the wound and began sucking.

And yeah, it was pretty bad.

She pulled back, spat violently, wiped her mouth with her hand and returned to the wound. Eeeeeuuuuwww. *Think tequila*.

Once again she bent to Adriano's groin and sucked for all she was worth.

And *that*, in the way of all the best romantic adventures, was the *perfect* moment for Philippe to find her.

Chapter Twelve

Philippe's world roared to a screaming halt as he swooped down into the small glade. Ripple—*his* Ripple— was sucking off *another guy*. Her head turned as she spat, and then went back to it. *In front of him!*

His heart froze and his breath choked him. A foggy haze obscured his vision and he staggered as he landed, feeling the life drain from his body to be replaced with a savage and overwhelming agony.

He blinked it away and then noticed as Ripple spat, something bloody was flying from her lips.

He frowned. "Ripple…"

She jumped and turned, a smear of blood on her mouth. "*Philippe…*" The joy in her eyes was enough to start his body functioning again. "Help me. He's hurt."

The two HORNETS who'd landed behind him thrust past Philippe. One of them tapped his antenna. "We need medics. Triangulate on these coordinates."

The other gently eased Ripple away from her task. "Ma'am. Step aside please. Let me look."

"It's venom. Poison from some frickin' ant." Tears ran freely down her face as she turned to Philippe, letting the HORNET take over. "He saved me, Philippe. Adriano got me out of the Gewürztraminer's compound, and flew me out on his Portia." Her words tumbled over themselves and she swiped a hand across her mouth. "He brought me here and fed me and I couldn't fuck him because of you and then we fell asleep and when we woke up that ant was here and they fought…and…and…"

"Whoa." Philippe grabbed her and hugged her as hard as he could. "It's okay, Ripple. It'll be all right. Slow down. Take a breath." He stroked her wings soothingly. "Adriano has a Porsche?"

Ripple thumped his chest with her fist. "Don't be a *guy* right now, okay?" She pointed to the side of the glade. "That…thing. I took it out with a base hit, but I don't know if it's still alive. And if it killed Adriano, I swear I'll exterminate the entire fucking species. Environmentalists be damned. It'll be my lifetime mission, okay?" She stabbed his chest with that finger. "You *got* that?"

"I got that." Philippe released her. "Let me go and see. Stay here."

He walked away from Ripple and the HORNETS to a crumpled heap of red armor. Urgh. Fire ants. He really hated fire ants. Didn't run into them too often, but when he did it always led to trouble.

This one was seriously injured. It twitched, back legs jiggling a little. Philippe sighed. Better to be merciful in this instance. He picked up the sword that had fallen by the body and neatly severed the head. The rest of it continued to twitch. Typical ant. Didn't die even after they were killed.

He turned his back on it, returning to Ripple who was again bending over Adriano. *Adriano*, of all people. Thank God he'd been there when needed, but he was a tad too handsome for Philippe to be real comfortable with the thought of him being alone with Ripple.

He pushed it away for now. There were more important matters to be dealt with. Like keeping Adriano alive so he, Philippe, could kill him again if he'd touched Ripple.

Merde. Life was complicated these days.

Suddenly the clearing filled with wings and fairies. Several large bats landed and disgorged the HORNET MedEVAC units, who efficiently prepped Adriano for transport.

"Where to, Sir?" A HORNET stepped smartly up to Philippe. "The nearest medical facility?"

"No. Take him to the Chateau. My mother is a healer, among other things. She'll know what to do." Philippe crossed mental fingers. Adriano didn't look good to him, but if anyone could help, it was Shiraz.

"Oh God, *Philippe…*" Ripple flung herself into his arms once more.

He forced himself to relax as she plastered her body against his. He had her back where she belonged — next to his heart. The pain of seeing her between another man's legs, the panic of knowing she'd been kidnapped — all faded away as her warmth and her scent surrounded him.

He sniffed. "You smell of garlic."

She giggled a little and glanced up at him. "I love you, too." Then she stilled, as if shaken by the words that had tumbled willy-nilly from her mouth.

What else could he do? He kissed her. Hard.

* * * * *

"So how'd you find us?"

Ripple was tucked up on Philippe's lap, sitting comfortably in the upholstered seat attached to the back of a huge butterfly. It sure wasn't built for speed, like Portia, but for comfort it was unsurpassed. "Uh, this thing wouldn't be called Lincoln, would it?"

Philippe looked puzzled "What?"

"Never mind. Tell me what's been happening. How you knew where we were."

His arms tightened around her. "Not much to tell, really. As soon as I found you weren't where I left you, I sounded the alarm. One of the good things about being Monseigneur — and there aren't that many — is that when I yell, people listen."

"Mmm. I'll bet." Ripple grinned against his chest.

"What's that supposed to mean?"

"Nothing. Go on."

"So I called out the guard, put a squad of HORNETS on the case, discovered you were at the Gewürztraminer place, and they went to rescue you."

"Ah." Ripple was silent for a moment. "You didn't want to come get me yourself?"

"I…er… I had to make some command decisions, Ripple. Those guys knew their job. I had to let them do it."

"Oh. Okay. So then what?"

Philippe swallowed, his chest rising and falling beneath Ripple's ear. She smiled quietly to herself. *Suuuuure*. He made some "command decisions" all right. They probably involved him being locked away someplace so he couldn't get in the way.

"We soon found out that you'd managed to rescue yourself, with Adriano's help, of course, and once I heard it was him with you, I knew where he'd go. I hopped the nearest bat and…*voilà*. Here we are."

"Simple, huh?"

"Yes indeed. Clearheaded thought, excellent strategizing and a case of fortuitous circumstances."

"Mmm-hmmm."

"What?" Philippe tried to look at her face.

"Nothing."

"You're thinking something. I can hear those wheels turning in here…" He tapped his chin on the top of her head.

"Well…" She paused. "I saw your face when you landed in that clearing, Philippe. There wasn't one damn *clearheaded* thought going through your brain right at that moment, babe. Can't fool me. You were ready to kill the both of us."

Philippe cleared his throat. "Honestly, Ripple. You're jumping to conclusions. I might have been—momentarily distracted by the sight of you…um…doing what you were doing…"

Ripple snuggled into his heat. "I'm gonna have to say it again, you know."

"What?"

"I love *you*. Sorry, but there it is. You're stuck with it."

Philippe's heart beat steadily against her and there was a long silence.

"Er…Philippe? You're supposed to—like—*say* something here?"

"Like what?"

Ripple sighed. "Like if you have any…feelings or anything for me, this would be a good time to mention it?"

"Feelings?"

Ripple started to get a little tense. "Yeah, dude. Feelings. You know…perhaps an 'I like you, Ripple' might work here. Or 'you ain't bad for a tourist-type fairy' thing."

"You want me to tell you how I feel? Is that what this is about?"

Ripple rolled her eyes. "Fucking A. Daylight dawns."

He peeled their bodies apart. "You want me to *tell* you how I feel about you?"

"That's the general idea. But God forbid I should put you on the spot or anything. It's not like I'm asking for a commitment here." Ripple pulled away from him.

He ground his teeth together so hard, Ripple could hear it. "Damn it, woman. I've just spent the worst twenty-four hours of my life. I've turned my entire vintage upside down, called out more professionals than I knew we had, practically declared war on the Gewürztraminers and nearly died when I thought you were sucking off my old friend." He glared at her. "And you *dare* ask me to *tell* you how I feel? Haven't I fucking *shown* you?"

Ripple chuckled, burrowed back into his body and wiggled her ass on his lap. "Shit, Philippe. You're such a *guy*."

He huffed out an exasperated breath. "If we weren't in such a public place I'd make sure you remembered that fact." His cock hardened beneath her bottom. "I'd have had you screaming out my name long before this. But you had to go get yourself into trouble, into Adriano's shirt and miles away from my bed. Where you damn well belong."

Ripple slithered around on his lap until she was straddling him, breast to chest, nose to nose. "Really?"

He snorted and moved his hips, rubbing her naked pussy with his distended breeches. "Do you doubt it?"

Oh yeah. There it was. The flood of arousal swamping her, turning her insides to mush and her muscles to high voltage power lines. She dropped her hands to his waist and undid the fastenings. "Show me."

"Uh…here?" Philippe blinked.

"Yeah. Right here. Right now." Ripple freed his cock and stroked its length, loving the hard velvety feel of his skin. "The butterfly's gotta look where he's going and anyway he's big enough to class as a stretch-butterfly. He's not gonna peek."

She pulled the shirt hem away from her body and rubbed her pussy against him. "Now, Philippe. I want you now. So fucking much I'm gonna die if you don't want me back."

"That'll never be a problem, *cherie. Ever*…"

Philippe slid his hands beneath the thin fabric and caressed her bare flesh, sending shivers of pleasure through her and making her nipples harder than marbles. He raised his hands and cupped them, teasing them with his thumbs.

"Aaah—*Ripple*…" He brought their heads close and licked her mouth with his tongue.

"Philippe…" She muttered his name against his lips. "Do it, babe. I'm so fucking hot for you I'm about to explode here…"

She wasn't the only one who was hot, either, since Philippe's touch burned as he radiated his own need like a solar flare. Between the two of 'em, they were probably registering as some sort of Unidentified Fucking Object on NASA's radar screens.

Then Philippe's hands slid around and behind her and found her ass. All thoughts of scientific observation flew out of Ripple's head.

"So do it. Explode for me, *cherie*."

He lifted her a little as he nudged the swollen head of his cock between her pussy lips. *Oooh Mama*! When he did that, it was all over but the screaming. And screaming was certainly on the way.

Ripple moved, helping him slide himself deep inside her. At the same time his fingers moved between her buttocks, tracing her cleft and finding her ass, teasing, circling and finally intruding—soooo good.

He filled her, aroused her, and turned her brain inside out at the same time. He held her like that for a long moment. "Ripple. Feel me. I… I don't know where I end and you begin…"

His gaze was dark and intense, piercing into her soul much as his cock pierced her body. "Make love to me, Ripple. Fuck me with your body and love me with your heart…"

"Yessss…" She closed her eyes against the naked emotions she could see roiling in Philippe. They overwhelmed her, touched her in raw places that stung with the newness of it all.

Slowly she began to move, sliding on Philippe's cock with ease, rising until he was nearly separated from her, then sinking back down with a sigh of pleasure. All the while he kept his hands and fingers busy, playing in dark and sensitive places and heightening her tension past its already-pushed limits.

This, she realized, *this* was truly making love. They'd passed fucking and moved into someplace new where so much more than the body was involved.

Maybe having a wingmate wasn't such a bad thing after all. Not when she could do *this*! She held tightly to his shoulders, as they blended, parted then returned to blend again, her pussy tight against his groin. Ripple wanted more of him—*all* of him—

thrusting herself onto his cock in an effort to suck him into places that had never been filled before.

She gasped as her clit grazed him, and he chose that moment to slide one hand away from her ass and up her spine to her wing bud. Mimicking the actions of his cock and his other hand, he slid a finger into the tiny space between her wings.

Ripple did as she'd promised.

She exploded.

And so did Philippe.

Chapter Thirteen

Chaos reigned at the Chateau Pinot Noir when the flotilla of bats landed in the Courtyard bearing the injured party.

Shiraz's heart stopped for a moment at the thought that it might be her son.

But it started up again as soon as she got a look at the patient bundled in soft moss. This wasn't Philippe. She wasn't sure who it was, but he was white as a ghost and his breathing was rapid and shallow.

"Fire ant venom, Ma'am," said one of the HORNETS. "We gave him a small dose of digitalis, sublingually."

"Good." Shiraz nodded, brain whirring. "Bring him along. Put him in my suite. I can rid him of this poison." *I think.*

And so she found herself alone with a strange fairy who was critically injured, and quite likely to die if she didn't do something. *Fast.*

Shiraz mustered her wits about her and stripped her patient, finding the exact location of the wound.

Part of her mind appreciated the body she was uncovering, but her focus at this moment was on the damage done by the venom and how best to counter it. She had to draw it out of his system, and pray that it hadn't gone too far.

He moaned and moved his head a little, beads of sweat breaking out on his pale forehead. God, he was so clammy. There was no time to waste.

Rushing to her medicine chest, Shiraz rummaged for bottles, powders and pastes. It had been quite some time since she'd had to administer healing balms to anyone this badly hurt, and her hands shook as she mixed things together and stirred the resultant concoction into a paste.

There. Aloe of course, along with comfrey, bayberry and some slippery elm. She was guessing at the quantities, but at this point, speed seemed more important than accuracy.

He sighed as she laid the salve over the wound and spread it thickly over the reddened flesh. It was the only color left on his body, with the exception of his hair. Now all she could do was wait.

And watch.

Heaving a sigh, Shiraz pulled a chair next to the bed and let her eyes roam over her patient. He was one good-looking man. She reached out and found his pulse, fluttering beneath her gentle fingers at the base of his wrist.

He groaned again, surprising her as his hand turned to hold hers.

"I'm here. Do not worry. All will be well." She whispered the words as she stroked his hair away from his face. Such a handsome face, too. Strong cheekbones, a firm jaw… Shiraz had always had a weakness for men with beards.

She let her hand wander down past his ears to his neck and gently rub his shoulders. Now that was a nice place for a woman to sink her teeth into.

Good heavens. What brought that on?

His wings lay limply on the bed, a dull red, suffering the ill effects of the poison along with the rest of him. But it didn't take a genius to figure out they'd be a vibrant crimson when he was well.

Shiraz swallowed. He *must* get well. All of a sudden she yearned to see those wings restored to their full glory. To see his eyes open and look at her. To see…her hand trailed down his chest to his navel, and paused. To feel this part of him against her.

Holy heck. She was having lustful thoughts about a complete stranger, and one who was seriously wounded to boot.

This was so unlike her, she attempted to back away from the bed, but his grasp tightened. It seemed he was unwilling to let her go.

Hmmm.

In spite of herself, Shiraz allowed her gaze to check out the rest of his body. The wound was covered with salve, and still angry, but not too far away, his cock rested on its nest of dark pubic hair, flaccid and pale.

On another man, it would have been unattractive, but on him? *Ooooh.* Shiraz licked her lips. Here was a cock worthy of respect. Even in repose it was nicely muscular, ridged in that deliciously masculine way that would bring the most pleasure to a partner. It was pretty impressive in size, too, given that it was currently napping.

What she would give for the chance to wake it up.

Shiraz sighed. *Get him well first. Then see if he's interested in some recuperative fucking. I think it would do us both good.*

A light tap on the door startled her from her sensual reverie, and she could feel her cheeks heating as she turned to see her son enter.

"How is he?" Thankfully, Philippe had eyes only for the man on her bed.

"It will take time. I don't know if I've managed to draw enough of the poison out yet…we must wait."

"Mother…" He turned worried eyes to Shiraz. "Heal him if you can. Please. He's an old friend."

"Nobody told me. Who *is* he, Philippe?"

"Count Adriano Collio Goriziano."

"Aaaah." Shiraz nodded as she recalled the name. "You spent some time with him when you were younger, yes?"

"Yes. A good friend, a good teacher… I'd lost touch with him recently, but apparently *he* was still in touch with just about everything. He got to the Gewürztraminers first and rescued Ripple before the HORNETS had landed."

"Oh—" Shiraz stared at Philippe. "I clean forgot to ask. Ripple. Is she all right?"

He smiled. "Oh yes." Then, surprisingly, he blushed. "She's fine. Just fine."

"Good." At least one matter is settled. She sank back in her chair and nodded at another. "Tell me about it." Her hand remained firmly intertwined with her unconscious patient's.

Philippe rested wearily on the upholstered seat. "The HORNETS landed in Gerhard's place, just as planned. There was some kind of party underway, and I don't even want to *begin* to imagine what that must have been like."

Shiraz winced. "Yes. Never mind. Go on."

"They realized, after storming in, that Ripple was gone and Adriano's name was on everybody's lips." He paused. "The ones who were talking, that is."

"Oh Philippe." Shiraz felt the color recede from her cheeks. "They were *torturing* people?"

Philippe's gaze shifted away. "Not exactly."

"Oh?" Shiraz raised an eyebrow.

"Ahem." Her son cleared his throat. "Look, Mother. You know what the Gewürztraminers are like. What they—er—*do*. Let's just say that those who were being tortured were—um—enjoying it."

"Ah." Shiraz nodded. A thought occurred to her. "How about the HORNETS?"

Philippe grinned. "Only a couple came back with me. It seems that they got rather interested in some of the interrogation *techniques* the Gewürztraminers were using. And the interest was mutual. So…" He stifled a chuckle. "Our friend the Lieutenant…"

"Le Coq?" Shiraz *had* to know.

"Yes indeed. He decided that it would be a politically appropriate move to temporarily suspend hostilities and—um—

learn from each other." Philippe bit his lip. "Last I heard, he was learning something himself from someone named Schatz."

Shiraz felt a bubble of laughter welling inside her. "Oh Lord. I'll just bet he went five-by-five on *that*!"

"That's a big green light." Philippe laughed along with his mother. "Anyway, they did report in first, thank God, and as soon as I heard Adriano's name, I had a good idea where they might be headed. A place I'd been, and not far from the Gewürztraminers."

He glanced at Adriano. "Unfortunately, I was almost too late."

Shiraz stared at her patient. "I will heal him, Philippe."

He stood. "I must go back to Ripple. I hope you're right, Mother. He's a good man. He has his odd moments, but he's a good man."

Shiraz said nothing, more moved by the emotion in her son's voice than his words.

Her hand remained entwined in Adriano's. It seemed right.

* * * * *

Ripple paced the floor of her room, battling any number of tensions, problems, worries and stress. Any more and it would be near time for her to start singing.

She was fresh from the ministrations of Bee17 who'd arrived full of hustle and bustle and what passed as tough love in the bee world. Philippe had been shooed away with enough forcefulness to send him hightailing it out the door, and Ripple herself had been thoroughly scrubbed, lathered, rinsed and repeated.

"Enough, already. I need what little skin you've left me, ya know…"

"Did you throw up, young lady?" Bee17's hands were approximately on her hips as she stared at Ripple.

"No I did not. So *there*." She came close to sticking her tongue out, but grinned instead. "Although I gotta tell you there were a couple of times at the Gewürztraminers that I came damn close."

Bee17 huffed and stepped away from Ripple's glowing body, passing her a soft white gown.

Oh Lord. Where are my jeans? A kingdom for my jeans…

"Put it on and stop worrying about those silly jeans of yours. They look ridiculous with wings, anyway."

"Do not."

"Do too."

Ripple opened her mouth to follow through with this line of thought, but got a very fierce stare from Bee17. She shut up and slid the gown over her head. Goddamned frou-frou stuff. It slithered down over her clean skin and she caught a glimpse of herself in the long mirror.

"Holy cow. Where did those come from?" She stared at herself, a vision in white silk, with a very nice cleavage showing. Cleavage she hadn't exactly had when she'd hit the New York high spots.

Bee17 chuckled, in a bee-like sort of way. "Sex, dear. The right kind of sex makes one glow. Can't you tell?"

Glow, huh? Ripple blinked at her reflection. Her short brown hair fanned out in a soft halo around her head, the blonde highlights reflecting the sun. The silk clung to her newly discovered curves, and her wings glittered pink and frosty white. *Holy fucking – fairy.* "Sex, huh? Who knew?"

Bee17 snorted. "Well, you would have if you'd been doing it right."

"Hey, I resent that. I've been doing it right…" Her protests tapered off as she stared at the new Ripple. "Okay. So maybe it's the air or the water or something."

Bee17 shuffled things around. "Ripple, I have to…"

"What?" Ripple absently lifted a bit of skirt and let it swish back down around her shapely ankles. *Coooooool.*

"I have to apologize." Bee17 sighed. "For Gerda."

Ripple blinked. "Why? It's not your fault she's a slut." She grinned. "And I mean that in the truest sense of the word, of course."

"Yes, but we bees, we do stick together, you know. I should've seen something, noticed something. I should've caught on that she wasn't...wasn't..."

"Normal?"

Bee17 chuckled again. "What's normal anyway?" She folded towels and tidied up the room. "No, I should've noticed that she was becoming too politically involved with the Gewürztraminers. Nobody bothers about a bit of leather now and again, but kidnapping you...well, that was really too much."

"Yeah, that did kind of push things to extremes, I guess." Ripple paused. "So, you...uh...you don't mind a bit of leather?"

Bee17 tutted and turned away from Ripple. "Stop. You'll make me blush."

"Honey, unless you do some serious waxing on those cheeks of yours, I ain't gonna be able to tell."

The bee scurried to the door. "Damn. Look at the time. And I have so much to do before tomorrow."

Ripple's spirits plummeted. "Oh yeah. The Choosing. It's tomorrow, right?"

"Yes indeed, and I have a million things to do—chambers to prepare...oh my."

"A lot of guests?" Ripple stared blindly out of the window. "Everybody coming to watch this thing?"

"You have *no* idea." Bee17 disappeared from the room in a flurry of bee fuzz.

I really don't have any idea. The thought appeared in Ripple's mind. She had no idea how she was going to make it through this damn ceremony and watch Philippe…well, there was no question about *that*, at least. She just flat *couldn't* watch.

All the talk about wingmates, all the fantastic sex, and the itchily awkward feelings that grew every time she saw Philippe—nope. She wasn't about to watch him fuck somebody else.

She wondered if there was a fairy convent in the area. If they'd take previously decadent fairies from New York. Ones who couldn't be decadent anymore.

Fuck. It wasn't even the "giving-up-decadence" thing that bothered her. Sure, she'd miss the parties, the wild and wonderful nights of sublimely drunken fun. Not to mention the Prada knockoffs, Fashion Week, New Year's Eve and the Fourth of July fireworks.

And her jeans. She'd miss those the most.

What really bothered her was the fact that she didn't *care*. That all these things were suddenly just that—*things*. Next to a lifetime without Philippe, they were nothing.

Well, okay, maybe there'd be a serious pang or two for the jeans. They'd really made her ass look fine. But if Philippe wasn't there to appreciate her fine ass, what was the point?

She paced the length of the room and back again, trying to come to terms with the fact that she was seriously in—in love, dammit. The stuff of rock songs, poetry and great literature. Not that she'd spent much time reading any, of course, but the books were nice to sit on. She'd had a couple of cute photographs taken that way. She wondered where they were.

Philippe would probably like to see them. *Sheeeit*. There he was again, intruding into her every thought.

"Get the fuck out of my head, you bastard." She whispered the words to her image in the mirror.

"Too late," Her image whispered back. *Holy heartbreak*. This love shit was a real pain in the ass.

Ripple reached for her hairbrush and cleared her throat. She tipped her head back, closed her eyes, and let a song fill her throat. But instead of the contemporary tune she expected, she found herself crooning an old love ballad, like a cheap lounge singer.

Aaaaargh!

* * * * *

Philippe grimaced as he neared Ripple's door and heard the dreadful sounds from within. His wingmate was singing again. He loved her screams of passion and her whimpers after she came, with him deep inside her.

However, *this*…this noise left a little something to be desired. Like melody perhaps, along with the ability to carry a tune. He sighed. It didn't matter that her voice was unlikely to be featured at the Milan Opera House anytime soon. It did matter that she was nervous.

Because so was he.

The Choosing ceremony was upon them. The conditions were right, the moon exactly where it was supposed to be, the weather would apparently fulfill all the necessary requirements—according to the woolly caterpillars—and they had a "go" for tomorrow.

It was time for Philippe to face his destiny. He'd been chosen by the grapes, and he had to choose a Chardonnay to repay them for that honor. He had to choose someone else when his heart had already chosen Ripple. "*Merde, merde, merde.*"

He ran his hands through his hair, sucked in a breath and opened Ripple's door.

"*Eeeek*…" She dropped the hairbrush and blushed.

Philippe wasn't sure if that was part of the song or not, and promptly forgot to ask as her face broke into a welcoming smile.

"Hey." Her welcome was a lot more musical than her song.

"Hello. You look…clean." She looked more than clean. She was glowing.

"I got the bee treatment. Scrubbed and fuzzed. I gotta tell you, if they opened a spa on Fifth Avenue, they'd do land office business."

"Your hands are cold." He pulled her close against him and she nuzzled his bare chest.

"Mmm."

He grinned. "Nice dress. How does it come off?"

With a smile as wicked as any he'd ever seen, Ripple stepped back, reached behind her and fiddled with something. Her dress slid to the floor in a swish of silk. "Like this."

She stood before him, naked and perfect. He swallowed.

Then she was against him again, her breasts squashed up against his skin. "Nice pants. How do they come off?"

"You know." He looked at her face, so honestly lustful and telling him every single thought that was going through her mind. She wanted him. Just about as much as he wanted her.

And the wanting was made even more evident when she whisked the drawstrings free on his pants and they joined her dress on the floor.

"Oh yeah, babe." She rubbed her body against his, pulling his cock upright between them. "Oh *very* yeah."

Chapter Fourteen

Adriano stirred and groaned as shards of consciousness stabbed at his mostly dormant brain.

Cazzo. He felt like shit.

"Ssssh, I'm here." A quiet voice spoke close to his ear and a hand softly smoothed his face.

"Grrrghfff…" He worked his mouth. Nothing at all happened.

"Drink, *mon amour.*" A hand raised his head and something cool was pressed to his lips.

He sipped, letting cool water trickle past his parched tongue. Aaaaah. Better. His head was eased back onto a soft pillow and he risked an attempt at opening his eyes.

Hmm. He must be dead. A woman was bending over him. But not just any woman. This woman was—was…for once, Adriano found himself bereft of speech. And not just because of the dryness in his mouth, either.

Flowing purple hair with glints of silver cascaded over her shoulders and down to a bosom that promised much. Since she was leaning towards him he knew the curves were soft and full, and a whiff of her scent rose from her heated skin to tickle his nostrils.

Her face was stunning, serene and yet with a sensual mouth that seemed to be asking for something. Something he might well have—in abundance.

"How do you feel?"

He thought about her question. "Strange." It was the best he could do, given the circumstances.

She smiled. *Dio Mio.* Her eyes lit up like candles and her expression heated his body all the way to his…*ouch.* He squirmed.

"Relax. Rest easy, Count Goriziano. You have been injured. Poisoned. Even now the venom is leaving your body. It will hurt for a little longer."

Memories flooded back into his brain. "The ant. The duel. I remember…" He frowned. "Ripple? How is she?"

The woman patted his shoulder. "She is well. Better than you, actually. She sucked out most of the venom, and thank God she did. I have been able to deal with the remainder, I think."

She made to pull away, but Adriano wasn't having any of *that*. He reached for her hand and stayed her with what little strength he had. "Where am I?"

She rested her hip on the bed beside him. "You are at the Chateau Pinot Noir. I am Shiraz, Philippe's mother. He brought you here from the clearing where you and Ripple had taken care of that damned fire ant."

"You are Philippe's *mother*?"

"I am."

"You don't look old enough to be anyone's mother. Let alone Philippe's." It wasn't smooth or courtly. The words just tumbled out on top of each other.

She blushed a little. "*Merci.* That is a nice compliment." Her gown stirred on her shoulders as she shrugged, and Adriano noticed the slight tremble in the delicate silvery wings arching behind her.

"I should've known. Philippe got his looks from you." He raised an eyebrow at her. "You are a very beautiful woman, Shiraz."

"Thank you again. Fortunately, I have some knowledge of healing. That has helped you more than any beauty possibly could."

He acknowledged the truth of that statement with a brief nod. "My life is now yours, I believe. You have saved it, *si*?"

She grinned. "Yes, but don't get all honorable around me, please. I wouldn't want that."

"What *do* you want?" He watched her throat move as she swallowed and glanced at her eyes. They were wandering down his body and back up to his face.

Shiraz blushed again, more heatedly this time. "We'll discuss that when you're well."

His cock needed no more than that to awaken. He felt the sting of his wound in his groin as his arousal grew. "I think I am on the road to recovery already."

Shiraz frowned a little. "Count…Adriano…you should not…not yet. You will disturb the healing process."

Oh certainly. Tell a man not to get an erection when he's got a dream woman with perfect breasts within licking distance. And she's staring at him like he's the vintage of her dreams and she wants to drain the bottle.

He heaved in a breath, letting desire pour through him and strengthen his muscles. It was a better tonic than all the herbs she could have used. He pulled her hand to his body and rested it on his chest, intertwined with his own. "My heart beats strongly now, Shiraz, thanks to your tender care."

She kept her gaze fastened on his face. "I know."

"And your touch…makes it beat faster still." His other hand crept up to cup her cheek. "Perhaps you might bring some feeling back to my lips…"

Her head neared his face with little or no encouragement from him. Eyes burning, she brushed her mouth against his. "Like this?"

He savored the gentleness and slipped his tongue out, drinking her sweetness. "It's a start…"

Shiraz bent to him once more. "And perhaps this would help…" Her lips parted on the words and she pressed them against his.

He pulled her head hard against his face, devouring her mouth. *Dio Mio*. She was every flavor, every taste, everything he'd ever dreamed of. His body throbbed with life and need and passion along with an overwhelming urge to lose himself inside her.

It also throbbed painfully in his groin. His cock was instantly hard and tugging on the wound. Regretfully he let his head fall away from hers.

She blinked at him and then raised a hand, touching her fingers to her lips. "*Adriano*!"

He smiled. "You felt it too." He glanced at her breasts. There was no need for her to answer. Her nipples were sending him an affirmative message in their own unique way.

"You…this…we…" Shiraz stumbled over her words, eyes wide.

"Yes, yes and yes, *mi amore*. Most definitely." Adriano knew, without a doubt, that he would forever owe a certain ant a debt of gratitude.

* * * * *

Shiraz's thoughts tumbled around like leaves floating down through a waterfall. Once Adriano's dark eyes had opened and fixed on hers, a flood of emotions had damn near drowned her. Just like she could've drowned in those deep pools that were as close to black as possible. Yet there were glints of gold lurking around his pupils, glints that sparked a fire inside her.

Oh heaven help her, she was so hungry for this man she wouldn't have been surprised to hear her stomach rumble.

The touch of his mouth, the feel of his body beneath her hands, nothing had assuaged this hunger, merely fueled it. She knew, with every fiber of her being, that had he been well, he'd be inside her by now.

And he knew it too.

His cock was hard, standing proudly away from its base of dark curls, a contrast to the wound which was too close for her to bear thinking about. The flush of venom was fading, and Adriano's color was returning.

It wasn't anything near the color she knew flooded her own cheeks, of course, but at least he wasn't as white as a ghost any more.

She fought to retain some kind of sanity. "You must relax, Adriano."

"I can't. Not now. Not anymore." His gaze swept her, heating her with its intensity. "I shall not relax again until we have explored this…this *thing* that is between us. And you know it."

Shiraz bit her lip. He was putting too much tension on the wound with that arousal of his, but she also believed he meant what he said. Fucking him was out of the question of course. But perhaps…

A tap on the door made her jump. *Merde.* Always interruptions. She sighed. "Enter."

A small fairy pushed the door wide and stepped aside, allowing something black to pass. "Laura is here, Madame."

"Ahhh. Very good." Shiraz smiled. The last tool in the healing process had arrived.

"Uhh…Shiraz?" Adriano looked at her with an arrested expression on his face. "What's that?"

The black creature waddled into the room and Shiraz rose to lay her hand on its head. She petted it. "This is Laura. She's a leech and will close your wound for you."

"Oh." Adriano definitely gulped. "She will?"

"Positively. She is the best at what she does—the most skilled. There will be no scar at all." Shiraz gave the critter a final pet and lifted her up onto the bed next to Adriano.

"Oh." His response was less than enthusiastic.

"She cannot see, Adriano, but she can feel the edges of the torn skin. She will knit them together in her own special way."

He said nothing, but watched Laura warily as she maneuvered her body onto his, unerringly seeking out his wound.

"Trust me, *mon amour*. This will work, and work well."

Adriano opened his mouth to respond, only to choke as Laura draped herself into his groin.

"Turn onto your uninjured side a little." Shiraz helped him position himself. "Laura will fasten herself to your skin. It will not hurt."

Her breasts brushed his arm and she suppressed a shudder of desire. Adriano couldn't suppress his response. "Shiraz…" He groaned out her name as Laura settled on his hip, draped from his wound around to his buttocks.

"Oh *Dio Mio*. What is she *doing*?" The leech was busying herself with her task, body sprawled in exactly the right place. Which put her two tiny antenna against his balls. Shiraz bit back a grin. There was nothing she could do—Laura knew her job and did it, regardless. Leeches were pretty much immune to the physical responses their work often aroused. They did have one small eccentricity, but Shiraz realized this might not be a good time to mention it.

She rested her hand on Adriano's shoulder. "I'm sorry. She must heal you."

"Then help her. I cannot stand this…need…" He grimaced as his cock leaked tiny pearls of desire. "Shiraz…please…"

Well, *merde*. How could she refuse a plea like that? Especially when it was what she wanted to do anyway. With Laura in place, she could rest assured that the wound was closing. Her way had been cleared.

She did give herself a little mental slap, but it was overridden by desire. *It's my time now. This is the man, and this is the moment.*

She slithered down the bed and took Adriano's cock into her hands.

* * * * *

If Adriano could've leapt off the bed, he probably would have at the moment Shiraz's mouth touched his cock. Hot and wet, she kissed her way up from base to head, then back down again.

And as she did, that damned Laura Leech critter picked up the rhythm with those poky things of hers and rolled his balls softly between them. It was *unbelievable*.

He moaned. A sound dragged from his guts by the actions of these two between his legs.

"I am hurting you?" Shiraz raised her head.

"*Non, no… Dio Mio, no…*"

She returned to her task with enthusiasm, opening her mouth and taking him inside. Slick and heated, her tongue played with him, teasingly and expertly flicking his most sensitive places with an uncanny accuracy.

He wasn't going to last very long at this rate. He panted, knowing that he probably looked more like a thirsty caterpillar at that moment than a lover. He didn't care. Just as long as she kept on doing what she was doing…

A slight movement distracted him.

"Shiraz? She… Laura…*umm*…" Incredibly, the leech's tail end was moving. Seeking out his ass and delving between his buttocks.

"Relax, Adriano." Shiraz encouraged him with a long swipe of her tongue. *Right. Relax.*

"Laura is taking care of you. And in return, she asks only that you take care of her."

Something tucked itself between his tight ass muscles and his buttocks clenched. "What do you mean?"

Shiraz sighed a gust of air against his wet cock and he shivered. "Leeches use their resources to heal. As they do, their body temperature is lowered. They get…er…cold tails."

"Oh." This was probably more than a fairy getting a blowjob could absorb.

"She needs to warm it." Shiraz sucked him, sending his eyeballs rolling back in his head. "She will use whatever nook or cranny she can find to do it."

And she'd found *his* cranny. Not to mention his nook.

Shiraz began to pull at his cock with her lips and her tongue, as the coolly smooth tail of Laura Leech slid snugly around his ass. He squeaked in surprise. Then gasped. "Holy fucking *merda*."

The not-entirely-unpleasant sensation of his butt being touched, combined with Shiraz and her extraordinarily talented tongue, sent Adriano out of his usually ordered Italian mind.

His balls were being fondled, his cock sucked and something was moving next to his ass, also contributing in no small measure to his level of arousal.

Which was now beyond belief and threatening to erupt like Mount Vesuvius.

"*Shiraz*…" He cried out as Laura's tail tickled him and Shiraz's mouth pulled his cock deep into her throat.

"Mmmm." She hummed.

That was all it took.

The lid blew off the caldera that was Adriano. Hot jets of lava spurted down Shiraz's throat as he came on a shout that emptied his lungs. His ass clamped down next to Laura's tail, his balls throbbed and his cock…well, it was blissfully spewing every drop of come he possessed as Shiraz continued suckling him dry.

He slumped, drained, trying not to squash the helpful leech, or push her tail into any place it shouldn't be.

His mouth gaped, and his renowned Italian address completely deserted him. "Wow."

Shiraz gave him a last loving lick and moved back. "You sound like Ripple."

"Who?"

She smiled. "How do you feel?"

"Yeah, dude. How *do* you feel?"

Both Shiraz and Adriano jumped. Well, Shiraz jumped. Adriano could manage little more than a twitch at this point.

Two fairies were standing in the door, grinning at the group on the bed. The man nudged the woman. "See, babe? I told you these Europeans could teach us a thing or two. A three-way with a leech. Now did *you* ever think of that?"

Adriano closed his eyes. This couldn't be happening.

"Hey Adriano-buddy. I'd ask you how it's hangin', but it's pretty plain for all of us to see." The tall man grinned, his glittering wings nearly stroking the ceiling high above. A small crown sparkled around his black hair.

The woman next to him nudged him back. Hard. "You are such an asshole, my love." She grinned apologetically. "I am so sorry we disturbed you, Shiraz. We came as soon as we could."

"So did our Addy here." The man snickered.

Adriano closed his eyes and seriously considered praying for death. He'd been poisoned by a fire ant, sucked off by the woman of his dreams, nearly fucked up the ass by Laura Leech and now — *now* an old friend was going to rag him about it for the rest of his life.

Oberon, King of the Fairies, was known for his atrocious sense of humor.

Chapter Fifteen

Philippe was as hard as he'd ever been. He was getting used to it, of course, since one whiff of Ripple and—*boingggg*. There it was. The hard-on to end all hard-ons. And the fact that she was rubbing her naked body along his cock merely accentuated it.

She was grinning. He grinned back.

She kissed him. He kissed her back. Enthusiastically.

They stood clasped together for long minutes, enjoying each other's mouths, then Ripple eased away from him. "Watch this, big fella." She fluttered her wings a little, closed her eyes and rose off the floor.

Automatically, Philippe's hands reached for her, letting her hips slide through his palms. She stopped in exactly the right place. Her pussy, that wonderfully appealing bald pussy, was inches from his mouth.

He licked his lips and prepared to snack on snatch.

"Wait."

Philippe blinked. "*Pardon?*"

"Ssssh. I gotta concentrate here."

Concentrate? On what? Surely it was Philippe who needed to concentrate. To get his tongue into those glistening pink folds that trembled about three inches from his nose. To seek out that teeny nubbin that would send Ripple into screaming shudders of ecstasy and make him feel like a God while doing it.

Her scent dazed him and words failed him. He simply did as he was told. He waited.

Her body twitched a little, her wings vibrated, and then…slowly, very slowly…Ripple began to rotate.

"*Mon Dieu*." Philippe's jaw dropped as she pivoted neatly around an invisible axis, ending up with her head between *his* legs. His eyes bugged out of his head as her pussy returned to his face, upside down this time, between widely parted thighs.

"*Ripple*!" He squawked out the word. "Fairies aren't supposed to be able to hover like that."

"Oh yeah?" Her voice was muffled since it was now coming from someplace around his crotch. "Helps to hang around the circus, ya know."

"But…the blood…it rushes to your head. You pass out…"

A giggle sent shivers of pleasure through Philippe. "Not if you do it *right*, babe."

Fuck! She was doing it *right*, no question about it. She'd found his cock—not a difficult task since it was now the size of the Eiffel Tower and growing— and…*merde*…yes, she was sucking it.

Philippe figured death was imminent. This was— extraordinary. No mere fairy could possibly survive this kind of pleasure.

"Mmmm…" She mumbled around him, hands busy with his balls.

He gasped for air, truly astounded at the talents of this wild and wonderful woman. *God Bless America*. Her pussy nudged his face. Time for *Vive La France*.

He reached for her, pulled her tight against him and buried his face in her smooth folds.

Taking her like this was unique. Upside down, inverted, probably perverted, and in violation of the laws of physics. It was also amazingly wonderful and required his full attention. No wonder she'd said she needed to concentrate.

He was torn between what she was doing to his cock and what he needed to do to her pussy. For once, his brain became fully involved in this amazing airborne fuck, and the world faded away as he fought for balance between the physical, the psychological and the pleasurable.

Finally, he gave up, buried his face in her cunt and just sucked for all he was worth.

So did she.

Within moments they exploded. They cried out, almost simultaneously, and Ripple's legs scissored shut around Philippe's ears as she pulsed into his mouth. She screamed around his cock—which was a unique sensation all by itself since he was coming down *her* throat at the time.

Yes, this was surely going to kill them both.

But what a way to go.

Their final tumble to the floor wouldn't have earned either of them any points for elegance. Wings clashed and tangled, knees thumped painfully on the carpet, and sticky limbs clung, separated and clung once more.

Oh *merde*. *What* a woman!

Philippe panted for air, his breaths matched by Ripple, who was lying limply half on top of him.

Something sounding suspiciously like a chuckle came from across the room. "Now *there's* something you don't see every day."

* * * * *

The voice made them both jump and Ripple clenched her teeth with what little strength she had left. "*Fucking A*. Is there no such thing as *privacy* on this whole goddamned *continent*?"

She struggled to her knees and glared at the four people who were standing by the door. Their heads were cocked, to the right and to the left. Yep. They'd caught the whole thing. "*Jesus Christ*. What a bunch of pervs and voyeurs. Wanna pay for the privilege? At least we could make a few bucks here. You all enjoy the show or what?"

"Uh, Ripple?" Philippe was scrambling for his pants.

"Yeah, yeah. I know. It's your mother. *Again*. And Adriano." She grinned. "Glad you're up and about, dude."

"Uh, Ripple?" Philippe pushed her gown at her.

She snorted. "Look, for the record, I'm not into this doing-it-for-an-audience thing, okay? I dunno who you two are, but Shiraz, I'd be obliged if you'd just take 'em away and show 'em grapes or something. Let 'em go spy on some other poor fuckers."

"*Ripple…*" Philippe's tone was urgent now.

"*What*?" Exhausted from her flying trick and consequent orgasm, Ripple was in no mood to be placated, ordered around or otherwise fussed. She wanted a nap. With Philippe, preferably.

The unknown woman laughed delightedly. "You're pretty much fucked out, aren't you, honey?"

The man grinned too. "After that neat trick I'm not surprised." He turned to his companion. "See?" He waggled his eyebrows at her. "I *told* you we should've gone to see that French circus show. But noooooo…you had to go to that frickin' Hugh Jackman movie…"

Ripple's eyes widened. "You're *Americans*? Holy fucking coincidence. You get caught up in a tornado too?" She finally took the gown Philippe was shoving into her hands and struggled into it.

Philippe grabbed her arm and held her steady as she teetered amongst voluminous folds of white silk. "Ripple." His voice was shaky. "May I present Oberon and Titania?" His grip tightened. "The *King* and *Queen* of the Fairies."

Ripple peeked one eye out of the neckline. "Oh fuck." She pulled the dress down and straightened her wings, shooting a sideways glance at Philippe. "You're kidding, right?"

He shook his head and made a respectful bow to the couple standing next to his mother.

"Oh double fuck." Ripple cleared her throat. "Uh…" She thought for a moment. "I didn't think you guys were for real."

Philippe choked.

Before she could dig herself in any deeper, Adriano staggered a little, and everyone went into major fuss-mode, getting him into a chair. Ripple noted with interest how Shiraz fluttered around him, tending to his every need. *Hmmmm.*

Finally, they were settled to everyone's satisfaction, and Ripple's gauche comment had been forgotten. She thought.

"So you didn't think we were real, huh?" Oberon's eyes twinkled at her.

Sheeeit. "Look, your Majesty, Sir… Mister King…" She waved a hand. "Sorry about that. No insult intended there."

"None taken." Titania smiled in her particularly attractive way. God, the woman was gorgeous. Not your movie-star gorgeous, but just…hell. Just gorgeous.

"It's just that…well, *King* and *Queen*, ya know? That stuff sooo isn't part of East Elmhurst. New Orleans at Mardi Gras, maybe, but New York? Nah…"

Oberon sighed. "I've been telling Tits here we should hit the Big Apple for a vacation. Perhaps now she'll listen to me."

Ripple giggled. "Tits?"

Philippe rushed into the conversation. "May I ask to what we owe this honor, Sire?"

"Your mom, kid." Oberon nodded at Shiraz. "She put in a call for a little assistance."

"Whoa." Ripple held up her hand. "Time out. You folks have *phones*? I though only humans had phones. I know we've tapped into their DSL lines but…"

Shiraz looked smug. "We're experimenting with high-level bat technology. Fit them with silvered dishes and send them as high as they'll go."

"And then?" Ripple was fascinated.

"A long piece of string and a tin can." Shiraz wrinkled her lips. "We've got some work to do on that."

"Whatever." Oberon waved the subject aside. "We got the message. We're here."

"Yeah, but why?" Ripple raised her brows.

"We're the cavalry, sweetie. Here to save your ass in the last roll of this fancy foreign flick."

"That's nice." Ripple's brain trampled along an odd and convoluted path as she fought with the concept of royalty, international travel and bat communication systems. "So you're stuck here now, too?"

Titania giggled. "Hell no. It's a nice place to visit, but with all due respect, I'm gonna miss Fairyland before too long. There's a new show coming into our favorite Gnome Gnightclub, and I have no intention of not being there when it debuts."

"But…but… I thought we couldn't go home from here. The prevailing wind thing…" Ripple frowned.

Oberon chuckled. "Winds? Who needs 'em? Just pick a nice ship heading west, and you're all set." He stretched his arms over his head. "I've been thinking of taking that big new Queen-something liner home. And fucking my big old Queen all the way. There's something about the sea air…"

Titania narrowed her eyes and thumped his shoulder. "Watch it with the *old* Queen bit, my love. You might wake up to find yourself a tadpole for the entire trip."

He nipped her ear affectionately. "As long as my pole can find your tad, honey, I'll be a happy invertebrate."

Titania, to Ripple's amazement, blushed.

So this was Royalty, huh? Who knew?

She cleared her throat and got down to the important stuff. "Okay. Letting the travel thing go for a minute here, how — exactly — are you guys…excuse me…your *Majesties*…gonna save my ass?"

"Turn around and lemme see it, babe. Gotta make sure it's worth saving." Oberon's eyes glittered.

Titania sighed. "You are *such* a dickhead."

Oberon hugged her. "But you love me anyway, right, sweet pea?"

Ripple gave up. It was all too much. Philippe, this whole wine thing, weird fetish fairies, fire ants, Italians and now, to top it all off, horny Royalty. There was only so much one fairy could stand, even one from East Elmhurst.

She slumped. "*Fuck*. I need a *driiiiink*."

"Me too." Oberon looked hopeful. "Anyone got any tequila around this place?"

* * * * *

Shiraz and Adriano snuggled together in a lump of wings and bodies. For the umpteenth time, Adriano marveled at how well they fit together. He sighed.

"Tired, *mon amour*?"

Her voice came from somewhere over his heart, where she belonged. He cuddled her even closer. "I'd be a fool to say no."

She chuckled. "You are no fool, Adriano."

"Only for you. And for not finding you 'til now." He dropped a kiss on the top of her head as she nipped his chest and licked him.

"At least we have found each other. The wait is over. For us both." Shiraz yawned. "So you think Oberon and Titania have a plan that will work?"

"Of course." Adriano snorted. "If they don't, Oberon will simply get one of those awesome *kingly* expressions on his face and bully everybody into submission."

"He can do that?"

"Oh yes, *cara*. I have no doubts about that at all." Adriano grinned to himself. "You have seen the fun and personal side of

His Majesty. There is another side, the formal monarch who rules Fairyland. One doesn't want to fuck around with that man. Not at all."

"I agree. I *don't* want to fuck around with him." Her hand slid lower, playing with his navel and moving on, gently, to his groin. "I'd much rather fuck around with you."

Adriano rested his head against the pillow and smiled, offering a prayer of thanks to fire ants in general, leeches, Ripple and the Gewürztraminers, all of whom had conspired to land him in bed with his perfect mate.

"Speaking of leeches…" His brain wandered over the subject.

"Who was?" Shiraz had found his cock and was teasingly running her fingertips up and down its length. Seeing as it had just performed in what Adriano considered an exhaustingly admirable fashion, he was quite surprised to find it responding once more.

"Um…yes, leeches." He bravely soldiered on, clinging to his train of thought. "You know that thing that Laura did with her poky antennae…"

Shiraz's hand dipped between his thighs and found his balls. "You mean…*here*?"

Adriano swallowed and closed his eyes. "Oh yes. *There*."

The conversation degenerated into sighs and moans as darkness filled the Chateau Pinot Noir and three couples finally got to fuck in privacy.

Adriano and Shiraz took their time.

Oberon and Titania took each other, several times. Loudly and royally.

And Ripple and Philippe? They *gave*. Shared their bodies and their hearts in a mutual joining that was exclusive to wingmates and new lovers the world over.

All of them deliberately refused to even *think* about one very important fact.

The Choosing was to take place the next day.

Chapter Sixteen

The following morning found Philippe, Adriano and Oberon staring blearily at each other over breakfast. They'd been shoveled out of their respective rooms and into a small salon at the Chateau, which had apparently been deemed appropriate for feeding the male of the species.

"Kicked you out too, huh?" Philippe grinned at Oberon.

"Yeah." He stretched. "No respect from these damn bees. I'm a *King*, for chrissake. Shouldn't be turned out of my own bed at the crack of dawn, or scolded for not looking where I dropped my pants."

"You're not *their* King, my friend." Adriano smiled.

"They made that fact damned obvious." Oberon frowned into his coffee. "Haven't been talked to like that since…well, I don't remember."

"Don't take it to heart. We all got the same treatment. Seems the women are up to something." Adriano raised an eyebrow. "Anybody got any idea *what*?"

Philippe stood and paced the room. "The Choosing, obviously."

"Ah yeah. This Choosing thing." He watched Philippe. "You gotta get a hard-on for some Chardonnay chick, huh?"

Adriano leaned back in his chair and stared at his friends. Oberon he'd met many years ago, and liked enormously. Theirs had been a brief but lasting friendship and he was very glad Shiraz had thought to contact him.

Philippe, on the other hand, was close to being the son he'd never had. The summers they'd spent fucking their way around exotic vineyards had been a gift to Adriano, and one he'd cherished.

And to think in all that time, he'd never met Shiraz.

He sighed.

"Quit it. You're thinking sex again." Oberon flashed him a glance from under lowered eyebrows.

"And you're not?"

Oberon gave up and chuckled.

Philippe stopped pacing and stared at Adriano. "Listen, should I ask about this thing with you and my mother?" He paused, blinked and then shook his head. "Never mind. Forget I said that."

Adriano stared back. "I will. Consider it forgotten. However…" He thought carefully about his next words. "If it were possible for me to find a wingmate, it would be her. Are we clear on that?"

Philippe's jaw dropped. "*You*? A *wingmate*?" He staggered and clutched his chest dramatically. "To think I should live to see the day…"

Adriano annoyed himself by blushing.

"You gonna give me a baby brother or sister…*mon père*?" Philippe's grin was pure mischief.

"What, so you can have someone your own age to play with?"

"Oh, nice one, pal." Oberon applauded politely. "But can the crap, will ya? We got ourselves a little problem here to settle."

The three men sobered and Philippe returned to his pacing. "I don't see an immediate solution, Sire. The Choosing is a ceremony rooted in centuries of tradition. And given today's political situation, turning around and picking Ripple would be disastrous."

"What happens if the old joystick lets you down, boy?" Oberon steepled his fingers together contemplatively.

Philippe sighed. "Then there is no Noble Mold flight. No champagne grapes for this harvest. And the prestige of the Pinot Noirs goes down the *pissoir*."

Adriano nodded. "Not to mention the fact that the Cabernet Sauvignons would immediately press for Philippe's replacement—with one of theirs, no doubt—and the Merlots would instigate even more rumors about the lack of abilities in House Pinot Noir. It's ticklish at best, fraught with political landmines at worst."

"And the Gewürztraminers?"

Philippe chuckled. "Well, I have to admit they're probably a bit occupied right about now. The HORNET team that went in to extract Ripple is still there."

Adriano shared his laughter. "I'd love to be a fly on the wall for that one."

"Would the Chardonnays get upset?" Oberon asked the question thoughtfully.

"*Merde*, no. They don't care one way or the other." Philippe huffed. "Ironic isn't it? The one vintage that makes the best champagne with the Pinot Noirs is unapologetically gay. They have to be bribed to breed, for heaven's sake, let alone participate in this Choosing ceremony."

"So the fate of the champagne rests squarely on your Johnson, young Philippe."

Philippe nodded. "*Oui*. And it's a thought I don't like very much. Not now. Not after Ripple."

"What exactly happens?" Adriano tilted his head as he looked at Philippe. "I've never been to a Choosing."

* * * * *

"It's really a rather lovely ceremony." Shiraz passed the croissants over the table to Ripple. "Eat, *cherie*. You need something."

"I can't." Ripple sat in the sunny suite with Shiraz and Titania, sunk in gloom. "The only man I've ever developed a real case for, and he's gotta save the world with his cock. And another woman."

Titania burped politely. "Damn, those are good croissants. Pass 'em over here if you're not gonna eat 'em. The hell with the calories." She buttered her fourth. "But the ceremony itself…what happens?"

Shiraz gathered her thoughts. "The Choosing takes place at sundown in the vineyards. One particular lane is shielded with flowers and boughs of leaves. The Chardonnay women stand on one side, and a small space is cleared around their wingbuds so that they show through to whoever is on the other side." She sipped her coffee.

"So is there like a parade, or something?" Titania continued her questions. "Gimme the skinny here, Shiraz. I need every detail."

"Hmm." Shiraz thought. "*Non*. No parade. The point is to make sure that no one sees which Chardonnay is which. They gather off by themselves, then enter this leafy tunnel place, all under cover. One bee, or perhaps two, escorting them. That's it. It's very important to maintain anonymity here, since it's Philippe's…er…" She broke off and glanced at Ripple.

"Go ahead. You can say it. It's my guy's cock that's gotta get a serious stiffy for some other babe." She sighed loudly. "This would *never* happen in New York."

Titania ignored her. "So this all happens at dusk?"

"Yes." Shiraz nodded.

There was silence for a few moments as all three women worked the situation over in their minds.

Finally, Titania developed a small smile. Which grew larger as Shiraz watched.

Ripple noticed it too. "What? *What*? You got a certain look about you, babe. Er…your Majesty…"

Titania waved the apology aside. "Does anybody know we're here, yet? Me and Oberon?"

Shiraz blinked. "Well...no. We didn't make a big thing about it. Security issues and all that."

Titania looked smug. "Good."

"Good? How good is good? Define *good*." Ripple's wings twitched.

"Patience, sweetie. I have to think through the details." Titania rose and the others followed suit. "First, I need a shower. I stink. You got any wing smoother?"

Shiraz nodded.

"Good. I think this occasion calls for some pretty spectacular grooming. Can't let the monarchy down with frizzed wings, can we?"

"Uh... I guess not."

"And I need a bee."

"Funny." The irrepressible Ripple glanced at Titania's bounteous cleavage. "I'd have said you were more of a D myself."

Titania clouted her upside the ear with a wing. "Don't get fresh, missy. These girls are what got Oberon slobbering in the first place."

Ripple giggled. "In that case, they have my undying respect."

Shiraz did her best to ignore the byplay. "You have a plan then?"

Titania looked enigmatic. "I have an idea. That may well become a plan. That will also work quite well, I think. Providing Ripple is indeed Philippe's wingmate." She dropped her humor and stared hard at Ripple. "Tell me, child. *Is* Philippe your wingmate?"

Shiraz watched as Titania the fun-loving sensualist became Titania, Queen of the Fairies. There would be no messing around with this woman when she was in this mood. A certain underlying strength of will shone from her beautiful eyes and she was regal in every sense of the word.

Ripple gulped and straightened her shoulders. "I don't know what a wingmate really is. For most of my life I figured it was some kind of joke. We don't go in for that shit where I come from." She swallowed. "But if it means that I don't ever want anyone else to touch me again but Philippe, then hell, yeah. He's my wingmate."

She warmed to her topic. "If it means that every time I see him a little bit more of me falls head over ass for him, then yeah, he's my wingmate. If it means that he only has to look at me to get me wetter than…uh…" she trailed off, blushing.

Shiraz listened with half of her brain. The other half was sitting up, and drumming its heels on her grey matter. *That's how you feel about Adriano.*

Could it be possible? Could a woman be lucky enough to have two wingmates in a lifetime?

Ripple boldly went on. "I'm totally freaked out by this guy. Philippe does things to me that turn me inside out. I've been around the block, Ma'am. I'm not your virgin Victorian elfin sprite. Uh-uh. Not me. I've had me my fun, New York City style. There isn't much I haven't tried. But Philippe…" Her voice faltered.

"Yes? Philippe?" Titania encouraged her.

"Philippe?" Ripple slumped. "I'm so crazy in love with him I can't stand myself." She shrugged. "There. It's out. The famous party girl from East Elmhurst has gone and done it. Used the 'l' word and survived." She brushed a hand across her eyes. "Almost survived."

Titania grinned. "All *righty* then. Time to get devious."

Shiraz tried to follow the conversation. She really did. But seeing as she'd just gotten the biggest mental shock of her life, it was hard. Ripple's words mirrored the emotions she'd experienced with Adriano.

The first time she'd looked at him, touched him, bells had clanged from Calais to Leningrad. She'd drooled, lusted, and generally behaved like a wanton fairy half her age. With the additional benefits of experience, the sex had been…well, *merde*. There weren't enough words in the dictionary to describe it.

She shivered.

"Quit it, Shiraz. You're thinking about sex again. I can tell." Ripple's voice sounded amused now. "The Queen here has a plan. You on board, or what?"

"Uhh…" Shiraz jerked herself out of her confusion. "Of course. Anything." She looked at Titania. "What's the plan?"

The Queen ran a thumb over her bottom lip as she thought. "I need to talk to Oberon. Get his input."

Ripple bit her lip as Titania shot her a look. "Don't even *go* there."

"Sorry. Okay—you need hubby. What else?"

"Like I said. I need a bee. A trustworthy bee."

A slow grin spread over Ripple's features. "Oh babe. I got the *best*. Just don't tell the Pentagon about her, okay?"

Chapter Seventeen

That enchanting time known as "dusk" to Europeans was falling rapidly. A time when the sun fades from sight, but darkness has yet to envelop the land. Philippe looked around him nervously. And there was a whole lot to get nervous about.

He was standing self-consciously on a dais at one end of his vineyard in front of what seemed like thousands of fairies. Long lanes of budding grapes were stretched almost as far as the eye could see. Had he been on ground level, it would have looked like a forest, but from his current vantage point, it must appear much as it did to human eyes. Orderly rows of foliage about to produce one of the world's greatest pleasures—wine.

And if he got it up for a Chardonnay, they jerked each other off mid-flight and the winds were right—champagne.

Everybody there that night would be watching, too. Fairies must have traveled for weeks to get here, since there were many he didn't recognize. Why did there have to be such a huge crowd? Tonight of all nights?

He mentally slapped himself upside the head. They had come because of the rumors. Probably started by the Merlots. Rumors that the Monseigneur of the Pinot Noirs was going to seriously fuck up and *not* be able to pick himself a Chardonnay.

He clenched his teeth and bit down on a pang of anxiety. He had to do his duty. He knew it and Ripple knew it too. She'd been the one who'd pointed that out last night when he'd awoken her for the third time. His need for her seemed overwhelming and nothing but her body could assuage it. He'd talked her around to his way of thinking, of course, much of the talking being done while his mouth was against her sweet pussy.

And *merde*, there it was again. A tickle in his balls, a shot of something sizzling running to his cock, and all he had to do was think of her. His Ripple. Perhaps he could get it up for a Chardonnay by thinking of Ripple? Oh *bon Dieu*. What a fucking mess.

"Philippe? Are you all right?" Shiraz and Adriano were standing a little behind him, and he felt his mother's hand on his arm.

"No. Yes. I don't know…" He ran his hand through his hair.

"Have faith, my son. Trust in what you feel." Shiraz's voice was soothing.

Philippe refused to be soothed. "There's so much at stake, *Maman*. Not just the wines. Oh I know…" He snorted. "I'll do my duty. But it's the rest of my life I'm thinking about. And…and Ripple."

She squeezed his biceps. "I know."

Adriano moved closer. "If you can't trust in fate, Philippe, do what men everywhere do. Listen to your cock."

Philippe rolled his eyes. "Riiiiiight." That was *really* helpful.

A rustle of excitement whispered over the dais and the entourages from the other vintages entered with a great deal of pomp. The Cabernet Sauvignons looked down their noses at Philippe, one even going so far as to shake his head a little as if in distaste.

Merde. What assholes.

The fireflies were gathering now, circling overhead and adding a sparkling light to the proceedings. Their illumination heralded the entrance of the Merlots, only four of them, but enough to stir things up if they so chose.

Philippe's lip curled. It looked like they were going to be spared the presence of the Gewürztraminers, thanks to a squad of happy HORNETS. He wondered briefly who was winning in the red-cheeks derby that was probably taking place over at their compound.

Then the Chardonnay contingent arrived and he recalled his disordered thoughts. Philippe watched the colorful fairies as they giggled and grinned and waved to their friends. They brought laughter and joy with them, thank the good Lord, and Philippe was very, *very* happy to see them join the group on the dais. Especially when he noticed Soix in the middle.

His friend gave him a "thumbs-up" signal, but could not exchange words, since more excitement was underway.

The Chardonnay women were assembling.

Not that anyone could see them, of course, but the fireflies had divided up and one group was now frantically circling a small and secluded area off to one side of the gathering.

Shiraz stepped forward and raised her hand for silence. As Mistress of the Chateau Pinot Noir, it fell to her to get the proceedings underway.

It's now or never. Philippe heaved in a breath, only to cough it out again as a giant blast from some invisible trumpets made everyone jump.

The crowd on the dais parted, staggered actually, and made way for a glittering mass of wings.

Philippe blinked. The crowd was silent.

"Friends, fairies…our ceremony this evening is honored by two very special guests." Shiraz's voice rang out over the faces turned expectantly toward her.

Philippe frowned in confusion. It wasn't like his mother to be quite so dramatic. Not in public, anyway.

"It is my pleasure to welcome—on your behalf—King Oberon and Queen Titania."

Shiraz dropped into a deep curtsey as gasps of excitement and wonder rippled through the throng. Everyone, including the

Cabernets, bowed deeply. Apparently royalty counted for something, even with them.

Philippe stared in awe as Oberon and Titania stepped out onto the front of the dais.

Gone were the two squabbling lovers, the hotheaded horny fairy and his lusty mate. In their places were—monarchs.

Oberon's black wings glittered with a thousand shards of light, almost painful to look at. Tall and straight, he surveyed the gathering with just the right amount of friendly disdain, his black silk tunic falling to just above his knees. His crown was a thing of beauty, featuring a multifaceted black jewel, ringed with hammered gold, resting in the center of his forehead.

And beside him—Titania. Her wild hair had been tamed into a sleek knot, her wings were vibrant and multi-hued, and her diadem flickered with each move she made. Her gown was elegant and flowing, and she stood alongside her husband looking every inch of what she was…the Queen of the Fairy kingdom.

With one accord, the crowd dropped to its knees and bowed.

And there was a small fuss and bother in the secluded glade a short distance away, which nobody noticed, since they were in the august presence of their rulers.

"Greetings, fairies." Oberon's voice boomed across the vineyard. "We are here to help you celebrate this time of Choosing. To join with you in this joyous occasion which unites *all* vintages in a single goal."

Philippe noted, with a certain degree of amusement, that the Merlots looked uncomfortable at the tone of King Oberon's words. To judge by the slight quirk in Oberon's lips he was fully aware of that fact, too.

"It has been too long since my Queen and I traveled to this fair land. Too long since we have had the pleasure of reacquainting ourselves with old friends and making new ones.

And too long since we have all sat together and shared our joys, our sorrows and our wisdom."

Polite applause greeted this statement, and Philippe wondered for a moment if Oberon was planning on running for office anywhere. The King was a fine politician along with everything else. This, supposed Philippe, was why Oberon *was* the King, of course. He listened as Oberon continued.

"Tonight, we shall watch as a Pinot Noir makes his choice and takes a Noble Mold flight. We shall share your happiness as we do his. Tomorrow, we shall spend in conference with all your vintages. We look forward to learning of your progress, your growth and your future plans. We hope to be able to help in whatever small way we can."

Merde. That will put the cat amongst the pigeons, and no mistake about it. Philippe managed to stop himself from gasping. Oberon obviously intended to set everyone straight in no uncertain terms.

But that was for tomorrow. Tonight—tonight he had to give it his best shot, find himself a mate if he could, and figure out how to live with the consequences.

He squared his shoulders as Oberon concluded his remarks, Titania gave a little queenly wave to the cheering crowd, and both took their seats on makeshift thrones hurriedly prepared for them.

This was it.

Choosing time.

* * * * *

The crowd was buzzing excitedly, a thousand fairy wings fluttering in the quiet evening air. To have this Ceremony honored by the presence of their King and Queen was a treat indeed, and tales of this night would be told for generations to come.

Philippe bit his lip. He didn't know if he'd be producing any of those generations himself. Or if the tales would include the bit about how he'd been a total disaster, failed to get it up for any of the Chardonnay brides, and disgraced both himself and the Pinot Noir vintage.

Shiraz nodded at him, and he stepped forward. It was time to show himself, literally, to the assembled crowd. Nudity was no big deal to fairies as a rule, but tonight, *especially* tonight, Philippe felt a pang of embarrassment as he reached for the drawstring on his pants. He had to make this walk stark naked. It was the only way to verify that he'd used no trickery to choose his mate for the Noble Mold flight.

With a sigh, he dropped his drawers, stepped out of them and faced the crowd.

Murmurs of approval, a couple of sighs and a smattering of applause greeted his "show", and he did his best to ignore all of them. This was a time for contemplation, concentration, duty and not thinking about anything, including one smart-ass New York fairy who'd stolen his heart.

His cock stirred. *Merde*. Not *now*.

He quickly turned away towards the steps leading to the secluded glade, only to be halted by Oberon's hand. "With your permission…" The King rose from his seat and turned to the crowd. "It would give me great pleasure to act as observer on your behalf during this ceremony. May I have your approval?"

Philippe blinked as the crowd cheered and roared with delight. Usually, the role of "observer" was filled by a senior member of another vintage. He saw the Cabernets grinding their teeth, and the Merlots frowning. He would've picked a Chardonnay, himself, probably Soix, but at this point he was confused enough. He simply nodded.

"Shall we?" Oberon beckoned Philippe. The King's face was calm and unusually expressionless. Nothing could be gleaned from his eyes or his demeanor. The two men stepped down off the dais and made their way to the glade.

It was much darker now, in spite of the fireflies, and Philippe stopped in front of a large bee in the shadows. Who, surprisingly, was grinning at him. "They're ready, Monseigneur." She bowed and stepped back. A long dark lane lay in front of him, with a thick hedge up one side. He knew what he would find within that hedge.

He gritted his teeth, offered up a prayer for guidance, and stepped out along the soft grass.

Sure enough, within the first five feet, a small opening had been cut into the foliage. There, shining at him, was a wing bud. A pleasant enough one, to be sure, but not one that called to him or stirred his loins.

Another couple of wing buds followed…the Chardonnay fairies themselves as quiet as mice on the other side of the hedge.

He stopped at one, touched it gently, and noted the shiver that went through the body. Nice, but nothing special. Once again he moved on. There would be a dozen of these apertures, a dozen wing buds displayed for his delectation. And a dozen times when his cock would not respond.

He slumped wearily as he neared the end of the lane. This was certainly going to go down in the history books as an appallingly bad Choosing. Perhaps Oberon could salvage the political situation. Perhaps he himself could hitch a ride to someplace far away where he and Ripple could…

He'd reached the last wing bud. Soft and sweet, it seemed to glow slightly amidst its frame of leaves and vines.

He paused. There was something…different about this one. Something…arousing. He stepped closer, reaching out a hand and stroking the soft gathered skin. A slight sigh accompanied the shudder caused by his touch.

To his astonishment, he felt his balls throb and his cock tighten. Holy *merde*. This couldn't fucking be happening. Could it? But it was. Almost involuntarily, his cock lengthened and thrust forward, as if it too wanted to touch. He couldn't restrain the urge, and leaned in, brushing himself against the wing bud.

He gasped. It was almost electric—stunning in its intensity. A cry from the other side of the hedge let him know that he wasn't the only one feeling this sensation.

"We have a *choice*." Oberon's voice rang out across the vineyard, and the sound of cheering followed it.

Philippe wanted to scream with anger. His own cock had betrayed him. He'd gone and gotten a hard-on from some Chardonnay, when all he wanted was Ripple. Forever. He clamped down on his horror and forced himself to back away and complete the ceremony. Duty. He had to think of duty now, nothing and no one else. He would return to the dais, and his bride would be led to him, veiled until the last moment. Then they would marry, and make their flight together.

Oh fuck, oh fuck, oh fuck.

"Well done, lad." Oberon clapped him on the shoulder. "I knew you wouldn't let the team down."

Philippe just looked at him. What could he say?

Slowly he made his way back to the dais in Oberon's wake. His life was crumbling around his ears and it took a great deal of effort to keep his wings from drooping miserably.

He dressed, not even hearing the cheers and applause from the crowd, or noticing the glares from the Cabernets. He didn't even see his mother as she stepped to the side of the dais and welcomed a veiled figure.

"My son." Her voice brought a measure of quiet to the vineyard. "We shall now reveal the bride you have chosen. I take it the Choosing meets with the approval of the observer?"

Oberon stepped forward. "All was done according to custom, Madame. You may rest assured that this was a genuine Choosing."

Shiraz nodded her thanks to the King. She led the veiled figure to the center of the dais next to Philippe.

He raised his eyes and sighed. His life was over.

Shiraz whisked off the veil and revealed…

"*You!*"

His very own Ripple was grinning at him.

"What the *fuck*..." Philippe's brain was screeching into a U-turn and leaving skid marks inside his skull.

"Hey, lover boy. I've had better proposals of marriage, ya know." She put her hands on her hips. "I know it's kinda public, and I wasn't exactly expecting you to get down on one knee, but shit, dude...you could at least look *pleased*."

"I...uh... I..."

"Oh fuck it. And here I figured you French guys were so smooth." Ripple stepped close to him, grabbed him by the ears and kissed him passionately.

The crowd, as the saying goes, went wild.

Chapter Eighteen

But then the mutterings began. Started no doubt by Merlot nuisances who had nothing better to do than point out that the woman currently chosen by the Monseigneur was about as far from being a Chardonnay as it was possible to get.

Ripple ignored them and kept doing what she really liked doing, which was kissing Philippe for all she was worth. *I must be getting used to the doing-shit-like-this-in-public thing.* She didn't even throw a blush.

However that bold attitude began to melt as Philippe's cock hardened between them and his hands roved over her butt. She returned the favor, grasping those lovely taut buns and hanging on for all she was worth.

A loud clearing of the throat behind them made the lovers jump apart, and this time it was Philippe who blushed.

Ripple smiled at Oberon. "Ooops."

He winked at her. "If you two'll cut it out for a minute, I've got a mess to straighten out here so you can get on with the fucking, okay?"

"Sire, I…I…don't know what to say…" Philippe still looked a little shell-shocked at the whole deal.

"So just shut up and let me deal with it. There are advantages to being King, ya know." He grinned at Titania who had moved to his side. "Besides the obvious ones."

The Queen rolled her eyes. "Then quit your nonsense and get on with it before a riot breaks out."

Ripple and Philippe stepped back, allowing the Royals to take center stage. Ripple chuckled to herself and dug Philippe in the ribs. They both watched as, out of sight of the crowd, Oberon's hand slid to his wife's bottom and administered a light pinch.

Yeah. It probably was good to be the King.

A hand slipped into hers and grasped it tightly. She looked up at Philippe, his dear face smiling at her, glowing with the love she knew was written all over her own features like a neon sign. *So who needs Fifth Avenue anyway? And the winters suck as well.*

A thought crossed her mind. "Hey Philippe…" She leaned closer and whispered to him. "You ever go to Paris for the fashion shows?"

"Sssssh." Shiraz held a finger to her lips. Ripple obediently shushed.

"This is a wonderful night for the vineyards." Oberon began his speech. "A wonderful night for *every* fairy of *every* vintage. The Pinot Noir Monseigneur has chosen a fine bride, and yes, she's not a full-blooded Chardonnay."

There were murmurs and chatter from the throng, which fell silent as Oberon raised his hand. "But are we not *all* from the same vintage? Are we not all *fairies*, with jobs to do, lives to lead, duties to perform and pleasure to be taken?"

Ripple stared as Oberon seemed to grow larger in front of them. His wings glittered fiercely now, almost as if lit from within. "Over the generations, you vineyard fairies have become fragmented. Separated into factions, each with their own responsibilities, their own grapes to tend. This is acceptable to us, but only up to a point."

He *was* growing larger. An aura began to pulsate around him. *Holy headlights.* This dude had a shitload more power than Ripple could even begin to guess at.

Even his voice had become stronger, more vibrant, holding the large crowd in thrall to his words. "It is time for change to blow fresh thought through these ancient vines. Time for not only the Pinot Noirs to choose, but for *all* fairies to choose."

There was dead silence. Then an elderly Cabernet moved. "Sire…with all due respect…"

Oberon ignored him. "The man behind me is about to argue that such a course of action is improper. That the blending of vintages in a careless way will result in different wines, strange and new grapes, and probably some disasters." Finally he glanced over his shoulder, the fire in his gaze reducing the Cabernet to a stuttering idiot.

"He is, in essence, correct."

Ripple blinked. Where the fuck was Oberon going with this stuff? She glanced at Philippe who looked as puzzled as she felt, and then at Shiraz and Adriano who were just smiling. And standing *real* close.

"But…" Oberon now dominated the glade. Hovering above the dais and surrounded by a brilliant rainbow of colors, he was magnificent. "It is time for you all to remember what you are, first and foremost. *You are fairies*. It is your job to bring light and joy into the world. To illuminate dark places, to tend that which you are, by nature, fit to tend, and to love with passion and boundless desire."

He gestured to Philippe and Ripple. "This Choosing ceremony ends tonight. There will be no more parades of wing buds. No more arguing over who should marry whom. Or whose job it is to make the Noble Mold flight."

Gasps now fluttered over the trembling wings of the throng.

"I know." Oberon nodded at them. "It's a drastic idea. And there will be a Monseigneur for each vintage. But that Monseigneur will choose the bride of his heart. He needs no ceremony to tell him which woman will make him complete."

"He's on a roll." Titania mouthed the words to Ripple, who nodded, still a little awestruck at the image of Oberon as the Power Ranger King.

"I shall be meeting with your Elders in the morning, and we shall reorganize things to everyone's satisfaction. Even…" He stared into the crowd. "Even the Merlots."

Several fairies squirmed uncomfortably, and a number of wings drooped.

"There will be problems. There will certainly be difficulties, and probably a lot of challenges. But you will overcome these things with the strength I know you all possess. There will be wonderful new wines, healthy new grapes and vines, and the world will see the dawn of better beverages."

"Hoo boy, he's running dry." Titania sighed. "Honey? Drop the soda commercial bit, okay?"

Oberon quivered slightly, but steadfastly kept his eyes on the crowd. "My Queen and I are proud of you all. We hope we can continue to serve you well. And we shall certainly return someday soon to see the results of our…discussions. In the meantime, we have a wedding to celebrate and a Noble Mold flight to watch."

Slowly, he touched down on the dais and the glow faded. "And I think it's time for the party to start."

A smattering of applause began somewhere, growing into a roar as a chant sounded low. Ripple had a sneaking suspicion that Soix had started it, too. He looked extremely smug. "*All hail Oberon…*"

"All hail *O-ber-on*. All hail *O-ber-on*…" The refrain was taken up by hundreds of voices and Ripple's skin tingled with goose bumps.

This sure beats the shit out of the Ritz-Carlton for a wedding reception.

She turned to Philippe. "So. Are we like officially married now, or what?"

Philippe raised his eyebrows. "You're asking *me*? I haven't a clue at this point."

Oberon moved to them. "Uh-uh. No fucking yet. Me and the Missus gotta say the magic words."

317

"What…like 'may all your troubles be flitter ones' or something?" Ripple grinned at him. "You ain't gonna tie tin cans to my wings or anything are you?"

Titania guffawed. "Nope. But it's a helluva thought."

Shiraz and Adriano shepherded the guests on the dais back, creating a small oasis for the King and Queen to face Philippe and Ripple.

"Here we go, kids. You ready?" Oberon looked at them intently.

"Yes, Sire." Philippe answered firmly.

"You betcha, dude." Ripple blinked. "Er, Sire, that is."

Titania turned a giggle into a cough as Oberon nodded at them both. "Friends, fairies, enchanted beings. It is our joy to bless the Nuptial flight of our devoted subject Philippe Pinot Noir and his chosen mate, Ripple…er…"

"*Smith*." She stage whispered her last name.

"Right. Ripple Smith." Oberon rolled his eyes. "*Smith*? You want a proper fairy name? Lacewing or Websparkle or something?"

"Nah. It'll be Pinot Noir shortly, anyway." Ripple rubbed her arm against Philippe. "And I'm *real* good with that."

"Okay." Oberon shrugged. "What*ever*." He cleared his throat and continued. "Their love will be sealed by this flight and their lives intertwined forever. As will their spirits when their wings fail and they move to the next great adventure."

A muttered sob followed by a loud nose-blowing sound came from beside the dais. Ripple saw Bee17 sniffling happily into a large handkerchief. She blew her a kiss. Dear Bee17. Bless her fuzzy little heart. She'd been the one to smuggle Ripple into the lineup under cover of the fuss caused by the arrival of Royalty.

Ripple wouldn't be standing where she was right now if it wasn't for Bee17. She wondered if she might get her a nice leather thong or something as a thank-you gift.

But Oberon was still speaking. Damn, this dude liked the sound of his own voice. Still when you were King…

"Philippe Pinot Noir. Will you pledge your magic to this woman for eternity? Will you salute her with your wings, worship her with your body and cherish her with your heart?"

Philippe tapped his wingtips together as he stared deeply into Ripple's eyes. "In front of our monarchs, I do so pledge."

Awwww. What a guy.

"My turn." Titania elbowed her husband out of the way. "Ripple Smith. Will you pledge your magic to this man for eternity? Will you worship him with your body, cherish him with your heart and bear his children in your womb?"

Ripple's throat clogged. There were so many cute ways of saying yes. Of whipping out her New York sass and making everybody laugh. But this just wasn't the right moment. Not when Philippe's emotions were in his eyes, and making her world shiver with joy.

She reached out and took his hands, entwining their fingers. She brought one pair to her chest, and the other rested against Philippe's heart. They were joined as one. "In front of our monarchs, I do so pledge." She too tapped her wingtips together.

Shiraz sniffled. "Oh, that's beautiful."

Even Titania surreptitiously brushed away some moisture from her cheek.

Oberon sighed. "You have pledged yourselves to one another. We recognize and honor this pledge on behalf of Fairyland. May your union bring joy and fulfillment. May your mating be fruitful, and may your line continue unbroken for generations to come." He stepped back. "I have now turned off the no-fucking sign. You are free to move around the sky, and boink your little fairy brains out."

"Oh *Jesus, Oberon*…" Titania screeched.

"*Whaaat?*" He turned his grin to her. "It's the truth, isn't it?"

* * * * *

After *that*, things sort of went downhill. Instead of the stately, procedurally correct stripping, followed by the decorously silent launch of the newlyweds, Philippe was astounded to see the party explode around him.

Fairies of all vintages mingled, drank, laughed, groped and even climaxed a few times right off the bat. He blinked at the sight of a Chardonnay fairy rubbing her breasts over a Merlot. And a guy to boot.

A Cabernet was downing a huge tankard of something and trying to feel up another Cabernet, who was busy kissing…*merde*, he couldn't even figure out what the hell vintage the other guy was.

"It's Titania." A resigned voice came from behind him and he turned to Oberon.

"What?"

"It's Titania. She sheds this sexual power. Turns everyplace we go into a screaming orgy when she does it." He looked around and then grinned. "Rather a cool trick, actually."

"Er…yes. I would imagine so." What else could he say? The vineyard glade now resembled something out of a porn movie. With wings.

"Kinda looks like X-rated greeting cards, doesn't it?" Ripple giggled beside them.

"Yeah…" Oberon narrowed his eyes. "And it's making me horny." He looked around. "Where's my woman?"

"Uh…Sire?" Philippe's voice was polite. He didn't really want to be a nuisance, especially since Oberon was clearly having difficulty with the large bulge distending the front of his pants.

"What?" Oberon's attention was elsewhere.

"We're going to leave now, with your permission."

"Sure. Go ahead. Do whatever. Aaaaah…" He spied his wife and headed her way, already tugging at his drawstring. "I got me a woman to fuck."

And so the newlyweds crept quietly away from the orgy that was unfolding amidst the vines, slipping unnoticed into the shadows.

"Whaddya know? I'm married!" Ripple's voice was light. "Who'd a thunk a girl from East Elmhurst would end up in a fabulous Chateau in France with the guy of her dreams?"

"Am I?" Philippe took her in his arms. "Am I the man of your dreams, Ripple?"

"Oh *babe*. Yes, yes and so much more than just yes." She rubbed herself against him as she kissed his chin and his neck.

"Good. Let's fly." Philippe efficiently stripped them both, batting Ripple's hands away from his cock as she reached for him. "Touch me now and there won't be a show, *cherie*. I'm too far gone here…"

Ripple pouted. "Then start the countdown, big fella. I'm about ready to dump my stage two rocket boosters and achieve orbit myself."

Philippe fluttered his wings and Ripple copied his movements, smiling as they left the ground below and headed for the dark, star-dotted sky. He reached for her, holding her close. "So how did you do it?"

She sighed with pleasure as their bodies brushed against each other. "It was a setup, of course. The King and Queen provided such a huge distraction, that nobody noticed when Bee17 slipped me into the chorus line and removed a Chardonnay gal."

"They didn't mind?" Philippe knew he wanted to hear the whole story before he got down to business. Although his determination was weakening rapidly as a nicely budded nipple fluttered close to his lips.

"Well, sure they minded. There were a couple of Chardonnays who nearly duked it out to be removed from the team, so to speak. I swear to God they'd *all* have vamoosed if given half the chance. I'm so glad that particular ceremony is done with. It really wasn't a good idea."

Philippe surrendered to his impulses and suckled her breast. "Mmmm. I know."

She groaned with delight and held his head close, wings fluttering madly as the air cooled around them. "Oh God this is divine, Philippe. How come we've never done it on the wing before?"

"Dunno." *And at this point, I don't care. I just want to do it.*

"It's kind of like skinny dipping, ya know? I did that once, in a fountain in Central Park. Did I ever tell you…"

"Ripple."

"What?"

"Shut up." Philippe slid his mouth down her body and opened it wide, sucking on her pussy for all he was worth.

"*Hoooooookay…*"

His tongue sought out the moisture, the folds, the slick silk of her clit and played with it, making her cry out with pleasure.

"Jesus, Philippe… I'm going to come…"

"Not yet, *cherie*." Philippe pulled back, wincing a little as he wrenched her fingers from their death grip on his hair. "Wait for *me*…"

He worked his way back up her body. "This one is for the vineyards. The rest of them will be for us. Forever."

He kissed her deeply, letting her taste her own juices and tasting her in his turn. His cock brushed against her, sliding through the wet folds of flesh between her thighs. But he did not, would not, enter her. Not this time.

Their hips moved in counterpoint, and as they soared high into the night sky, Philippe Pinot Noir and his new bride, Ripple Pinot Noir, *nee* Smith, orgasmed in a mighty explosion that showered the grapevines beneath with an abundance of magic.

It was the Noble Mold flight to end all Noble Mold flights.

At least that's what they were told later.

Of course, those doing the telling were pretty unreliable, since Titania's sex magic had be-spelled everybody present, and they were all otherwise occupied at the time. Just about everything they did and saw was touched with wonder and the sparkle of joy.

They ignored their King, who had pulled his wife off to a spot way beneath the dais and was making her hit high C time after time.

They ignored the now-former Mistress of the Chateau Pinot Noir, who was learning her own music, an Italian aria, from a rather handsome man who resembled a Musketeer and certainly seemed to know how to use his sword to the best effect.

But some of them did notice the trails of light that lit up the sky, not once, but four times. The first one was spectacular, and even the grapes on the vines seemed to turn towards it. The other three were smaller, but no less spectacular. One Chardonnay stopped what he was doing to another very handsome Chardonnay for a moment and blinked as the third explosion dappled the night sky.

"*Mon Dieu*, Philippe. *Four* times?" Soix smiled then sighed. "I think I shall have to practice being an uncle." He blinked and turned back to the gorgeous ass that hovered in just the right place. With a shout of pleasure, he drove himself deep, as his partner cried out in delight.

Thanks to fairy magic, the wines and the vineyards would thrive. And thanks to love, so would a slick gal from the Big Apple.

Epilogue

"Ripple, you're whining." Philippe glanced over to his wife, who was drying herself off after a shower.

"Am not."

"Are too." He grinned and lay back on the pillows. "You know you won't be able to fit into those jeans much longer even if we could find them."

Her belly had yet to swell, but Philippe was already ecstatic at the thought that their child even now slept safely within her body.

"But *Philippe…*" She rubbed her head. "They were such *nice* jeans." Spikes of frosted hair stuck out softly as she tossed the towel away.

"I like the ass they covered better. And I'd only have to keep taking them off you anyway."

"Well, there is that." Ripple grinned back at him. "You still like my ass, huh?" She turned around and waggled it at him, making his eyes cross. They'd already made love once this morning, but if she kept that up he'd be happy to go for another round.

"*Oh oui*, cherie. It's a *fine* ass. And I'm glad you're keeping your pussy bald, too." He swallowed as she jumped onto the bed and straddled him, putting the aforementioned pussy about three inches from his nose. Ahhh. *Breakfast.*

She paused. *Merde.* Just as he'd opened his mouth, too.

"You know, babe, I just had the oddest feeling."

"Oh?" Philippe couldn't look at her face, not with those soft pink folds beckoning him and making his mouth water.

"You think there's a chance I could get a few limes around here? I got me the strongest craving for tequila…"

* * * * *

New Year's Eve — several years later

The ball dropped in Times Square to the usual fanfare, cheers and fireworks, and once again, the human world marked the passage of one year into another by celebrating, drinking themselves into a stupor and fucking anything that stood still long enough.

A large portion of the population carefully eased the corks from their champagne bottles. It was a new brand, from France, and had been imported just for this occasion.

"Mmm. Tangy."

"Tart with a hint of dryness?"

"Youthful, but not impetuous."

The connoisseurs of such things frowned, tutted, rinsed their mouths and tasted once more. This vintage had a distinct flavor—best described as "sassy" by the experts—and everyone agreed that it was a fine addition to anybody's wine cellar.

There'd been a few new wines earlier that year. Some had worked, some hadn't. A couple had been appallingly bad. Others surprisingly good.

Overall, the wine world had concluded that weather conditions had provided a unique collection of grapes for several years now, and the wines they were producing bode well for the future of the European vineyards.

None of the humans could possibly have known that those same vineyards hosted an interesting mixture of sex-mad fairies. Nor did they know that the special champagne had a healthy dash of "Ripple" in its makeup.

And all things considered, it didn't really matter. Good wine was, and always will be, good wine. Good champagne is even better.

And finding the right lover is the best thing of all.

The End

Why an electronic book?

We live in the Information Age—an exciting time in the history of human civilization, in which technology rules supreme and continues to progress in leaps and bounds every minute of every day. For a multitude of reasons, more and more avid literary fans are opting to purchase e-books instead of paper books. The question from those not yet initiated into the world of electronic reading is simply: *Why?*

1. ***Price.***   An electronic title at Ellora's Cave Publishing and Cerridwen Press runs anywhere from 40% to 75% less than the cover price of the exact same title in paperback format. Why? Basic mathematics and cost. It is less expensive to publish an e-book (no paper and printing, no warehousing and shipping) than it is to publish a paperback, so the savings are passed along to the consumer.

2. ***Space.***   Running out of room in your house for your books? That is one worry you will never have with electronic books. For a low one-time cost, you can purchase a handheld device specifically designed for e-reading. Many e-readers have large, convenient screens for viewing. Better yet, hundreds of titles can be stored within your new library—on a single microchip. There are a variety of e-readers from different manufacturers. You can also read e-books on your PC or laptop computer. (Please note that Ellora's

Cave does not endorse any specific brands. You can check our websites at www.ellorascave.com or www.cerridwenpress.com for information we make available to new consumers.)

3. *Mobility*. Because your new e-library consists of only a microchip within a small, easily transportable e-reader, your entire cache of books can be taken with you wherever you go.

4. ***Personal Viewing Preferences.*** Are the words you are currently reading too small? Too large? Too… ANNOYING? Paperback books cannot be modified according to personal preferences, but e-books can.

5. *Instant Gratification.* Is it the middle of the night and all the bookstores near you are closed? Are you tired of waiting days, sometimes weeks, for bookstores to ship the novels you bought? Ellora's Cave Publishing sells instantaneous downloads twenty-four hours a day, seven days a week, every day of the year. Our webstore is never closed. Our e-book delivery system is 100% automated, meaning your order is filled as soon as you pay for it.

Those are a few of the top reasons why electronic books are replacing paperbacks for many avid readers.

As always, Ellora's Cave and Cerridwen Press welcome your questions and comments. We invite you to email us at Comments@ellorascave.com or write to us directly at Ellora's Cave Publishing Inc., 1056 Home Avenue, Akron, OH 44310-3502.

THE
⚜ ELLORA'S CAVE ⚜
LIBRARY

Stay up to date with Ellora's Cave Titles in
Print with our Quarterly Catalog.

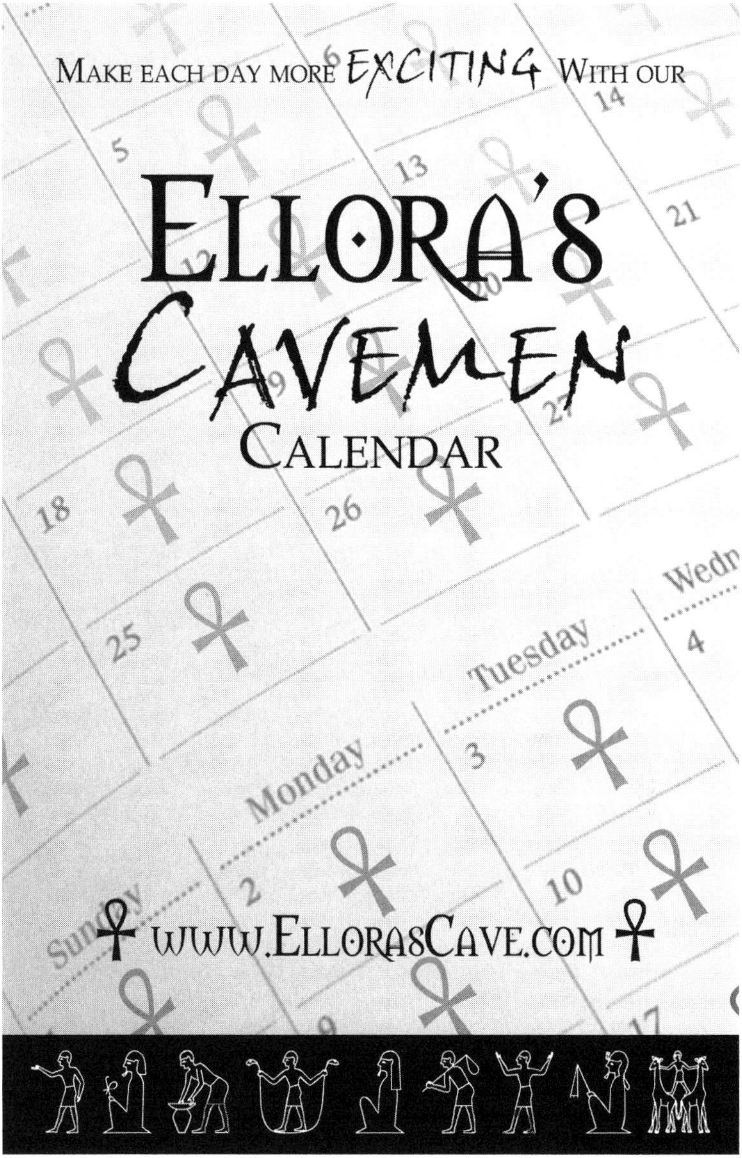
Make each day more EXCITING with our
Ellora's
Cavemen
Calendar
www.EllorasCave.com

COMING TO A BOOKSTORE NEAR YOU!

ELLORA'S CAVE

Bestselling Authors Tour

erridwen, the Celtic Goddess of wisdom, was the muse who brought inspiration to storytellers and those in the creative arts. Cerridwen Press encompasses the best and most innovative stories in all genres of today's fiction. Visit our site and discover the newest titles by talented authors who still get inspired - much like the ancient storytellers did, once upon a time.